An Absence Of Forgiveness

(A DI Townshend investigation)

by

Gary Cann

CHAPTER ONE

Rain. How he hated rain, particularly heavy, constant rain on dark winter evenings. Rain was part of a policeman's lot, he knew that. The worst cases always seemed to come up when it was raining. He remembered winters as a young copper; day after day and night after night, wet, miserable and cold. They don't do that anymore, he reflected sourly. A policeman on the beat was a rarity these days. He pulled the collar of his overcoat up as he walked, hoping it would give him just a little bit more protection. It didn't. The rain was still going down his neck.

It was an evening off, as much as he ever had time to himself; somehow the rain seemed worse on his own time. He stepped carefully around a puddle and joined the queue inside the chip shop. He hadn't eaten since breakfast and there was still plenty of time to sit in the car and get through a portion of chips. And maybe tonight a nice piece of cod or haddock to go with it, the smell of the fryers behind the counter tantalising his taste buds.

He would never have described himself as a gourmet; fish and chips was as good as anything, and better than most. His first wife, a lovely girl, would have agreed. Whatever else he'd married her for, it hadn't been her cooking. With his second wife, it was a different matter. Food, and in particular wasted food and missed meals, another part of a copper's lot, were a constant source of arguments between them. Both marriages had fallen foul of many aspects of the job, but mainly his single-minded approach to it. Little else mattered when he was working on a case.

He took his order back to the car, hungry and hurrying once more through the rain. Once inside, he turned the radio on, and started on his food, wishing, not for the first time, that his thoughts wouldn't keep turning back to the past; an unfortunate side effect of growing old when you're on your own. There's more life behind you to think about than there is future to look forwards to. And there's another reason to hate the rain, he thought, it makes you miserable so you think miserable thoughts. But maybe that was one of the reasons why he threw himself body and soul into his work. Something else to think about.

The food finished, and thoroughly enjoyed, he started the car and pulled out into the road, turning out of Ewyas Harold heading towards Pontrilas. His destination for the evening was the showrooms belonging to Wards Auctioneers to hopefully indulge his passion for old 78 rpm records. Not just any old 78s. It had to be the blues. Mississippi Fred McDowell, Blind Lemon Jefferson and the rest, evocative names of another generation. Finding anything by Robert Johnson would be like winning the lottery, and just about as likely. The blues was what he liked; he knew it narrowed down the possibilities; but he was always hopeful.

The showroom was in the old yard of Pontrilas station, on the Hereford to Abergavenny line, and as he parked in the car park, almost on cue, a train went rumbling past. It was a viewing evening for the main sale the following day, but perhaps because of the awful weather, the car park was almost empty and thankfully, he was able to pull the car up fairly close to the entrance. He still had to go out in the rain again; only a short distance, but enough to get wet. It was a relief to get inside the building.

Directly ahead as he entered was an office with a counter, where tonight's sealed bids would be handed in, and where, tomorrow, the staff would be busy taking payments from successful bidders. The display rooms were to either side. He turned right and began strolling up and down the aisles. There weren't many people around, which gave everyone a chance to take a closer look at the items for sale. The first room was mainly filled with furniture and computer equipment while off to one side was an area which seemed to have been reserved for luggage and large trunks, which he ignored completely. They simply weren't of interest.

He turned back out of the room, re-crossed the foyer and went in to the other showroom, laid out in a similar fashion, but with smaller items on rows of tables. He wandered up and down the rows with no success, and then it was up a short flight of stairs, admiring a model galleon which had seen better days, but still caught the eye. The stairs led to another room predominantly used for art and pictures, but with shelving in the middle containing boxes and boxes of books, records and importantly, 78s. He ignored the pictures.

Occasionally, he'd tried to analyse his collecting. Was it the search, the anticipation of the find? Was it the actual feel of the old records? Was it the story behind them, who'd owned them, who'd played them? The music was of course important, but the sound quality was much, much better on CD. Finding a box of possible treasures, he dismissed the thoughts, but the records in the box were a disappointment. Guy Mitchell, Ruby Murray, even Mantovani; all very good in their own right, but not what he was looking for. Then he heard the scream. A woman's scream, loud and piercing, and suddenly cut off, coming from the direction of the first showroom he'd looked in. He was on the move without thinking.

A small crowd had gathered by the time he reached the source of the scream, as they always seem to when something untoward happens, a morbid fascination with other people's misfortunes. It was mainly showroom staff, along with the few customers who'd braved the weather, all speaking at once. He pushed his way through to the front to discover they were standing around a woman who'd collapsed to the floor in a faint. There was already a female member of staff with her, ably dealing with the situation. But it wasn't the woman on the floor his attention was really focused on. One of the huge trunks he'd seen earlier had been opened, and inside was a body, the body of a man, all too obviously dead. He pushed closer.

"Just who the hell do you think you are, pushing your way in like that?" It was a young woman speaking, indignation in her voice.

"Detective Inspector Derek Townshend, West Mercia Police," he replied politely, showing her his warrant card.

CHAPTER TWO

Richard Bexton-King. The name of the victim meant nothing to Derek Townshend. But then they never did until an investigation was under way. It was then that the details of their lives and their characters began to meld into the picture of a real person. Townshend would soon come to know Mr Bexton-King almost as well as he knew himself. That was the way he worked, understanding the personality of the victim.

There had been no identification on the man's body when it was found in the trunk. He'd been recognised by one of the showroom staff and Townshend already knew some sketchy details about the victim by the time his Detective Sergeant, David Ingleby, had arrived on the scene along with uniformed back-up and a scenes of crime team. Bexton-King was a local businessman, well known and well-liked, but with a reputation for upsetting people in business. On hearing that, Townshend immediately thought to himself that investigating the death of a man who had a reputation for upsetting people wasn't going to be easy. He said as much to Ingleby when he filled him in on the scanty details, but the young detective, still filled with enthusiasm for his work and the job, seemed keen to get on with it.

"So where is it you want me to start, sir?" he asked. Townshend looked around. The 'Do Not Cross' tapes had already been set up around the area where the body had been found and the staff and customers who'd been present were now sitting in a small cafeteria area.

"Get uniform onto the usual stuff, David. Names, addresses, that sort of thing, from everyone who was here. Then let everyone but staff go home. As for yourself, have a chat with the porters. See if they noticed anything unusual about that trunk. Find out if they thought it was unusually heavy when they brought it in. I want to know if the body was in it when it arrived." He paused. "I'm going to have a chat in the office.

They must have records of where it came from and who was selling it." Ingleby made to turn away. "Oh, and David, let me know when the pathologist arrives, will you?"

"Yes, sir." Townshend sighed as he watched his Detective Sergeant go into action, talking first to a pretty young WPC. Ingleby was still new enough to be fired by the thrill of the chase, a murderer to be hunted down and captured. Like a young foxhound, Townshend thought, while he himself was more like the old, wise and somewhat disheartened leader of the pack. Maybe he was getting too old and blasé for the job. Was it time to think of retirement or a desk job? Leave all the running around to the young bloods? No. Not yet, anyway.

The staff in the front office, two youngish girls, were more than helpful, but very keen to direct Townshend into a much smaller back office where details of the lot and the seller were quickly produced for him.

"It was part of a job lot from High Lawns here in Pontrilas, Detective Inspector," said the clerk, a middle aged woman, who'd been introduced to him by one of the girls as Mrs Morgan, 'the lynchpin of the office.' She seemed charmed by Townshend's friendly smile. "From the notes it looks like a house clearance and the seller had made arrangements for it to be delivered to us."

"Does it say who the seller was, Mrs Morgan?" Townshend asked.

"Oh, yes. We don't accept anything for sale anonymously. It was Mr Bexton-King himself who made all the arrangements, or at least his office in Hereford." That was a surprise for Townshend, but he'd long ago learned to hide things that surprised him.

"I don't suppose you know the transport firm that brought the items to the saleroom?"

"We were told to expect two large vans from 'BKM,'" she said after another quick look at her computer. "That's Mr Bexton-King's own haulage firm."

"Two large vans?" he asked. She nodded. "So a good deal of the items in tomorrow's sale were from Mr Bexton King?"

"Yes."

"Do you have an inventory of the items that I could have?"

"Oh, yes, Detective Inspector. I can print one for you."

"If you could, Mrs Morgan. Thank you." As he finished speaking and Mrs Morgan began printing the list of items, a small angry looking man appeared in the doorway of the office.

"Just what the hell is going on here? Some policeman has just tried to stop me coming in. Mrs Morgan?" The woman, now flustered, was just about to explain when Townshend interrupted.

"And who might you be, sir?" he asked politely.

"I'd like to know who's asking me!" the other man demanded. Townshend sighed. Why is it always the little men who get so angry so quickly? Little man syndrome, they call it, he thought. "My name's Townshend, sir, and I'm a Detective Inspector with West Mercia Police. Now, you are?"

"Police? What the hell do the police want here?" The man's raised voice was beginning to grate on Townshend a little. There was simply no need for it.

"Sir, I'll be more than happy to explain," Townshend said, "as soon as you tell me who you are."

"David Neville. I'm the manager of this saleroom. Now, what the hell is going on?" Neville repeated, obviously incapable of moderating his tone. Townshend made a point of taking out his notebook and carefully writing in the man's name. He didn't need it. He had an excellent memory for names, but the man was annoying him.

"Well, Mr Neville, a body has been found in your saleroom, in a large travelling trunk, so I think you'd agree it's a good thing the police are here."

"A body? A dead body, you mean?"

"Yes."

"Oh, God. It's not one of the staff is it?" Townshend shook his head. "Then who is it?" Townshend was reluctant to say, but as it was a member of staff who'd identified the body, it would soon be out anyway.

"It looks as though it may be a gentleman named Richard-Bexton King," he said. Both men turned as there was a sharp gasp from Mrs Morgan, who appeared to have gone pale. Of course, Townshend thought, she didn't know. "Did you know Mr Bexton-King, Mrs Morgan?" Townshend asked.

"No." Was that a hesitation? Townshend wasn't sure, but he had a feeling Mrs Morgan might not be telling him the whole truth. He'd come back to it later.

"How long is this all going to take, Detective Inspector?" David Neville appeared to be calming down slightly and considering the effects of this on his business. "We have got rather a busy day ahead of us all tomorrow, what with the sale?" Townshend couldn't help but stare at the little man. Did he really think the sale was going to go ahead?

"This is a crime scene, Mr Neville and until I'm satisfied it has nothing left to offer us in the way of clues or evidence, it will remain that way. There will be no sale tomorrow and after we have finished talking to people who were present this evening, the building will remain closed to visitors and staff alike until I say so."

"But what about the sellers?" Neville spluttered. "They'll be expecting…"

"Contact them and explain," Townshend interrupted. "Yes, David, what is it?" he continued as Ingleby appeared in the doorway behind Neville.

"Karen Welby's here, sir," he said. "The pathologist. You said to let you know."

"Thank you, David. Show her the body will you? I'll be out in a minute."

"She's already looking at it, sir," Ingleby said. It didn't surprise Townshend. From what he'd heard, Karen Welby was a no-nonsense and very efficient woman. If there was work to be done, she got on and did it. No small talk, no chit chat, just get the job done. That put her very much on the same wavelength as Townshend himself and he had a lot of respect for her, without even having met her. "David?"

"Yes, sir?"

"Make sure the constable on the door knows not to let any unauthorised people in, will you?" Ingleby nodded and Townshend turned back to David Neville and Mrs Morgan. She was holding out a number of pieces of paper to him.

"This is that list you wanted," she said. "It is quite a long one."

"List?" asked David Neville.

"A list of all the items being offered for sale by Mr Bexton-King," Townshend said, not knowing why he was explaining even as he was speaking. "Thank you, Mrs Morgan," he said, giving her a smile. There was no doubt about it, she was clearly upset. Looking down the list. Townshend was very aware that what he was about to say was going to upset the saleroom manager again. "Mr Neville, am I right in assuming you've got secure storage here?" Neville nodded. "Good. I'd like you to put everything on this list in there."

"What?" Neville exclaimed.

"Everything from this house High Lawns, Mr Neville and then give the keys to either myself or my sergeant," Townshend repeated. Neville moved as if to get the job done immediately. "No, Mr Neville. Wait until scenes of crime have finished. They'll let you know. Now if you'll both excuse me, I have things to do."

CHAPTER THREE

"So what have we got on our victim, David?" Townshend asked, sitting in his small office in Hereford Police Station, coffee in hand, with his Detective Sergeant sitting on the other side of the desk.

"Nothing of much interest yet, sir, but Sarah has dug up a bit of stuff for us," Ingleby said, yawning. Sarah Miller was the only female member of Townshend's team. Dark haired and slim, she was a new arrival in the office, having arrived only a few weeks before Townshend himself. She was friendly and helpful, but Townshend was a little worried that there seemed to be friction between her and David Ingleby.

Ingleby yawned again. It had been late the previous evening when Townshend and Ingleby had finally left the incident van at the sale rooms and for the tired David it was irritating that the late night seemed to have little effect on his older boss. The two men had only been working together for a couple of months, since Townshend had transferred to West Mercia from Cambridge, and they were still finding out about each other.

"Everything's of interest when there's a dead body involved, David. You'd do well to remember that." Ingleby winced a little. Maybe Townshend was feeling tired and irritable after all. "Don't dismiss things because they seem to be unimportant." Townshend paused. Even to himself he sounded like a harsh schoolmaster. "So what has she found?"

"It seems Mr Bexton-King was rather a law-abiding citizen, sir. Parking tickets and a large number of speeding fines."

"Anything else?"

"An RTC when he was a teenager. A girl was killed in the crash." Townshend looked interested.

"Killed? Was he to blame?"

"Not according to the inquest, sir. There was no blame apportioned to him at all. The verdict was accidental death."

"But? The tone of your voice says there's more, David."

"Not really, sir. The girl's mother and father didn't agree with the verdict."

"Naturally," Townshend said. Of course they wouldn't. Losing their daughter, they'd be looking for someone to blame.

"There was a bit of harassment but nothing serious, from what I can gather."

"How long ago was all this, David?"

"Twenty eight years ago, sir." He yawned again, unable to stifle it.

"Did you get any sleep at all last night?" Townshend asked.

"A few hours, sir." Townshend didn't comment on that. "Are the parents still alive?"

"They emigrated a year after the inquest, sir. New Zealand."

"Check on whether they're still alive, will you? Now, anything else?"

"No, sir. Sarah's making more checks now."

"Don't forget, David. It's all lists. Possible enemies to start with. Who has he upset, who has he ripped off in business. Anything unusual that's happened, especially in the last few weeks." The DI took a long sip from his mug and pulled a face as he tasted the now cold coffee. "What we also need to know is if anyone benefits from his death. Insurance policies, that sort of thing. Who gets the business for instance? What about his house? Who's in his will?"

"I'll get Ken on all that, sir, when he gets back from Pontrilas," Ingleby said. "He's overseeing the storage of all that furniture." Ken Collings was the fourth and final member of the small team, a big lumbering giant of a man, with a dry sense of humour.

"Good. Did you send someone with him to get prints from the staff who are doing it?" Townshend asked.

"Yes, sir," Ingleby replied.

"Right. Anything on next of kin for the victim?"

"Yes, sir. There's a brother and an ex-wife, and we've not been able to contact either of them yet. There was a mother until very recently, but she died a few weeks ago - it was her house in Pontrilas that all the furniture came from."

"Shame about the relatives. It's already out on social media that he's dead. Did you know?"

"Yes, sir, but there's nothing we could do about it when he was recognised at the sale room."

"You'd think people would have more bloody sense, but there you go. That's the age we live in. Everyone lives their lives publicly," Townshend said. "Get these checks underway, David, and grab yourself a coffee before you fall asleep. Then we'll be off to Burghill to have a look at Mr Bexton-King's own house."

"Not High lawns, sir? That's where the trunk came from."

"No. I've got a forensics team out there now, so we'll have to wait and see if they find anything. No, Burghill it is. Now get those checks organised and don't forget the coffee." Townshend pushed his own cold cup towards Ingleby as a hint.

An hour later, after a speedy coffee and an equally quick catnap in an empty interview room, David Ingleby was driving the pair of them out of Hereford to Burghill, a quiet little place just a short journey of four miles to the north west of the city. A sprawling meandering village of narrow lanes and little traffic, it was a sought after place to live, but because of its proximity to the city, it ran the danger of being enveloped in any future developments, Ingleby explained as he drove.

"There's money out here, David," was Townshend's only comment as they passed the church of St Mary the Virgin. Ingleby nodded. That was a belief held by many people in Hereford.

The driveway of Richard Bexton-King's house was already cordoned off with the obligatory 'Police – Do Not Cross' tape, but as Ingleby and Townshend pulled up, a uniformed constable waved them through. The drive sloped downhill through neatly cut lawns dotted with well-tended circular rose beds to a large three storeyed building flanked on the left by a single storey stable block. Townshend noticed that the whole area was surrounded with high hedges to ensure privacy. Ingleby parked the car in front of the house and the two men got out.

"Are we looking for anything in particular, sir?" Ingleby asked. "Signs of a struggle or something like that?"

"Was there a struggle, David?" There was a long pause. Ingleby was becoming used to this habit of Townshend's, but this time the other man just looked at him, as if expecting an answer.

"I don't know, sir," was the answer Ingleby gave.

"No, David, nor do I. Karen Welby said it was most likely a heavy blow to the head that killed him, but how did that happen? Was it deliberate or an accident? Hopefully her report will help when she's had a good look at the body."

"Did she give you any idea of when it might have happened, sir?" Ingleby had been interviewing the sale room staff when Townshend was talking to the pathologist.

"It got a bit technical at one point, but basically the body had passed through rigor mortis. She thinks that he was put in the trunk before rigor mortis had started, or at least before the major muscle groups began to contract, mainly because whoever put him in there wouldn't have been able to change the body position. So he went in there within two to four hours of dying." Townshend paused. "She made a rough guess that he might have died on Tuesday evening or early Wednesday morning," he said, finally answering Ingleby's question. Then something seemed to occur to him. "Can you make a note to find out when the items from High Lawns were delivered to the sale room?" Ingleby nodded, and made an entry in his notebook. "And while you're at it, do a little bit of checking on the sale room secretary, Mrs Morgan. She seemed rather upset at finding out that the victim was Richard Bexton-King. It might be nothing, but you never know."

"So what we need to know is whether he was in the trunk when it arrived at the sale room?" Ingleby asked.

"Yes, because if he wasn't in it when it was delivered, then how did whoever put him in it get him in there? If he was in it, then where did he die?"

"High Lawns is the logical place, sir, because otherwise the body would have had to have been moved." Townshend nodded.

"I agree, David, but why put him in a trunk that was heading for a sale room? Either the person who hid him didn't know that's what was happening to everything at High Lawns or they just hid him quickly hoping to come back for the body. Both would fit your theory of High Lawns being the place." There was another of what Ingleby was beginning to recognise were Townshend's characteristic pauses. "Come on, let's go inside."

The two men had been standing by the front door talking and as he spoke, Townshend turned the door handle to let them in. The first thing they both noticed was how clean and tidy the place was, even in the hallway. That impression grew as they moved from room to room on the ground floor. It was as if the place had been thoroughly cleaned from top to bottom.

"We need to find out if Bexton-King has a regular cleaner or housekeeper and on what days they normally come," said the DI. Ingleby made another entry in his notebook. "And while you're at it, David, find out about a gardener or handyman as well. We'll see if either of them have noticed anything unusual going on recently. His secretary as well," Townshend added. "Now let's see if we can find a study."

Bexton-King's study was, unfortunately for them, as tidy as the rest of the downstairs. No loose papers had been left lying on the desk, but the desk drawers were unlocked, as was a large wooden filing cabinet. The two policemen lost track of the time in what turned out to be a fruitless search for anything that might be of interest. The upstairs, when they searched it proved to be as tidy as downstairs.

"You know, sir, it's almost as if no one lives here. It's like a show home," said Ingleby from the en-suite bathroom.

"I was thinking the same thing, David. It's almost too perfect."

"I think our Mr Bexton-King was a bit of a ladies' man, sir," Ingleby said a few moments later, with a slight laugh in his voice. "There's four boxes of condoms in here." Townshend smiled, but made no comment. He thought again, sometimes it's odd pieces of information that can turn out to be important, a lesson he'd learned early on in his career.

The house gave them no clues so Ingleby led the way to the stable block which turned out to have been converted into a massive garage. Inside were five flashy sports cars, identified by an excited Ingleby as two Porsche 916s, a Lotus Elise, an ostentatious bright yellow Lamborghini Aventador and an Aston Martin DB9.

"No wonder he gets speeding tickets," Townshend said sourly. "I would imagine not many people in this area drive this sort of car, do they, David?" Ingleby laughed.

"Supercars like this? No, sir. In fact my Mum told that up until the late Sixties and early Seventies there was a doctor in Hereford who still did his rounds in a horse and trap. Francis, I think his name was." Townshend looked at him in disbelief.

"Really?" Ingleby simply nodded. It was quite crowded in the garage, with the cars parked alongside each other like a starting grid, It prompted another question in Townshend's mind. "David, we need to find out whether Bexton-King had any other cars. Ingleby made yet another note in his notebook; there certainly wasn't space in here for another car, he thought.

"Don't you think these would be enough for anybody, sir?" he asked.

"Oh, yes, David. But I wouldn't give you tuppence for any of them. As far as I'm concerned, they're rich boys' toys, but it's something else to consider. If Bexton-King died somewhere else, then how did he get there if all of his cars are here? And if he did die here, someone has gone to an awful lot of trouble to clean up, haven't they? The cleaning of this place is up to professional standards." He paused for a few moments, apparently thinking. Ingleby waited, admiring the cars. Whatever the DI thought, Ingleby would love to own any one of them, let alone all five. And he'd jump at the chance of driving them.

"This place isn't giving us anything, David," the DI said finally and Ingleby turned back to face him. "We'll get forensics over here after they've finished at High Lawns, but my guess is that they won't find anything." Ingleby nodded, trying unsuccessfully to stifle a yawn. He was mortified to find Townshend almost grinning at him. "Let's get back to the station, and you can get somebody on to those notes you've made. Then you can get yourself home for some rest, David."

CHAPTER FOUR

The fact of it being a Sunday morning makes little difference to the hustle and bustle of a city centre police station. For Townshend, there was a string of messages, on e-mail. Seated at his computer screen, gazing at his e-mail inbox, he longed for the days not so long past when people would actually write notes on pieces of paper. There was something more satisfying about dealing with a piece of paper and filing it or throwing it away rather than just pressing the delete button on his keyboard. He started reading them anyway.

The first one he opened was about Richard Bexton-King's ex-wife. Marcella, not a name he'd come across before, but one that sounded vaguely Italian. Townshend had read somewhere that names quite often reflected a person's personality and he enjoyed checking on the meanings of people's names. Not quite a hobby, but definitely an interest. A quick check on his computer and he was proved right. Italian. He smiled as he read the meaning and thought he might just let Ingleby interview the woman. She was apparently 'warlike, martial and strong.' God preserve us poor men from strong warlike women, he thought. Now for the message. Apparently a neighbour had reported to the visiting constable that she was spending a few nights away in Ross-on-Wye with a friend, said the e-mail. But there was still no contact with her. The euphemism made him smile, but he decided Marcella Bexton-King could wait until she was at home.

Robert Bexton-King, the victim's younger brother, was the subject of the next e-mail. He smiled. Sarah Miller was very sensibly keeping each person separate in her reports. Bexton-King had apparently been away in Lichfield on a business trip since Wednesday. Townshend's suspicious mind immediately switched on. If Karen Welby's estimate as to the time of death was anywhere near correct, that still gave Robert Bexton-King the opportunity of having killed his brother or at least been involved in hiding the body before travelling. Would he benefit from his brother's death? Almost certainly with no other relatives, but the only way to be sure was to find out what was in Richard Bexton-King's will.

That brought his thoughts back to the victim's house at Burghill. He'd been both surprised and disappointed not to find any personal papers there. As far as a will went, it would possibly have to wait another day until Monday morning to discover the beneficiaries. Townshend had no qualms about rousing a solicitor over the weekend if he had to, but there wasn't much benefit to be gained in antagonising them unnecessarily. Then he smiled. Without any personal papers he didn't actually know which solicitor he'd have to rouse anyway.

The brother Robert would have to be the one to identify the victim's body, being the nearest relative, and he'd have to be interviewed as well. David Ingleby could handle the viewing, which would be at the hospital mortuary, and then they could both interview Robert afterwards. He thought about it for a few moments longer and decided that as the man would be in the city to see the body, the interview might as well take place at the station, as long as Bexton-King himself was agreeable. Townshend made some notes to pass on to Ingleby. On a piece of paper.

The third e-mail from Sarah contained more details about the car crash Richard Bexton-King had been involved in when he was a teenager. Townshend had wanted them just to see if they would help him form a more complete picture of the victim, but he didn't have a chance to start reading it. Ingleby, looking much more refreshed than the previous day, came rushing into his office, having just answered a phone call in the main office.

"Something up, David?" Townshend said, looking up from his computer screen.

"Yes, sir. There's been a fire."

"Where?" Townshend asked. His immediate thoughts were High Lawns, Burghill or at the very worst, the salerooms at Pontrilas.

"Richard Bexton-King's business out on the Worcester Road. BKM is the name of the place. It started in the early hours of the morning, apparently."

It took the two men only twenty minutes to arrive at the scene, with Ingleby driving again. Townshend was still unsure of his bearings in the Hereford area. On the way, Ingleby filled him in on the nature of Bexton-King's business. Initially a garage and car sales company, it had been started back in the 1930s by Arnold King, the victim's grandfather. His son, Ronald Bexton-King, had taken his mother's maiden name to hyphenate the family name, and had expanded the business to include road haulage as well, taking advantage of the decline of the railways in the early Sixties.

"Dr. Beeching," Townshend said idly. Ingleby ignored the comment and carried on.

"When the father died, the business passed to Richard Bexton-King, the eldest son, but his brother's also got a stake in it, sir."

"You've done your homework, David. Well done."

"Thank you, sir."

"So as far as the business is concerned, it would be Robert's now?" Townshend asked.

"I would think so, sir, yes." Ingleby swung the car on to a large forecourt, beyond which what used to be the business premises were a smouldering mess.

"It must have been some business, David," Townshend said, looking at the extent of the property.

"It was, sir, and worth a bit too," Ingleby replied, as the two men got out of the car. A fire officer came rushing over to them, obviously intent on preventing them from going too close.

"Sorry, gents, but no further. As you can see, we've got the area cordoned off. Press, I presume?" He apologised as both Townshend and Ingleby showed him their warrant cards. "Sorry, we've been expecting the TV people here at any time. The local press have already been and gone." He held out his hand. "I'm the Station Officer, Tony Butler." As the three men shook hands, he carried on talking. "It's been a hell of a shout, this one. We've had to get the standby crews in from Peterchurch and Ewyas Harold to help out. One of the guys found a whole bundle of cylinders in a storage area, so we had to evacuate those houses over there," he gestured at some houses on the perimeter of the premises, "and cordon everything off. We thought they were acetylene, so we couldn't take any chances. Turned out to be oxy-propane. Thankfully, it doesn't burn as hot as acetylene, so it was less of a problem than we thought it was going to be. Still had to drag the Haz Mat Officer out here, though."

"What started it? Any ideas?" Townshend asked.

"Not yet. You'd have to have a chat with Andy Sheppy about that. He's the Fire Investigation Officer. I'll see if I can find him for you, but it's probably for the best if you wait here." He went off in search of the other man.

"Don't you think it's strange that the business of a man whose murder we're investigating should be burned to the ground, David?" Townshend asked while they were waiting.

"It does seem a coincidence, sir." Townshend snorted at the suggestion.

"In a murder investigation, there's no such thing as a coincidence, David. Mind you, I don't believe in them anyway."

"So you think it was deliberate, sir?"

"I'd stake my pension on it," Townshend said, "and I'm closer to mine than you are to yours. Now, the question is, why would someone burn down the business of someone who is already dead, David?" Townshend asked. Ingleby shook his head.

"Trying to hide something, sir?" he said.

"Exactly. But the question is what? And why the business, why not the man's home?"

"It must have had something to do with the garage or haulage business, sir."

"I would think so, David. Something to do with the vans, I think. They were due to be checked over today by forensics. And it's also possible that Bexton-King kept personal papers here, because we didn't find any at the house, did we?" He paused. "And remember, we haven't got any reason for the victim to be murdered, have we?"

"You think there might have been a clue in the office here, sir?" Townshend shrugged.

"We'll never know now, will we, David?" he said. They were joined by a smoky and grimy fire-fighter as they talked. He introduced himself as Andy Sheppy.

"Tony said you wanted a word," he said.

"We wondered if you had any idea how this might have started." Ingleby said. "It's a hell of a mess."

"Well, all the whole area was well ablaze when the crews arrived. It's a big place with a number of buildings and yards and there wasn't a lot they could do. The only problem is that they've covered the place with foam because of those canisters they found."

"How did the fire spread over such a wide area?" Ingleby asked.

"That's what we're trying to work out," said Sheppy.

"Even the office area?" Townshend asked. Sheppy nodded.

"Yes. It seems a couple of spare canisters were stored in a back room."

"How convenient," Townshend muttered, more to himself than to the others, but they both heard.

"It is a bit strange," Sheppy said, "because they weren't there a month ago. I did a bet of checking before I came out and the place was given a full safety certificate then. Still, the foam isn't making my job any easier. It could be a couple of hours before I can find anything." Townshend gave him a business card, and Sheppy gave him a puzzled look. "Cambridgeshire Police? Aren't you a little off your patch, Detective Inspector?" Ingleby noticed with amusement that Townshend seemed slightly embarrassed as he gave the Fire Investigation officer a West Mercia Police card, taking the other back.

"I've only been here a couple of months," Townshend explained. "I thought I'd binned all of those. Give me a ring when you know anything." As the Fire officer returned to his search, Townshend and Ingleby got back into their car.

"What now, sir?" Ingleby asked as he pulled out onto the main road.

"Robert Bexton-King. I need you to take him to identify his brother's body, and then bring him into the station for a chat," Townshend replied.

"Into the station, sir?"

"Yes, it makes sense if he's in town to see the body. Ring him when we get back."

"Yes, sir." Ingleby hesitated. "About viewing the body, sir…"

"What about it, David?"

"Well it is Sunday, sir."

"The last time I checked, David, hospital mortuaries weren't working nine to five office hours. There'll be someone there."

CHAPTER FIVE

Viewing a corpse was not the way David Ingleby would have chosen to spend a Sunday afternoon, but the matter was out of his hands. It needed to be done and that was all there was to it. Robert Bexton-King had at least agreed to identify the body and Ingleby couldn't imagine he felt any better about it either. Thankfully, Bexton-King had also agreed to be interviewed at the station afterwards, although Ingleby felt he didn't seem too happy about it.

As the hospital was fairly close to the police station, Ingleby had decided to walk and it was only a short stroll down Kyrle Street and into the hospital grounds off Union Walk, cutting behind the bus station. It was cold, but at least it wasn't raining, and the freshness of the air woke him up. He'd been sitting at his desk in front of a computer since he and Townshend had returned from Bexton-King's burnt out business, and he was feeling stiff and drowsy.

He entered the hospital through the main entrance, having agreed to meet Robert Bexton-King in the coffee shop in the foyer. It was only a few months since he'd last been through those doors, but that had been to the maternity unit when his wife had given birth to their baby daughter.

Bexton-King was easy to spot, sitting at a table on his own in the hospital coffee shop, a half-finished cappuccino in front of him. He was obviously waiting for someone, but looked relaxed as he rose to greet Ingelby.

"Mr Bexton-King? Detective Sergeant Ingleby. Are you ready?"

"Ready as I will be, Detective Sergeant," Bexton-King said in a well-spoken voice. "Although I have to admit this has all come as a bit of a shock." Bexton-King was quite a big man, casually and expensively dressed, but his voice was higher pitched than Ingleby had expected for his size.

"I can imagine, sir," he said sympathetically, "But if you'd like to come this way." Bexton-King finished the last of his coffee and followed Ingleby through the hospital to the mortuary. This was not an experience the Detective Sergeant had often had as part of his duties and he disliked it. Seeing bodies in car accidents was one thing, but when they were laid out on a mortuary table, it was completely different. They were cold empty shells, almost inhuman, and despite his age, it always made him far too aware of his own mortality.

When the mortuary attendant pulled back the sheet for Robert Bexton-King to identify his brother, Ingleby shivered slightly and knew it was having the same effect on the other man. Bexton-King turned to him and nodded, having taken quite a mournful look at the body, but Ingleby still had to ask the question; he needed a verbal response.

"Is this your brother Richard, sir?" The other man, nodded again.

"Yes, it is," Bexton-King said shakily. Ingleby motioned the attendant to cover the body again and the two men left the mortuary to make their way out of the hospital. The short walk did them both good and Robert Bexton-King seemed to have regained his composure when they arrived at the police station, Ingleby took him to an interview room.

"I'll arrange a coffee, sir. I'm afraid it won't be a cappuccino or up to Costa Coffee standards, but we'll do our best. I'll tell Detective Inspector Townshend we're here."

Townshend had spent his time reading the e-mails he'd been taken away from earlier but when Ingleby walked into his office, he was relieved to stop.

"He confirmed the identification, sir," Ingleby said in response to Townshend's question.

"How did he take it, David?"

"It shook him, sir, and he went a bit pale, but all in all he took it very well."

"How was he when you left him in the interview room? Nervous?"

"No, sir, quite calm and waiting for a coffee."

"Before we see him, tell me what your first impressions of him were, David," Townshend said, rising from his seat and putting his jacket on as he spoke.

"First impressions, sir?"

"Yes, David. What opinion have you already formed of him?" Ingleby gave this some thought before answering.

"Self-assured, fairly confident, well-built and obviously keeps himself in shape. Also a little effeminate, sir." He hesitated. "Why do you ask, sir?"

"First impressions can be important, David," was all Townshend said. "Now, let's go downstairs and talk to him, shall we?"

The room Bexton-King was waiting in was dull and featureless and Townshend thought it was in dire need of a coat of paint. But then again, it was an interview room; it wasn't supposed to be cosy and comfortable. He could imagine that it would inspire a sense of alarm in suspects and interviewees. Townshend noted however, that just as Ingleby had said, Robert Bexton-King seemed relaxed enough.

"Good afternoon, Mr Bexton-King. My name is Detective Inspector Townshend. Thank you for coming in." He seated himself across the table, and Ingleby sat next to him. "I realise it's a difficult time for you, but we do unfortunately have some questions," Townshend began.

"That's not a problem, Detective Inspector." Bexton-King smiled. His voice, soft-spoken, confirmed for Townshend what Ingleby had said. It did give the impression of the man being effeminate. "Are we going to have the tape recorder on?" he added, reaching out for his coffee.

"No, sir," said Ingleby. "That's only if you're here under caution, but I will be making some notes." Was that relief Townshend saw on the man's face as he took a sip from his cup?

"Now, Mr Bexton-King," Townshend said. "Shall we start with the obvious question?" Townshend didn't wait for an answer. "Can you think of anyone who might have wished your brother dead? Did he have any enemies? People that he might have upset in business?"

"In a word, Detective Inspector, no. I can't think of any enemies. The closest he ever came to that was when his girlfriend died in a car crash years ago. Her mother went a bit strange. In business, again no. He was hard but fair. It didn't seem to upset people."

"When was the last time you saw your brother alive?"

"Last weekend," the other man replied, then paused. "No, actually it was last Monday afternoon, but not to talk to."

"And where was that?"

"In Hereford, by Greyfriars car park. He was on the pavement with Marcella."

"That'll be his ex-wife?" Townshend confirmed.

"I suppose you could call her that, but legally, they're still married, as the divorce hasn't gone through yet."

"But they were separated?" Townshend asked.

"Oh, yes, and had been for some time. Anyway, I was in my car and they were on the opposite side of the road, by St Nicholas' church. Having a hell of a row, by the looks of things."

"Do you know what the row was about?"

"No, as I said, I was in my car so I couldn't hear anything. I did see her slap him, though," Bexton-King said.

"Slap?"

"Yes, and it looked pretty hard to me. It certainly rocked him back on his feet a bit." Another sip of coffee. "Then the lights changed, and I had to drive off. I don't think either of them saw me."

"Had you seen anything like that between them before?"

"Arguments, yes. When they were together, Richard and Marcella fought like cat and dog most of the time, but I don't ever remember seeing them come to blows. But you know what they say, Detective Inspector, 'what goes on behind closed doors...'" Townshend nodded and Ingleby looked up momentarily from his notebook.

"Were these arguments about anything in particular?"

"No, it seemed to be about anything and everything. It wasn't a happy marriage, right from the start. They were totally unsuited to each other. I would imagine, knowing Marcella that most of their arguments revolved around money, or at least started that way."

"Around money?" Townshend said.

"Yes. They were such different personalities, like chalk and cheese. Richard's only real extravagance was his cars..."

"We've seen them," Townshend interrupted.

"Then you'll know what I mean by extravagance," Bexton-King said. "Richard liked a bit of speed. He kept the ones at Burghill mainly for track days. It was coming home from them he'd get speeding tickets. It was almost a standing joke with us that traffic police don't like flashy cars."

"Only if they're breaking the law," Townshend said drily. "Did your brother have a day-to-day car, Mr Bexton-King, or just the ones at Burghill?"

"Yes. A white Audi A3."

"Thank you. Now, you were saying about money differences."

"Yes, of course. I'd just like to say that Richard might have been a fast driver, but he never did anything stupid. He was very confident behind the wheel of a car."

"But what about that crash you just mentioned where his girlfriend was killed?" Townshend asked.

"That was a long time ago, Detective Inspector. It wasn't his fault, you know, even though Kim's crazy mother thought it was. It was the best thing they could have done, emigrating. She was making Richard's life a misery."

"What about these differences over money?" Townshend persisted.

"Apart from the cars, Richard didn't really throw his money around much. He wasn't tight, but he was careful. That was the problem between him and Marcella. When they met, she was impressed by the cars and the house at Burghill and decided Richard was a playboy type who could give her the jet-set lifestyle she wanted. He didn't and wouldn't." Townshend was quiet, apparently thinking about what Bexton-King had said. When he spoke, however, he changed tack.

"What happens to the business now? Who does it go to?"

"There's not much business left, is there Detective Inspector?" For the first time, Bexton-King seemed less than relaxed, leaning forwards in his seat. "I take it the fire is being investigated?"

"Oh, yes," said Townshend, "as part of our investigations into your brother's death. Now, you didn't answer my question as to who the business, or what's left of it, goes to."

"I don't know," said Bexton-King. "I presume me."

"You don't know? Did you and your brother never discuss it? You did have a share in the business, didn't you?"

"Yes, I did have a share of the business, thanks to Richard and not my father, but Richard and I never talked about such things."

"I take it that you do know what the contents of his will are?" Townshend asked.

"No, I've no idea." Another pause from Townshend.

"You didn't talk about that either?"

"No, but I do know it's lodged with a solicitor," said Bexton-King.

"Who?"

"Lacey and Bartholomew in Leominster."

"Leominster? Why not a Hereford solicitor?"

"Richard could be funny about things at times. He said he didn't want anybody in Hereford knowing his business. Ridiculous I know, but he was adamant about it. They were the solicitors for BKM as well." It was Bexton-King's turn to pause. "When Dad was around, we used a Hereford solicitor, old Michael James, but when Dad and Michael James retired at the same time, Richard changed solicitors straight away." He finished his coffee and looked at Townshend waiting for the next question. It took him by surprise.

"Was your brother a ladies' man?"

"What on earth makes you ask that?"

"Just a question, Mr Bexton-King, just a question," Townshend said.

"Yes, he was, but he would only ever see one woman at a time," Bexton-King said.

"How did his wife feel about that?"

"There wasn't a lot she could say, Detective Inspector. She slept with any man who so much as smiled at her."

"Including you, Mr Bexton-King?"

"Marcella? And me? God, no." He laughed at the very thought of it.

"Just a few final questions, Mr Bexton-King, if you don't mind," Townshend said.

"Of course. What is it?"

"It's just about your business trip to Lichfield."

"My alibi you mean?" Bexton-King laughed again, while Townshend just smiled.

"Something like that, yes."

"It's not a problem, Detective Inspector. Ask away."

"When did you leave?"

"Early Tuesday evening. I'd been at home all afternoon and I wanted to be in Lichfield in time to have an evening meal at the hotel."

"Which hotel were you staying in?"

"Swinfen Hall, on the outskirts of the city."

"And who were you seeing?"

"Two private sellers, Detective Inspector. They were both selling cars Richard was interested in for the showroom. I've got their details on my laptop at home. I can e-mail them if you like."

"Send them to the Detective Sergeant, if you would." Townshend smiled and then continued. "Finally, Mr Bexton-King, would you agree to providing fingerprints and a DNA sample for us? The records of these will be destroyed after the investigation is complete," Townshend said. Bexton-King nodded, although Townshend noted something about the man which said he was a little reluctant. When Ingleby had finished, Townshend spoke again, before rising from his seat. "I'm sorry for your loss and I'd like to thank you for taking the time to come in and talk to us, Mr Bexton-King. The Detective Sergeant here will see you out and give you details of his e-mail address."

CHAPTER SIX

"Let's have a look at how those checks are doing, David," Townshend said, "before we get stuck into anything else."

"Yes, sir." Townshend smiled. Ingleby had pre-empted him and was already primed with notes.

"First, have we found out anything about the victim's cleaner and gardener at Burghill?"

"Yes," said Ingleby. "Ken managed to get hold of Bexton-King's secretary at BKM, a woman called Sharon Doherty on the phone. She told him the cleaner's name is Valerie Pereira and she lives at Belmont, here in the city. She cleans for a number of other people as well."

"Is she self-employed or does she work through a cleaning company?"

"Self-employed, sir."

"OK. What about the gardener?"

"A guy named Stephen Warner. Apparently he's a bit of an odd-job handyman and does a bit of cash-in-hand work for the haulage part of BKM as well."

"Doing what?"

"A driver's mate, sir. Basically shifting and carrying."

"Did Ken do any background checks on them?

"He's doing them now," Ingleby replied.

"Good. Well, we'll need to talk to both of them. Did Ken get their addresses?"

"The secretary didn't know them. They were all kept at BKM, sir. She told Ken that all the important stuff like staff details was kept in a fire-proof box at the office," Ingleby added as the expression on the DI's face fell.

"Some good news," Townshend said. "There might be something of interest in there. Has it been found yet?"

"We've already got it downstairs. The fire people brought it into the station last night," Ingleby told him.

"So I take it we need this secretary, Sharon something or other…"

"Doherty, sir."

"Yes, Sharon Doherty, to get the thing open?"

"Yes, sir, it's a combination lock."

"I presume he's got her address, so get Ken to pick her up, will you David? He can finish those background checks later. We could do with knowing what's in that box and we need to talk to her anyway." Ingleby disappeared into the outer office to give Ken his instructions, quickly returning to Townshend's office with a cup of steaming hot coffee in each hand. It had only taken the team a few days to discover that Townshend had what was verging on an addiction to coffee.

"Thank you, David," Townshend said, gratefully taking the offered cup. "Now, let's talk fingerprints."

"There are unidentified prints on the trunk, sir. We've ruled out the porters at the auction rooms and the woman who actually opened the thing and found the body."

"Sarah checked with the Liaison officer who saw her. She's fine apparently. She certainly wasn't on Friday night after finding the body, that's for sure." Ingleby had been the one to interview her when she'd recovered from her faint.

"Hardly surprising. It's not every day you find a body in a trunk," Townshend said drily. "What did she have to say to you when you spoke to her? We haven't talked about it."

"She said she liked the look of the trunk and wanted to see what condition the inside was in, so she just opened it up. As simple as that, sir." Ingleby took a sip from his coffee. "I would think that at least some of the prints that are left are from the guys who delivered it," he added. Making suggestions didn't come easily to him. It had been frowned upon by his former boss.

"From the BKM Haulage men? Yes, I agree," said Townshend, nodding. "Another reason to talk to Sharon Doherty, then, David? To find out who they were." He took a sip of his coffee, which was now at a drinkable temperature. "Anything in from Karen Welby?"

"Not yet, sir, but it's still a bit early in the day," Ingleby said.

"If you've not heard anything by lunchtime, chase her up, will you? There might not be much she can tell us that will help, but you never know." Townshend paused while Ingleby made some more notes. It was an admirable trait in a young copper. That way you never forgot anything. "What about Robert Bexton-King?" he asked when Ingleby had finished writing.

"What about him, sir?" Ingleby looked vague for a moment.

"Has he sent you the e-mail I asked him for?"

"Yes, sir. He must have sent it almost as soon as he got home yesterday. Sarah's checking out the names and addresses he gave us."

"Good, but I've got a feeling they'll check out, David," Townshend said. "It's the timing of his leaving Hereford and the time of his brother's death that interests me. Did he have time to do it or not? That's the question that will decide whether or not he's a suspect."

"And hopefully Karen Welby's report might shed some light on times as well," Ingleby said.

"Yes, but there are a few other things to check. For instance, how long does it take to get to Lichfield from Hereford?"

"It's not as far as it seems, sir, and at that time on a Tuesday evening he'd probably do it in under two hours."

"Which would get him there in plenty of time for an evening meal. Check his arrival time with the hotel, will you?" Ingleby noticed

Townshend had taken to twiddling a pencil in his fingers while he thought, but he'd still not become used to the Detective Inspector's habit of skipping from one thing to another without pausing. "Have Forensics put in a report yet, David?"

"From High Lawns, sir, or from the saleroom?"

"From High Lawns and Burghill," Townshend said. "They should have finished there as well. They won't start on the saleroom unless we need them to."

"I'll check, sir." Another note in the notebook, Townshend noticed. Ingleby was just about to rise from his seat, and then thought better of it as a question occurred to him. "What about Marcella Bexton-King, sir? When are we going to see her?"

"I'd really like to know what's in the victim's will before seeing her," Townshend said. "Hopefully we'll find a copy in this fireproof box thing later. If we don't, you'll have to get on to the solicitor in Leominster. When you do, we also need to find out if divorce proceedings had been started and by which one of them. The brother knew they were separated but I don't think he knew the actual state of affairs so we need to get that cleared up."

"If they haven't, won't that make her still the next of kin, sir?" Ingleby asked.

"Yes, which would make her entitled to his entire estate, unless of course the will says different. We have to remember as well that until the decree absolute is granted by the court, they're still married. If they hadn't already reached a financial settlement, it would give Marcella an excellent motive." Albeit an obvious one, Townshend thought to himself.

"Could that have been what the argument between them was about, the one that the brother said he saw?"

"Very possibly, but we'll find out about the state of things from his solicitor first. It's still early days."

CHAPTER SEVEN

Unusually, even though Sarah Miller and David Ingleby were both on the phone, the office was fairly quiet, so Townshend returned to his e-mails only to read a reminder from his boss, Detective Chief Inspector Logan, that David Ingleby's annual review was due. He absently picked up his coffee and took a long drink. It was stone cold and he pulled a face as he swallowed it. Lukewarm coffee was passable, but this one was just a bit too cold. He resisted the temptation to call out to Sarah for a fresh cup. For some reason, probably to do with his predecessor, they didn't think allowing their DI to make his own drinks was right and it was something he was having trouble getting used to. But then David Ingleby stuck his head around the door.

"Robert Bexton-King's contacts all check out in Lichfield, sir," he said, "just like you thought they would."

"Thank you, David. What time was his first meeting?"

"Nine in the morning, sir, and he was on time."

"And what time did he reach his hotel on the Tuesday evening?"

"He checked in at seven forty-five, sir. The receptionist was very precise about it. Apparently it's recorded on their computer system. He went in to eat about half an hour later."

"That fits with the time he says he left Hereford, doesn't it?"

"Yes, sir, even allowing for traffic. I also asked the girl if their system showed the time he went into breakfast, and it did. She explained it showed everything that was signed for against a room number."

"God preserve us from Big Brother, David. What time was it?"

"Quarter past seven. Again it checks out with his first meeting in the city." It was Ingleby's turn to pause. "There's something else as well, sir."

"What, David?"

"The hotel records show there was a call to room service for coffee at quarter to five in the morning."

"Well that shows he was there, doesn't it?" Townshend said, waiting to see what Ingleby was going to suggest.

"Well, yes, sir, but is it possible that after eating, he drove back to Hereford, killed his brother and then returned to Lichfield and had a coffee before going to bed?"

"Everything's a possibility until it can be proved otherwise, David, so yes it is possible. I think it's a little unlikely, but we can't dismiss it. Most murders committed by family members, particularly siblings, are spur of the moment things, done in anger. Driving to and from Lichfield in the middle of the night just doesn't fit that pattern. It would take a fair amount of calculation and planning. But, yes it is possible. What we need to know is what time Richard Bexton-King died. It might clear his brother from any suspicion." Townshend held out his cold coffee. "Any chance of someone making a hot one, David?" It came quickly, and thankfully, he'd finished it when the phone rang.

"DI Townshend," he said. "How can I help?"

"Hello, Detective Inspector. It's Karen Welby. I thought it would be a good idea to ring about our murder victim before I have my report typed up and sent to you."

"I take it you've found something, then Dr Welby?"

"Yes. Despite that large bruise on the victim's head, I believe he was poisoned. The bruise was caused, or so I think, simply by him being banged about as the trunk was moved."

"What makes you think that?" he asked the pathologist. This was a result Townshend hadn't expected.

"His stomach was full of a drug called oxycontin," she replied in a matter of fact way.

"Which is?" Townshend had no idea.

"It's what they call a slow-release pain-killer for extreme pain."

"Slow-release? And it would have killed him? How long would it have taken?" The questions poured from the detective.

"It's only slow-release when it's in its over-the-counter form as a capsule. As a powder, it's quite deadly as an overdose and there was enough inside him to kill one of our local Herefordshire bulls."

"Well, Dr Welby, we can assume that as he was found in a trunk that he didn't take it himself," Townshend said.

"Definitely not," Karen Welby agreed, "and anyway, the taste is diabolical."

"So how could someone get him to take it? Force feed him?"

"I can't think of any other way," she said. "It could be mixed with strong tasting drinks, but that isn't what happened in this case, Detective Inspector. There are marks on the victim's wrists and ankles that indicate he was restrained."

"Restrained? Tied up or handcuffs, you mean?" Townshend said.

"It looks like rope," she said. "My guess is that he was tied to a chair or something like that." There was a pause on the phone, then she continued. "You asked how long it would take, Detective Inspector. Well, how long is a piece of string? Judging by his build and he was a fairly big man, it would have taken a fair while."

"So it certainly wasn't a heat of the moment crime," Townshend mused.

"No. It was a long, drawn-out process which would have taken some planning. And it would have had to have been planned by someone who knew the effects of oxycontin. What was the victim taking oxycontin for, Detective Inspector? Do you know?"

"No, I don't, Dr Welby. Does the autopsy show anything?"

"No, it doesn't, but we haven't finished yet. I just wanted to let you know the probable cause of death."

"So, that brings us to the important question. We know how he probably died, even if it wasn't the struggle I assumed it might have been, but can you give me any idea of when he died?"

"Not precisely," she began, and Townshend felt his heart sink a little," but even given the nature of oxycontin, I'd think late Tuesday evening or early Wednesday morning. That fits with the rigor mortis. There is something else we check, called livor mortis, or post-mortem lividity..."

"Isn't that something to do with the settling of the blood?" Townshend asked.

"Yes. It gives us some idea of if or when the body was moved after death," she said. "The blood starts to settle in the lowest parts of the corpse within twenty minutes to three hours of death. In this case, the settling is all around the victim's bottom and feet, so he was moved into that trunk fairly quickly after dying or possibly even as he was still dying."

"Which still leaves the question of why would someone take such a long time killing him and then hide him away in a trunk," Townshend said.

"I'm afraid I can't help with that one, Detective Inspector, but I'll let you have a full report when we're done with the body." She rang off, leaving with him thoughts.

This wasn't a killing done in anger; the way it had been done ruled that out, with the victim being restrained and force-fed a toxic drug. He agreed with Karen Welby that it showed signs of being well-planned. But what about this hiding of the body inside an old luggage trunk? Did it mean that whoever killed Richard Bexton-King was disturbed and was forced into hiding the body quickly? If so, who might have disturbed the killer?

With Karen Welby telling him that the body had been moved very shortly after death, it did narrow one thing down for him. The murder almost certainly took place at High Lawns and not Burghill. It didn't help him with who or why, though. They also had to find out about the oxycontin as well. Why was Richard Bexton-King taking it and who would have known he took it? He sighed. Lunch was starting to seem like a good idea when David Ingleby disturbed him, knocking lightly on the door frame.

"Sharon Doherty is downstairs, sir."

"OK David. Thank you. Before we go down to see her, will you ask Ken to go out to Pontrilas and have a chat with the neighbours around High Lawns? The usual stuff. Did they see or hear anything unusual on the night Bexton-King was killed."

"I take it you've heard from Karen Welby, then, sir?" Ingleby said.

"Yes. She thinks he was killed on either Tuesday evening or in the early hours of Wednesday morning, so we need to get somebody out there to start asking questions. He can do it while we're having a chat with Sharon Doherty."

CHAPTER EIGHT

When the two detectives entered the interview room, Sharon Doherty was sipping at a cup of tea. Smartly dressed and seemingly not bothered by her surroundings, she appeared a slim and slightly built woman. Townshend placed her in her early forties, but he was well aware of how wrong men can be at estimating women's ages, even trained policemen. As they entered, she looked up and gave them both a friendly but tired looking smile and Townshend noticed dark rings around her eyes despite make-up. Was that lack of sleep or possibly grief? Ingleby switched on the tape recorder and she swept an imaginary loose hair away from her face with a well-manicured hand.

"Thank you for coming in, Miss Doherty. My name is Detective Inspector Townshend," Townshend began, but she interrupted before he could say any more.

"Mrs Doherty," she said, firmly but politely correcting him. A well-spoken voice, he thought, probably very good on the telephone.

"Sorry, I didn't realise," he said gesturing at her left hand, where there was no sign of a wedding ring. She smiled.

"I'm a widow," she said, "and my married name is the only thing I have left of my husband." Townshend nodded, thinking to himself that he would need to keep this lady on track and not let her wander away from what he wanted to talk to her about.

"I'm sorry to hear that," he said.

"Thank you, Detective Inspector, but it was four years ago now," she said. Townshend introduced Ingleby and then continued.

"I hope Detective Constable Collings explained to you why we needed you to come in, Mrs Doherty?" She nodded. "But we'd also like to take the opportunity of asking you a few questions about your employer, Mr Bexton-King." She nodded again and Townshend noticed a quick look of sadness cross her face.

"It was a shock to hear about Richard's death and the fire over the phone, Detective Inspector. Rather upsetting." There was a definite note of complaint in her voice.

"I can imagine, Mrs Doherty," Townshend said and paused for a few moments before carrying on. She was an employee, he thought to himself, not a relative. As far as he was concerned, they hadn't done anything wrong, no matter what she might think. "Detective Sergeant Ingleby here will be making some notes as we talk." She took a sip of tea. "Can you tell me exactly what your position is in BKM?"

"Company Secretary, Detective Inspector," she answered.

"And what exactly does that involve?"

"Just about everything Richard and Robert don't want to do," she said, "which was quite a lot. Admin, staff management, accounts, dealing with customers. You name it, I did it."

"So what did the brothers actually do in the company?" asked Townshend with a vague suspicion that she was building up her role.

"Richard was a networker, a charming man. He brought in the customers. But he was more interested in the next deal, or where he could make more money than the actual business itself. Robert was the salesman. Buying and selling cars is his life, his passion."

"So as far as the day-to-day running of BKM was concerned, you did it?"

"Yes, but Richard and Robert made the decisions," she said.

"If you don't mind me asking, did they pay you well for all this responsibility?"

"Yes, Detective Inspector, they did. Both men are very caring of their staff and appreciate loyalty and hard work, Richard particularly." For just a second her feelings sounded as if they ran deeper for Richard

Bexton-King than just those of a loyal employee for her boss. Was her constant use of Bexton-King's first name an indication of something to pursue?

"Did either of them make enemies in business, Mrs Doherty?"

"Richard and Robert? No." She seemed to find the idea amusing.

"And you can't think of any reason why anyone might want your boss dead?"

"No."

"When did you last see him, Mrs Doherty?" Again that fleeting look of grief.

"Last Tuesday, early in the afternoon, at the garage. He left at about three o'clock to meet an antique dealer at High Lawns. You know, his mother's house in Pontrilas," she added.

"Do you know who the dealer was? We might need to talk to them."

"I'm afraid I don't. Richard made the appointment himself." That was the third or fourth time she'd referred to her boss by his first name, Townshend thought.

"Never mind," he said. "Did you actually see your employer leave BKM?"

"Oh, yes. I even booked the taxi for him. He was going to stop at his doctor's for his medicine on the way."

"Taxi? Didn't he use his own car?"

"It was in our workshop. He'd said it wasn't running properly, so one of the boys was going to have a look at it for him."

"And that would be the Audi?" Townshend asked.

"Yes, a lovely car." That was one issue resolved, Townshend, thought. He'd been wondering what had happened to the victim's car.

"Even compared to the others?" he asked.

"Oh, yes. I much preferred it. I thought Richard drove too fast in the others." Townshend considered this for a few moments. It fitted with what the victim's brother had said.

"Have you spoken to him since last Tuesday afternoon, Mrs Doherty?" She seemed to hesitate before answering, looking down at her hands before meeting his gaze.

"Yes. He rang and asked me to meet him at High Lawns on Tuesday evening when I'd got home from Cardiff."

"Cardiff?"

"Yes I was going to the University Hospital after work to see my daughter. She's just had another baby, and I've not seen it yet. Another grand-daughter," she explained proudly.

"What time did you arrange to meet?" Another slight hesitation.

"Half past eleven. That gave me time to get back and freshen up before…" Her voice tailed off.

"That seems late," Townshend said. She said nothing, but he noticed her colouring up a little as she looked at him. "Were you in a relationship with Mr Bexton-King?" She nodded, and this time tears appeared in her eyes. She fumbled in her bag for a tissue. He gave her a moment, then continued. "What happened when you got to High Lawns, Mrs Doherty, if the last time you saw him was in the afternoon?"

"He wasn't there. The place was dark and all locked up, and I didn't have a key."

"Did you notice anything strange?"

"Strange?"

"Anything unusual or out of the ordinary, Mrs Doherty."

"Not that I can think of, no. I was angry and upset, Detective Inspector. It wasn't like him when he'd made an arrangement. I just drove home."

"And you didn't try to contact him the next day?"

"No." She went to pick up her cup, found it was empty and pushed it away.

"Can we get you another cup, Mrs Doherty?"

"No, thank you."

"Can I ask you why you didn't try to get in touch with him?"

"I told you. I was angry and upset," she answered a little snappily.

"Didn't it worry you that you didn't see or hear from your boss for so many days?"

"No. He's done it before," she said testily. It was obviously a sensitive subject.

"Hopefully, we won't have to take up much more of your time, but can we get you to open this box for us?" he asked and then indicated to Ingleby to put it on the table. She opened it quickly, obviously confident with the combination.

"What do you want to know?" She seemed to have regained her composure.

"Just some names and addresses, please, Mrs Doherty, unless of course, there is some personal documentation in there, or perhaps even a copy of Mr Bexton-King's will."

"I'll need a computer or a laptop for the addresses," she said, holding up a CD. "It's all on here." Ingleby was sent for a laptop. "There won't be any of Richard's papers in this box, Detective Inspector. He kept them all at home in Burghill."

"Do you know where?" He didn't explain that he and Ingleby hadn't been able to find anything. He was surprised when she laughed.

"Yes. He used to joke about having a secret drawer in his desk," she said and explained how to open it. Ingleby, having just returned with a laptop, was given the instructions and sent back upstairs to the team office to arrange for someone to go out to Burghill. He was back before the CD had loaded.

"I sent Sarah, sir," he said. "Ken's already left." Townshend nodded and turned his attention back to Sharon Doherty.

"Whose details did you want?" she asked. Townshend looked to Ingleby to answer her.

"For starters, Valerie Pereira. Somewhere on Belmont, I believe," Ingleby said.

"Here we are. Beattie Avenue," giving him the full address.

"How long had she been the cleaner at Burghill?" Townshend asked.

"About two years. She started cleaning there soon after she started at BKM."

"She cleaned there as well?"

"Yes, and at High Lawns. Richard was so impressed with her that he arranged for her to help his mother out. Now, who else did you want?"

"The gardener at Burghill, Stephen Warner," Ingleby said.

"That might be a bit more difficult. I'm not sure of his address or a contact number. I don't think it's on file, either. He was someone Robert met in one of his clubs, and he was never actually on the books at BKM. As well as the gardens at Burghill and High Lawns, he did do some work on the haulage side, but it was all cash in hand stuff." She was checking the records as she spoke. "No. Nothing for him, but I'm pretty sure he had lodgings somewhere near Cargills, possibly out on Yazor Road, but I wouldn't swear to it."

"Do you know much about him?" Townshend asked.

"He was one of Robert's pets, just like Valerie was one of Richard's. They both seemed to bump into people who were struggling a bit and give them a helping hand. I know he had a strange accent. Robert might have told me where he came from, but I can't remember."

"Did he tell you anything else about him?"

"Apparently he's travelling; a back-packer, Robert called him, but I thought he seemed a bit old for that. And there was something about him working his way from country to country."

"How old would you say he was?"

"I'd put him in his early thirties, but it would only be a guess."

"Who was clearing High Lawns, and who was on the delivery to the auction rooms?"

"Tim Stevens, the haulage foreman was in charge and he would have been driving one of the vans. Ron Broad would have been the other driver. Keith Evans was up there, and Robert had asked Tim to take Stephen Warner along for a bit of extra cash in his pocket."

"We'll need to talk to all of them," Townshend said. Mrs Doherty read out their details. Tim Stevens might be able to tell you where to find Stephen Warner," she added.

"Just before we let you go, Mrs Doherty, we need a DNA sample and fingerprints."

"What for?" She sounded defensive but relaxed when Townshend answered.

"Just for our initial enquiries," he said.

"What happens to them afterwards?"

"They'll be destroyed," Ingleby said.

"Very well," she said, but there was still a noticeable reluctance in her voice. When Ingleby had finished, Townshend thanked her again for coming in. He wasn't overly surprised that she looked relieved the interview was over.

CHAPTER NINE

The outer office was empty. Sarah Miller was in Burghill, Ken Collings in Pontrilas and David Ingleby had gone out with the fingerprint team to visit the BKM men who'd been working at High Lawns. And even better, the phones hadn't rung. It had given Townshend some peace and quiet to have a late lunch at his desk. Although only a sandwich and a coffee it had helped settle a grumbling stomach. Experts of all sorts were of the opinion that you should get up and walk away from your desk at lunchtime, even if it was just for fifteen minutes, but during the course of an investigation, Townshend couldn't bring himself to do it.

The interview with Sharon Doherty had opened up some interesting questions, but had at least settled his mind about the victim's car. The lack of an ordinary road car had for some reason been nagging at him and sorting it out had been like ticking an item off the long list of things to be checked, even if the car in question had gone up in flames at BKM. Little snippets of unexpected information had been added to the pieces of their jigsaw puzzle. That's what a murder enquiry is, he thought flippantly, a massive jigsaw puzzle where not only did you have to fit the pieces together to get the complete picture, you had to find the damned things first and then work out what the picture was. Still, as he'd said to David Ingleby earlier, it was early days.

There was every chance that Sarah would find something useful at Burghill, in this desk drawer that he and Ingleby had missed, and that might give them some more pieces of the puzzle, particularly relating to the will. She seemed to Townshend to be a keen young woman and he hoped she was going to relish being sent out again to visit Val Pereira with David when he got back. But meanwhile, someone had to ring Marcella Bexton-King to arrange for an interview. Despite thinking he'd get David to do it, he knew the best thing was for him to do it. No time like the present. The call went straight through to an answering service.

"Hi, you've reached Marcella. I'm probably off doing something exciting and can't get to the phone, so please leave your number and I'll get back to you." Townshend did so, leaving a short message as well. He'd been half expecting her voice to sound slightly exotic and it was almost disappointing when it didn't. In fact, he thought, it sounded rather like someone trying to make themselves sound more cultured than they were. Well-spoken but with flaws. There was something about the message that seemed to say 'I think I'm better than you' and that nettled him more than it possibly should have. He started on the e-mails. The Forensics report was in for High Lawns, but gave him nothing useful. The place was as clean as a whistle.

"Shit," he muttered. He couldn't help himself. Something, no matter how tiny, would have been helpful, but they'd found nothing. It was hardly unexpected in a house that was being cleared. He wasn't surprised when the report ended with the conclusion that the place had recently been professionally cleaned and was half expecting the same result for Bexton-King's house in Burghill. When he and Ingleby were there, the place had almost been too clean. Some gut instinct told him that Val Pereira, just one person, wouldn't have been able to clean them to that sort of standard, but it would be interesting to see what David Ingleby and Sarah Miller reported when they interviewed her. The question that nagged at him was why Burghill was so clean.

The next e-mail was one he hadn't been expecting so soon, preliminary findings from the Fire Investigation Officer. The garage fire had been started deliberately, using accelerant, of which there had obviously been plenty available on the site. It had been a thorough, comprehensive job, with three separate buildings, a storage yard and all their contents completely destroyed. Apart from that they were still investigating. He resisted the temptation to swear again. There was only a few more minute's peace and quiet before voices in the outer office alerted him that someone was back. Townshend rose from his desk and went to see who it was, finding Sarah, accompanied by a uniformed constable, carrying a large document box.

"Is that thing full, Sarah?" he asked, thinking that this secret drawer of Bexton-King's must have been a big one.

"No, sir," she said, smiling. "There's only a few things in here, but it's all I had in the car to put them in." The constable put the box on Sarah's desk. "He offered to carry it upstairs for me, sir," she explained as the young man left. Townshend wasn't surprised. Sarah was, after all, a very pretty young woman.

"Grab yourself a coffee and we'll see what's inside, shall we?" he said.

"Are you having one, sir?" she asked, picking up the coffee jug. Just for one uncharacteristic moment, he considered saying no, but nodded instead. Then they started on the documents. A couple of them looked bulky. They were business, home and personal life insurance documents with fairly detailed policies, which he passed to Sarah to have a good look through. How much small print can you fit into one document, Townshend thought. He wasn't expecting much of real interest in the business and house policies, but the life insurance policy might be a different matter, so he directed her to look at that one first.

The document he'd been hoping to find, however, Richard Bexton-King's will, was tucked away underneath the policies. He held the envelope in his hand, turning it over and over, noticing immediately that it wasn't sealed. How important it would be to the case he wasn't sure, but there was only one way to find out. He opened the envelope, surprised to find that there was only a single sheet of headed notepaper inside, from Lacey and Bartholomew in Leominster, the solicitors Robert

Bexton-King had said his brother was using. It was dated just a week before, the day before Karen Welby was suggesting Richard Bexton-King was killed, and the same day Robert Bexton-King had said he saw his brother arguing with his wife Marcella in Hereford. Before he had a chance to start reading it, the main phone into the office began to ring. Sarah answered it, almost immediately putting her hand over the mouthpiece and turning to Townshend.

"Phone call for you, sir," she said quietly.

"Who is it?" he said, hardly making a sound, more mouthing the words.

"Someone from the Hereford Times wanting a statement about the enquiry," she whispered.

"Tell them it's an on-going investigation and as soon as we have something to say to them, we'll be in touch." The last thing he wanted to do, with so little information, was talk to the press.

He turned his attention back to the will and its date. Was it a coincidence? Townshend didn't believe in them. When he read them, the contents led him to believe there was a connection, at least between the argument and the will. The sole beneficiary of the will was the victim's brother Robert. His complete estate, the house at Burghill, the business, the cars; everything, lock, stock and barrel. Marcella was getting nothing and would be bound to be annoyed if the will had been changed. But the only way she could have found out that quickly was if Richard had told her that afternoon. Sarah interrupted his thoughts, pointing at a page in the life insurance policy she'd been reading.

"This might be interesting, sir", she said. "The beneficiary of this is Marcella Bexton-King."

"For how much?" Townshend asked.

"£250,000, sir. A quarter of a million pounds."

"A lot of money, Sarah," Townshend said. So Marcella would receive a large amount on Richard's death, as would his brother Robert, who'd said he wasn't aware of the contents of the will, a will which would make him a rich man. Had he been lying? Was the estate enough to kill for? Was the insurance enough to kill for?

CHAPTER TEN

Ken was the next to return to the office, which was hardly surprising when David Ingleby had three men to visit. Townshend, still sitting at a desk in the main office, greeted him and then gave him a few minutes to get himself organised.

"How did it go, Ken?"

"Not bad at all, guv, but there weren't too many people to talk to," Ken replied.

"No?" Townshend was surprised. "Were people out?"

"No, it wasn't that, guv. It's just that High Lawns is the last house on a lane that turns into a bridleway. After turning off the road, there's only three houses up there."

"It's quite private up there, then, Ken?" Townshend asked. He was thinking about the private layout at Burghill.

"Very much so, guv. I reckon it would cost a few bob to live up there," Ken said. "The neighbours keep themselves to themselves. The people in the first two houses, the ones nearest the village, hadn't noticed anything at all that night. They only knew there was something wrong through gossip in the village and when they saw the Scenes of Crime vans in the lane."

"And the third house? Did they see anything?"

"It's a Mrs and Mrs Wright living there. It's about fifty yards down the lane from High Lawns. A lovely couple. They invited me in for a cup of tea. Nice bit of cake as well. Even though they're quite an elderly couple themselves, they liked to keep a lookout for the old lady up the lane, as Mr Wright put it."

"Yes, Bexton-King's mother," Townshend said. Ken nodded and carried on.

"The two of them thought the world of her and were really upset when she died, guv. Even though they knew the house was empty, they kept a bit of an eye on it. The old fella told me that when he was out on Tuesday evening with his dog, the animal was unusually noisy on the way up the lane, barking all the time. Coming back down from the bridleway he saw a car come speeding out of the drive from High Lawns. He said it was going that fast it scraped the front wing against the gate post."

"So there'd be a scratch?" Townshend asked.

"No, more than that. He said the car hit it quite hard and the gate had been missing for a while. It scraped along the hinge bracket which was sticking out a bit. He reckons there'd be a bit of a dent as well."

"Well, that's good news," said Townshend. "Any idea of what time?"

"Oh, yes. Mr Wright's as regular as clockwork at taking his dog out for a walk. Never misses, no matter what the weather is. Around eleven o'clock every night without fail."

"What about the car? Could he give you any details?"

"No, guv, apart from saying it was a two-seater job, a bit flashy and black, but black could mean any dark colour at that time of the night."

"Did he see how many people were in it?" Townshend asked.

"No, guv. He couldn't see."

"Oh well. Anything else, Ken?" Townshend asked.

"No, guv. That's it. The old man's quite sharp and I don't think he's forgotten anything."

"Thanks for your good work, Ken. Get it all typed up, will you?" The information Ken had picked up seemed to confirm what Karen Welby had suggested, but the details on the car were unfortunately vague. He was still thinking about it when David Ingleby came back.

"We only managed to get two of them, sir, Ingleby said. "Tim Stevens, the foreman, was out. His wife said she'd tell him to come in and see us when he got back. I don't think she was very pleased at having the police on her doorstep," he added, grinning.

"That's understandable, David. My mother would have been mortified at having policemen turn up at our front door, and I was in the bloody force!" Townshend laughed at the thought. "Still, it's a shame he wasn't in. He's the one who might be able to tell us where we could find this Stephen Warner guy, isn't he?"

"Yes, sir," Ingleby said.

"Never mind. It'll wait until we talk to this Mr Stevens," Townshend said. "I take it Forensics are already eliminating the prints you did get?"

"Probably after a cup of tea, yes, sir," Ingleby said, smiling. It somehow seemed easier to be light-hearted with Townshend than with his predecessor.

"You'd better get yourself a drink, David, because I want you to go back out with Sarah and interview the cleaner, Mrs Pereira."

"With Sarah?" Ingleby seemed reluctant.

"Yes, David. It'll be good experience for her." Townshend needed to get to the bottom of this issue between David and Sarah. Possibly a word with Ken while they were out of the office to see if he knew anything. He didn't have long to wait. Ingleby decided against a drink, wanting to get on with the interview. As they left, Townshend noticed that the frostiness between them all seemed to be on Ingleby's side, not Sarah Miller's.

"It's the sergeant's wife, guv," Ken said when Townshend asked.

"His wife?" Townshend hadn't met Mrs Ingleby and didn't even know her first name, but he understood the couple to be happy and enjoying life with their young baby. He said as much to Ken.

"They are, guv, very. The problem is Claire's quite an insecure person and Sarah's a very pretty girl…"

"So she thinks she's a threat?" Townshend asked, interrupting, "and she's giving Ingleby a hard time over it?"

"That's the way I read it, guv," Ken said. "She's got no need to worry about the Sarge, he's besotted with her, and as far as Sarah's concerned, the Sarge isn't her type at all."

"But it's making life a little difficult around the office," Townshend commented. Ken nodded and returned to his typing. Townshend sighed and went back to his own desk and the refuge of his office. It was a situation he'd not had to deal with before and he'd have to give it some thought.

CHAPTER ELEVEN

"Mrs Pereira's definitely an upset woman, sir," Ingleby began when he and Sarah Miller had settled themselves in Townshend's office.

"Upset? Why?"

"I think she had a thing for Richard Bexton-King, sir," said Sarah Miller. In the few short months he'd been in Hereford, Townshend had decided that this young woman, only recently made a Detective Constable, had quite a future ahead of her in the force.

"What makes you say that, Sarah?" he asked.

"Female intuition," said Ingleby before Sarah could explain. Townshend frowned. Even after his conversation with Ken, he wasn't sure if his Detective Sergeant was having a dig at Sarah's expense; it wasn't only older men who showed some resistance to female detectives. He decided to give him the benefit of the doubt. "She didn't actually say so, sir," Ingleby continued, ignoring the glare from Sarah Miller.

"But did you ask, David?"

"Well, no, sir." Ingleby went quiet.

"So, Sarah, what makes you think she had 'a thing' as you put it, for our victim?" Townshend asked, turning back to her.

"She was much more upset when we told her about his death than I would have expected his cleaner to be. He might well have been a good boss, but there seemed more to it than that." Townshend smiled. Those were exactly the thoughts he'd had about Sharon Doherty. It seemed that Richard Bexton-King might have been quite a charmer.

"Mm, that seems fair enough. Seeing how people react is just as important as what they say when you ask them questions. Did either of you notice anything else?"

"A couple of other things, sir. I don't think she was that good a cleaner," Ingleby said. Sarah agreed.

"Why?"

"Her flat was a bit of a mess, sir," Sarah said. "It wasn't a very good advertisement for a cleaner."

"It could be a case of spending all her time cleaning for others and not being bothered with her own," Townshend said. "Just look at how clean Burghill was, David." Neither Ingleby or Miller looked convinced. Townshend had to go along with them. They'd been to her flat and he hadn't.

"She was quite dramatic in her grief, sir. Loud sobbing and tears." Sarah sounded as if she didn't approve.

"Mrs Pereira is Spanish, sir," Ingleby interrupted, as if that explained. Sarah Miller continued as if he hadn't spoken.

"Did you ask her when she last cleaned High Lawns and Burghill?"

"Yes, sir. The previous weekend to when he was killed sir, so almost a fortnight ago. She hadn't done it since because both houses were going to be professionally cleaned."

"Both houses?" Townshend asked.

"Yes, sir," Sarah said. "High Lawns and Burghill."

"And what about BKM? When did she last clean there?"

"She cleaned the offices and showrooms every evening when they'd closed," Ingleby said, referring to his notebook. "Half past five to half past six."

"What about Saturdays?" Townshend asked.

"Yes, that includes Saturdays as well, but she says she didn't notice anything strange last Saturday, sir. She did say there were still some men in the haulage office, but that was all."

"Did she by any chance know who did the final cleaning at High Lawns?"

"Yes, sir, we asked her. She said it was a company called Absolutely Spotless. Apparently she's worked for them in the past."

"God, where do people get the names for their businesses from these days," Townshend muttered. "Sarah, will you get on to them, ask them if they spotted anything strange at either High Lawns or Burghill?"

"Yes, sir," she said, rising from her seat.

"And ask Ken to chase up the fingerprinting people about the prints David brought back," he added as she left the office. Townshend then updated Ingleby not only on the contents of the will and the life insurance policy but also what Ken had found out in Pontrilas. He'd just finished when Ken Colling's bulk filled the office doorway.

"The fingerprint boys have done their checks, guv," he said. "They check out with prints on the trunk".

"Thanks, Ken. Let me know when Stevens arrives will you," Townshend said.

"Either of you want coffee?" Ken asked." Both Townshend and Ingleby took up the offer.

"What do you think of all this, David? Is it all about money? Or is there something lurking in the background we haven't picked up on?" Ingleby didn't answer straight away. His former DI hadn't tended to talk things through very much.

"Do you think it could have something to do with women?" he asked. "There were all those condoms in his bathroom."

"I think he might just have been sexually active, David. Robert was quite vague when we asked about him being a ladies' man. He was certainly a charmer if Sharon Doherty and Val Pereira are any indication. He might just have been a 'love 'em and leave 'em' type."

"But at the moment, sir, the only woman we know of for sure is Sharon Doherty," Ingleby said.

"But is that because we're not asking the right questions?"

"Are you thinking of Val Pereira, sir?"

"Yes, her and Mrs Morgan," Townshend said.

"Mrs Morgan? Who's she?"

"She's the secretary at the auction rooms where the body was found," Townshend said. "Until now, she'd slipped my mind. It's a similar situation to Sarah's feelings about Val Pereira. There was something under the surface when she found out who the body was."

"Shall we get Sarah to talk to her, sir? She seems quite sympathetic," Ingleby suggested. Townshend nodded, surprised.

"Good idea, David. And of course, there's Val Pereira."

"What about her, sir?"

"I think we need to know for sure if she was having a relationship with Bexton-King."

"Sarah again?"

"I think so, don't you?" Townshend paused. "I think we need to expand things a bit, David. Get Ken on to Bexton-King's social life. I want to know where he socialised and who with."

"Who's likely to know, sir? His brother, Sharon Doherty?"

"They're as good a place to start as any other. In the meantime, the two of us will have a chat with Tim Stevens when he comes in." Ingleby left the office to talk to Sarah Miller and Ken Collings while Townshend settled back in his chair to reflect for a few moments. And remembered that Marcella Bexton-King hadn't returned his call. He sat forward again and reached for his phone. As before, the call went through to the answering service.

CHAPTER TWELVE

"Sorry I wasn't in when your guys called earlier," Tim Stevens said when Townshend and Ingleby had settled themselves in the interview room. "The wife said something about you wanting my fingerprints?"

"That's right, Mr Stevens, but don't worry about us missing you," Ingleby said. "It's actually worked out quite well, because there are a couple of questions we wanted to ask you as well."

"Well, anything I can do to be of help," Stevens said. "What about the fingerprints? What do you want them for?" Tim Stevens was a man in his early forties, Townshend guessed and he seemed quite a confident person, quite skinny, with well-cropped black hair, and a friendly open smile. He didn't sound anxious, just curious.

Townshend had decided on the way downstairs from the office to let Ingleby lead the questioning and the Detective Sergeant had seemed quite pleased at the idea. Townshend was going to take on Ingleby's role and do the note-taking.

"We need your prints to eliminate them from fingerprints found at High Lawns, Mr Stevens," Ingleby explained as he took the man's prints. "They'll be destroyed at the end of the investigation." He didn't go into any more detail than he had to, Townshend noticed.

"Speaking of High Lawns, can we start there, Mr Stevens?" Ingleby asked as Stevens was wiping his fingers clean.

"Richard's mother's house? He asked a group of us to crate stuff up and get it down to the auction rooms in Pontrilas. He said he'd rather get that sorted himself than arrange for a house clearance company. It gave him more control, and if there's one thing he liked, it was to be in control."

"How many of you were working there?"

"Just four of us. Myself, Ron Broad, Keith Evans and Robert's little friend Stephen."

"Stephen Warner?"

"Yes. Robert asked me to take him up to give him a bit of work."

"You sound like you weren't very keen on him," Ingleby asked.

"He's a good enough worker, that's for sure, but there's something about him I'm not quite sure about. Of course, I'm Hereford through and through. It might just be his accent that puts me off."

"His accent?"

"Yes. Australia, New Zealand, possibly even South African, I can't really tell the difference. He did tell me, but I wasn't really interested as long as he did his work."

"He was back-packing around the world, wasn't he?" Townshend interrupted.

"Yes," said Stevens, turning to look at him rather than Ingleby. "But back-packing always makes me think of teenagers, not a grown man in his mid-thirties. He should be settled down with responsibilities like the rest of us. But like I said, as long as he did his work it didn't matter."

"How long had you, Ron Broad and Keith Evans been working for BKM, Mr Stevens?" It was back to a question from Ingleby.

"All three of us were taken on by Ronald, Richard and Robert's father. We've been there a while."

"And you say you were packing the crates at High Lawns? Were they being stacked in the house, or put straight on the vans?"

"As soon as each one was packed, it was put on a van. We had a couple of long wheel base transits up there. We were storing the stuff at BKM because there was CCTV on the premises. It wasn't due to be taken to the auction rooms until the Thursday before the sale, so Richard was insistent that the loaded vans be stored at BKM. We took the vans back up on Wednesday morning to finish the job."

"Was there anybody there or any vehicles when you arrived on Wednesday?"

"Yes, the cleaning company, Absolutely something, were there, already cleaning the rooms we'd cleared the day before."

"Did you see Mr Bexton-King on Tuesday afternoon, Mr Stevens?" Ingleby asked.

"Yes. He turned up in a taxi just before a dealer from Leominster arrived. There was a bit of an argument between those two. From what I could gather the guy from Leominster was offering silly money for some good antiques. Richard sent him packing. He won't be messed about when money's involved."

"Was he still there when you left?"

"Yes, in the kitchen. On his phone to Sharon and drinking a cup of coffee."

"Sharon Doherty?" Ingleby asked.

"Yes. He was knocking her off at one time. I don't blame him. Things weren't right in his marriage. Everyone in the company knew. It was like an open secret."

"Was that the last time you saw him?"

"Yes. He seemed his usual self."

"Do you recall an old-fashioned travelling trunk?" asked Ingleby.

"A huge brown thing, with leather straps? It was old fashioned when the Titanic sank."

"That's the one."

"It was under the stairs gathering dust and cobwebs. The brute was bloody heavy, but Richard had told us it would be. Ron and I thought we'd be able to manage it, but we almost had to drag it out. Getting it up into the van was the worst part. At least it had been cleaned off by the time we moved it."

"Cleaned?" Townshend asked, looking up from his notebook.

"Yes, somebody had wiped the dust off. I presumed Richard had done it. Didn't make it any lighter, though," he joked.

"Had he said what was in it?"

"Nothing, apparently. It was just a very heavy piece."

"Did anyone else handle it, apart from you and Mr Broad?"

"Yes. It took all four of us to get it up into the van. It was the last thing we put on before we came back to the yard."

"And the cleaning company were there when you left?"

"Yes. They had keys which they were going to return to Sharon when they'd finished."

"You said that Richard Bexton-King was having a relationship with Sharon Doherty," Ingleby said.

"Yes."

"Do you know if he was seeing anyone else?"

"Knowing Richard, no. He would only ever see one woman at any one time."

"What about his brother?" asked Ingleby. Townshend glanced at him. Where did that question come from?

"Robert? No. He's a gambler, and as for women, that isn't his inclination. It's why he fell out with his father."

"He's homosexual?" Ingleby asked.

"Yes, but he prefers the word 'gay'."

"Is he lucky at his gambling?"

"Not usually. It was another point of contention with Ronald. Robert always seemed to be needing money." Well done with that line of questioning, Townshend thought. Then Ingleby returned to the subject of the vans.

"On the Thursday, who took the vans to the auction rooms?"

"Just me and Ron. The auction rooms had said their guys would help unload, so we didn't need Keith and Stephen."

"When we talked to Sharon Doherty, she said you might know how we can get hold of Stephen Warner," Ingleby said. "We just want his prints to eliminate him, the same as you."

"Yazor Road. He's got lodgings in a guest house with a Mrs Bellamy. Funny bloody woman she is. I've had to pick him up a few times."

"Hasn't he got his own transport?"

"He used a pushbike usually and sometimes Robert let him use one of the fleet vans. He does a bit of gardening and odd jobs for people, so I'm not sure when you'll catch him in."

CHAPTER THIRTEEN

There were road-works on Aylestone Hill, their three-way traffic lights causing havoc with the early morning traffic coming in to the city as office and shop workers headed towards their daily grind. Townshend and Ingleby were both grateful to be travelling in the opposite direction, but with the road-works sited on the mini-roundabout, there was still a lengthy delay. Ingleby was proving to be a not very patient driver in the slow traffic, while the DI sat calmly in the passenger seat, apparently lost in thought. Their destination was near the summit of the hill, just before the road started dropping away in a fairly straight run to join the Worcester road. Townshend breathed a sigh of relief as Ingleby pulled off the main road into the drive of a large Georgian mansion where Marcella Bexton-King had a luxury flat. Ingleby stopped the car near the porticoed front door.

"Have you done the police driving course, David?" Townshend asked, undoing his seat-belt.

"The driving course? No, sir," Ingleby replied. "It was suggested when I was still in uniform, but then I joined CID."

"Get in touch with HQ at Hindlip and organise one for yourself when this case is over, David."

"I don't think there's anything wrong with my driving," Ingleby said, irritated at the implied criticism. "And it's twelve weeks long."

"Treat it as a target from your job review. It's not just about driving, David. It'll do you good in your career." Townshend got out of the car and walked up to the front door, Ingleby following, unhappy about this suggestion from his boss. "What number flat is it, David?"

"One, I assume, sir. She lives in the ground floor apartment." The name card on the intercom by the door confirmed Ingleby's assumption.

Townshend pressed the relevant button and a foreign-sounding voice answered, distorted slightly by the speaker.

"Who is it, please?"

"Detective Inspector Townshend, West Mercia Police. I'm here to see Mrs Bexton-King.

"Police? Wait a moment please." The metallic voice sounded worried, but a buzzer sounded unlocking the heavy front door. Townshend noticed Ingleby was looking strangely at the intercom.

"I'm sure I recognise that voice, sir," he said as they walked into a large hallway with a polished tiled floor and an elegant wooden stairway leading upwards. In the centre sat an ornate oak table supporting a large floral decoration. Various pictures hung on the walls, mostly landscapes.

"Well, I'm assuming it wasn't Marcella Bexton-King," Townshend said, looking around. "It sounded nothing like her answering machine message."

"No, sir. I think it was…" He didn't have a chance to finish as a door opened to the left, and a slim petite dark haired woman appeared, looking in their direction. "As I was saying, sir," Ingleby continued, "Mrs Pereira." She in turn obviously recognised him and gave him a smile.

"Ah, you are the young man who came to see me with the nice police lady," she said, her English good but accented.

"Yes, that's right, Mrs Pereira, and this is my boss, Detective Inspector Townshend," Ingleby replied. Townshend nodded and extended his hand to the woman, who shook it uncertainly, looking a little awed by what she considered to be his authority. He allowed Ingleby to continue leading the conversation. "We're here to see Mrs Bexton-King, Mrs Pereira," the Detective Sergeant said.

"That's what he said on the intercom," Mrs Periera said, glancing at the DI, and Townshend smiled. "She's still in bed."

"We do rather need to speak to her," Ingleby insisted.

"She's not alone. She has someone with her."

"That doesn't change the fact that we need to talk to her," Townshend said. "Will you please tell her we're here and that we have some questions for her?" Mrs Pereira still hesitated, plainly concerned about disturbing her employer. "And Mrs Pereira, will you also tell her that if she doesn't agree to talk to us, I will arrange for uniformed officers to escort her to the police station."

With a slightly shocked expression, the cleaner now quickly ushered them from the vestibule and through the front door of the flat. Leaving them in the living room, she went off down a passage, presumably to announce their arrival to Mrs Bexton-King. The two men sat down to wait on an expensive-looking leather sofa, both unable to stop themselves looking around. To Townshend the room was luxurious, but tasteless beyond belief, an ostentatious display of money. He compared it to his own much more humble flat on Whitecross Road and shrugged. He could hear voices and a mumbled conversation through a bedroom door and touched Ingleby on the arm.

"I'm assuming she didn't say she was working here when you saw her, David?"

"No, sir. She didn't mention it."

"It might be interesting to find out how long she's been doing it," Townshend said and Mrs Pereira came back in the room at just the right moment.

"About three weeks," she said in response to Ingleby's question. "Mr Bexton-King recommended me, when his mother died and I wasn't needed at High Lawns." She paused. "I have told Mrs Bexton-King you are here. She is not a happy woman, but she says she's coming." There was no time for her to add anything before the woman in question burst angrily along the passage wrapped in a silk dressing-gown. The two policemen rose politely. Despite the anger in her face and her messed-up hair, Marcella Bexton-King was undeniably an extremely attractive woman and the dressing gown left little to the imaginations of the two policemen. Ingleby seemed particularly uncomfortable. The description of her name as warlike and strong that Townshend had idly looked up seemed to fit her perfectly and he knew he was going to have trouble with her.

"Just what the hell do you think you're doing coming to my home at this time in the morning, making threats? It's intolerable!"

"Good morning, Mrs Bexton-King," Townshend said calmly. "My name is Detective Inspector Townshend and this is Detective Sergeant Ingleby."

"I don't care who the hell you are! I don't want you here. She shouldn't have let you in," she added, gesturing at Mrs Pereira. "Now get out!"

"No, Mrs Bexton-King, we won't get out. We have some questions for you and you haven't been returning our calls," Townshend said, still calm.

"I'll answer your damned calls when I'm good and ready and not before. Just go!" Before Townshend could answer a man's voice called down the passage, a voice both policemen recognised immediately.

"Is everything all right, Marcella? Who's here?" Robert Bexton-King, wrapped in only a towel, stopped as he entered the lounge and saw who she was arguing with. "Ah," was all he could say as he recognised the two detectives.

"Good morning, Mr Bexton-King," Townshend said to the embarrassed man, trying not to show his surprise. "This is rather unexpected."

"Yes, it certainly is, Detective Inspector," Bexton-King said and then turned to Marcella. "I really think you ought to talk to them rather than make a fuss, Marcella," he said.

"It would be for the best, Mrs Bexton-King," Townshend agreed. "I'm sure it would be embarrassing for you if uniformed officers arrived on your doorstep. Now, I would suggest that both you and Mr Bexton-King get dressed while Mrs Pereira makes us all a cup of coffee." Val Pereira, who had been hovering in the background and presumably listening, Townshend thought, disappeared in what he assumed was the direction of the kitchen. Robert Bexton-King put his arm around the shoulders of a still fuming Marcella and guided her back down the passage to her bedroom.

CHAPTER FOURTEEN

"Well, Detective Inspector, you've certainly got Marcella wound up," said Robert Bexton-King, returning to the lounge. "She's in there like a bomb waiting to go off," he said, gesturing down the passage. "Hopefully a quick shower will help calm her down." He poured himself a black coffee from the pot which Val Pereira had provided before discreetly going back to the kitchen, and sat in an armchair, looking sheepish and uncomfortable.

"That's as may be, Mr Bexton-King, but before she appears, there are a few more questions we need to ask you," Townshend said quite sharply. Ingleby took out his notebook.

"And the first of those, I imagine, is about Marcella?" Townshend nodded and waited for an explanation. "It's been going on for some time," Bexton-King said.

"You told us on Sunday that you hadn't slept with her," Townshend said. "You were even quite dismissive of the idea. Why lie, Mr Bexton-King? I don't hold very well with people lying to me."

"For the same reason anyone lies. To make things look better for myself."

"Better for yourself? In the circumstances, I hardly think it's achieved that. How does Mrs Bexton-King feel about your homosexuality?" Townshend asked suddenly. The question seemed to come out of the blue, but Robert Bexton-King took it in his stride.

"You've been told about that? No matter, it's no secret," he replied very matter-of-factly.

"Nothing in a murder inquiry is a secret, Mr Bexton-King, but you haven't answered my question. How does your sister-in-law feel about your homosexuality?"

"I have no idea and I haven't asked her, but it doesn't seem to bother her. Rather than homosexuality, I think the word you're really looking for is bi-sexuality, Detective Inspector. As long as they're attractive enough, I'll sleep with a man or a woman."

"And is that why your father left the business solely to your older brother?"

"Oh, he absolutely hated the idea of me being gay," Bexton-King said, "But that wasn't the reason Richard got the business. My father was a traditionalist, Detective Inspector. Everything left to the eldest son and any other sons don't get a look in, not even a silver bloody teaspoon. Primogeniture, they call it."

"How did you feel about that?"

"To be honest, it didn't bother me. I'd known right from my childhood that it was going to happen and Richard wanted it more than I did. It didn't seem fair, but it's just the way it was. I definitely didn't feel bitter towards Richard over it. He'd decided when we were both young that no matter what the old man's will said, he would make sure I got half of the business."

"Half? I thought it was his and you managed the showroom and sales."

"Yes, I do, but I own half the business, not that there's ever much ready cash."

"For your gambling?" Townshend asked. Bexton-King laughed.

"You really do your homework, don't you?" he said. "Yes, Detective Inspector, my gambling has meant that life is one long and constant financial crisis." He smiled self-depracatingly.

"Why do it if you keep losing?" Ingleby asked, looking up from his notebook.

"You're not a gambler, are you, Detective Sergeant?" Ingleby shook his head. "If you were, you'd know it's always about the next bet or game of cards. It'll be the big win that puts everything right."

"So what's the set-up here?" Townshend asked. "Is it just about sex, or money, or was it about getting one over on your older brother?"

"Sex, Detective Inspector, nothing more. It didn't start until Richard and Marcella's marriage was over."

"Not money to help with the gambling?"

"No. But that's not to say Marcie isn't rather well-off." Townshend noted with amusement Bexton-King's use of a pet-name. He imagined she would hate it.

"Well-off? Is that courtesy of your brother?"

"Yes, I suppose you could say that. Marcie suggested a settlement, quite a large one, in agreement for not contesting the divorce. He jumped at the chance to keep everything private and even said she could carry on living here rent-free."

"Was he paying the rent for her?"

"No. Richard owns, or rather owned the place. It's part of his property portfolio. He had places all over the county, usually about this size. It's the only one worth anything."

"What about this settlement? Was it a legal agreement? Were solicitors involved?"

"Solicitors? No. It was a gentleman's agreement," Bexton-King said.

"So was the divorce being handled by solicitors?"

"As far as I know, Richard was doing it himself. He didn't talk to me about it."

"He was pushing it through because Marcella had agreed not to contest it?"

"Yes."

"And that was in spite of all his assets and investments?" Townshend asked.

"Yes. As I told you, Richard and Marcella sorted out an agreement between themselves," Bexton-King said. Townshend wasn't really satisfied with the answer, but it depended on the size of the agreement. He put it to one side for the moment.

"I think that because of your relationship with Mrs Bexton-King, we need to re-address some of the questions we asked you on Sunday." As he spoke, a door opened along the passage and a now fully-clothed Marcella Bexton-King appeared. A favourite phrase of his mother's from long ago slipped into his mind as Marcella entered the room: 'mutton dressed as lamb.' The woman was simply dressed in a style inappropriate and much too young for her age. He took the opportunity to pour himself and Ingleby another coffee from the pot while watching her. If her anger had abated, it wasn't by much.

"Let's get on with this," she snapped. "Then you can get the hell out of my home."

"If you could give us just a few more minutes, Mrs Bexton-King," Townshend said politely. "We have a few more questions to ask your brother-in-law." He immediately sensed her bristling at his words but Robert Bexton-King butted in before she said anything.

"Just take a few minutes out in the bedroom, Marcie. I'll give you a shout when they've done with me," he said. Townshend could only describe the way she stormed from the room as 'flouncing', making him think he was right about her not liking Robert's pet name for her. "Ask away, Detective Inspector," he said, smiling.

"It's about your brother," Townsend began.

"Yes?"

"Did he take prescription pain-killers for anything?" Bexton-King looked puzzled at the question, obviously not expecting it. Had he coloured up a little at it? Townshend wasn't sure.

"Yes, he did and had done since that bad crash where Kim McAuley died. He did some damage to his neck and shoulders and it was constantly giving him gyp."

"Do you know what it was?"

"No, but you could ask his doctor. I know it was a strong one, though."

"Who is his doctor?" Townshend asked.

"Dr Graham. He's got a private surgery on King's Acre," Bexton-King replied.

"Thank you. Now tell me again about your brother's will, Mr Bexton-King. Were you telling the truth about not knowing what was in it?"

"Not quite," Bexton-King admitted. "I was telling you the truth when I said I didn't know what's in it, but I do know what's not in it and that's anything for Marcella." Townshend waited. "She's not getting a penny."

"How do you know?"

"She told me. I saw her for dinner on Wednesday evening after my Lichfield trip. She was still angry about it."

"When did she find out?"

"On Monday," Bexton-King replied.

"So was that what their argument was about?"

"Yes."

"Why did she think she'd still be in the will, with your brother divorcing her?" Townshend asked. He found it difficult to believe she could be so naïve.

"I know it seems silly, but that's what she's like. She was convinced he'd leave her something in his will. Some chance. He was glad to get rid of her. Because he told her about the will, she was trying to get more out of him for the settlement."

"And he said no, I presume," Townshend said.

"Not only that, he told her she'd already had more than she was worth. That's enough to upset any woman." Bexton-King hesitated, obviously uncertain about something. Townshend sipped his coffee, waiting. "She was that angry with him that she had another go at him about it," Bexton-King continued.

"When was that, Mr Bexton-King?"

"On Tuesday evening at High Lawns, our mother's house in Pontrilas."

CHAPTER FIFTEEN

Marcella Bexton-King was still fuming with anger when her brother-in-law sent her into the lounge from the bedroom. She almost collided with Mrs Pereira, who was coming in from the kitchen to see if fresh coffee was needed. Marcella furiously waved her back in the direction of the kitchen with instructions not to bother them and remained standing until the cleaner had left the room. Then she exploded.

"How dare you come bursting uninvited into my home?" she demanded.

"I've no wish to argue with you, Mrs Bexton-King, but we did not come bursting in, as you well know," Townshend said.

"You're throwing your weight around. It's no wonder the police have such terrible reputation and people have lost all respect for you. This is an invasion of privacy and you're bullies. I want you out of here, now!"

"Have you quite finished, Mrs Bexton-King? I have some questions for you and the sooner I can ask them, the sooner we can leave," Townshend said calmly. He was well aware that she would quieten down, but just wished it could be sooner rather than later.

"I don't care about your questions and I don't see how I can help you."

"That's for me to decide, Mrs Bexton-King. As I'm sure your brother-in-law has pointed out to you, this is a murder investigation relating to the murder of your ex-husband. I suggest you take it seriously."

"As you said, Detective Inspector, my ex-husband." She stressed the 'ex'. "He's not my responsibility or my concern. We're separated and that's an end of it as far as I'm concerned. Now please leave. She paused for breath, then said "I want nothing to do with it." Could this woman be as cold as she appeared to be, Townshend thought, or was she hiding something? Whether or not she wanted anything to do with it, he was determined that she was going to answer his questions.

"Mrs Bexton-King, I have been informed that just a day before your husband…" She glared at him. "Sorry, ex-husband, died, you were seen arguing with him on the city streets and that you actually struck him. Circumstantial of course, but enough for me to take you in to the station for questioning. On the other hand, if I considered your attitude as somehow obstructing me in the course of my enquiries, I could have you arrested." It was Townshend's turn to pause to gather himself. It would do neither of them any good if he got angry. "Now, we can either do this like civilised adults," he said, despite a growing belief that despite her age, he was talking to a petulant teenager, "or we can continue this at the police station. Which is it to be, Mrs Bexton-King? I have no strong feelings one way or the other as long as I get answers to my questions." He poured himself another coffee from the almost empty jug and gave her a little time to think over his words. After a few minutes of silent fuming on her part, she sat down in an armchair opposite him, an expression on her face that somehow mixed anger and resignation. He made her wait just a little longer before asking his first question.

"Was your divorce amicable, Mrs Bexton-King?" She glared at him before answering.

"No."

"Was it you or husband who initiated it?"

"My ex-husband." Again, she stressed the 'ex'.

"On what grounds, Mrs Bexton-King?"

"This is very personal, Detective Inspector, and almost intrusive."

"Please answer the question, Mrs Bexton-King."

"The breakdown of our relationship." She seemed pleased with the vagueness of her answer. Townshend decided not to pursue that angle of the divorce. At this point of the investigation, it wasn't that important. He could come back to it later if he needed to.

"Were you contesting it?"

"No."

"Why not?"

"Richard and I agreed on a settlement," she said, after a moment.

"What was he doing? Buying you off?"

"Well, it looks like it, doesn't it?" she snapped. Each question was increasing her anger. It showed all the signs of being a difficult interview and he might yet have to take her to the station.

"And you thought it wasn't enough." It was a statement not a question. She looked surprised, but he didn't give her a chance to speak. "Was there another man involved?" He asked. "Other men?" The look he received could have shattered rock, but she nodded. "Was it any one man in particular?" he asked.

"Any one man in particular?" she flared. "What do you think I am, some kind of whore?" He made no apology, angering her even more.

"Was it?"

"Yes." It seemed to almost hurt her to say it and she snapped the answer out.

"And the settlement with Richard was to keep this man's name off the divorce papers?" A nod was the only response. "Was that your idea or his?"

"Mine. But he was happy to go along with it; he hated to be in the public eye."

"Go on," Townshend prompted.

"I told Richard I wouldn't contest the divorce if he gave me a settlement and kept the man's name out of it. Otherwise, I threatened to fight him every inch of the way and take him for as much as I could. I think his solicitors persuaded him it was a good idea in the end, though," she explained. Almost a kind of reverse blackmail, Townshend thought, but stayed quiet. It might be worth pursuing. He thought the whole scenario strange, but then on the occasions he'd divorced, he'd never had enough money for his ex-wives to worry about.

"Was it really that important? To the other man, I mean?"

"Yes," was all she said. Important enough to kill, wondered Townshend. He didn't know. Yet.

"I'm going to need to know this man's name, Mrs Bexton-King" he said.

"I'm not prepared to say," she said, shaking her head firmly. "I'd need to talk to him first." Confident that he would find out one way or another, Townshend changed tack.

"So tell me about his will," he said.

"What about it?" she asked, puzzled.

"How did you feel about being written out of it?" Sometimes Townshend felt like a psychotherapist with the questions he asked.

"What do you think? Angry, of course. He promised me."

"Promised you what?" Townshend asked.

"Promised to keep me in his will no matter what," she said, confusing Townshend.

"When did he promise that?" It seemed strange behaviour for a man divorcing his wife over adultery.

"When we married."

"And you didn't think that might have changed with the divorce?"

"No. Why should it?" It was said in such a matter of fact way that it gave Townshend a real flavour of her way of thinking. Richard Bexton-King was a possible source of further income to this silly woman while alive, but that had to be balanced against the life insurance pay-out.

"So you were angry and that's what the argument was about on Monday."

"Yes, but I wasn't angry enough to kill him, if that's what you're getting at," she said.

"Let's talk about his life insurance," Townshend said. "Do you know anything about his life insurance policy?" he asked.

"I knew he had life insurance," she said. "That would be absolutely typical of Richard. Always so sensible. He was very organised."

"Do you know who the beneficiary is?"

"No."

"You, Mrs Bexton-King, for a rather large sum."

"Me?" He nodded, noticing the look of surprise clouded by avarice.

"When did you last see him alive, Mrs Bexton-King?" There was no hesitation in her answer.

"On Tuesday evening, at his mother's."

"Can I ask why, especially after your argument the previous day?"

"After him telling me about the will, I wanted more money in the settlement."

"I thought he'd already said 'no.'"

"He had, but I thought I might be able to change his mind."

"Did you?"

"No. He wasn't very talkative and we argued again. But he was still very much alive when I left. He just wanted me to go."

"Could he have been waiting for someone?" Townshend asked.

"No, I don't think so. Knowing him, he had work to do."

"What makes you say that?"

"The business was everything to him. It's all Richard ever thought about. And he never wanted to go anywhere but his precious golf club and just one particular pub. He just never wanted to have a life, even though he had the money."

"Do you know which pub?"

"No. I didn't care and I never went with him," she snorted. The anger was still there.

"What time did you leave High Lawns?"

"About half past seven."

"You've been very helpful, Mrs Bexton-King, thank you," Townshend began.

"If we've done, you can leave," she said, not acknowledging his thanks.

"Not quite, Mrs Bexton-King," said Townshend.

"But if you've no more questions…" she began.

"I haven't, but we need to take fingerprints and a DNA sample from you, please."

"DNA? What for?" she demanded. Townshend sighed. Why did people always react that way when DNA was mentioned?

"To rule your DNA out from any we might find, Mrs Bexton-King. We will of course destroy both the prints and the sample as soon as the investigation is complete," he said. People had become almost paranoid about DNA since the government had mentioned a national DNA database. Her agreement came in the form of another glare, but she at least allowed Ingleby to take the sample.

CHAPTER SIXTEEN

Townshend felt almost relieved when the interview with Marcella was over. She made no effort to move and show him and Ingleby out. No matter, he thought, they knew the way. He rose and walked around the sofa to the huge lounge windows. The promising early morning sunshine had already disappeared, leaving in its wake the inevitable grey rain clouds. A question occurred to him, prompted by the sight of the well-kept, tidy garden.

"Who does the gardening here, Mrs Bexton-King? I presume there is a gardener?" All he received was a glare.

"I thought we'd finished," she snapped.

"It's just a simple question," he said.

"One of Robert's little darlings. Can't say that I like him, but I haven't seen him since last week."

"Is his name Stephen Warner by any chance?" Townshend asked.

"Yes, I think it's something like that. I don't have much to do with him."

"And you say you haven't seen him lately?"

"He's usually here on a Monday, but he didn't turn up yesterday."

"Why one of Robert's little darlings, Mrs Bexton-King?" Townshend said after a pause. It was a strange phrase, he thought.

"Why do you think, Detective Inspector?"

"I take it they're having a relationship?" he said, answering her question with a question.

"I'd hardly put it that strongly, but yes."

"And despite that, you're still sleeping with Robert?" Townshend asked.

"Yes, Detective Inspector," she said, laughing at what she took to be discomfort on his part. "We both enjoy sex a lot, so why shouldn't we? Does that shock you?" Townshend didn't reply, turning instead to Ingleby.

"Can you get Mr Bexton-King back in here, David? I think we'll have a few final words before we leave." As Ingleby went in search of Robert Bexton-King, Marcella was clearly unhappy about this further delay to the two policemen leaving, but she didn't say anything.

"More questions, Detective Inspector? I thought we'd done," Robert Bexton-King said as he followed Ingleby back into the room. "Wasn't there a TV detective who had a habit of always asking questions just as he was about to leave a room? Columbo I think it was." He smiled. "Anyway, what can I do for you this time?"

"Stephen Warner, Mr Bexton-King. How do you know him?"

"I met him at a club."

"A club? Can you be more specific?"

"A private club, Detective Inspector. A gay club."

"So is Warner gay?" Townshend asked.

"Yes and no. I think he's happy either way," Bexton-King said.

"And you got him work at BKM?"

"Yes. I mentioned him to Richard and he had a word with Sharon. She always accepted his judgement as better than mine and as she did the hiring and firing, it seemed the best way to go about it." Townshend nodded and looked at Ingleby. "I think we're done here now, David."

"And about bloody time, too," he heard Marcella mutter, but ignored her.

"Thank you both for your help," he said to both Robert and Marcella. "If we have any further questions we'll be in touch." They didn't wait to find out Marcella's reaction to Townshend's words.

The rain had started again as Ingleby pulled the car out onto Aylestone Hill to head back into the city centre. It was quieter than when they'd driven out, but there was a still a hold-up at the road-works.

"What did you make of that, David?" Townshend asked.

"Robert and Marcella?"

"Yes," said Townshend.

"Well, they're certainly a strange pair, sir." Townshend nodded in agreement.

"There's too many loose ends and too much we don't know, don't you think?"

"Like what, sir?" This was not a way of working he'd encountered before. His previous DI had always just thrown out instructions, whereas Townshend seemed to like to discuss things.

"This man Marcella Bexton-King's hiding for starters. Why's she doing it? What is so important about him?"

"Married man, sir?"

"Almost certainly, David, but that's not enough for him to be this keen on keeping his name out of a divorce. It's not exactly a social stigma any more. I suppose it could depend on who he's married to." He paused. "Could it be his career in some way? Is he in the public eye?"

""Do you think he's a possible suspect, sir?" Ingleby asked.

"Wanting to keep something a secret so badly can be a very good motive for murder, David, especially if there's a real possibility of that secret coming out." Townshend paused again. "We're not going to know until we find out who he is and what the big secret is."

"What about Marcella?" David asked, starting to pull away as the traffic lights changed and then swearing as the car in front stalled. The lights switched back to red before the unfortunate driver could get it going again.

"Yes, David. What about her?" Townshend was quiet for a few minutes, lost in thought and not speaking again until Ingleby parked the car in the police station car park. "Let's get the team together when we get upstairs, David, and talk this out. It might help us to sort our thoughts out and it'll bring them up to speed as well."

There was a delay before they could talk, though. When the two men reached their upstairs office there was a message for Townshend. A woman named Ginny Marston, a journalist from the Hereford Times, wanted him to get in touch.

"Couldn't you have passed this on to the Press Office, Ken?" he said, a bit irritated. "She probably only wants an update on the case."

"She was insistent, guv," Ken replied. "Said she wanted to talk to the officer in charge of the investigation."

"Go straight to the top for a proper story, eh?" Ingleby joked.

"No," said Ken, serious for once. "She said she had some information relating to the victim."

"Something about Bexton-King? And she only wants to talk to me?"

"Yes, guv."

"OK, Ken, leave it with me. I take it she left her number?"

"Yes, guv and said something about having sent you an e-mail." Townshend nodded and sighed.

"Sarah not around yet?" he asked, looking around the office.

"Not at the moment. She said something about seeing that Morgan woman in Pontrilas. You know, the one from the auction room you wanted us to talk to. She'll be back a bit later."

"Good. When she gets back, let me know. It's a meeting around the white board to pool our ideas, OK? In the meantime, Ken..." Townshend left the rest unsaid, grinning.

"Yeah, I know, guv. Get the coffee on," Ken replied, laughing.

CHAPTER SEVENTEEN

Not wanting to proceed with anything until Sarah Miller returned and the team had been a given a chance to consolidate what they'd already learned, Townshend took a deep breath and rang the Hereford Times offices. He didn't like talking to the press, always aware that a slip of the tongue or a wrong word would certainly end up in an article.

"Hello, Hereford Times News Desk," a voice said.

"Is Ginny Marston available please?" he asked politely.

"Speaking," said the person who'd answered. It was a friendly voice, and if the word could be used appropriately, a smiley voice. "How can I help?"

"It's Detective Inspector Townshend, Mrs Marston. You wanted to talk to me?"

"Miss," she said.

"Sorry?"

"It's Miss Marston, Detective Inspector."

"Oh, right. Sorry again." She laughed, a pleasant laugh which brought a smile to his own face.

"I've got some information relating to the Bexton-King murder," she said without any preamble. It wasn't what he'd been expecting and he picked up a pen and pulled a pad of paper closer. He was much more used to journalists wanting information than giving it up, but he refrained from saying so.

"OK, I'm ready," he said. "What have you got for me, Miss Marston?" There was a pause while she seemed to be thinking of what to say.

"Have you read the report going into the paper this week?" she asked.

"No, I haven't." It was his turn to pause. "Let me guess. You've sent it to me as an e-mail."

"Yes," she said.

"I haven't read it yet." It sounded like a confession.

"Never mind," she said. "Can we meet, Detective Inspector?" The question seemed to come out of nowhere.

"Meet?" he asked.

"Yes. So we can talk face to face. Shall we say Ascari's at two this afternoon? It'll be much easier than trying to talk on the phone."

"Yes, that'll be fine, Miss Marston. I'll see you then." Even as he put the phone down, Townshend found himself wondering why he'd agreed so readily. It just wasn't like him. Was it something about her voice? It was very nice. He smiled, feeling a little like a teenager for no reason that he could put his finger on. Then he settled to looking at his e-mails, starting with one from the forensics team sent earlier in the morning when he'd been talking to Marcella Bexton-King. In addition to checking fingerprints, they'd been looking for DNA evidence in Richard Bexton-King's clothing and the trunk in which he'd been found.With nothing of any use having been found at either Pontrilas or Burghill, they were almost a last hope.

He was disappointed but not surprised to find that the trunk was as clean of any DNA evidence as both houses, apart from that produced by Richard Bexton-King's body. The fingerprints of the three workmen from BKM had matched, leaving one set unidentified which Townshend felt quite sure would turn out to be from the elusive Stephen Warner, if ever they got hold of him. There was no report yet on the clothes, but if there was something there, he was confident forensics would find it. His thoughts were disturbed by a polite cough from the doorway. David Ingleby was standing there, holding a cup of coffee.

"Did you get a chance to look at the e-mail I forwarded to you from the New Zealand police, sir?"

"No, David, I haven't. Tell me about it instead, will you? I take it there was something of interest," he said, gratefully taking his coffee and trying not to show his irritation. This reliance on technology really irked him. What was wrong with just talking to each other? But this was the way things were now. Not just in the force, but everywhere, and of course, he thought cynically, e-mails leave an accountable trail. Ingleby had carried on talking, so Townshend forced himself to concentrate.

"The Macauleys went to Auckland when they left Hereford and apparently settled in the city," Ingleby began. "The police checked their records, and it turns out they're both now dead. The father, Brian, died first some time ago, and the mother, Marsha, just two years ago." Ingleby looked at his boss. "Why did you want to know, sir?"

"It's the small things, David. If you leave something hanging in a murder investigation, it might come back and bite you on the backside. And remember, that car crash in his teens is the only black mark we've discovered about Richard Bexton-King, isn't it?" The Detective Sergeant nodded.

"So you were thinking that revenge for the daughter was a possibility?"

"Only very remote, especially after this length of time, but it had to be ruled out, no matter how unlikely. Thanks for checking it, oh, and thanks for the coffee." A thought crossed his mind. "Call Ken in for a moment, will you?" Townshend's office was quite small, and when Ken joined them, it seemed almost overcrowded. "What was the name of Bexton-King's doctor on King's Acre, David? His brother told us earlier." Ingleby flicked through his notebook.

"Dr Graham, sir. Runs a small private practice."

"That's him. Ken, get on to this Doctor Graham and have a chat about our victim's medication and what dosage he was on, will you? And don't take any crap about patient confidentiality. Tell him it's a murder investigation."

"OK, guv," Ken said.

"If you do get any problems, Ken, just go round there and stand over him until he tells you. You'll be enough to scare the shit out of him," Ingleby said, laughing. He turned to Townshend, a puzzled look on his face as Ken walked back out into the main office.

"Karen Welby told me Richard Bexton-King had enough of this oxycontin stuff in his system to kill a bull," Townshend explained. "Why so much? Was it even his? That's why we need to know what he was being prescribed." The phone rang, and Townshend picked it up irritably. "Townshend here," he said and then paused, listening to the voice on the other end. "Yes sir. When?" Another pause. "Things are a bit busy, sir, but now would be OK." He slammed the phone back down. "Shit!"

"Something wrong, sir?" Ingleby asked, something he would never have done with his previous boss.

"Logan wants to see me," Townshend said, rising from his seat.

"Good luck, sir," Ingleby said with feeling. He didn't have a very good relationship with Detective Chief Inspector Logan. Townshend grunted, slipping on his jacket. His own relationship with his boss was still in its infancy, but could do without seeing him just at the moment. He walked upstairs, subconsciously straightening his tie and tapped on the Detective Chief Inspector's door.

"You wanted to see me, sir?" he asked politely, entering the office, which, due to the privileges of rank, was much larger than his. DCI Logan was a thin, wiry man, his height hidden as he sat behind his desk, but Townshend knew him to be well over six feet. A receding hairline and grey patches at his temples gave him an air of gravitas, but he wasn't a particularly well-liked man around the station.

"Yes, Derek. I thought it might be a good idea to have a quick word about this Bexton-King affair. Seems you're kicking up a bit of a stink." He gestured for Townshend to sit down.

"Does it, sir? I've only just started trying to get to the bottom of things."

"So I gather," Logan said drily. "I've had the Police and Crime Commissioner's office on the phone, hinting rather heavily that we ease off on Mrs Bexton-King." There was an edge to his voice that indicated he didn't approve of the outside interference. It gave Townshend reassurance that he wasn't about to be reprimanded.

"Mrs Bexton-King? Christ, she's on the ball. It's not an hour since I left her." He hesitated. "I thought the PCC's office weren't supposed to interfere in cases, sir?" he asked.

"Yes, well," Logan said. "She's obviously got contacts, but that's the problem about this bloody county, Derek. Everybody knows everybody else. They all move in the same social circles. You'll learn, the longer you're here." He paused. "So what's the story? Are you harassing her? Is she a suspect?"

"She's got a possible motive with a life insurance pay-out and a misplaced grievance over changes to his will, sir, but otherwise, no. She's hiding something though, something she's not willing to tell me, and that always makes me suspicious," Townshend said. He noticed the DCI's eyebrows rise a little.

"Is it a 'what' or a 'who', this something that she's hiding?"

"Definitely a 'who', sir. The victim, Richard Bexton-King, was divorcing her because of an affair she was having," Townshend explained. "It seems she's doing all she can to keep this other man's name out of things, including accepting a settlement in the divorce. The bottom line is, I want to know this man's name."

"It's not unusual for people to make settlements in divorces," Logan said.

"It just doesn't seem right in this case, sir. Marcella Bexton-King appears to be very money-oriented. I don't know yet what this settlement is, but I'd think she'd probably stand to get a lot more if she fought the divorce."

"So is it all about keeping this man's identity quiet?"

"It would seem so, yes, sir."

"Well, be careful, Derek. The Commissioner's office does have a bit of clout."

"Yes, sir. I'll bear that in mind. Just out of interest, do we know who in the PCC's office wants me to ease off?" Logan shook his head.

"No. Just try to stay clear, Derek."

"Whatever you say, sir. Was there anything else?"

"Yes, Derek. Just when are you going to get around to giving Ingleby his job appraisal? I know Rawlinson was supposed to do it, but HR are chasing it up."

"Pressure of work, sir, but I'll get to it when this investigation's done," Townshend said, smiling and rising from his chair. Job appraisal reviews. Surely to God there were more important things in police work. He had no time for them. Next thing, they'll be giving coppers a bonus for every arrest they made, and then God help the public.

"Just don't forget it, eh, Derek?"

"Yes, sir," replied Townshend, sensing the note of dismissal in the other man's voice and turning for the door. As he walked down the corridor and down the stairs to return to his own office, there was only a single thought in his mind. Who was it in the Crime Commissioner's office who was interested enough in Marcella Bexton-King to get involved?

CHAPTER EIGHTEEN

"Right, let's start with our victim," Townshend said. He was standing in front of a blank white board, with a marker in his hand. Ken Collings, Sarah Miller and David Ingleby were sat at their desks facing him, making him feel a little like a lecturer. As they spoke and discussed things, Townshend added notes to the board. "Richard Bexton-King, aged forty seven. A well-known and relatively wealthy local businessman, he owned BKM Ltd, a car sales, garage and haulage business on the Worcester Road. He also had a very healthy property portfolio. He liked fast cars and was, according to his brother, a bit of a ladies man, although we haven't really found much evidence of that." He ignored the little snort of amusement from Ingleby. "The only thing we've dug up on him so far is a number of speeding fines and a car crash when he was nineteen, in which his then girlfriend, Kim McCauley died. He's divorcing his wife Marcella, which is something we'll come back to, and at the time of his death was involved in a relationship with the company secretary at BKM, Sharon Doherty." He added the names of Kim, Marcella and Sharon to the board. "David, can you fill us in on the details of this crash?" Townshend asked.

"At the inquest, Bexton-King was cleared of any blame for the accident," Ingleby said. "Kim McCauley's parents, particularly her mother, Marsha, didn't agree. Mrs McCauley was very public in her opinions that Bexton-King killed her daughter and was actually given warnings about her behaviour by police at the time. She and her husband emigrated to New Zealand and according to local police, they're both now dead," Ingleby concluded.

"As a result of injuries he sustained in the crash in his teens, Bexton-King was taking a strong painkiller, oxycontin," Townshend said. "According to the post-mortem report, he had abnormally high levels of this in his stomach, which is almost certainly what killed him. There were also signs on his wrists and his ankles that he was restrained, probably by being tied to a chair. Oxycontin is a prescription-only drug." He turned to Ken. "What did you get out of that doctor?"

"To start with, guv, despite sounding like a real snobby arsehole on the phone, he turned out to be quite a nice guy," replied Ken. "He was a bit reluctant at first, but finally told me what we needed to know. Bexton-King had just been to see him for a new prescription. His dosage was increased to two sixty milligramme tablets a day as he'd said the pain was getting worse. Dr Graham gave him two months' worth of tablets and Bexton-King collected them from the pharmacy at the surgery on Tuesday afternoon."

"Thanks, Ken," Townshend said. "I couldn't work out why he had so much of this medication at Pontrilas and not at his own home. Now, who knew the victim was taking oxycontin?"

"Only people who knew him well, I should think," ventured Sarah Miller. They all agreed.

"That fits with what his brother said about him not liking other people knowing his business," Ingleby said.

"So who have we got?" Townshend asked.

"His wife, his brother and possibly his secretary," David Ingleby said. "At the moment, it doesn't seem like there's anyone else that close to him."

"Don't forget the doctor and the pharmacist," added Ken Collings. Townshend nodded.

"That brings us to our main problem," Townshend said. "We don't really know enough about our victim. Who were his friends, his enemies? What were his interests, his weaknesses?" He explained his theories about needing to know a victim inside and out to proceed properly and then came back to the board. "His wife told us he never went out unless it was to his golf club or a pub she couldn't remember the name of. We need to find out where these places were, pay them a visit and see what we can dig up about our victim. Ken, I want you and Sarah to see Sharon Doherty. She was in a relationship with him and will probably know about his social life and the people he knew. Hopefully, she'll be more helpful than his wife. OK?" They both nodded. "David, I want you to go to Leominster to Bexton-King's solicitors. They acted for the business and for him personally. See if there were any problems that they knew about with the business or any concerns Bexton-King might have had, business or personal." He paused. "Sarah, you had a chat with the woman from the auction rooms this morning, didn't you?" She nodded.

"Yes, Mrs Morgan."

"How did it go?"

"Nothing there, sir. Her family had known the Bexton-Kings for years. Hearing of his death was just a shock to her. There was no relationship between them and nothing that she seemed to be hiding."

"OK, thanks. It was just a hunch, but at least it's cleared up. Now, before we move on to Marcella Bexton-King, just a couple of things from forensics. There were fingerprints on the trunk the victim was found in, but matches have been made to the porters at Pontrilas and the guys from BKM. There's one set of unidentified prints, but I'm sure they're going to belong to the one BKM guy we haven't been able to get hold of yet, Stephen Warner. There's no DNA on the trunk, and forensics are still checking Bexton-King's clothes. Both houses, in Pontrilas and Burghill were as clean as a whistle. Some company called…" He looked at Ingleby, but it was Sarah who answered.

"Absolutely Spotless, sir."

"That's it. Bloody stupid name, but I think I said that at the time. Sarah, while you're out with Ken, pop in to see them and ask a few questions about the job."

"Yes, sir."

"And David, while it's on my mind about Stephen Warner, on your way back from Leominster, stop off at his digs on the Yazor Road and find out if anything's been seen of him. I don't like the fact we don't know where he is." Ingleby nodded. "Right then. Marcella Bexton-King is our victim's wife. Forty-three years old, she likes to think of herself as much younger. She appears very money-orientated. The marriage was an unhappy one, something she's admitted and which was confirmed by the victim's brother Robert. It seems she was expecting a jet set lifestyle with the victim because of the cars, his house in Burghill and his money. She didn't get it and turned to other men. She's having a relationship with the brother, which is not something I think we need to worry about, but it wasn't that relationship that led to the divorce. It appears that the victim had turned a blind eye to his wife's affairs, but something changed his mind and he wanted out of the marriage. We don't know what. Marcella says the divorce was because of the breakdown of their relationship, but something there doesn't tie up. There's another man involved, whose name we don't know. The victim and his wife had agreed on a divorce settlement, whereby she wouldn't contest the divorce as long as he kept the other man's name out of it. She wouldn't tell us who the man was when we interviewed her. At the moment we've let that go."

"Could Sharon Doherty know, sir? Or the victim's brother?" Ingleby asked.

"They might, David, and we could have asked Robert this morning, couldn't we?" Ingleby nodded. "Never mind. Sarah, be sure to ask her later, will you? And no disrespect, Ken, but when you and Sarah are interviewing Sharon Doherty, let Sarah lead, will you?"

"Just in case you scare her to death," joked Ingleby.

"There's something strange about the idea of Marcella Bexton-King hiding this man's name," said Townshend. "Given the divorce laws, she'd probably have stood to get a lot more out of the divorce than the amount she's agreed to, whatever that is."

"Don't you think it's very much, guv?" asked Ken.

"No, Ken, Robert Bexton-King said it was a large sum, but Richard wouldn't have settled for more than she would have got if she'd contested, would he? She's also the beneficiary of his life insurance policy, to the tune of three quarters of a million pounds."

"Even though they were getting a divorce?" Sarah asked, almost incredulous.

"Well it's my guess he hadn't got around to changing it," said Ingleby. "Perhaps he was waiting for the divorce to go through completely. Still," he added, "if she knew he hadn't changed it, but was going to…"

"Yes, it might give her a motive for killing him," Ken finished for him. Townshend kept back, happy to see his small team discussing the case between them.

"She said she didn't know who benefitted from the policy when we asked her," Ingleby said, "but being his wife, I would've thought she would. I know about my wife's insurance."

"And me," said Ken. "My wife's goes to the bloody kids!"

"What about the victim's will?" Sarah asked. "Had he got around to changing that? Was she still being left anything?"

"No, he'd changed it. She wasn't getting a penny," Ingleby said.

"Well, that figures if they were separated and divorcing," said Ken.

"It does, but it was something they had an argument about the day before his death," Townshend added. "For some reason she thought she should still be getting something and even drove out to High Lawns on Tuesday evening to continue the argument. She was still angry when she left, saying he was expecting someone. She assumed it was Sharon

Doherty. And that means that unless something else comes up, she's the last person we know to have seen the victim alive, apart from the killer. But that's assuming that Marcella Bexton-King and the killer aren't one and the same person."

"So she's our first suspect?" Ken asked. Townshend nodded.

"As she doesn't have an alibi and freely admits she saw him at Pontrilas, she has to be a suspect," he said. "Now let's deal with the victim's brother, Robert. He was the first person we interviewed and it turns out he was a bit sparing with the truth. He's five years younger than Richard and was passed over in their father's will, getting no part of the business. That might have been a grievance, but Richard made him a partner and gave him half the business. Robert also has an alibi that seems to check out: he was in Lichfield that Tuesday evening. It's possible he could have done a return trip in the middle of the night and still made his appointments, but it's unlikely. The problem with Robert is motive. We've discovered he's the sole beneficiary of the will, getting everything, but he insists he doesn't know what's actually in his brother's will."

"Is Sharon Doherty not getting anything, sir?" Sarah asked.

"Not according to the copy of the will we've seen, but it's an interesting point and something we need to consider. Just how deep was their relationship?"

"Something else to ask her, sir?" Sarah said, making a note.

"Yes, but don't tell her about the will," Townshend said. "Coming back to Robert, one thing we do know about, and something he freely admits, are gambling debts, but we don't know how much, or if he's under any pressure about them."

"I've got someone who might be able to help with that, guv," Ken said. "I'll have a word."

"Good." Townshend knew better than to ask details about sources of information. "Just as long as they're reliable." He paused. "See if your source can find out who the money's owed to."

"What about his relationship with his sister-in-law, sir?" Ingleby asked. "I know it may not be pertinent, but he was very dismissive of her in his first interview and then we find he's sleeping with her. Could she be helping him with his debts?"

"From what he said earlier, it's a possibility, but I'd still like to know some more details," Townshend said.

"Could they be working together, sir?" Sarah asked. "Money seems important to both of them, and if he did happen to know about the will..." She let the words tail off.

"Money's a good motivator, but I'd have thought if they were, they'd have arranged an alibi that covered both of them, not just Robert," Townshend said. "He has to remain a suspect though, at least until we can prove otherwise." He paused again. "The other major player we've got to consider is Sharon Doherty, the secretary and, according to her, girlfriend." He looked at his watch. Already half past one. "As Ken and Sarah are paying her a visit this afternoon, I think we'll leave her until later. I'm meeting this woman from the Hereford Times at two." He looked at all three of them. "Anything else?" he asked.

"Yes, guv. This report I got from the neighbour in Pontrilas. He mentioned the car hitting the gatepost as it drove out of High Lawns," Ken said.

"Yes," said Townshend. "A dark car, wasn't it?" Ken nodded. "That needs checking, Ken. Check up on who drives what and whether any of their vehicles have got any damage. All back here for a quick recap about five." They all nodded, but Townshend noticed Ingleby about to say something. "It's alright, David, I know it's your anniversary and you've got a meal booked with your wife. It'll just be a quick chat and then back to the white board in the morning. Now, can anyone tell me the way to Ascari's?"

CHAPTER NINETEEN

Naturally, it was raining again. Townshend, never a fan of hats or umbrellas, turned his collar up, put his head down and walked quickly instead. Sarah had given him good instructions: up to High Town past the black and white house, straight through until he reached All Saints' church and then down into Broad Street until he reached Barclays Bank. Opposite the bank, it was into West Street and Ascari's was on the left hand side of the road. She'd even confidently added 'You can't miss it.'

The rain seemed to be keeping everyone indoors, although there were hardy souls in the open air coffee franchises, sipping their coffees and smoking their cigarettes under the huge umbrellas. Otherwise, High Town was uncharacteristically quiet.

He hadn't previously known where it was, but Ascari's proved as easy to find as Sarah had predicted. Even so, by the time he got there, he was wet and glad to get inside out of the rain. He quickly shrugged off his sodden raincoat while waiting to order a coffee, well aware that he was unfortunately dripping water on their floor. When he looked down though, it was already wet and dirty in a way that only tile floors can get in wet weather.

It must have been a post-lunchtime lull as there were only a few people scattered around the tables; none of them paid him much attention, so he took his coffee down the slight slope into the lower room and found himself a comfortable seat by the window, overlooking The Stagecoach opposite and giving him a reasonable view of the main entrance to the coffee-shop. People watching was an inevitable side-effect of his job, but for him it was also a pleasure in itself. Sitting where he was, he was able to indulge himself as much as the weather allowed. He decided he liked Ascari's; it was his sort of place.

He was just taking the first sip of his coffee when a woman stopped at the door and lowered her umbrella, shaking the raindrops off as she stepped backwards through the doorway. For some unfathomable reason, he just knew it was Ginny Marston. He lost sight of her for just a moment behind the wall until she re-appeared by the counter. Professionally, he took in everything. She was wearing smart but casual clothes and after his experience that morning with Marcella Bexton-King, he was rather thankful that she was dressed appropriately for her age, which he put at early forties; a pleasant, friendly looking face and nicely styled shortish hair. In Townshend's opinion, long hair on older women, tied back in a pony-tail or left loose, looked wrong; long hair was for little girls and young women.

"Hello, how are you today?" he heard the young man behind the counter say. A regular then, he thought.

"Fine, if a bit wet. How's business?" said the same voice he'd spoken to this morning. He'd been right. It was Ginny Marston.

"Slow," came the reply. "It's the rain."

"More room to sit then," she joked and they both laughed. As she came through to the lower room to where he was sitting, Townshend rose and gestured to the empty seat at his table.

"Good afternoon, Miss Marston, please join me." If she was surprised, she didn't show it as she sat down.

"Thank you, Detective Inspector. You're very punctual," she said.

"I tend to make a habit of it," he said. She smiled at a waiter as he placed her coffee on the table in front of her. "Table service," he joked. "I take it you're a regular here."

"Well now, that's a variation on 'Do you come here often,' Detective Inspector," she said smiling. "But yes, I'd rather come here than anywhere else in town. It's a place for locals rather than visitors. It's been here since the Fifties. My Mum and Dad even did their courting here."

"You're a Hereford girl, then?" he asked.

"Through and through, but I'd guess from your accent that you're not a Hereford man." A journalistic cast at finding out a little more about this man she was already feeling strangely attracted to. It was unusual for her; she prided herself on being cool and detached. He took the bait.

"No, I'm from the other side of the country, Cambridgeshire born and bred. I'm only a recent convert to the area and this is actually the first time I've been in here." He gestured around him. "But I had good directions."

"Sorry. I just assumed being in the Hereford police that you'd know where it was. Not for any bad reason, of course," she said. "It's not that sort of place." She stopped herself. "I think I'll shut up, I'm babbling." That wasn't like her, either. For his part, Townshend was beginning to like this woman.

"No, please carry on," he said. "People who are babbling quite often tend to say the most interesting things." He watched as she took a tentative sip from her hot coffee. "Now, Miss Marston, what was it you wanted to talk to me about?"

"Please, Detective Inspector, I feel so uncomfortable when people call me Miss Marston. It's Ginny, if that's OK?" He nodded. "It's about Richard Bexton-King and the Macauleys."

"Ginny it is then, which makes me Derek," Townshend said, smiling.

"Even though you're on duty?" she joked.

"Yes, even though I'm on duty," he joked back. He was surprised at himself. Working on a case, and here he was flirting with a potential witness who also happened to be a journalist. That should make him even more careful and circumspect than he usually was. She looked pleased, however. "What about them?" he asked. "It was all a long time ago."

"People in Herefordshire don't forget, Derek."

"That usually means grudges as well," he said, but she didn't appear to hear.

"I was part of the group that Richard and Kim hung around with," she said, "back in the late nineteen-eighties. They were both about two years younger than me." He did a quick mental calculation: that made her somewhere around forty-nine. She didn't look it.

"The crash must have been a big shock to everyone," Townshend said, slowly trying to feel his way to what she wanted to tell him.

"It was. My mum and Kim's mum Marsha were good friends, and Marsha took Kim's death very badly."

"There can't be anything worse than losing a child," Townshend said. Ginny Marston agreed.

"It's not the natural order of things," she said, falling silent for a few moments. "Do you have children, Derek?" she continued. "Sorry that was a bit personal, but as we were talking about children..." She stopped. "I'm babbling again, aren't I?" She picked up her coffee, embarrassed.

"No, it's OK," he said. There was something very appealing about her. "No, I don't have children, or a wife for that matter." Now what on earth made him say that? He was here officially, not to talk about his personal life, he thought. It was a subject about which he wasn't usually very forthcoming. "It just never seemed to happen," he added.

"Nor me," she said. "I try to convince myself that it was through choice." She stopped again, once more embarrassed and looking out of the window rather than at him.

"Tell me about Marsha Macauley," he said, trying to get the conversation back on track and still wondering what it was that she felt she could only tell him face to face.

"Did you read the report that's going in to this week's paper?" she asked instead. He had to admit he hadn't. "Well, it just mentions his body being found at Pontrilas auction rooms and that there is an investigation being carried out."

"Not just an investigation, Ginny, it's a murder investigation," he said.

"Of course," she agreed. "The article also mentions the car crash where Kim died."

"That's not a surprise. Her mother blamed Richard Bexton-King, didn't she? It's just the sort of connection papers make. So tell me, Ginny, was she justified in thinking that?"

"No. Richard was a safe driver even then. But it was much more than blame."

"You sound like you still know him," Townshend commented.

"No. We all drifted apart. I haven't spoken to him for years."

"Let's get back to Marsha Macauley," Townshend said. "I know a fair bit of harassment went on."

"Marsha was warned off by the police a couple of times, apparently and Mum said she was making death threats for a while. People around her thought she was actually capable of carrying them out. Kim's death twisted her mind."

"Ginny, while this is interesting, I don't know where it's leading to. Both Brian and Marsha Macauley are dead. We've had it checked out by the New Zealand police in Auckland."

"I know they are. Mum was quite upset by both their deaths. But there is more. Marsha had become so bitter about everything as the years passed that it affected her sanity. Brian left her, you know, and she reverted to her maiden name."

"I still don't see where this going, Ginny," Townshend said gently, with a gut feeling that he was missing something somewhere.

"When her husband left her, he tried to take their son with him, but he wouldn't leave his mother."

"Son? I didn't know they had one," Townshend said. "It's not in the reports."

"It does say 'family'," Ginny said, "but they're not specific. Nor is this week's report in the paper."

"A conscientious journalist? Not publishing everything that's known?" asked Townshend and then apologised immediately. "I'm sorry. That was uncalled for. Please carry on." Her only reaction to his words was a wry smile.

"Apparently, according to my Mum again, who kept in touch with both Brian and Marsha, Marsha's attitudes and way of thinking were starting to seriously affect the boy. He grew up thinking his dead sister was all the saints rolled into one and that Richard was the devil incarnate. Brian tried to get him away from all that, but failed. He was devastated when his son took his mother's maiden name as his surname." Townshend's mind was starting to make connections. The Macauleys had a son who apparently hated Richard Bexton-King as much as his mother did and although born in Hereford, would now have a southern hemisphere accent. It was a longshot, but not impossible.

"How old would their son be?" he asked.

"Stephen? About thirty eight, I think. He was a bit younger than us" Townshend's suspicions strengthened. Stephen?

"What would his mother's maiden name be?"

"Warner," she said, sipping her coffee,"and it was him I wanted to talk to you about." Townshend waited as she gathered her thoughts. "He came to see me," she said.

"When?"

"A few days ago, here in Hereford." Not such a long shot, thought Townshend. "You don't seem very surprised, Derek," she continued.

"Sometimes I think it's all about making the right links," he said, more to himself than to her. "No Ginny, I'm not surprised. A guy by the name of Stephen Warner has been working for Richard Bexton-King at BKM."

"At BKM? Right under Richard's nose?" she interrupted, a little shocked. He nodded.

"I just didn't know who he was and I haven't had a chance to talk to him yet. Now, tell me, what did he talk to you about?"

"A lot of catching up, really. About how things hadn't changed that much in Hereford while he'd been away, about life in New Zealand, how he was back-packing around the world…"

"Isn't thirty-eight or thereabouts a bit old for back-packing?" Townshend asked. "I thought it was the province of kids just out of university."

"No, all sorts of people do it, apparently. He said there was nothing left for him in New Zealand after his mother died and he wanted to see the world," Ginny said.

"Didn't he have a job, a family or responsibilities of any kind?"

"His mother was the only family he had," she said shaking her head, "and from what he said, he just gave up his job." She paused. "Look, Derek, I'm not going to get him into any trouble, am I? I just thought it was best you knew he was in Hereford. He seems nice, despite his mother…" Her voice trailed off.

"I just want to talk to him, Ginny. The only way he'll be in any trouble is if he's done something wrong." He reached out across the table without thinking to take her hand, but changed his mind when he saw her looking strangely at him. "You've done the right thing, believe me." She glanced at her empty coffee cup. "Can I get you another one?" he asked hopefully. She shook her head again.

"No, I really should get back to the office, Derek, but thank you for asking. Maybe another time?" she asked, sounding like she meant it. He certainly hoped so, but only smiled and nodded, saying nothing. It somehow seemed inappropriate just at the moment. He rose as she did and held his hand out. She shook it politely.

"It's been a pleasure, Ginny," he said, "and thank you for the information." She smiled and left the café, returning to the rain, and gave him a little wave as she passed the window. Townshend ordered himself another coffee and settled back down to think. There were more enquiries to be made about this Stephen Warner with the New Zealand police and questions to be answered closer to home. Did Robert Bexton-King know anything about this man that he was sleeping with and had Richard Bexton-King known who Stephen Warner was?

CHAPTER TWENTY

Townshend dropped the bombshell about Stephen Warner to everyone at the team meeting on the Wednesday morning. Everything the previous afternoon for David, Sarah and Ken had taken longer than he'd expected, so he'd told all three not to bother coming back to the office. In particular, he felt for David Ingleby. There were enough strains on police marriages; he knew that from his own experiences. This early on in an investigation, a little bit of leeway on his part towards one of his team about a wedding anniversary meal was no bad thing.

"The important thing to remember," he said, "is that even if a prime suspect seems to have been dropped into our laps, everything about him is, at the moment, circumstantial. I've e-mailed the Auckland police to see if they can give us more details about him. Until they arrive, we'll continue as we have been." He looked at his team and they all seemed to be in agreement. "We'll start with you and Sarah, Ken. How did you get on yesterday?"

"First off, guv, we didn't manage to get to Absolutely Spotless," Ken began.

"I'll get on to them today, sir," Sarah added. Townshend nodded, confident she'd get to it.

"We went to see Sharon Doherty," Ken continued. "According to her, Richard Bexton-King kept himself to himself and didn't have what you could call close friends."

"It sounds a little like what she told us, sir," Ingleby said, "and what his wife hinted at."

"She's consistent at least," Townshend agreed. "Go on, Ken."

"He was a member of the Rotary club here in town," Ken resumed, but Ingleby interrupted again.

"Presumably for the business contacts he'd make. Sharon Doherty told us they were important to him," he said. Ken nodded. "Mind you, they do a quite a bit of charity work as well, don't they?" Ken nodded again.

"OK," said Townshend. "David, find out who the President is and have a chat with him. It could help. These people all know each other and presumably each other's business as well," Townshend added.

"If you're a member of Rotary, doesn't that automatically mean your wife is a member of the Inner Wheel?" Ingleby asked.

"I think so, David, although I don't know much about these types of organisations." Townshend said. "Why?"

"I was just imagining Marcella Bexton-King associating with other businessmen's wives, sir. It was nothing pertinent."

"OK. Now, Ken, did Sharon Doherty have anything else to say?"

"Yes, guv. She told us he was a member of the golf club at Burghill and that the pub he used to go to was the Waggon and Horses out on the Leominster road. We went to both of them when we left her."

"Right," said Townshend, noting the details on the white board. "We'll get to those in a minute." He turned to Sarah Miller. "Did you ask her about her relationship with the victim, Sarah?"

"Yes, sir. She said it just seemed to develop over time until it became something quite serious. She also said that their relationship was the reason he was finally divorcing his wife."

"It was that serious?" Townshend asked. "She didn't even hint at that when we talked to her before."

"Apparently, sir, yes. And yet he wasn't leaving her anything in his will. It doesn't make sense."

"I think I might be able to make a little bit of sense of that, sir," Ingleby said. "When I was at Lacey and Bartholomew yesterday, the solicitor mentioned Sharon Doherty's name. Richard Bexton-King talked to him about her when he changed his will."

"About what?"

"He made over his complete property portfolio to her," Ingleby said. "The one his brother told us about."

"Why the hell would he do that?" Ken asked before Townshend could say anything.

"The solicitor, Martin Lacey, was actually quite helpful," Ingleby explained. "He said that while he couldn't be sure, he had the impression Richard Bexton-King had changed his mind about the divorce settlement with his wife. He didn't know why and wouldn't hazard a guess."

"That would confirm the truth of what Sharon Doherty was telling us about the depth of their relationship," Townshend said.

"It seems that way," Ingleby said. "According to Mr Lacey, the portfolio was worth over three million pounds, sir, and it certainly extended well outside the county."

"I'd say that's more than his brother thought from what he told us," said Townshend. "And I also thought Robert said his properties were all in Herefordshire. I take it that transferring it to Sharon Doherty was to prevent his wife getting hold of any of it?"

"I think so. The solicitor said it was watertight." Ingleby paused, a smile on his face. "Of course, it also means Sharon Doherty is now Marcella Bexton-King's landlord." Townshend decided to let that comment pass.

"Does Sharon Doherty know about this?" he asked.

"No. Martin Lacey was adamant about that. I think Richard was going to tell her on Tuesday night."

"It could be. Sharon Doherty told us he'd asked her to meet him in Pontrilas, didn't she?" Ingleby nodded. Townshend looked at his team.

"By her own admission, she was at Pontrilas, as they'd arranged, but she says she didn't see him. Could she have killed him? Any thoughts?"

"No, I don't think she could," said Sarah. "You only had to look at her when she was talking about him. She was devoted to him."

"That's the impression she gave me and David when we interviewed her" He looked at his team. "What would she have had to gain from his death, if she already had his property?"

"But she didn't know," Ingleby insisted. "At least according to the solicitor she didn't."

"If it was her that filled him full of oxycontin, David, he'd have had plenty of time to tell her. Wouldn't that have stopped her?"

"Not if she didn't want him around, so she could enjoy the money any way she wanted to," Ken said.

"I still go back to the way she seemed to feel about him, sir," Sarah persisted. David and Ken didn't seem quite so sure, but Townshend was inclined to agree with her.

"What concerns me," he said, "is whether or not Sharon Doherty could have managed to put Richard Bexton-King's body into that trunk on her own. She doesn't look like she's got the strength." There were nods of agreement. They'd all met her.

"No, guv. She'd have needed help," said Ken.

"The same applies to Marcella Bexton-King," Ingleby said. "She wouldn't have been able to manage either."

"I agree. At the moment, there's no one in the picture who might be a possible accomplice of Sharon Doherty's. We can't say the same of the victim's wife. There's this man involved in the divorce who she won't name. Is he a possible accomplice?" He left the question hanging in the air for a few moments as he made some more notes on the white board. He turned back to face them when he'd finished writing. "That brings me back to something you said a few minutes ago, David." Ingleby looked a little puzzled. "You said the solicitor had the impression that Bexton-King had changed his mind about the divorce settlement." Ingleby nodded.

"Yes, he did."

"We thought the argument Richard and Marcella had in Hereford was about her not getting anything in his will, yes?" Townshend asked.

"Yes, sir. That's what Robert said Marcella had told him," said Ingleby.

"What if it was about the divorce settlement as well?"

"She didn't mention it when we asked about the argument, sir, only that it was about the will," Ingleby said. "But then, getting anything out of her was like pulling teeth."

"Exactly," said Townshend, "but I don't think she would have mentioned it, because it might have led to more questions about this mystery man. There is one thing we can be sure of though. If our mystery man was that keen to keep his name out of things, he wouldn't have been very happy about Richard Bexton-King changing his mind." He turned to Sarah Miller. "Did you ask Mrs Doherty if she knew who this man was that had caused the divorce?"

"She didn't know. Apparently Richard hadn't said anything specific to her, but she did know the man was trying to make something of himself in public life."

"That would be why he wanted his name kept quiet," Ingleby said.

"Guv, she also said that Bexton-King had described the other man as a 'stuck-up prick with his head up his own arse'," Ken added with a smile on his face. Sarah frowned at him and he shrugged his shoulders. "Just saying," he added, still smiling.

"It's safe to say they didn't like each other, sir," Sarah said.

"We need to know who this man is," Townshend said firmly. "He's a loose end, and I don't like that. And he could be important."

"Sarah and I might have a clue about that, guv," Ken said, "although it's a bit tenuous. We went over to Burghill Golf Club when we left Sarah Doherty and had a chat with the Club Secretary, a Mr Markham. It's certainly a lovely place, I might have to try it myself."

"I didn't have you down as a golfer, Ken," Ingleby said.

"I try to keep my little secrets," Ken said, smiling again.

"Did you get anything interesting out of him, Ken?" Townshend asked, trying to keep things on track.

"He talked to us like he was writing an obituary or practising a eulogy," Sarah said.

"Apparently Richard Bexton-King wasn't much of a golfer, but Markham described him as, hang on, let me use the right words." He looked through his notebook. "Oh, yes. 'A man of integrity and honesty' was what he said, and he added he was the sort of person they liked as a member. He was well-liked at the club, but there had been an incident or two in the week leading up to the victim's death."

"Incident?"

"That makes it sound more dramatic that it apparently was, sir, but it was the word the Secretary used," Sarah said. "It seems more a case of arguments, raised voices and a bit of pushing and shoving than anything more violent or aggressive."

"Who was doing the pushing and shoving? Bexton-King?" asked Townshend.

"No, guv," said Ken. "According to Markham, Bexton-King was the one being pushed around and earned himself some real respect at the club for not retaliating and escalating things. The other man has been suspended from the Club until he's seen by the Club Committee. I also had the impression that Markham wouldn't be sorry to see him go." Sarah nodded in confirmation.

"Do we have a name for this other man?"

"Nicholas Eddison, sir," said Sarah.

"Did this man Markham have anything to say about him?"

"He wasn't quite so complimentary about him as he had been about Richard Bexton-King. He described him as pushy, ambitious and well, just a little bit loud. He's apparently a family man, with a home on the outskirts of Weobley, where the properties are a bit pricey because of the incomers, sir," said Sarah. "He's a qualified solicitor, but he's not practising, as he's working with the Police and Crime Commissioner's Office at Hindlip up near Worcester."

"What?" asked a surprised Townshend. Could this be another unexpected link? Sarah repeated what she'd just said and Townshend made some more notes on an increasingly crowded white board. Then he filled in his team about the conversation he'd had the previous day with Detective Chief Inspector Logan.

"Don't you think it's a bit of a coincidence that the victim was having arguments with someone from the PCC's office and that someone from that same office was complaining that you were putting undue pressure on the victim's wife?" said Ingleby.

"It seems like it, David, but I think I've told you before that I don't believe in coincidences. Sarah, see if you can find out anything more about this Nicholas Eddison when we're done here, will you?"

"Yes, sir."

"Now before we move on to Stephen Warner, how did you get on at this pub Bexton-King used to go to?"

"More of the same, guv, and a very nice half pint of Butty Bach as well. He was a nice man according to the barmaid, but she did say that her father, who's the landlord, knew him a bit better," said Ken.

"And what did he have to say?"

"Unfortunately, he was out, but the girl told us that her father had described him as a good-hearted man who could always be relied on to put his hand in his pocket if there was any charity do or fundraising going on. She also added that he just seemed to enjoy the company, but on his own terms."

"So nothing new, really," said Townshend. "It all seems to match with what we already know about him and it's filling out our picture of Richard Bexton-King."

"Yes, guv," Ken said. Townshend turned to David Ingleby.

"Are we done with what you learned at Bexton-King's solicitors, David, or was there anything else?"

"I asked Martin Lacey if he knew of any problems connected with the victim's business like you said. If there were any he insisted Lacey and Bartholomew weren't aware of them. As far as they were concerned, the business was running well, or at least well as could be expected for an independent company."

"Fine. Thank you, David." There was a slight pause, while he made a few more notes on the board. "Right, then," said Townshend, "let's all take a short break before we talk about Stephen Warner, shall we?"

CHAPTER TWENTY ONE

It wasn't a break as such. There was always something to do. For Townshend, it was checking e-mails, but for a change, Townshend wasn't moaning or complaining about them. He was keen to see a reply from the New Zealand police with more information about Stephen Warner. The first one that came up was instead from the Fire Investigation Team in Hereford, about the fire at BKM on the previous Sunday morning. It didn't make for good reading.

He wasn't happy to find out that they couldn't find any evidence of an alien accelerant, but as the e-mail pointed out, there was any number of inflammable liquids and gases both in the workshops and the garage. It ruled out one avenue of investigation. A starting point for what might be arson was always to search for traces of some accelerant that shouldn't have been there. The Fire Officer had also pointed out that it looked very much as if separate fires had started in each of the buildings rather than spreading from one or two points. It appeared to be the only explanation for the speed of the blaze and the destruction caused throughout the site. Other than that, they could offer nothing. Townshend sighed. It was probably as much as he could have hoped for.

The fire at BKM had slipped to the back of his mind while other strands of the investigation were being pursued, but now it came to the forefront again. It still seemed likely that the fire at BKM was an attempt to destroy evidence of some sort connected with Richard Bexton-King's murder. He realised he'd been hoping for something helpful or obvious to emerge from the fire team's investigation into the blaze, something that might point him in one direction or another. That wasn't going to happen according to the contents of this e-mail. The fire had been in the early hours of the morning, so there were almost certainly no witnesses, apart from the person who'd originally called in raising the alarm. It was frustrating.

"David!" he called out. Ingleby was quickly in his office. "There are some houses behind where BKM was, aren't there?" Ingleby nodded.

"Yes, sir. Bulmer Close," he answered. "That's where the fire was reported from."

"Good. Ask uniform to send a couple of constables for a door to door, will you? Get them to find out if anyone saw or heard anything on Sunday morning when this fire started."

"Yes, sir. I take it the Fire Team didn't find anything useful?"

"No, they didn't, but they're prepared to hazard a guess that it was arson." Ingleby laughed. "Yes, I know," said Townshend. "Anyway, get uniform out there as soon as possible, will you, David?" Ingleby left the room to arrange the door-to-door and Townshend turned back to reading his e-mails, this time opening the reply he'd been waiting for from Auckland CID. It didn't tell him much he didn't already know, but Stephen Warner hadn't quite walked away from everything as Ginny Marston had said. When he'd left New Zealand nearly eighteen months ago, some months after the death of his mother, he'd arranged for his house to be let for an undefined and extended period. That indicated to the Auckland police that he was intending to return at some point. Townshend agreed with their assumption. But it was the section about Warner's business that caught Townshend's attention. Not the fact that he'd sold it, and for quite a reasonable sum, that made sense if he was intending to travel the world. No, it was the nature of the business he'd been in. Stephen Warner was a qualified pharmacist and that meant he knew about drugs.

Townshend was aware that the New Zealand police force had what they called the Automated Fingerprint Identification System database of fingerprints and had requested in his e-mail that they check for Stephen Warner's prints. They'd come up trumps and before resuming the case discussion with the team he passed them on to forensics to see if they matched the remaining unidentified set of prints from the trunk. He restarted the team discussion by telling them about Stephen Warner before they started on anything else.

"I said earlier we should be wary of getting carried away by having such a prime suspect dropped in our laps. That still stands. There are things that don't add up about Stephen Warner."

"Like what, sir?" Ingleby asked. Townshend thought he detected a tone of 'This is our man, why can't we go and get him' in his sergeant's voice. He was also aware that at Ingleby's age and at the same point in his career, he'd probably have felt the same.

"Well, for starters, there's the fact that he didn't sell his house, only rented it. He obviously had every intention of returning to it. And think about it. If he'd been planning on revenge for his sister's death, that would be the first place police would look for him." Townshend paused for a moment to let that sink in before continuing. "And why spend eighteen months tootling around the world if he was planning on coming back to Herefordshire? If you were intending on committing a murder, wouldn't you want to get it over and done with?" He saw Ingleby nodding. "There's also this idea of him working for BKM that bothers me. Didn't he think it was possible Richard Bexton-King might have recognised him? Or Robert for that matter? Ginny Marston did."

"But would Robert have known him years ago, sir?" Sarah asked.

"And would Richard have recognised him after all this time?" Ken added.

"Warner might not have hidden his identity, sir, but he's not exactly publicised it either," Ingleby said.

"Would you, David?" asked Townshend. "After twenty odd years away, would you go walking into Richard Bexton-King's office and boldly announce that you were the brother of the girl that died in a crash your mother held him responsible for?"

"No, sir, but on the other hand, why associate yourself with the Bexton-King brothers?" David asked. "I'd have thought that even if some sort of nostalgia had brought him back to the area, with the way his mother felt and the apparent effect it's supposed to have had on him, he'd be more likely to avoid them than end up working for them." Both Ken and Sarah nodded in agreement with him.

"Are you saying that it was deliberate to keep quiet about his identity to get close to them?" Townshend asked.

"It's a possibility, guv," said Ken.

"But what about the possibility of Richard recognising him? Isn't that taking a risk if he intended anything?" Townshend paused. "If he had some sort of revenge on his mind, even if it was planted there by his mother, it seems brazen and foolish to march openly into BKM."

"Could it work the other way, sir?" Sarah asked. Townshend gestured for her to continue. "Well, by going to them openly, it might have the effect of lowering any feeling of threat. We have to remember that even if Robert Bexton-King didn't know who he was, nor Sharon Doherty, we don't know that the victim wasn't aware of who he was."

"That's a good point, Sarah. David, how much younger than his brother is Robert Bexton-King?" Townshend asked. He waited as David flipped through his notebook.

"Five years, sir."

"So Sarah's point earlier was quite right. There's no reason Robert Bexton-King would ever have known Stephen Warner, is there?" Townshend said. He turned to the white board and drew a link between the victim and Stephen Warner, with the words 'Did he know?' written along it. "Ken, can you pull over that second board? I think we need a to-do list." He squared up to the new board. "First things first," he said. "We need to talk to Stephen Warner more than ever. There's a lot of questions we need answers for, so we need to give some urgency to finding him."

"Don't you think that's suspicious in itself, sir?" Ingleby asked.

"Suspicious, David?"

"Yes, sir. The fact that we've not been able to find him. Is he lying low somewhere?"

"You're assuming his guilt, David. If you remember, his landlady was asked not to tell him we'd called; you even told her so yourself. We need to make enquiries about him in different places and not jump to conclusions when we've not been able to talk to him yet."

"What sort of enquiries, sir?" Sarah asked.

"Well, Ken is making enquiries about Robert Bexton-King's debts." He wrote as he spoke. "I'm assuming we're no further forward yet, Ken?"

"No, guv. I'm seeing my source later, so I should know something then."

"Good. I think I mentioned it, but in case I didn't, we need to know not only how much, but who to, and where he ran these debts up."

"Yes, guv."

"OK, thanks. Now, Sarah, when you've had a chat with the cleaning company, do some research on this Nicholas Eddison, the guy our victim was having arguments with at the golf club. It would help to know what they were arguing about. We also need to know more about him and his family life." She scribbled some notes. Re-iterating what he'd mentioned earlier, Townshend added a comment about waiting for a forensics team to analyse Stephen Warner's fingerprints to the board and then turned to David Ingleby.

"David, chase up the Rotary angle and find out if uniform got anything out of their door to door behind BKM." More notes were added to the board.

"Yes, sir."

"For now, that's it. I know it looks as if this Stephen Warner is our prime suspect, but I want all of you to bear in mind that it could be any of the people on this board. We need more facts."

CHAPTER TWENTY TWO

It wasn't until the following morning that forensics gave them an answer about Stephen Warner's fingerprints. Townshend was sitting in his office quietly gathering his thoughts when they rang. It was almost a week since Richard Bexton-King's body had been found and apart from having a list of possible suspects, they weren't a lot further forward with the case. The early days of a murder investigation were the most important and not a lot was happening. The results from forensics didn't help. As he'd expected, the prints from New Zealand matched the unidentified set on the trunk. That completed the group of four men from BKM that had been dealing with the clearance of the Bexton-King house at Pontrilas, as well as the porters at the auction rooms. Another loose end tied up without taking a single step closer to a resolution, Townshend thought.

Despite Ingleby's promptings and reminders, there'd also been no response on the DNA samples that had been sent for analysis. With very little going on in the county, Townshend had hoped the labs would have been quiet and able to turn the results around quickly, but that didn't look like happening either.

He sat back in his chair, his eyes closed and for just a few minutes, tried to put the case out of his mind. Somewhere he'd read that a change of problem and thinking about something else could bring you back refreshed to your original problem. Or had that been taking a long walk? Opening his eyes, he decided to concentrate on David Ingleby's review, guilty that it was overdue and annoyed that it had fallen in his lap. It should have been done by his predecessor before he retired, he thought as he pulled the forms out from his desk tray.

"We've got a result from uniform's door to door, sir," said Ingleby from the doorway, interrupting Townshend's thoughts before they'd even really got started. He pushed the forms back into the pile of other papers and looked up at his Detective Sergeant.

"Yes, David? What have they found?"

"It turns out that all of the houses in Bulmer Close have their own CCTV, sir. It was apparently something put in by the developers to attract buyers. It's monitored centrally by a private security firm."

"Anything to sell a house, eh, David?" Townshend said drily.

"Yes, sir," Ingleby replied. "It was a bit of a disappointment at first, as all the cameras were pointed at doors, drives and gardens, as you'd expect, but the officers got lucky. It seems that one of the cameras on Number Eleven had a broken bracket which the security firm hadn't fixed. It had swung out of position, pointing directly down the yard at BKM." Townshend straightened up in his chair.

"And?"

"We've had to do some image enhancing, sir, but one of the PCs is a bit of a whizz at it apparently and we've got good pictures of someone in the yard in the early hours of Sunday morning."

"Anyone we know, David?" Townshend asked, his hopes rising.

"Yes, sir." Ingleby placed some still photos on Townshend's desk. It only took one glance at the top picture for the Detective Inspector to recognise the figure caught by the camera. Robert Bexton-King.

"Well, that's a surprise, David," he said.

"Yes, sir."

"I presume you've checked the rest of the footage yourself? There's no one caught by the camera after this?"

"No, sir. The only thing that happens after this is him leaving and the fires starting. I can't see that there's any doubt about him starting them, sir."

"Neither can I, David. We'll bring him in to explain himself," Townshend said.

"Shall I send uniform, sir?" Ingleby asked.

"No. Grab your coat and we'll handle this ourselves. I want to see his reaction." Robert Bexton-King was very surprised to see them on his doorstep and, Townshend thought, more than a little dismayed. He gave the distinct impression that he'd been expecting someone. Nevertheless, he invited them in, closing the door with a quick anxious glance up and down the short street.

Unlike his brother Richard, Robert was a city dweller, and had made his home in a fashionably refurbished Georgian town house in what must have some time have been a mews. As they stood in the hallway, both Townshend and Ingleby took in the tasteful decoration and ornaments, Townshend in particular mentally comparing it to Bexton-King's sister-in-law's apartment.

"Would you like to come through to the lounge?" Robert asked politely as he turned back to them from closing the front door. "We'll be more comfortable in there." And out of the way when the visitor you're expecting arrives, Townshend thought.

"No thank you, Mr Bexton-King," said Ingleby. "We're here to ask you to accompany us to the police station. We have more questions for you." Bexton-King, slightly confused, looked from Ingleby to Townshend and back again.

"About Richard's murder? I've told you all I can," he said.

"No, sir, not about your brother," Ingleby said. "These questions are related to the fire at BKM." Townshend kept quiet, happy for his sergeant to handle the situation. He didn't have to be watching Bexton-King closely to notice his reactions. The man visibly paled and his shoulders sagged.

"And they have to be asked down at the station?" Ingleby nodded. "Am I allowed a solicitor?" Bexton-King added quietly.

"I think a solicitor is probably a good idea, Mr Bexton-King," Townshend said. "You can arrange for one now, before we leave, if you'd prefer, so that he can meet you there." It wouldn't do David Ingleby any harm in his career to learn that these situations can be handled with a little decorum.

"Thank you, Detective Inspector, I appreciate that. I'll just make a call from the other room, if you don't mind and then I'll fetch my coat." Bexton-King turned away and then looked back at the two policemen. "Am I being arrested?" That one question was as good as a confession, Townshend thought.

"No, sir," said Ingleby, significantly adding "not yet." Townshend hadn't thought it possible for Bexton-King's face to lose any more colour, but he paled even further at Ingleby's comment. Then he disappeared through a doorway, closing the door behind him just as the doorbell rang on the outer door. Townshend answered it to a man in his mid-thirties. The visitor was obviously surprised to be greeted by someone he didn't know.

"Hi. Is Robert there? He's expecting me." Townshend smiled. The accent gave the man away immediately. He invited the man in.

"He's a bit busy at the moment, but please come in," Townshend said, gesturing the man to come inside. With a pleasant smile, the newcomer stepped through the doorway. Townshend closed the door behind him. The visitor seemed taken aback by the presence of another man in the hallway. A worried look crossed his face immediately.

"Is everything alright?" he asked. "Where's Robert?" He sounded quite anxious about him. Townshend ignored the questions.

"David, please meet Mr Stephen Warner. Mr Warner, this is Detective Sergeant Ingleby and my name is Detective Inspector Townshend."

"Police?" Warner asked, even more anxiously. "How do you know who I am? And what's happened?"

"Simple deduction, Mr Warner. The accent, about the right age, and a friend of Mr Bexton-King," said Townshend. "And as for your second question, Mr Bexton-King's making a phone call and fetching a coat, Mr Warner. He'll be with us in a moment." He gestured towards the room Robert Bexton-King had gone into.

"Mr Warner, we've been waiting for a chance to talk to you," Ingleby said, "and I'd be grateful if you could come to the station with us and Mr Bexton-King".

"To the police station?" Stephen Warner didn't have a chance to ask anything more. A single gunshot made them all turn to the closed door and gave the lie to Ingleby's words that Robert Bexton-King would be joining them shortly.

CHAPTER TWENTY THREE

"He's not dead, David," Townshend said, leaning over the body on the floor and checking the pulse on his neck, "and we can thank our lucky bloody stars for that. We've got enough trouble on our hands with one dead Bexton-King. It looks like he's tried to top himself and only managed to shoot himself through the cheek. Phone an ambulance, will you?" Townshend was angry, with himself more than anything else. He should never have allowed Bexton-King to be left on his own, but the man didn't seem like someone who'd try to blow his brains out. He was getting complacent.

"I didn't think for one minute that he'd do something stupid like this, sir, or I'd have gone with him," Ingleby said apologetically, putting Townshend's thought into words, which didn't help much. Still, Townshend thought, the younger man shouldn't bear any of the blame or the guilt.

"Not your fault, David. I didn't either. Now just phone for an ambulance." The gun Robert Bexton-King had used in his failed suicide was lying close by him on the floor of his study. Townshend picked it up carefully and dropped it in an evidence bag. He always kept them in his pocket, just in case. Stephen Warner meanwhile had dropped to his knees on the other side of Robert's unconscious body and was confidently carrying out some emergency first aid to stem the bleeding.

"I didn't know that pharmacists were given medical training," Townshend said to Warner as he worked.

"We aren't. It's just that I'm a fully qualified first aider, Detective Inspector. I had to be for my mother in her last months. She started to self-harm." He didn't explain any further, but instead asked: "How did you know I was a pharmacist?"

"Courtesy of Auckland police. We've been doing some background checks on you."

"Mmm, so it would seem." There was a pause. "Is that to do with a dead Bexton-King? I presume it's Richard?" Townshend was surprised at the question.

"Did Robert not tell you?"

"No. I've not seen him for a week. I've been staying in a hostel in the Forest of Dean. It was a chance to visit Chepstow and Tintern."

"I'll need an address," Townshend said.

"To vouch for me telling the truth? So I'm a suspect, am I?" He laughed. "I've got the phone number on my phone. Just give me a second to finish here."

"Richard Bexton-King was found dead last week, so I'd say, given your family's history with him, that yes, you were a suspect, Mr Warner." The younger man, having finished stemming the flow of blood, was quite pale as he straightened up and looked at Townshend, who continued calmly. "We've been trying to contact you to ask you some questions relating to the investigation, but if you were away, it would explain why we've not been able to. But it's strange that you didn't bother to tell your landlady, isn't it?" Warner nodded, but before he had a chance to answer, the doorbell interrupted their conversation.

Ingleby answered the door and a paramedic appeared in the lounge, removing a motorcycle crash helmet and carrying a small case. Ignoring Townshend and Warner, he knelt by Robert Bexton-King and examined the two wounds in his face.

"He'll live. What happened here?" he asked Townshend. He and Ingleby both produced their warrant cards. "Police? You got here quick."

"We were already here," said Townshend, earning a puzzled look from the paramedic, who then glanced at Warner.

"Gunshot wound, self-inflicted," Ingleby said in answer to the question. "The idiot tried to kill himself. He needs to be hospitalised." The paramedic just nodded at Ingleby's stating the obvious.

"How long will the ambulance be?" Townshend added.

"Any moment, sir. We got the shout at the same time, but it's always quicker for me to get anywhere on the 'bike. Anyone else hurt?"

"No, it's just him you have to worry about," Townshend said.

"Well, if you can just give me some details, when the vehicle gets here, we'll get him off to County." Townshend obliged. "Bexton-King? Any relation to that guy whose body was found last week? I read about it in the local paper. Terrible thing. In a trunk!"

"His brother," Townshend said wearily, wanting to get Robert Bexton-King dealt with so he could talk to Stephen Warner now he had him at hand. He was rescued from any more questions by the arrival of the ambulance crew, who took charge. The three medics quickly had Robert Bexton-King on a stretcher and on his way to A&E. "David, get on to the station and have uniform send a man down to the hospital to keep an eye on Bexton-King. I don't want anything stupid happening like him discharging himself before we've had a chance to talk to him. It's a damned shame we couldn't arrest him unconscious," he added, more to himself than to his sergeant.

"Yes, sir," said Ingleby, with the glimmer of a smile. He picked up the phone to make the arrangements, wondering if Townshend was joking or not. The DI turned to Stephen Warner when the younger man asked him a question. He'd obviously heard Townshend's muttered comment as well.

"Arrest him? You were here to arrest Robert?" Warner asked. "Are you saying that Robert killed his brother? I can't believe that."

"No, Mr Warner, we're not arresting him for murder," Townshend said, raising his hand as if to stop the flow of words. "Let's find somewhere else to sit and talk, shall we?" He was very conscious of the large bloodstain on the floor and he wanted Warner's full attention when he questioned him. David Ingleby joined them as they adjourned to a modernistic fully fitted kitchen, with chairs designed more for style than comfort.

"Can I ask what you are arresting Robert for?" Warner asked.

"Yes," Townshend said, much to Ingleby's surprise. What business was it of Warner's? "He's being arrested on suspicion of arson, Mr Warner."

"Oh, God. Not BKM? Did he actually go through with it?" Townshend nodded.

"It certainly looks like it from the CCTV footage we've got," he said.

"I thought he was all talk. I didn't think he'd really do it. I mean, I know he had problems, but to burn down his own business…" Townshend turned to Ingleby before replying.

"David, put the kettle on and make us all a coffee, will you. It'll do us good to have something to drink while we're talking and I'm sure Mr Bexton-King won't mind."

"I'll do it," Stephen Warner said, rising from his seat. "I know where everything is. But let me give you this phone number first." He read out the number of the Forest of Dean hostel to Ingleby to record in his notebook. "OK?" he asked him.

"Yes, thank you, Mr Warner," Ingleby said. "Just out of interest, when did you go down there?" he added.

"On the Wednesday, after we'd finished at Pontrilas," Warner answered.

"Let's get back to Robert," Townshend said as Warner turned back to the kettle. "What problems did he have, Mr Warner?"

"It was all to do with money, but he wasn't very specific about them. He owed money to some pretty undesirable people, or so I gathered from what he did say."

"Did he say who?" Warner shook his head.

"No." The answer came very quickly, Townshend thought. Did Warner know or not?

"How did you meet him?" he asked instead. Ingleby glanced up from his notebook. He was becoming used to sudden changes of direction from his boss, but had still expected him to pursue the debts angle.

"Meet him?" asked Warner. "We were introduced at a club in town. It was recommended to me and I was trying it out."

"What was the name of this club?"

"The Monday Club. Hardly appropriate when it's open every night of the week, but there you are," Warner said. Townshend looked at Ingleby, hoping for some local knowledge.

"Is that the one in Union Street?" Ingleby asked as Warner sat down with three mugs of coffee.

"That's the one. Not so good on the outside, but very well done on the inside," Warner said.

"Is it a gay club?" Townshend asked and Stephen Warner laughed.

"You're very direct, aren't you, Detective Inspector?" he said. "But yes, it is."

"And a casino?" Warner nodded, the look on his face saying that he was all too aware of where these questions were leading.

"Is that where Robert did his gambling?" Townshend asked. Another nod. "A little or a lot?"

"A lot. It was a problem for him. He couldn't stop." It was Townshend's turn to nod. "But the Monday Club was the only place he gambled," Warner added.

"Yes, he told us it was a problem. Usually that's the first step in sorting things out. I'm interested in your travels, Mr Warner," Townshend said, changing tack again.

"My travels?"

"Yes. Someone said you were back-packing around the world." Warner laughed.

"Back-packing? Hardly that," he said. "I'm wandering, yes, but with a certain amount of comfort, Detective Inspector, not roughing it."

"But you are working your way around the world?"

"In a manner of speaking, yes."

"Only in a manner of speaking? What does that mean, Mr Warner?"

"My main intention was always to come back to visit Hereford, and I decided to see parts of the world while I did it. I had no ties, and if I wasn't going to do it now, then I probably never would. If I found a place I liked, I stayed for a while, got myself a little bit of work, and replenished some of my funds."

"So Hereford was always your destination?"

"Yes. I was born here and I wanted to see the place again. From here, it's a return journey directly to New Zealand."

"And you got a job with BKM?" Townshend asked.

"Only when they needed an extra pair of hands. Robert arranged it through that stuck-up secretary in the office."

"Sharon Doherty," Townshend said.

"Yes, that's her."

"Stuck-up?" Ingleby asked.

"Oh, she's just so full of herself," Warner said dismissively. "Not my sort of person."

"And Richard Bexton-King gave you some work cutting grass at some of his properties." It was a statement, not a question, but Warner answered it anyway.

"Yes, and loaned me a van to carry around the mower and the other stuff I needed."

"Wasn't that a bit strange?" Townshend asked. A puzzled look crossed Stephen Warner's face.

"Strange? Yes, I suppose given the background, it is," he said.

"Did Richard Bexton-King actually know who you are, given the change of name?"

"Yes, he did." There was no hesitation.

"Did that cause any problems?"

"No, Richard's a nice guy – sorry, was a nice guy. My mother had a real problem with him, which I know you'll be aware of, but when I introduced myself in the BKM office, he even asked after her and my father."

"Your mother's attitude didn't rub off on you? She felt very strongly about him." Again, Stephen Warner didn't hesitate before answering.

"No. Not a bit." He paused and looked Townshend directly in the eye. "You think she was trying to groom me to take the revenge she couldn't have herself? Isn't that a bit far-fetched, Detective Inspector?" Townshend didn't reply. Warner shook his head. "Richard Bexton-King couldn't have been nicer to me. Let's face it, that damned car-crash, which I've heard about all my life, was nothing more than an accident."

"But it made your parents leave the country, taking you with them," Townshend said.

"No, it didn't. They were going anyway and Kim was supposed to be coming with us. Emigration takes time to arrange. You can't just do it at the drop of a hat. Look, Richard was good in giving me some work to let me get some money. There was no bad feeling either way." Townshend paused before speaking. Some of the things Warner was telling him didn't match up with things he'd already been told. He decided to leave it for now.

"Before we finish up, Mr Warner, we need to take more fingerprints and a DNA sample. Then you can go. We'll lock up here on our way out. Thank you for your help."

CHAPTER TWENTY FOUR

"It doesn't look very good for the Force at all, does it, Derek?" said Detective Chief Inspector Logan, his attitude decidedly icy.

"No sir."

"In fact, it looks downright sloppy," Logan said. "What are the press going to make of it?" Townshend had to agree it was a problem. He'd explained what had happened, but it all boiled down to two detectives, one an inspector and one a sergeant, allowing a man who they were bringing in for questioning to shoot himself. No, it didn't look good.

"It might have been worse, sir," he found himself saying, taking a slight risk.

"Worse? How can it have been worse?"

"He could have succeeded, sir," Townshend said drily. Thankfully, it brought a slight smile to his superior's face and the tension relaxed.

"Let's get back to the beginning, shall we? What were you doing there anyway, Derek?" Logan asked.

"We wanted to bring him in for questioning under caution, but obviously we didn't get that far."

"What were you bringing him in for? More questions about the murder?"

"No. We had some serious questions about the fire at BKM. We've turned up CCTV footage that places him there and of the fire starting just after he left." There was a short silence while Logan thought about what Townshend had just told him. Townshend meanwhile looked around the office, waiting. It was functional and lacking in personality, very much like his own. Despite not having been with Hereford CID long, Townshend had picked up on the fact that Logan had the same attitude to work as he did. Townshend's own fully absorbed approach to work had cost him two marriages; Logan had come to it the other way around. He was a widower and had thrown himself into his work at the expense of everything else in life on his wife's death. The rumours around the station were that his home was a shrine to his dead wife, not that anyone had been there, but here in his office there wasn't even a single photograph.

"Is the fire related to the murder, Derek, or a separate investigation?" the DCI asked.

"When it happened, so close to the victim's body being found, I thought it had to be related, sir. It looked every inch as if someone was trying to cover something up, but now I'm not so sure."

"Any reason?" Logan asked.

"Robert Bexton-King was up to his eyeballs in debt. It seems he had a real gambling addiction. We're still working on how much and who he owes it to, but my guess at the moment is that whoever he owes the money to is putting a lot of pressure on him to pay up and that he cracked and did something stupid."

"And set a fire at BKM?" Logan said and Townshend nodded. "Presumably for the insurance, then?" Logan added.

"That's what it looks like, sir. I really don't think there's a link between the fire and the murder now, but until we can talk to Robert Bexton-King, I can't dismiss it as a possibility either, sir," Townshend said.

"Well, with the wound you say he's managed to inflict on himself, it's not very likely that he's going to be speaking to anyone for some time, if ever, is it?" Logan said.

"I'd thought of that, sir. He may not be able to speak, but as soon as the hospital are prepared to let us in, there's no reason he can't write down his answers to my questions. There's nothing wrong with his hands or his hearing." Logan nodded in agreement.

"Now, what about this Stephen Warner person? How are you getting on with tracing him?"

"He walked right into our laps while we were at Robert Bexton-King's, sir. It seems he's been away for a week in the Forest of Dean. Ingleby and I had a chat with him after Bexton-King was taken to hospital. Everything about him seems plausible and hangs together, but like all the others, he's got to remain a suspect until proved otherwise."

"Anyone you haven't talked to yet, Derek? Any other leads?"

"I'm still waiting on DNA results from the victim's clothing and body, sir, and I've got the team busy on some enquiries. There is one man I want to talk to, this man who is so keen to keep his affair with Marcella Bexton-King quiet. She's not going to tell me, and I'm rather hoping Robert Bexton-King might know."

"Had you not asked him that before?" Logan asked.

"No, sir," Townshend admitted. "It was one of the questions I had lined up for him under caution." He paused, feeling a light air of disapproval re-appear. He was well aware that it was a question he should have asked the last time he saw Bexton-King, in Marcella's flat, but at the time, it just hadn't occurred to him. The niggling thought that maybe he was getting a little old for the job came back into his mind; it certainly wasn't the first time he'd thought it. "There's also a man who we've been told the victim was apparently having arguments with at his golf club," he continued, "someone named Nicholas Eddison. According to the club secretary, the arguments between the two of them had been getting quite heated. It's just a shame he didn't know what they were about," Townshend added with a smile. "It might have helped us move forward."

"Did you say Eddison, Derek?" Logan asked sharply.

"Yes, sir. It seems that he and Richard Bexton-King were fellow members of the Burghill golf club and of Rotary. David's pursuing the Rotary angle at the moment."

"First name Nicholas?" Logan persisted.

"Yes, sir. He works at the Police and Crime Commissioner's Office in Hindlip."

"He certainly does, Derek," said Logan, looking serious. He's the man who rang me about you harassing the victim's wife. I don't think I mentioned his name at the time, which I apologise for. I should have done, but I didn't think it was relevant. If you're going to question him, be careful how you handle it, Derek. The PCC's office wouldn't like any hint of a scandal."

"No, sir." Townshend was quiet for a few minutes, wondering if Logan's mind was working in the same way as his. He voiced his thoughts. "Is it even remotely possible that this man Eddison is the man Marcella Bexton-King is having an affair with and keeping quiet about, sir?" He paused. "I know it's a bit of a leap in the dark, but it fits in with him wanting to keep quiet about it. From what we know already, he has a wife and children and a good career so if he is the man she's seeing it would be in his interest, wouldn't it?"

"It would, Derek. The man's not making a secret of wanting a career in politics. He's telling anyone who'll listen or might be of any influence that he intends to run for Parliament at the next election. He's probably got his targets set even higher than that."

"Can I ask if you happen to know him personally, sir?" Townshend asked. It would complicate things considerably if Logan did, but thankfully the Detective Chief Inspector was shaking his head.

"No, Derek, the man's nothing more than an acquaintance, so no problems there," Logan replied. "But for God's sake, just remember to tread carefully and keep your ideas under your hat until you've got any sort of proof that he might be involved."

"Of course, sir. It's just another thought that might go nowhere." He got up to leave.

"Derek," Logan began, as Townshend opened the office door.

"Yes, sir?"

"Keep me informed about this man Eddison. And don't let any more suspects shoot themselves."

CHAPTER TWENTY FIVE

"I've been on to the hospital, guv," Ken said as his DI walked into the team office. It was now Friday morning, a week after Richard Bexton-King's body had been found and Townshend had been ruminating on the case during his morning walk to work. "They're keeping Robert Bexton-King sedated today. When I said we needed to talk to him, they weren't happy. The nurse I was talking to passed me on to some stuck up sister. She said that under no circumstances would she let us see him today and that however important it was we'd have to wait until tomorrow when the doctors see him on their rounds. And even then it would be their decision." The burly detective didn't sound impressed.

"Thanks, Ken," Townshend said with a smile. "We'd better do as we're told. It wouldn't do to upset the sister before we've even set foot on the ward, would it?" he added, grinning. He started to take off his wet overcoat. It had been raining for the last part of his walk from Whitecross Road and he couldn't wait to get his car back. He was just turning towards his office when Ken continued.

"I've checked on cars, guv. There are no matches to a dark car with any of our suspects. In fact, as I can see, Sharon Doherty doesn't own a car." It was then Sarah Miller's turn to stop Townshend as he turned away.

"I've done the background checks you wanted on Nicholas Eddison, sir," she began. "The only thing in our records is a gun licence."

"A gun licence?" That surprised him. He hung up his coat and ran his hands over his damp hair.

"Yes, sir. For a pistol. He's had it for five years and is apparently a member of a gun club." She glanced down at her notes before continuing. "Leominster Rifle and Pistol Club, sir." Something clicked in Townshend's mind, a question he hadn't pursued. Karen Welby, the pathologist, had told him that Richard Bexton-King had shown unmistakable signs of being restrained, both at his wrists and his ankles, but she hadn't mentioned any signs of a struggle. That prompted the question of why a grown man would allow himself to be tied to a chair without resisting or putting up a fight. Could it have been a sexual thing or was he somehow forced into it without being able to resist? If he was forced there would need to be some sort of weapon involved. Such as a pistol. It was a long shot, but with a week gone and no real leads to go on, he couldn't ignore anything.

"Sir?" Sarah Miller was obviously waiting for him to say something.

"Where's the gun licensed to?" he asked.

"Sir?" She looked puzzled.

"If the weapon's licensed to his home address, he can use it between home and the gun club, but if it's licensed to the gun club, he can only use it there," Townshend said. She nodded.

"It's his home address, sir."

"OK. Get on to the gun club secretary and see what he says about Eddison as a person, what sort of character he is."

"Yes, sir."

"And Sarah, find out whether the gun is stored at the club or whether he keeps it at home."

"Would he do that, sir? With two young children?" she asked.

"If it's kept safely, you never know," Townshend replied and turned towards the coffee jug. Before he could walk away, she had another question for him.

"Are we treating this Nicholas Eddison as a suspect, sir?"

"He's someone who's been having arguments with our victim in the weeks leading up to the victim's murder, so he has to be, Sarah. But just like the others, we've got nothing concrete against him at the moment." He raised his voice so that both Ken and David could hear as well. Now was as good a time as any to pass on Logan's instructions. "Will you all bear in mind that because of Eddison's position in the PCC's office, we have to go quite gently with any enquiries that concern him. Nothing too direct, please." He left Sarah to make her phone call to the gun club, and having collected a much-needed coffee, went to sit in his office, looking vacantly at the rain steadily falling outside his window. It was strangely relaxing.

Now that his train of thought was focussed on the manner of Richard Bexton-King's death, something else had occurred to him. He'd been working on the basis of there being one person, one killer, but the scenario just didn't support that. In the same way that Richard Bexton-King wouldn't have allowed himself to be tied to a chair, he certainly wouldn't have willingly drunk something he knew would kill him. Could one person have managed that? The answer, even if they were determined enough, was almost certainly no. It would be so much easier with two. And that brought his thoughts round in a circle. Was Richard Bexton-King a willing participant in being tied up?

If he was happy to be secured to a chair for some sex game, it would have had to have been someone with whom he was intimate; a woman. From what they'd heard about their relationship, that ruled out his wife, leaving only Sharon Doherty, who'd insisted during her interview that Richard was absolutely faithful to her. But was he? Both his brother Robert and Tony Stevens, the BKM foreman had said in their interviews that he was a bit of a ladies man and Ingleby had been quite amused about the large supply of condoms at Burghill. So he was certainly sexually active. But his brother had also said he only ever saw one woman at a time, never two-timing any of them.

What was it Sarah Miller had said about the cleaner, Val Pereira? He racked his brain for a few seconds. Oh, yes. Sarah had said she'd had the feeling that Val Pereira had a thing about Richard Bexton-King, but neither Sarah nor Ingleby had asked her outright about any possible relationship. That needed to be checked out. He'd had a similar feeling about Sharon Doherty before she admitted to a relationship, so if Sarah was right with her female intuition as David had described it, then Val Pereira could be another element in the investigation, if not a suspect. If Sharon Doherty had been in Cardiff, seeing her daughter and grand-daughter, could it have been Val Pereira playing sex-games with Richard Bexton-King?

He was starting to feel uncomfortable about the number of questions that either hadn't yet been answered or worse, hadn't been asked in the first place. And there was another one. Had anyone checked on Sharon Doherty's alibi? Had she actually been in Cardiff on that Tuesday evening? He started making some notes, consoling himself that it was still early days in the investigation and that there were many pieces of the puzzle yet to be found.

"I've managed to get hold of the Rotary Club president, sir," David Ingleby said from the doorway.

"Good, David, come in and sit down," Townshend said, gesturing to the chair on the other side of his desk. "What did he have to say?"

"Much the same as the secretary at the golf club. The two men had fallen out a couple of times and he'd stepped in to reprimand them and ask them to keep their differences away from meetings."

"Did he say what the arguments were about?"

"He didn't know and didn't really seem to care. He said that it seemed personal so it was none of his business, but that whatever it was, he wouldn't have it affecting the work of Rotary."

"Fair enough, I suppose," said Townshend. "We're certainly seeing a consistency in the relationship between Bexton-King and Eddison." He paused to smile at Ingleby, before adding "As only one of them can tell us what these arguments were about, we need to have a quiet chat with Mr Eddison, don't we?"

CHAPTER TWENTY SIX

The two detectives moved on to discuss Sharon Doherty's alibi and after asking Ingleby to chase it up with the University Hospital Cardiff, Townshend decided to phone Nicholas Eddison himself. He had no concerns about what his boss had said to him; he was sure that in spite of the man's apparent temper, he could deal with him diplomatically. On the other hand, it could be that Eddison was just argumentative with Richard Bexton-King. He'd soon find out. Not knowing Eddison's direct line number, he rang the main PCC office number. The phone was answered promptly by a young-sounding receptionist.

"Good morning, Police and Crime Commissioner's Office. Can I help?" she said in a friendly voice.

"Can you put me through to Mr Nicholas Eddison, please?" Townshend asked.

"I'll just see if he's available. Can I ask who's speaking, please?"

"Detective Inspector Townshend, Hereford CID."

"Please wait a moment, sir." The phone line went dead for a few seconds before the receptionist came back on the line. "I'm sorry, sir, but Mr Eddison's answering machine says he's out of the office and won't be back in until Monday morning. Would you like me to put you through so you can leave a message for him?"

"No thank you, I'll try him again after the weekend," said Townshend and put the phone down. Another delay. He considered his options. Would a visit at home be treading softly enough for Logan? Of course it would, he decided, getting up from his desk. Looking sourly at the rain that was still falling outside his window, he grabbed his coat. "David," he said, from his office doorway, "get Eddison's home address. We're going to pay him a visit." Ingleby nodded, reaching for his own coat as Sarah Miller passed him a piece of paper on which she'd scribbled the address. "Have you got hold of Eddison's gun club yet Sarah?" Townshend asked her.

"No, not yet, sir. Just their answering machine."

"OK, keep trying." he said, then he and Ingleby left the room for the car park. He turned to Ken. "Can you chase up the hostel in the Forest of Dean where Warner was supposed to be staying and check it out?"

"Yes, guv," Ken answered, reaching for his phone.

"Is visiting Eddison a good idea, sir? Particularly after what the DS said," Ingleby asked as they walked out to the car, thinking as he said it that he would never have dreamed of questioning DI Monroe like that. He'd have hit the roof. But Townshend was a different person entirely. His new DI just gave him a quick glance as they dashed through the rain. Townshend answered the question when they were both sitting in the car.

"A good idea, David? I don't know, but we'll go with it anyway. Nicholas Eddison is a loose end and we've got to get the loose ends tied up to make any progress. Let's just see what happens, shall we? If there's any flak, it'll come my way."

"Yes, sir." Ingleby hesitated before continuing. "It wasn't that I was questioning your judgement, sir…"

"I know that, David, but even if you were, it wouldn't be a bad thing. If you've got questions or doubts, voice them. You never know, it might save us having problems later."

The rest of the journey was quiet, with Ingleby concentrating on his driving because of the rain and Townshend thinking about Val Pereira. They needed to talk to her again, and he was wondering if would be better to send Sarah Miller or to do it himself. He decided to let Sarah handle it. There were questions to ask Sharon Doherty as well and he needed to find out, either from Marcella Bexton-King or Robert Bexton-King, just who this mystery man was in her life.

Nicholas Eddison's house was on the edge of Weobley and would probably have been extravagantly described by an estate agent as a 'country cottage.' With its size, it looked more like two cottages knocked into one with an extension added on for good measure. It was a good-sized property. A closed five bar gate prevented them from pulling onto an immaculately kept gravel drive so Ingleby parked the car on the road alongside a hedge. As they climbed out, grateful that the rain had stopped, at least for a short time, a dog started barking on the other side of the hedge.

"Sounds like a big one, doesn't it, David?" Townshend said with a grin.

"Yes, sir. Let's hope it's tied up. It doesn't sound very welcoming." Ingleby wasn't a great dog lover. The barking increased as they opened the gate into the drive way, but the dog, a golden retriever, was confined behind a side gate into a rear garden. Townshend wasn't surprised at the breed. They made good family dogs.

"He's just doing his job," Townshend said. "He'll be friendlier than he sounds, David. Retrievers usually are. They'll lick you rather than bite you."

"I'll take your word on that, sir," Ingleby said, glancing the direction of the still barking dog before ringing the doorbell. It chimed faintly a long way away from them, and it took a short while for it to be answered by a woman who Townshend took to be Eddison's wife. She looked harassed and tired and as if to match her appearance, the rain started again. Both men sheltered under the porch.

"Yes, what is it?" she said shortly as she opened the door to them, continuing quickly before they had a chance to speak. "If you're here selling something, I'm not interested and if you're Jehovah's Witnesses, I haven't the time or the inclination."

"Mrs Eddison? We're police officers and I'm sorry to bother you at what's obviously an inconvenient time," Townshend said, showing her his warrant card. "Is your husband in?" She didn't seem daunted by who they were.

"No, he's bloody well not in and probably never will be again," she said. "What do you want with him? He's at his office, I would imagine."

"No, he's not there. We've tried," Townshend said. "We just wanted a word about his gun licence." He ignored the glance he sensed he got from Ingleby. "Could we possibly come in out of the rain for moment?" She invited them in, but only as far as the carpeted hallway. The dog had carried on barking outside, and as they stepped through the door they could hear a child shouting from the kitchen. Frowning, she shrugged her shoulders and motioned for them to follow her through to the source of the noise. A young toddler in a high chair immediately fell quiet as soon as it saw the two men, its eyes not leaving them as they entered the kitchen.

"What did you mean by saying your husband probably won't be here again, Mrs Eddison? He has a gun licensed to this address. If he's moved, he should have told the police," Townshend said.

"It might be where the damned thing's licensed, but it's not here and I'm glad to see the back of it. I never wanted it here. I don't like guns and I never have. My father was killed in a shooting accident and I didn't want one in the house. Nick was adamant, like he often was. 'Guns don't kill, people do,' was all he said when we argued. Bloody rubbish." She seemed to realise she was ranting. "Sorry," she said, then added: "He took it with him."

"Took it with him?" Townshend asked.

"Yes. When he left. Look, you might as well know. We're getting a divorce. He's decided that me and the children would get in the way of his career or some other stupidity like that and he's filed for a divorce."

"If you don't mind me asking, is there another woman involved?" Mrs Eddison shook her head at Townshend's question.

"No. He said something about the irretrievable breakdown of our relationship or whatever the proper words are."

"Do you know where he is or where he can be contacted, Mrs Eddison? We really do need to get this matter of the licence sorted out. The weapon needs to be kept in a secure place."

"No, I don't and to be honest I don't really care. If you want me to, I can ring him on his mobile and tell him you want to see him, but I think that even for the police, he'd be very angry if I gave you his personal mobile number." Townshend nodded. "I do know he's got a secure box in the boot of his car, if that's any help. He said he needed it when he was taking the gun to the club."

"If you could ring him, I'd be grateful, Mrs Eddison," Townshend paused, glancing at the still quiet toddler. "We'll see ourselves out and thank you for your help. I'm genuinely sorry to hear your news and again please accept my apologies for disturbing you."

"Don't be. For all his faults and his temper, he's looking after his children and me as well, for that matter, as long as I don't contest the divorce. To be honest, I'm almost glad to be seeing the back of him." The two policeman left her in the kitchen and let themselves out through the front door, closing it carefully and also ensuring the driveway gate was securely shut. Their steps were accompanied once more by the barking of the dog. They were in the car before either of them spoke.

"A waste of time, sir?" Ingleby asked as he started the engine.

"Oh, I don't think so, David. It's further confirmation that our Mr Eddison has a temper and is a secretive man."

"Secretive, sir? I don't understand."

"He's treating his wife very well in the divorce, isn't he?"

"Yes, sir, but I don't see…Oh yes I do. As long as she doesn't contest the settlement. It's almost like a gagging clause, isn't it? He's covering his own back."

"Doesn't that sound familiar?" asked Townshend.

"Yes," said Ingleby, nodding. "The victim and his ex-wife. She was using a similar tactic on him, but promising to keep quiet if he didn't mention a co-respondent."

"Yes, David. Something that she was put up to by her mystery man," said Townshend.

"It could be coincidence, sir," Ingleby.

"Yes, David, it could be."

CHAPTER TWENTY SEVEN

As he obviously wasn't going to have the chance to interview Nicholas Eddison before Monday at the earliest, Townshend decided on the journey back into town from Weobley that the rest of the day would have to be spent in chasing up loose ends. But where to start? There were too many.

With a fresh coffee on his desk, accompanied by a very enticing jam doughnut courtesy of Sarah Miller, he opened his e-mails. He was pleased to find a response about the DNA results found on Richard Bexton-King's body. Taking a bite of the doughnut, he read the e-mail eagerly, looking for something that would push the case forwards. The victim's hair and fingernails showed signs of DNA that didn't match any of the samples he and his team had supplied so far, as did, interestingly, the inside of his mouth. There were signs of Sharon Doherty's DNA, which wasn't a surprise given what she'd said about her relationship with Bexton-King. A quick phone call to the lab established that they hadn't yet had a chance to run comparison tests on Stephen Warner's DNA. So, results with another loose end hanging on their tail. He finished his doughnut and began to work through his mental to-do list. After just a few moments, he went into the outer office and stood looking at the white boards, drinking his coffee.

The cleaning company, Absolutely Spotless, still had a question mark against it. Why were those houses, the one in Pontrilas and the one in Burghill, so clean? High Lawns was understandable. It was being cleaned out after Bexton-King's mother's death. Who ordered the work done? It was incredibly convenient for a killer that the murder scene was to be cleaned and a real pain in the neck for the police. But why the victim's own house in Burghill as well?

"Sarah?"

"Yes, sir?"

"That cleaning company, Absolutely Spotless. Did you get any details of the work at Burghill and Pontrilas?" Townshend asked.

"Yes, sir. A deep clean was ordered for both properties, one as a house clearance and the other because the owner was going away."

"Going away?" That was interesting, Townshend thought. Nobody had mentioned anything about Richard Bexton-King going away, least of all Sharon Doherty and if anyone would know, she would.

"That's what they said, sir."

"Did they say what a deep clean involved?"

"Yes, sir. Basically everything. Insides of cupboards, all that sort of thing. The most thorough clean they do. It's usually done at the end of tenancies. Nothing is left untouched."

"And any forensic evidence would be wiped away," Townshend said, almost to himself. How convenient, he thought for the second time in just a few minutes.

"Yes, sir," Sarah agreed.

"Who ordered the clean?" he asked, knowing what the answer would be. She did everything else.

"Sharon Doherty, sir," Sarah confirmed.

"I thought it might be." It left that question of the cleaning company being told about Richard Bexton-King going away.

"Presumably they used their own staff?" he asked.

"I would assume so, sir. That would be the norm."

"Thank you, Sarah," he added, then turned back to her. "What about Leominster gun club? Did you get anything?"

"Well, from what the secretary said, he's not a popular member," she began.

"Which I'm not surprised about," Townshend interrupted.

"But he did add that he seems to keep himself very much to himself, sir. He only goes four or five times a year," she continued, "and keeps his pistol at home."

"OK, Sarah. Well done on that. Now, can you go to see Val Pereira again? Push her a bit on her feelings for Richard Bexton-King. I need to know whether there was anything going on there. Just you this time. A woman to woman chat might be more productive. She might open up more," he said. "Oh, and as she was his cleaner, see if she knew anything about plans for Bexton-King going away." Townshend turned back to the white board and David Ingleby interrupted before he could get his thoughts in any order.

"I've just had an interesting call with Cardiff University Hospital, sir," he began. Townshend turned to face him, sipping at his coffee. "It's a bit of a strange story. The girl is actually Sharon Doherty's step-daughter, not her daughter." His three colleagues all registered differing degrees of surprise.

"So her late husband had been married before," Townshend said. It was a statement rather than a question, but Ingleby replied anyway.

"It looks that way, sir."

"What was it Sharon Doherty said to us about him the first time we interviewed her, David?" he asked. Townshend was coming to rely on Ingleby's excellent memory.

"She said that she was a widow and that her married name was all she came away from the marriage with, sir. She didn't elaborate on anything." Was it that Sharon Doherty wasn't very forthcoming or that they hadn't pursued something that at the time didn't seem important? It might just be now, Townshend thought, with Sharon Doherty's alibi not standing up to close scrutiny.

"Yes, I thought it was something like that. Thank you."

"Anyway," Ingleby continued, "the step-daughter was in there a week ago last Tuesday and because of complications, she's actually still there. Sharon Doherty hasn't been to see her. In fact, according to the hospital, she had no visitors on that evening."

"So it looks as if she lied to us," Townshend said.

"Yes, sir, but there is more. It seems that the two women are estranged from each other and the hospital were under instructions from the step-daughter not to let her in even if she had turned up. So despite what she told us, Sharon Doherty was nowhere near the place."

"Well, she wasn't at Pontrilas with the victim, because Marcella Bexton-King told us she was there," Townshend said. "So what was she doing on that Tuesday evening that she doesn't want us to know about? And why did she lie to us about her step-daughter?"

"But she did say that she went up to Pontrilas to see Bexton-King later on and there was no one there," Ingleby said. "Do we need to see her again, sir?" he added.

"Yes, she might just know something about Robert's debts as well." That prompted him to turn to Ken. Robert Bexton-King's debts and actions might still be a factor in all this. "Well, Ken? Anything come up on that?"

"Yes, guv," Ken said. "It appears that Robert Bexton-King is in hock up to his proverbials, to the tune of nearly half a million quid."

"Do we know who to?" Townshend asked, trying to hide his surprise. It was a lot of money.

"Initially to Karl Singleton, the owner of the Monday Club in Union Street, but then he started to get involved with some serious gamblers from London. These were high stake private games and it seems the only thing Bexton-King was good at was losing." Townshend nodded. That fitted with what they'd been told. "These guys are bad men to cross, and it seems our Robert hasn't been keeping up with his payments. My source says the word is they've been exerting pressure and quite a lot of it."

"Enough to make him want to burn down his own company to get the insurance money?"

"I would think so, guv, especially if he couldn't get the cash any other way. He'd be getting desperate."

"He's going to be more desperate now," Ingleby muttered.

"And you say he still owes this Singleton money as well, Ken?"

"Not now, Singleton sold the debt to the firm from London."

"OK, Ken, thanks. Don't forget that hostel, will you?" said Townshend. "Now let's pay a visit to Sharon Doherty, shall we?" he said to Ingleby.

Sharon Doherty's flat was one of a number in a three storey late nineteenth century house of red Hereford brick in the Broomy Hill part of the city, near the cemetery. It didn't take Townshend and Ingleby long to get there, even though they had to cross the town. As with the house in which Marcella Bexton-King had her flat, each flat had its own individual doorbell outside the main door to the building. Being turned into flats seemed to be the way with these large old Victorian houses, Townshend thought. They were simply too big and expensive for modern families. Ingleby selected the buzzer tagged 'Doherty' and pressed the button. There was no response. He pressed it again, with the same result.

"Looks like we might be out of luck, sir," Ingleby said, turning to Townshend.

"Who are you after, gentlemen?" an older-sounding female voice said from behind them before Townshend could reply. Both detectives turned, startled. Neither had heard anyone come up behind them. The person facing them was indeed an elderly woman. "Mrs Armstrong," she said, introducing herself. "I live in the downstairs flat. If you tell me who it is you're after, I might be able to help. I know all of the other residents."

"We're looking for Mrs Doherty," Townshend said.

"Mrs Doherty? In flat number three? Lovely woman, but you won't find her in. She's gone away for the weekend with that man of hers. They went out earlier."

"What time would that have been, Mrs Armstrong? Do you know?"

"Yes. Mid-afternoon. I was just on my way to get the bus into town. I can't walk as far as I used to be able to, you know."

"You said there was a man?" queried Townshend. Sharon Doherty had told them she was in a relationship with Richard Bexton-King and she couldn't possibly be going away for the weekend with him. Was this something else she was keeping from them?

"Oh yes. He's quite often around here for her. Always got a smile or a friendly word for me as well," the thought bringing a smile to her own face.

"I don't suppose by any chance you know this man's name, do you, Mrs Armstrong?" Townshend asked. She seemed hesitant about answering. Townshend showed her his warrant card to encourage her.

"Oh, she's not in trouble is she? She doesn't seem the sort." The old lady seemed genuinely concerned.

"No. no, Mrs Armstrong. We just wanted to talk to her about the fire at the company she works for," Townshend reassured her. "She's certainly not in any trouble. Now, that name?"

"Oh, yes. Of course. I don't know his surname, but his first name's Nick. Short for Nicholas, I think."

CHAPTER TWENTY EIGHT

Why was Sharon Doherty estranged from her step-daughter? What had happened between them? Townshend couldn't stop asking himself the questions. But what did they really know about Sharon Doherty? Marcella Bexton-King hadn't been complimentary about her, but on the other hand hadn't run her into the ground either. She seemed to be an efficient and conscientious worker who seemed to be almost single-handedly running BKM for the two brothers, but Robert Bexton-King had said very little about her in any of the interviews they'd had with him and Tim Stevens, the foreman at BKM, hadn't passed any opinion on her. Stephen Warner, although he hadn't known her long, didn't like her. Sharon Doherty herself had said she was a widow. But what else? Very little was the answer. Who was the real Sharon Doherty? He reviewed the wash-up with the team on the white board about the case so far and they'd almost skipped over her. Yet Richard Bexton-King had made a property portfolio worth three million pounds over to her. Surely you don't do that to a woman you're not serious about, he thought.

Townshend kept coming back in his mind to her relationship with Bexton-King. A relationship she'd asserted was serious. Yet now it seemed they'd discovered another man in her life, one that she had apparently been seeing regularly at the same time as she was supposedly in a relationship with Richard Bexton-King. And this man had the first name of Nicholas. That was enough to start alarm bells ringing, even though the name was common enough. A link is a link in a murder case, however tenuous it may be and it had to be checked out. If it was Nicholas Eddison and they missed it because they thought it was too much of a coincidence, there'd be all hell to pay. Townshend was too cynical and experienced to not investigate anything that didn't make sense.

The old lady, Mrs Armstrong had given them a description: tall, handsome and muscular, with short cut blond hair and piercing blue eyes. Almost Scandinavian, Ingleby had commented as they walked away. In the office, they'd compared the description to the photograph Sarah Miller had in her file. It matched, so to be sure, Townshend had sent Sarah to Broomy Hill to have a chat with the neighbour and show her the photograph. Mrs Armstrong had confirmed it was the same man. Sharon Doherty was seeing Nicholas Eddison and if the neighbour was to be believed, had been for some time. That certainly threw another level of complexity into the case that they could probably have done without.

"Obviously Eddison's wife doesn't know about Sharon Doherty, sir," Ingleby said, "not from what she said to us this morning."

"Or doesn't care, David," Townshend said. "She hesitated a bit over that question and she seems to be getting what she wants out of the divorce."

"Divorce?" Ken said. "That seems to be a recurring theme in this case, doesn't it, guv?"

"Can I interrupt here?" Sarah Miller asked. "When I went to see Val Pereira, she was in a much more talkative mood than before." Townshend noticed her glance at Ingleby with an 'I told you so' look on her face. There was that undercurrent between the two of them again. Both were good officers, but he wasn't going to have petty rivalries or jealousies affecting the team. For now, though, it appeared under control.

"So what did she have to say that she didn't say last time, Sarah?" he asked.

"She was adamant that Richard Bexton-King was divorcing his wife for her, not that scheming bitch Sharon Doherty – her words, not mine, sir." Someone else who doesn't like Sharon Doherty, Townshend thought.

"Did she give any reason for saying that, Sarah?" Townshend asked. "It goes against what Sharon Doherty told us. Was she saying she was in a relationship with the victim?"

"Yes sir, and she also said that Richard Bexton-King did have a fling with Sharon Doherty but it was all over," Sarah said. "She says they were going to the Greek Islands together."

"The woman sounds delusional to me, guv," Ken said.

"It sounds more than an employee's crush on her boss, doesn't it, sir?" Ingleby said. "More like an obsession."

"According to her Richard Bexton-King had an estate and villa out there on Hydra and just wanted to get away from everything in his life."

"Is she just not making all this up?" Ken asked.

"It sounds like Hollywood chick-flick stuff, the dreams of a woman who couldn't have what she wanted," Ingleby added, agreeing. "I can't believe you fell for it, Sarah."

"Check it out yourself," Sarah said, her anger barely controlled, passing him a file, "and then tell me if she's making it up." A couple of photographs fell out and Townshend picked them up from the floor. Val Pereira and Richard Bexton-King outside a white washed and sun drenched villa. Townshend felt his heart sinking towards the floor. Ken was looking over his shoulder as he gave them to Ingleby.

"Oh, hell," he said. "That doesn't make things any easier."

"No, it doesn't, Ken. What do you think, David?" Townshend asked.

"Could be Photoshop, sir," Ingleby said. Sarah Miller snorted.

"She doesn't own a computer," she said.

"What else is in there, David?" Townshend asked.

"Plane tickets and a credit card receipt, sir," Ingleby answered. Townshend took a deep breath. This was totally unexpected.

"OK. Check out the villa with the Greek police on Hydra will you? Just get them to confirm who owns it." Ingleby looked as completely dumbfounded as he was himself, but agreed, moving over to his own desk. Townshend turned to Sarah. "Good work, Sarah."

"Yes, well done, Sarah," Ingleby added. "She certainly opened up to you, didn't she?" Sarah Miller nodded, as surprised as Townshend at Ingleby's words.

So Val Pereira knew that Bexton-King was thinking of going away," Townshend said, almost to himself.

"Yes, sir," said Sarah, "but there is more," she said. Townshend sighed. He certainly didn't want any more complications.

"Go on, Sarah."

"Val Pereira was the person who did the deep clean on the house in Burghill and she admitted that it was her who told Absolutely Spotless the owner was going away."

"So Sharon Doherty probably didn't know," Townshend mused. "Why did the cleaning company use Val Pereira? Did she say?"

"She knew the property and the company knew her. If you remember, sir, she had worked for them. It was as simple as that."

"That seems reasonable," Townshend said. "Thank you," he added, turning towards the white board with an irresistible urge to wipe everything off and start again.

Just what sort of games was Richard Bexton-King playing before he was killed? That was the question that Townshend now had to get answered. There was something in this mess that he was missing. Why did he rewrite his will and leave everything to his brother but not tell him he was going away? Why, even more strangely, did he sign over his property portfolio to Sharon Doherty when he had every intention of leaving the country with another woman, a woman who was his cleaner? The solicitor in Leominster had told Ingleby that the property transfer was water-tight to stop Marcella Bexton-King getting her hands on any of it through the divorce. Is it possible the man was having some sort of breakdown? If the circumstances of his death, the restraint marks and his body being found in a trunk, weren't as they were, Townshend may well have been seriously considering the man had taken his own life.

CHAPTER TWENTY NINE

Saturday morning brought no relaxation of the gloom in the team office. If anything, it was marginally deeper. The complications of Richard Bexton-King's life and the decisions he'd been making seemed impenetrable, clouding the motives of any of the suspects. Who knew what? That was the question to be resolved. But that was what a detective's life was all about, peeling away the complexities of a problem layer by layer until you reached the core.

"Sarah!" Townshend called from his office cutting through the depressed silence.

"Yes, sir?" She was already on her feet, notebook in hand, heading for his office as she answered.

"Fancy a trip down to Cardiff?" Townshend asked. She knew very well the question was rhetorical.

"Sharon Doherty's daughter?" she asked in return. He nodded.

"Yes, we need to talk to her. See what you can find out about their relationship. It's better done face to face," Townshend said. That was one lead being followed, he thought as she turned from the doorway. Now for another. "Ken?" he called.

"Yes, guv?"

"Get on to the hospital again and find out if we can see Robert Bexton-King. He must have come round by now."

"Yes, guv," said Ken and then added, muttering "I bet I get that snotty sister again."

"If you do," said Ingleby from his desk, "then use your considerable charms on her," and laughed. The sergeant's phone rang, preventing Ken from making any reply to him, rude or otherwise. Townshend heard Ingleby simply say "OK. We'll come downstairs directly." After putting the phone down, Ingleby crossed the office to Townshend's door.

"What is it, David?" Townshend asked.

"Marcella Bexton-King's just come into the station, sir, asking for you personally. The desk sergeant's showing her into one of the interview rooms." Townshend tried not to show the surprise he felt. He had the nagging feeling that however complicated things were, they were just about to get a whole lot worse.

"We'd better go and see what she wants, then, hadn't we David? It doesn't do to keep a lady waiting," he joked. They were both quite shocked at her appearance as they entered the interview room. Gone was the well-groomed, heavily made-up Marcella trying to emulate the look of the women in the glossy society magazines. Gone also was the superior, 'I'm better than you' look on her face. Instead, she seemed deflated and looked older than she actually was, definitely not the person they'd first encountered less than a week ago. She looked up as they walked in looking almost relieved to see them and Townshend got a first good look at her face. Her cheeks were bruised and discoloured and there was a nasty black eye developing. He lip was also puffy from a cut. There was however, no disguising the anger in her eyes.

"Good morning, Detective Inspector, Sergeant," she said, addressing both of them. "Thank you for seeing me." There was no sign of her earlier dismissive attitude towards them.

"That's not a problem, Mrs Bexton-King," Townshend said, sitting down opposite her. "How can we help you? No perhaps we ought to start with a drink. Can we get you a tea or a coffee?"

"Coffee, please," she said and David Ingleby went off to organise drinks for all three of them. Townshend waited until he came back before carrying on.

"I think it might be good for you to tell us what's happened, Mrs Bexton-King. Apart from your obvious injuries, you seem rather distressed," Townshend began.

"I'm better now than I was yesterday," she said, anger flashing momentarily in her eyes.

"Yesterday?"

"Nicholas came to see me," she said. "Early yesterday afternoon."

"Nicholas Eddison?" Townshend asked. She looked surprised.

"Yes. How did you know?" He ignored her question.

"Is he the man you were having a relationship with?" he asked instead. She nodded, still looking a little puzzled. "The man who made the suggestion about you not contesting the divorce?" She nodded again. That seemed easy, thought Townshend. The last time they'd spoken, she was adamant about not giving them the man's name. "What happened yesterday, Mrs Bexton-King?"

"Isn't it bloody obvious? Work it out, you're the policemen." There was the anger again. She apologised. "I'm sorry, Nicholas came around, raving about how the police were looking for him, that you were looking for him, Detective Inspector. He accused me of giving you his name."

"And beat you up?"

"Yes. I told him it had nothing to do with me and that I didn't know how you'd got hold of his name. He didn't believe me."

"Has he ever threatened you or hit you before?" Townshend asked.

"No. I knew he had a temper, but he's never been less than kind to me before," she said.

"Why does he think we're looking for him, Mrs Bexton-King? Has he got something to hide?"

"He didn't say, just said that if anything came out about his involvement in my divorce from Richard, that it would ruin his chances of ever getting what he wanted out of life."

"And that was reason enough to assault you? It seems a bit of an over-reaction. People get divorced all the time these days."

"Apparently. He was very angry, Detective Inspector." She sipped her coffee, wincing as her lip touched the hot cup. "When we originally talked about it, he said it would be an unacceptable black mark against him."

"Mrs Bexton-King, it's my understanding that Mr Eddison is looking towards a career in politics. Politicians have done far worse than be involved in divorces. Is that really what this is about?" She just shook her head.

"As far as I know, yes."

"Have you seen anyone about your injuries, Mrs Bexton-King?" Townshend asked. She nodded, which surprised him. He'd had the feeling she might just be a little embarrassed about going to a hospital A&E.

"Yes, the hospital. They gave me an ice pack to help the swelling go down and some co-codamol for the pain," she said.

"And your injuries?"

"Two loose teeth, a broken cheek bone, bruising and as you can see, a black eye," she replied.

"Are you going to bring charges against Mr Eddison?"

"Yes, Detective Inspector, I am. I'm not going to let him get away with this."

"No, of course not. We'll get that organised when we've finished, but if you're OK with it, I would like to ask you a few more questions."

"Yes, that's fine. Is it more to do with Richard's murder?"

"Yes, but they might be a little upsetting," Townshend warned her.

"Then let's just get them over with, shall we, Detective Inspector?" she said with a flash of impatience he hadn't expected from the ready way she'd agreed to the questions.

"Let's stick with Nicholas Eddison for the moment," he said. "Were you aware that he was having heated arguments with your ex-husband? Apparently both at the golf club they belonged to and at Rotary meetings."

"No, I wasn't. I didn't even know they knew each other. Nicholas never said he knew Richard."

"So you'd have no idea of what those arguments might be about?" Townshend persisted.

"Not if I didn't know they were arguing, no," she snapped.

"How much do you know about Mr Eddison, Mrs Bexton-King?"

"In what way?" she asked.

"His home life. His social life, that sort of thing."

"He's good in bed, Detective Inspector, what does the rest matter? Just what are you getting at?" There were starting to be flashes of the Marcella Bexton-King they'd interviewed early in the week. Townshend paused. Were these questions that uncomfortable for her? There was almost certainly going to be some sort of reaction to the next couple, he thought, probably anger.

"Did you know he'd filed for divorce from his wife?" Her eyes widened a little, but apart from that she didn't react.

"No."

"Mr Eddison has been a regular visitor at Sharon Doherty's flat and has been for some time. Were you aware of any relationship between them?"

"No, I bloody well wasn't! He's been seeing that scheming conniving bitch behind my back?"

"And his wife's," Townshend commented.

"Who told you? How do you know?"

"A neighbour of Mrs Doherty's told us and gave us a description," Townshend said. "Of course, we've no idea of the sort of the relationship they've been having," he added. She laughed.

"No, of course not. Anything else, Detective Inspector? I'm feeling so much better for having come here, you know." The sarcasm was heavy in her voice.

"Just a couple more questions, Mrs Bexton-King, then DS Ingleby can get on with taking your statement about the assault." She nodded. "Firstly, about your ex-husband's property portfolio," Townshend began.

"His what?" She laughed again.

"His property portfolio," Townshend repeated.

"More like a collection of run-down properties that no one else wanted," she said. "He picked them all up at auctions. The grand idea was that he'd start a development company and do them all up, but it was all just a pipe-dream. They're all falling down."

"So they're not worth anything?" Townshend asked.

"No. Both Robert and I told him he was wasting his money and his time. It would cost millions to do them all up even to a state where they could be sold and then he probably still stood to lose money." She seemed to find the whole idea rather funny.

"Not worth three million pounds, then?"

"Not in their current state, no. It's about what it would cost to do them up, though."

"What about the house on Aylestone Hill? I was under the impression from your brother-in-law that your ex-husband was the owner," Townshend said.

"No, he wasn't the owner," she replied. "All of the flats are separately owned. Richard owned the flat, not the house, and it wasn't part of his so-called portfolio. As for the rest of the properties, they're a liability, not an asset. Why are you asking?" Townshend could see no reason for not telling her.

"He transferred them all to Sharon Doherty," he said. She laughed again, more loudly. A very un-ladylike belly laugh. When she calmed down, he moved on.

"We've also found out that your ex-husband had plans for going away, Mrs Bexton-King. Did you know anything about this?"

"No, but then you've got to remember we were hardly talking. He probably regarded it as none of my business."

"And finally, what about him having a villa in Greece, on one of the islands?"

"Again, no, I wasn't. It was a dream of his for his retirement, I know that, but I didn't know it had gone any further than that. I wanted him to get one on the Cote D'Azur, but it never happened. I didn't like Greece and he hated France. I'd write that one off as just a dream as well, Detective Inspector," she said.

"Thank you, Mrs Bexton-King. I'm sorry you've been through what you have and I'll leave you in Sergeant Ingleby's hands to deal with your complaint."

CHAPTER THIRTY

Townshend was able to feel a little more positive a few minutes after he returned to the office. Ken had some good news from the hospital and a message for David Ingleby from the Greek police. On top of that, Marcella Bexton-King's complaint about Nicholas Eddison's assault gave him an extra reason to interview Eddison and made it easier to justify to Detective Chief Inspector Logan.

"That snotty sister at the hospital I was talking to yesterday said that someone can see Robert Bexton-King this afternoon, guv," Ken said, "but we can't have long with him. Apparently, he's still quite fragile, as she put it."

"Fragile?" Townshend said, grinning. "OK, Ken, at least that's a start." But Robert Bexton-King could wait until David had finished downstairs, Townshend thought. "Anything else?"

"Yes, guv. Just after you both went downstairs, there was a phone call for Sergeant Ingleby from the police on that Greek island, Hydra. I could hardly understand a word of the guy's accent." Townshend poured himself a coffee from the always bubbling jug while Ken spoke.

"What did he have to say?" he asked, adding milk to his drink.

"Dunno guv. It was all Greek to me." Ken laughed at his own little joke, then continued. "It seems that this Pereira woman's above board, at least about the villa. Richard Bexton-King does own one on the island. The guy said he'd owned it about five years, although he hasn't visited it very often."

"Five years? That long, eh? His ex-wife doesn't know anything about it," Townshend said, but it was hardly surprising. The Bexton-King's marriage wasn't a good one, and from what he could gather, hadn't been from the start. There was no reason he would have told her, especially as she wanted one in the south of France. "When was he there last, Ken? Did he say?"

"About two months ago, and there was a woman with him," Ken replied.

"Did she match Val Pereira's description?" Townshend asked.

"Dunno, guv. All they knew was that Bexton-King had a woman with him. I don't think anyone took that much notice." Townshend nodded and walked through to his own office, sitting down with his coffee.

With the two people he really needed to talk to, Sharon Doherty and Nicholas Eddison, not available, there was a slight hiatus in the investigation. Townshend, still feeling guilty about it, thought he might be able to do a little work on David Ingleby's review, but he couldn't settle to it. There was so much else to think about. The investigation kept spinning round in his mind and he was convinced that there was something he was missing, some little fact he'd overlooked. He went back out to the main office and stood quietly looking at the crowded white boards. He was soon re-drawing links and adding questions and comments.

"Do you think Richard Bexton-King was the sort to indulge in sex games, Ken?" he suddenly asked over his shoulder.

"Sex games? He hardly seems the type from what we know of him, guv, but you know what they say: it's always the quiet ones who surprise you. What makes you ask?"

"It's this whole idea of him being tied up, presumably to a chair as he was being force-fed, Ken. If he wasn't willing, then it would have taken two people, one to tie him up and one to hold him down or threaten him with a weapon of some sort." The thought had been bothering him since the previous morning. Up until then he'd been thinking about the who and the why of the murder, but had, to an extent, been ignoring the how. The thing was, it might make a very big difference to the question of who did it and what the motives were. "The only reason I can think of for him being willing to be tied up is some sort of sex game."

"I see where you're coming from, guv, but was he dressed?" Ken asked.

"When he was found, yes, so I assume he was when he was killed," Townshend replied, then pulled himself up. You can't make assumptions. Not in a murder case. "On the other hand, he could've been dressed afterwards by the killer, couldn't he?" he said. Ken nodded.

"But don't you think it's unlikely to have been a sex game, guv?" Ken persisted. Townshend nodded, almost absently. Ken changed tack. "It's about the women. Sharon Doherty looks like she's lying to us about her relationship with Richard Bexton-King, guv, and he certainly wasn't having that sort of relationship with his ex-wife, was he?"

"There is Val Pereira, Ken," Townshend said.

"Who was about to go to Greece with him, if she's to be believed, guv. That doesn't seem to make her a good suspect."

"And that leaves us with needing two people," Townshend concluded.

"Yes, guv." Townshend started drawing lines. There was a link between Robert Bexton-King and Stephen Warner as they were having a sexual relationship. There was the same sort of relationship between Robert and Marcella Bexton-King. Then, with her, there was another relationship with Nicholas Eddison, who also happened to be seeing Sharon Doherty. Richard Bexton-King was naturally in the middle of all this. The only other person on the board was Val Pereira, who said she was having a relationship with Richard, but was also Marcella's cleaner. He stepped back from the board and Ken looked at the boards from his desk. "God, what a mess," he said.

"Yes, Ken and that's just their relationships. Now, what about possible motives?" Townshend said.

"Motives? I thought we'd been through all that the other day," Ken said.

"So we did, Ken. But that was individual motives and it's only half the picture. If we allow for two people, it complicates things. What we've got to think of then is what motives could possibly link any of these people together. A motive strong enough to pull them together to kill. You've really got to trust someone to be involved in a murder with them."

"That's got to make it one hell of a motive, guv. Or it could be something that would be powerful enough to give one of them a hold over one of the others. "

"Yes, but what? If we're to believe the stories about Stephen Warner's family and especially his mother, then revenge would motivate him, but having talked to him, I'm not so sure. He doesn't seem the type." He paused, and when he resumed, was almost talking to himself. "But do murderers ever seem the type? He seems plausible enough and was talking like Richard Bexton-King almost welcomed him back as an old friend."

"But we've only got his word for that, guv. The victim can't back him up, can he?"

"No and Warner would certainly know the capabilities of a drug like oxycontin," Townshend said. "But then there's the link. We've only got a link between him and the victim's brother."

"And that seems like it's only sexual," said Ken. Townshend nodded, agreeing.

"Would that be enough?" he asked and then answered his own question before Ken could say anything. "No, it wouldn't, would it, Ken? It wouldn't be enough to persuade a man to kill his brother."

"Unless he wanted him dead anyway, guv."

"Good point. If Robert Bexton-King wanted his brother dead and then found himself with a willing ally ..." He let his words trail off as he thought about it. "But what about Robert's motive? Money? Jealousy going back to their childhood? Remember that their father always favoured Richard over Robert. That could leave a lasting resentment. The psychologists would have a field day with it."

"Could it be both, guv?" Ken asked.

"Both?"

"Well, we know he's in deep trouble with money and with some nasty characters from London. If he can't get his hands on any readies because his brother won't help him, there's going to be some ill feeling. If he's already got some issues with the victim from his childhood, then that could be quite a potent mix."

"Robert told us he didn't know what was in the will, Ken," said Townshend.

"I'd say he could have worked it out. He was the victim's only relative and Richard Bexton-King doesn't seem to have been the sort of person to leave all his money to a cat's home."

"But remember as well, Ken, that the divorce between Richard and Marcella hasn't gone through. In the eyes of the law, she's his closest relative, not Robert. But if Warner and Robert Bexton-King were discussing Richard, they might have found some common ground for wanting him out of the way," Townshend said.

"That'd be some sort of pillow talk," said the down to earth Londoner, smiling.

"It gives us some questions to ask Mr Bexton-King while he's lying comfortable in his hospital bed, that's for sure," Townshend said. "But what about the others? Marcella Bexton-King, for instance."

"What about Marcella Bexton-King, guv? She seems to like having the trappings of money as well as the money itself, but what about a motive? She seemed to have been doing pretty well out of the divorce."

"I agree, Ken. She also knew she wasn't getting anything in her husband's will, so him being dead wasn't of any benefit to her, was it? Unless," he added, "he died before the divorce was finalised. Then she'd have a case for contesting it." It seemed to Townshend that as he and Ken talked, the possibilities grew ever more complex. The two of them were talking in circles and not getting anywhere.

"If he'd been killed in a more violent way I could possibly understand she might have done it in anger, because I think if roused, she could be capable of it, guv."

"This certainly wasn't a heat of the moment thing," Townshend said. "Do you know what her name means, Ken? Marcella?"

"No, guv."

"Warlike and strong," Townshend said, smiling.

"Doesn't surprise me, guv. What was she in for earlier?"

"Nicholas Eddison has assaulted her," Townshend said.

"Now that's interesting, isn't it?" Ken said.

"Yes it is, because it destroys one link between them." He didn't match his words by erasing the line he'd put on the board for their relationship, explaining to Ken that the links that mattered were those that existed when the murder took place.

"What about Sharon Doherty?" Ken asked. "Surely this relationship that's come to light with Eddison changes things."

"It does, very much so," Townshend said. "Why is she having a relationship with a man who is constantly picking arguments with the man she says she loves and who she says is divorcing his wife for her? It doesn't make sense. And there is something else." He paused to refill his coffee mug. "This property portfolio of Richard Bexton-King's is apparently worthless, at least according to his wife."

"So where did this figure of three million pounds come from?"

"From his solicitor. Marcella Bexton-King says that's how much it would cost to even make the properties worth selling. She didn't think it was possible to make a profit out of it, that's for sure."

"What does that mean? A confused solicitor?" Ken asked.

"I don't know, Ken. The solicitor insists that Sharon Doherty didn't know she was being given this portfolio, but I'm not so sure. If she'd found out she'd been given a dud, she'd be pretty bloody mad about it."

"Why would he do it, though," Ken asked.

"Well, it's only supposition, but think about it. If she was involved with Richard Bexton-King and he found out she was having affair with Eddison, he'd be angry, wouldn't he?"

"Yes, but wasn't he having a relationship with that cleaner, Val Pereira?"

"Was he? We've only got her word on that," Townshend said.

"But what about that photo and the plane tickets," Ken persisted.

"Yes," Townshend agreed. "There's still a lot to be resolved, Ken, and a lot of questions to be answered."

CHAPTER THIRTY ONE

Robert Bexton-King was in a private room on his own off to one side of the main ward, close to the nurses' station. Townshend and Ingleby had, before being allowed to go in and see him, been reminded in no uncertain terms by the sister, presumably the same one Ken had spoken to, that they were not to be in there too long and that they were not to cause him undue stress or to tire him out.

"Did you remember to bring the kid gloves and the grapes, David?" Townshend had said drily. The ward sister hadn't been amused by his humour.

"He is recovering from a dreadful shock," she said acidly.

"A self-inflicted one, Sister," Townshend replied. As they entered Bexton-King's room, a uniformed constable rose hurriedly from his chair in the corner of the room, folding a newspaper.

"Give us half an hour, constable," Townshend said. "Get yourself down to the coffee shop and have a drink." The man looked quite grateful for the break and hurried off. Bexton-King was apparently sleeping, propped up on pillows and heavily bandaged around the lower half of his face. A rather superfluous sign on the wall above his head said 'Nil by mouth' which made Townshend smile. They'd be lucky to find it under all those dressings, he thought.

"Do we wake him up, sir?" Ingleby asked quietly.

"Of course we do, David, we'll be wasting our time if we don't, and that sister has probably already got a stopwatch running." Ingleby leaned over and touched Bexton-King's shoulder. He woke up immediately, looking both surprised and uncomfortable at seeing the two detectives rather than a nurse. It was almost as if he felt ashamed being faced with them.

"Good afternoon, Mr Bexton-King," said Townshend. "I take it that Sister didn't tell you we were coming." Bexton-King gingerly shook his head. "We've a few questions we didn't get the chance to ask you the other day." Bexton-King nodded gently and reached for a notepad and pencil which lay on his bedside cabinet. Townshend raised his hand to stop him, pleased to see that someone had already had the foresight to decide on that as a way of communicating. Bexton-King placed the pad on the bed within easy reach. "No need to write anything just yet. Then you'll just need to answer my questions. We're not here for small talk, and a nod or a shake of the head might be enough for some of them. Is that alright?" Bexton-King nodded again.

"I'll get right to the point, Mr Bexton-King," Townshend continued. "We have clear CCTV footage of you entering your premises at BKM in the early hours of Sunday morning. You arrive alone and can be seen going in and out of the various buildings before leaving, still alone. Shortly after you leave flames and smoke can be clearly seen from those same buildings. Do you admit having been there then?" A slight nod of the head.

"I believe that your intention in visiting the premises at that time was to deliberately set them on fire. Is that correct?" Townshend was deliberately taking a very formal approach to the interview and trying to phrase his questions to give Bexton-King a chance to answer by either nodding or shaking his head. Ingleby was taking notes as usual. There was a long pause and then Bexton-King obliged with an almost imperceptible nod accompanied by a look that might have been acceptance or just relief.

"Did starting the fire at BKM have anything to do with your gambling debts, Mr Bexton-King?" Another nod.

"I take it you'd found no other way of raising the money, then?" Townshend asked. An emphatic shake of the head this time.

"Did you go to your brother for help?" Bexton-King nodded.

"And I presume he refused, leaving you with nowhere to turn." Townshend was momentarily confused by a shake of the head when he'd expected a nod.

"So he said he'd help?" A nod, accompanied by a smile. So why the fire, Townshend thought, although an idea was forming.

"How was he going to help you? Money?" A shake of the head. This was going to be difficult with yes and no answers, Townshend thought. He gestured at the notepad on the bed.

"How?"

"The fire," Bexton-King wrote.

"The fire? Did he have something to do with it?" Had the brothers discussed the possibility of burning down their own business? A nod followed by a short scribble.

"It was his idea," Townshend read out so Ingleby could hear.

"He suggested that you set fire to BKM?" Townshend asked. A very firm nod. "Can you explain that?" Bexton-King took up his notepad. Townshend waited until he was passed the sheet of paper. He read it aloud.

"The company was in trouble. We'd gained no new accounts for two years, but we'd not lost any. We weren't going anywhere. The problem was, we'd been told we were losing our two oldest and biggest accounts later this year. We were going to do it together, but I insisted I'd do it alone."

"Was BKM going to go under?" Townshend asked. Bexton-King nodded.

"Did anyone else know? Sharon Doherty?" A shake of the head. "The company solicitors certainly didn't know," Townshend said. "They told us everything was fine." Bexton-King nodded again and then wrote a few words. "We kept it from everyone," Townshend read out. "Richard wanted out as well, so we agreed on the fire."

"To get money from the insurance policy on the business?" It was a common enough scam, but the two men obviously hadn't realised it was an incredibly difficult one to get away with. The question was followed by another nod. It seemed to Townshend that Bexton-King was suddenly beginning to look tired. How much of that was put on to avoid further questions he could only guess. "I assume you'd both decided BKM couldn't be sold as a going concern?" Another weary nod.

"You said your brother wanted out, Mr Bexton-King. Did you know he was planning on going away?" A nod. "To his villa on Hydra?" Bexton-King nodded again, but looked surprised, an unasked question of 'How did you know that?' in his eyes. "Mrs Pereira told us." As far as Townshend could tell from his bandaged face, Bexton-King smiled. His eyes certainly twinkled. "She also told us that your brother was going there with her. She even had a photo of the two of them outside what I assume to be the villa." He pulled it from his pocket and showed it to the other man, who nodded. "Is she telling us the truth?" Bexton-King nodded and took up his notepad again. When he'd finished writing, Townshend again read out the words for Ingleby's benefit.

"Richard was comfortable with Val. She had no expectations and put no pressure on him. She'd have made him happy." Townshend looked up at Bexton-King again.

"Did Sharon Doherty know about your brother's involvement with Mrs Pereira?" The response this time was an uncertain shake of the head. "Did Val Pereira know about Mrs Doherty?" There was another shake of the head, followed by a noise which could have been a laugh but resulted in a fit of coughing.

"Just what is going on here?" The acid voice cut into the coughing as the ward sister burst into the room, crossed over to Bexton-King and immediately began fussing around him. "I told you specifically not to cause this patient any undue stress." The coughing fit subsided fairly quickly, but the sister remained protectively by the bed, between Bexton-King and Townshend, who'd remained seated. Glaring at the detectives, she seemed to reach a decision. "You're causing my patient distress. I'm going to have to ask you two gentlemen to leave. This is a hospital, after all."

"No, sister, we're not going to leave, not just yet, anyway," Townshend said firmly. He saw her stiffen at this refusal to acknowledge or accept her authority. "We still have one or two questions to ask Mr Bexton-King and I'm sure he's quite happy to answer them." Frowning, the sister turned to Bexton-King, who smiled and nodded his agreement at her. "We won't be any more than ten minutes, sister," Townshend added placatingly as she looked ready to protest.

"Very well, Detective Inspector," she said, "but no more." She still didn't seem happy and Townshend heaved a sigh of relief as she left the room. It seemed that Robert Bexton-King felt the same way. Townshend considered Bexton-King's reaction to his question about Sharon Doherty. Was he missing something again?

"You seemed to find my last question funny, Mr Bexton-King," he said. "Why?" Bexton-King was soon writing rapidly and then passed the sheet over to Townshend when he'd finished.

"From the moment she started with BKM," Townshend read out, "Sharon Doherty was all over Richard, throwing herself at him. Everyone thought it was quite funny, but Richard went for it. He was having troubles with Marcella and Sharon was there for the taking. It was stupid. She'd got her claws into him. He finished the relationship but she wouldn't accept it." Townshend looked up from what he was reading. This was in direct contradiction to Sharon Doherty's assertions, but it wasn't a thought he shared with Bexton-King.

"Couldn't he just have fired her?" he asked. More hurried writing.

"She threatened an employment tribunal, which we couldn't afford, because she'd almost certainly have won. So when Richard met Val, he had to keep it a secret from Sharon. But, yes, Val did know about Sharon. All about her." Conscious of the time and not wanting a reappearance of the sister, Townshend pushed on with his questions.

"What about your brother's property portfolio? We've been told it wasn't worth anything." Bexton-King shook his head while writing again.

"Worthless," Townshend read. "It was a waste of his money."

"Why did he sign it over to Sharon Doherty?" Townshend asked and Bexton-King looked as if he was about to start laughing again. Instead, he started writing again.

"I didn't know he had," Bexton-King had written. "It would either have been to keep her quiet or as a cruel joke." Townshend noticed that the constable was back by the door, and that the sister was with him.

"Two more minutes and we're done," Townshend said to both of them and they moved away. He sighed. Any more questions they wanted to ask Robert Bexton-King would have to be asked in the presence of a solicitor to stay within police procedures. He gathered together the sheets of paper Robert Bexton-King had written and turned to Ingleby. "Go ahead, David."

"Robert Bexton-King, I am arresting you for the crime of arson at the premises of BKM Limited," Ingleby said. "You do not have to say anything, but it may harm your defence if you do not mention when questioned something which you later rely on in court. Anything you do say may be given in evidence."

CHAPTER THIRTY TWO

Neither of the detectives spoke until they had left the hospital building and were walking across the car park. It was David Ingleby who broke the silence.

"That was a bit of a surprise, sir," he said.

"Which part, David?" Townshend asked, amused by the way his Detective Sergeant had broached the subject. He'd been thinking that interviewing someone who wrote down their answers was both an inconvenient and unsatisfactory process. It gave the interviewee time to think and inflections in a person's voice when they answered a question could be a good indicator of whether or not they were telling the truth.

"Well, all of it really, sir, but especially the fact that both brothers seem to have been involved in the fire." The two men stopped on the edge of the pavement to allow a speeding car to pass before they crossed the road.

"Bloody boy racers," Townshend muttered as they resumed walking, before agreeing with Ingleby. "Yes, David. The state of their business puts a whole new complexion on why Richard Bexton-King had decided to go away, doesn't it?"

"Do you think he was trying to get away from debt as well, sir?" Townshend shook his head.

"No. I think it's more likely that he'd just had enough of it all and had decided to get out and enjoy the rest of his life. It seems like he had the money to do so, didn't he?" He glanced at Ingleby. "Still, it does seem a bit rash burning your business down."

"And there's his will, sir," Ingleby said. "Do you think he changed it because he was going away?" Ingleby asked.

"His will? Yes. I would imagine he was simply settling his affairs and getting them in order before going to Hydra. But his will doesn't seem as important now as it did when we first found out about it."

"But it was the reason him and his ex-wife were arguing, sir. Don't you think that it would have given Marcella Bexton-King enough motive to kill him?" Townshend shook his head again.

"No," he replied. "With his will changed and her knowing she wasn't going to be left anything, it wouldn't have made sense. The insurance is a slightly different matter, although she insists she didn't know. It's strange that he hadn't changed the beneficiary on the policies, though. My guess is that he just hadn't got round to doing it. Mind you, he probably wasn't expecting to be killed," he added drily as they reached the front entrance of the police station.

"Presumably not, sir," said Ingleby, not knowing whether or not to smile at Townshend's last comment.

Townshend was surprised to find Sarah Miller already back in the office from Cardiff. She looked up from her computer screen as he entered the office and spoke to her.

"Useful trip, Sarah? You're back quicker than I thought."

"There wasn't a lot of traffic around and yes, sir, it was very useful," she replied.

"Well, that's a bonus," Townshend said. "You'll have to fill us in on what you've found out. Ken not around?" She smiled.

"Natural break, sir. He said he wouldn't be long."

"OK. We'll wait until he comes back, then we'll all catch up." As he spoke, Ken ambled back into the office, speeding up slightly as he caught sight of his boss. Townshend and Ingleby divested themselves of their coats and all four detectives gathered around the whiteboards once more. "Right," Townshend said, "let's get to it. There have been more developments and I think we need to pool our ideas and thoughts again. Everyone OK with that?" The other three all nodded.

"Can I start this one off, guv?" Ken asked and Townshend gave him the nod.

"The floor's yours, Ken," he said. "What've you got for us?"

"I mentioned the other day that Robert Bexton-King was involved with a nasty firm from London about his gambling debts and that he'd got himself in over his head. Well, a couple of their heavies have been sent up and they're hanging around town. My informant tells me he's heard they've been to see Bexton-King to put the frighteners on him about the money." He paused and looked at his colleagues. "It might put a little more importance on the fact that Richard Bexton-King left everything to him in his will."

"A ready source of money," Ingleby commented.

"What conclusion would you draw from that, Ken?" Townshend asked.

"If he needed money, then he was being left the houses and the business. All he needed was Richard dead," Ken said. David Ingleby and Sarah Miller both nodded in agreement.

"Yes, Ken? Go on," said Townshend.

"Well, we know that Robert Bexton-King was out of town on the night his brother was killed, but could these London guys have done the murder for him, or more importantly for their bosses? From what I'm told, they're both capable of it. Robert would have been able to fill them in about the oxycontin, wouldn't he?" Townshend glanced at David Ingleby.

"There's one little problem, Ken," Ingleby said. "The business was in trouble and only the brothers knew. They were due to be losing their biggest customers later this year. They couldn't sell and the fire was rigged up between them. Why would Robert still go ahead with that if all he had to do was wait for the money from his brother's will? It doesn't add up."

"I agree it's a bit strange, but what about the big houses in Pontrilas and Burghill and that garage full of expensive cars? They still belonged to Richard, didn't they? His brother would have had that as well as the insurance money," Ken said. Townshend looked thoughtful for a few moments.

"You think he might have got a bit greedy?" Townshend asked. Ken nodded.

"Yes, guv. It's certainly a possibility. He's got the gambling bug and having the money from the will and the insurance money would have given him something left over by the time he'd paid off this London firm, wouldn't it?"

"You said these heavies are capable of something like murder, Ken? It's a step up from putting on the frighteners, isn't it?" Ken didn't reply, just nodded, a serious look on his face.

"Could a visit from these guys followed by a visit from us be enough of a reason for Bexton-King to shoot himself, sir?" Ingleby asked, going off at a bit of a tangent.

"It could be a factor in it, David," Townshend answered. "With us investigating his brother's murder, he must have known we'd be digging deep. These sort of people he's mixed up with in London wouldn't take kindly to having the police around. My guess is he's as scared as hell about what he's got himself involved in."

"They wouldn't be the type of people to give much time or leeway in paying debts, guv," Ken said.

"Do we know who these heavies are, Ken?" Townshend asked.

"Yes, guv. I did some checking earlier while you were down at the County. Evan Colman and Mark Yeats. A couple of nasty characters by all counts, but the Met have never been able to pin anything on them, not even a parking ticket," he added, grinning, but sounding just a little disappointed.

"Did your informant tell you how long they've been around Hereford, Ken?" Townshend asked. It was important to know if they'd been in the area when Richard Bexton-King was killed.

"A couple of weeks is what I was told, guv."

"We need to be more specific than that, Ken. Richard Bexton-King died eleven days ago. If this Yeats and Colman arrived after that, we can forget about them. See what you can find out when we've finished this, will you? As quick as you can."

"Yes, guv," Ken said.

"Right, let's get back to what Robert Bexton-King told us this afternoon," Townshend said. "He was well aware that his brother was leaving the UK for his villa in Greece and also who he was going with. It seems that Richard Bexton-King and Val Pereira were very much an item, to coin a phrase." He drew a line between the two people on the now very untidy looking whiteboard.

"Doesn't that call into question the relationship that Sharon Doherty said she was having with Richard Bexton-King, sir?" Sarah Miller asked.

"Yes it does. Robert Bexton-King told us there had been a fling between the two of them. According to him, Sharon Doherty threw herself at his brother the moment she started work at BKM. He took her up on whatever she was offering but dropped her just as quickly."

"That would make for a really happy working environment," David Ingleby said, his voice heavy with sarcasm.

"Yes, hell hath no fury," Ken quipped.

"Exactly, Ken," said Townshend, "but there's more involved. What if Sharon Doherty found out about Val Pereira? And what if she found out that Richard Bexton-King's property portfolio was worthless?

His brother confirmed what Marcella told us about it. I think it would be likely to make her very angry." He paused to look at the other three. "But would it make her angry enough to kill?

CHAPTER THIRTY THREE

No one answered Townshend's question. They just didn't know enough about Sharon Doherty to be able to make a judgement. After a few moments of silence in the office, Townshend turned to Sarah Miller. Hopefully what she had to say might help to fill out the picture.

"What did you find out in Cardiff, Sarah?" The underlying unspoken comment was that anything might help. "Was her daughter helpful?"

"More than helpful, I'd say, sir," Sarah replied.

"Did you find out why Sharon Doherty and her step-daughter were estranged? What happened between them?"

"It was all about her relationship with the step-daughter's father, sir."

"A jealous daughter not liking a new woman in their father's life?" Townshend asked. It wouldn't be the first time.

"That's not the impression she gave me, sir. Lynn, that's the step-daughter, insisted that her and her brother only wanted their father to be happy. The issue seems to have been with Sharon Doherty. They didn't want their father to get involved with her in the first place. Sharon Doherty. And they especially didn't want him to marry her."

"Did she say why?"

"Oh, yes, she was quite open about it. For a start, neither of them trusted her, just an instinct, Lynn said, but it's the way they felt. According to her, their father was a fairly wealthy man, who'd had his own business, something to do with telecoms. He sold it about a year after employing Sharon Doherty."

"She worked for him?"

"And started a relationship with the boss?" Ingleby added. "Sounds familiar."

"Lynn and her brother were both convinced she was some sort of gold-digger and it was all about money. Neither of them thought she cared anything for their father."

"Couldn't it be just a case of them wanting the money for themselves, Sarah?" It was Ken who asked the question, but Townshend had been thinking the same thing.

"I'm not sure, but it certainly seems to have been a case of an older man falling for the charms of a younger woman. Lynn told me that even from the beginning of their relationship Sharon Doherty always seemed to be wanting the best of everything."

"She sounds like more than a match for Marcella Bexton-King," Townshend said drily. "No wonder Mrs Bexton-King doesn't like her much. Go on, Sarah."

"Apparently their father had always been a careful man with his money, but as soon as Sharon Doherty was on the scene, everything changed," Sarah said. "Lynn was quite bitter about it. She said he'd never spent money on her mum the way he did on Sharon Doherty."

"It sounds more and more like a case of jealousy to me, guv," said Ken. "The daughter's upset about her inheritance being spent on someone else." Townshend nodded and then turned as Ingleby spoke.

"People do change, sir. Surely it's possible for the father to have changed?"

"I agree, David, they do and every relationship is different," said Townshend.

"So do I," said Sarah, "but jealousy over the money being spent is still not the impression I picked up."

"Do we know how Mr Doherty died, Sarah?" Townshend asked. It was a question Sarah had been expecting and she had an answer ready.

"Yes, sir. Natural causes. A heart attack, Lynn said. Her father had suffered from angina for some time."

"Did the daughter suspect Sharon Doherty of having anything to do with it?" Ken asked.

"If she did, she didn't say anything," Sarah said.

"I just wondered," Ken said, "considering her attitude to the money."

"Did he have any other medical issues?" Townshend asked.

"Osteo-arthritis in his hands, sir," Sarah answered. "Nothing else."

"What medication was he on?"

"Oxycontin, sir," she said.

"Oxycontin?" he repeated. Sarah nodded.

"It's a common enough prescription pain-killer, sir," said Ingleby, despite agreeing with what Townshend was obviously thinking.

"Yes, it is, David," Townshend said. "Anything else, Sarah?"

"Lynn Doherty was very annoyed that she was being used as an alibi, sir," she said.

"I can imagine she was," said Townshend. "Did she have any idea as to how Sharon Doherty might have known she was there?" Sarah Miller shook her head.

"Not really, sir. I asked her and she said possibly friends, neighbours, something like that. Or one of these social networking sites. It could have been anything. Someone might have kept in touch with her. According to Lynn, she had a knack of making herself popular with people." Townshend nodded, thinking back a little.

"Especially her bosses," Ken quipped.

"What happened when Mr Doherty died, Sarah?" Townshend asked.

"How do you mean, what happened, sir?"

"His will, Sarah? What happened to his money, house, that sort of thing. What was Sharon Doherty left?"

"Nothing, sir. Apparently and remember that this is according to Lynn Doherty, Sharon had tried to persuade her father to change his will on a number of occasions, but he never did."

"Might he still have been going to?" Townshend asked, thinking aloud. "It seems that the father was putting his children before his new wife," he added.

"I don't know the answer to that one, sir," Sarah apologised.

"No matter, Sarah, no one would, but it certainly explains why she said she had nothing left from the marriage but her name," Townshend said.

"Keeping that name might have been more important to her than we think, sir," Sarah said.

"Why, Sarah?" asked Ingleby.

"There's something else about Sharon Doherty we didn't know. Lynn gave me Sharon Doherty's maiden name."

"And?" Townshend was intrigued. What else had Sarah managed to uncover?

"Before she married Lynn's father, her name was Sharon Lilley, so when I got back from Cardiff, I did some checking. I'd just finished when you and Sergeant Ingleby came back from the hospital. She's got a record and she's been inside, sir."

"What?" Townshend was surprised, to say the least.

"An eighteen month custodial sentence eight years ago. She served half before being released."

"What was she inside for?"

"Fraud, sir. According to the records, she was skimming money from a company payroll when she was in charge of their accounts office."

"No wonder she wanted to hang on to her married name," Ingleby said. "It's almost like having an alibi. She certainly sounds like a woman who's interested in money, doesn't she?"

"Show me a woman who isn't," joked Ken, ducking a playful punch from Sarah Miller.

"You've done some good work, Sarah. We know a lot more about Sharon Doherty now, that's for sure." Townshend said and then paused. "It brings us back to a problem, though. We need to talk to both her and Nicholas Eddison and they're away somewhere. Together, from what we can gather from Doherty's neighbour. It brings us to a halt." He looked around at the others. "At the moment, I can't see that we're going to get anywhere without talking to them." There were nods of agreement. "Ken, tomorrow I want you to chase up your informant about Yeats and Colman. Find out exactly when they arrived in Hereford. They're a loose end and it would be good to either rule them out or see if we need to worry about them. OK?"

"Yes, guv."

"Then while we've got the chance, spend a few hours with your family, Ken. Are you OK manning the office until about three tomorrow, Sarah?"

"Yes, sir," she replied. It was one of the penalties of being a single officer, Townshend knew that, but she seemed happy enough.

"When Ken gets in, I want you to go out to Sharon Doherty's flat in Broomy Hill and bring her in when she gets back from this weekend away. Wait until Eddison's gone. He'll only make difficulties and we'll talk to him later. Take someone from uniform with you, but make it an unmarked car."

"Unmarked, sir?"

"Yes. There's no point in giving the neighbours anything to talk about."

"Yes, sir." Townshend turned to Ingleby.

"David, unless I need you desperately, spend the day with your wife and baby, at least until about four o'clock. Then I'll want you here to talk to Sharon Doherty with me." Given the circumstances with the case, Townshend was trying to give his two married officers a chance at a little home time.

"Yes, sir, but what about Eddison?" Ingleby was confused as to why they weren't bringing in Nicholas Eddison for questioning as well.

"We'll talk to Doherty first, David and find out from her where he's staying at the moment. I think she's currently the more important of the two," Townshend said.

"Are Eddison and Doherty our prime suspects, sir?" Sarah Miller asked. Townshend shook his head.

"No, Sarah, we haven't got that luxury yet. They're still just suspects. Prime doesn't come into it unfortunately. There's still work to do."

CHAPTER THIRTY FOUR

Townshend waited patiently, listening to the ringing tone of the number he'd just dialled, hoping for an answer and not an answering service. It seemed to go on forever. Mid-morning on a Sunday was often the best time to catch people in, he'd thought. Now, with the phone ringing unanswered, he wasn't quite so sure.

"Hello, Ginny Marston speaking." Even though he was waiting for it, the sound of her voice still made him jump.

"Hello, Ginny, it's Derek Townshend."

"Oh, hello, Derek." She sounded pleasantly surprised and said so.

"Well, I just thought I'd ring on the off chance that you might be free for lunch," Townshend said, surprised to find himself feeling a little nervous. How awkward would he feel if she said no?

"Lunch? That sounds like a good idea," she replied, much to his relief. "Have you anywhere in mind?"

"Well…" His voice tailed off.

"I remember. You're still fairly new to the area, aren't you?" she said and Townshend could imagine the smile that would have appeared on her face.

"It's worse than that," he said, laughing. "I still don't have my car back yet, either." This time she laughed out loud with him.

"I see, Detective Inspector, just like a man," she said in a mockingly stern voice. "Ask a girl out on a date then leave it up to her to organise everything." She paused and he knew the smile was still there. She confirmed it with a little giggle which he found quite attractive. "Don't worry. I know just the place. It's called The Bell at Tillington, just out of town. On a wet Sunday lunchtime in February, we shouldn't have any problem with having to book. Where shall I pick you up?" And just like that, lunch was arranged. Townshend almost sighed with relief over how easily it had all gone. A middle aged man as nervous as a teenager. It was ridiculous. He couldn't believe himself.

Townshend had been thinking about the journalist off and on since they'd had coffee at Ascari's, but it still felt strange to have actually arranged to meet her for lunch as friends and not in an official capacity. She was punctual in picking him up, pulling up in a sporty black VW Golf. The car suited her. She had a big smile on her face as he climbed in next to her.

"Not out chasing criminals today, Derek?" she asked as she slipped the car into gear and drove off.

"No," he said, smiling back at her. "I'm sure even Sherlock Holmes had time off every now and again."

"Even in the middle of an investigation?"

"That sounds like a journalist talking," he said, laughing.

"No, not a bit of it," she said hurriedly. "I promise I've left my journalist's head, notebooks, tape recorder and secret camera at home," she laughed. "Seriously, I'm glad you called, Derek," she continued.

"So am I, but I really didn't know whether to or not," he admitted, "but I'm glad you said yes." They were quiet for the next few minutes as Ginny expertly handled the car around a roundabout and on to the Leominster road. "What's this place we're going to like?" Townshend asked.

"The Bell? Nice country pub, heaving in summer and a good reputation for food. At this time of year, even on a Sunday, it should be fairly quiet unless there are some dedicated walkers about," she replied. "They make their own cider, too. Tillington Belle. It's a nice drink. In moderation," she added with another laugh. He was beginning to enjoy hearing her laugh. It was a lovely, relaxed sound. Ginny turned off the main road and onto a narrower lane and they were soon pulling into the pub car park. Townshend could see the attraction of the place, even in the rain. It looked like a proper pub. It was quiet, just as Ginny had predicted it was likely to be, at least judging by the car park; there were only two other cars there. Inside, they found themselves to be the only customers. The barmaid was all smiles, pleased to see them, as if happy to have something to do.

"Oh, there's no problem about a table," the girl said breezily when Townshend asked. "We've got a couple of families booked in after they've been to Credenhill Park Wood, but otherwise sit where you want." That explained the two cars in the car park, Townshend thought, his policeman's brain working. It was an occupational hazard that he always liked things to fall into place.

Both he and Ginny decided on the pub's own cider and took their menus to a table about half way between the bar and the window. While they were still studying their menus, the two families appeared and the dining room filled with the sound of muted chatter, no one except the children wanting to talk too loudly.

"This is where we tell each other all about ourselves, isn't it?" Ginny said, smiling, as they sat facing one another across the table.

"Oh God, I hope not," said Townshend, with a grimace. "I'd hate to bore you." He was rescued by the appearance of the barmaid to take their orders. "I think it's actually the point where we choose what we're eating," he added, relieved and with a grateful smile at the barmaid.

"The lamb shank sounds good," Ginny said to the barmaid and Townshend agreed. "I can't believe a career in the police force can have been boring," she added, as the barmaid walked away.

"It's not all car chases, smashing in doors and stuff like the Sweeney," he said. "Oh God," he added with a smile, "that dates me, doesn't it?" He smiled again, thinking that it also summed up his current case as well.

"I remember it as well," Ginny said, "but I'm sure it's been more exciting than you're letting on," she said, persisting. "Where were you before you came to Hereford?"

"Peterborough. Another quiet little cathedral city."

"Hereford wasn't too much of a shock, then?"

"No." Townshend felt slightly uncomfortable talking about himself, even at this level. Part of his mind was insisting that she was a journalist and that all this questioning was probably for a piece on 'Meet The Detective' for the local paper. He paused, wondering what to say and dismissed the thought. Ginny actually felt like the sort of person he could talk to and seemed genuinely interested in him, which unsettled him a little. She filled the silence for him with a change of subject, almost as if she could sense his discomfort, but wanted to keep him talking. The new subject she'd chosen immediately put him on the defensive.

"I saw Stephen Warner yesterday," she began. "He told me you'd had a chat with him. Lots of questions, he said."

"Yes, we met on Thursday," he said guardedly. Then a thought occurred to him. "When we were talking, he said that his sister Kim was supposed to be going with them, but that's not the impression you gave me."

"Kim go to New Zealand? Not a chance. She had her sights set on the high life in London, Derek. It sounds like something his mother cooked up later on." She hesitated. "He told me what happened to Robert Bexton-King," she said, "but we already knew in the office."

"You already knew?"

"Yes, word travels fast in a small place like Hereford. One of our reporters was in the hospital when Robert Bexton-King was brought in. It's quite a story."

"I presume that means it'll be in the paper this week," Townshend said, a little more sourly than he'd intended. It was too much too hope for that Ginny hadn't noticed.

"Sorry, but yes. Our editor wouldn't pass up on an opportunity like that. A headline story probably. Prominent businessman attempts suicide, or something like that. Does it cause you problems?" She sounded genuinely concerned that it might.

"No. It's only to be expected, especially with his brother's death still fresh in peoples' minds." The arrival of heaving plates of food interrupted their conversation. The case wasn't really what he'd expected to be talking about. Ginny seemed to pick up on that.

"I'm sorry. It's almost business talk, isn't it?" he didn't reply, his mouth full of succulent lamb. He swallowed before speaking.

"It doesn't matter Ginny. I'd be talking about myself otherwise." Despite his concerns about talking to Ginny about the Bexton-King case, he was intrigued as to what Stephen Warner might have said to her. There was something about Warner that didn't seem to gel in Townshend's mind. He'd said that everything was fine between him and Richard Bexton-King and that he'd been welcomed almost as an old friend. But there was only Warner's word for that. The only man who could corroborate his story was the murder victim. He tried to put the thoughts out of his mind; he was here for a friendly lunch with a woman he was feeling quite drawn to, not to interrogate her as part of a murder investigation.

"Have you always been a journalist?" he asked her between mouthfuls of food.

"When I left college," she said, "I wanted to be a writer and I thought journalism was a good way of getting experience. I've been with the Hereford Times ever since."

"So what about the writing?"

"Three unfinished novels and a host of rejected short stories," she said laughing. "Still, working for the paper is a great way of meeting people."

"I can imagine you're good at that," he said.

"Well, so must you be," Ginny said. He laughed.

"Not many people like the police coming into their lives. It usually means bad news of some sort." After a pause while they continued eating, he changed the subject. "You were right about the food. It's good, isn't it?" She nodded, her mouth full of the succulent lamb.

"And so's the cider," she said after she'd swallowed. Townshend was surprised at how quickly they'd finished their food and washed the last mouthful down with his cider.

"Another one?" he asked. She shook her head.

"I would like a coffee, though." Townshend stood up to order their coffees from the bar and his mobile phone rang. He glanced apologetically at Ginny.

"Bloody mobile phones," he muttered. "I know it's rude, but I'd better take this," he said to her. She nodded, understanding. "Townshend," he said into the phone. It was Sarah Miller.

"Sir, we've had a report from uniform. Apparently there's been a quite serious break-in at Richard Bexton-King's house in Burghill."

"A break-in?"

"That's what they're saying, sir. Uniform are there now."

"OK, Sarah, thank you. I'll get over there straight away. I'm in Tillington, so it won't take long. I'll check in later." He disconnected the call and swore softly to himself again, then looked at Ginny. "Sorry," he said to her. "Duty calls. Can we take a rain check on coffee?"

"Of course, Derek, but I'll hold you to it. Where do you need to get to? I presume I'm giving you a lift."

"I'm sorry, Ginny. I rather took it for granted, didn't I?" Townshend said.

"It's not a problem. Just tell me where we're going." She was surprised at his reply.

"Burghill. Richard Bexton-King's house, but we'd better pay the bill first."

CHAPTER THIRTY FIVE

Just like the first time Townshend had been to Richard Bexton-King's house, he was met at the drive entrance by a uniformed constable. The man pulled the car to one side, seeing Ginny driving, but as he leant down to speak to her through the driver's window, recognised Townshend and waved them through. Townshend told Ginny to park the car near the garage next to the marked patrol car, whose blue lights were still flashing.

"It's certainly an impressive house, Derek," Ginny said, looking at the main building as she turned the engine off.

"Yes," he agreed, seeming a little preoccupied. He hadn't been expecting the garage to be the centre of attention. When Sarah Miller had said break-in, he'd naturally assumed it was the house. Another uniformed officer emerged from the garage and Townshend climbed out of the car to talk to him, motioning Ginny to come with him, much to her surprise. She'd thought he'd want her to wait in the car. As she joined him, Townshend was telling the uniformed officer to turn the flashing lights off.

"I know there's not usually much call to use them, constable, but there's no need now." The constable leaned into the patrol car and did as he was told. As he straightened up, Townshend continued. "Now, what exactly has happened here?" The constable took a quick glance at Ginny as if wondering if he should say anything in front of her, but it seemed to be all right with the Detective Inspector, so he told him.

"We got a call from an alarm company that the alarms were going off here, sir. Then they rang back to say the alarms had been switched off, which they thought was strange, because they'd been informed that the house was empty. They asked us to come out and investigate. It took a bit of time to get here, unfortunately. We got held up a bit by a couple of horse riders who were passing by and were complaining about people in sports cars driving through the village like it was a race track."

"It was the cars that were stolen, then, not anything from the house?" That made sense, Townshend thought.

"I assume so, sir. The garage doors had been forced and it looks very much as if whoever broke in knew the code to turn the alarm off. The garage was empty, as you can see for yourself, so if there was a car in here, it's what they took." They were all by now standing in an empty garage. Townshend was stunned. It had looked very different the last time he'd been in here.

"Richard Bexton-King was into his cars, wasn't he?" asked Ginny. "I'd heard he had quite a collection." Townshend nodded, looking at the empty space in front of him, still thinking of the cars that were there on his previous visit. For all of them to have been taken, this had to have been a fairly big and well organised operation. He looked at the constable.

"It wasn't just one car, constable," he said. "The last time I was here, there were five very expensive sports cars parked here."

"Can you give me details, sir, for my report on what's missing," the officer said. He pulled a notebook from his pocket.

"Of course." Townshend had no difficulty remembering. "Two Porsche 911s, a Lamborghini Aventura, an Aston Martin DB9 and a Lotus Elise." There was a sharp intake of breath from Ginny and the constable had the same look on his face that had been on Ingleby's. "I would imagine the collection was probably worth about four hundred thousand pounds second hand."

"My God," said Ginny. "He certainly knew his cars. But he was interested in them when we were younger."

"Somebody obviously knew what was here, sir," the constable said. Townshend didn't say anything. He was beginning to form an idea of what might have happened and if he was right, then Robert Bexton-King had some serious questions to answer.

"It certainly looks that way," was all he said to the constable. "When you file your report, officer, your sergeant needs to pass it through to me. This is linked to an ongoing murder investigation. Now get in touch with the station and tell them to get a forensics team out here as soon as possible. You and your colleague are to stay here until they arrive."

"Yes, sir." He turned to his car and put through the message, adding that Detective Inspector Townshend was giving the instructions. "It'll give it more clout, sir," the officer said smiling, turning to explain to Townshend. The DI smiled back.

"Well done. It'll save wasting too much of your time waiting." Townshend turned to face Ginny. "Come on Ginny, I still owe you a coffee and there's not really much I can do here. Shall we go back to the Bell?" Ginny didn't say anything until they were sitting in her Golf.

"Are you sure I should have heard all that, Derek?" He smiled.

"There are two ways of looking at it, Ginny. Either I ask you to forget what you've just seen and heard or I tell you to go ahead and file it as a story." He paused. "Ring it into your editor; it's not going to affect the investigation into Richard Bexton-King's death."

"No? How can you be so sure?" she asked. "You told the constable it was linked to it."

"Call it a hunch," he said, a smile on his face, but he wouldn't be drawn any further. "Now, I've got to make a call back to the office. Are we OK for the Bell?" She surprised him with her answer.

"No. Let's make it my place, shall we?" He nodded.

"You call in your story from there," he said and then called his office. Ken answered the phone.

"Ken, it's Townshend. You're in early. Is Sarah still in the office?"

"Yes, guv. Do you want her?"

"No. I just needed to know if she's still there. I've got a job for you. Get down to the hospital and ask Robert Bexton-King a few questions for me and take no messing from that stuffy sister. Somebody's made off with his brother's collection of cars and I think Robert's up to his neck in it." Townshend smiled as he felt, rather than saw Ginny's quick glance at him. "Find out if Colman and Yeats have been into the hospital to see him and check with the ward sister as well. I think he's let them have the cars to pay off his debt and that he gave them the code on the alarm system. They broke in, so he couldn't have given them a key. I also want to know if BKM had any creditors that would come chasing after him as well. I'll be in later, but tell Sarah to go to Doherty's flat and stay there until someone appears."

"OK, guv," was all Ken had the time to say before Townshend broke the connection. Ginny was looking at him as if she was weighing something up.

"Did I hear you say Colman and Yeats?" she asked him, a little cagily as she pulled the car out of the drive, turning down through the village.

"Yes. Surely you don't know them, or even know of them," he said.

"I don't," she said quickly, "but Stephen mentioned them to me when we were talking. I'm sure it was those two names."

"Warner? Did he have anything to say about them?" he asked. He couldn't keep the interest out of his voice and she picked up on it.

"Are they important to the investigation?" she asked without thinking. Of course he wouldn't be able to tell her. "Sorry, I shouldn't have asked," she said. He smiled and waited for her to carry on. "He told me Robert had described them as thugs from London. They seemed to unnerve Robert and Stephen from what Stephen said."

"So he met them at Robert Bexton-King's?"

"Yes."

"Did he say when, Ginny?" It felt like he was interrogating her, but he needed to know.

"A couple of weeks ago."

"I know it seems like I'm pressing you and I don't mean to, but can you be more precise?" Townshend asked.

"More precise? How do you mean?"

"Was it before or after Richard Bexton-King's death?"

"I'm sorry, Derek. I just don't know. But it wasn't the only time he met them."

"He met them more than once?"

"So he said. I don't know where or when he met them, but he gave me the impression they were keeping quite a close eye on Robert."

"Did he say anything else?" Townshend asked. She shook her head, concentrating on the traffic on the junction to the Roman Road. She'd given him a lot more to think about, with Stephen Warner having met Colman and Yeats. Was it just about Robert and his debts or could there have been more to it? A suspicious mind was part of the job and every possibility had to be explored. Stephen Warner had been slipping down his list of suspects since it came to light that Bexton-King's murder would have needed at least two people, but could he have done it with Colman and Yeats? Or could it have been just the two London-based thugs? The train of thought remained unfinished as Ginny stopped her car outside a smart modern semi-detached house not far from the Roman Road.

"Time for that coffee," she said. "Then I'll give you a lift back to your office."

CHAPTER THIRTY SIX

Despite spending a pleasant forty five minutes at Ginny's, Townshend's mind was still working overtime when she dropped him off at the police station in Gaol Street. As he walked through the entrance, he glanced at the clock. Nearly four o'clock. Ken and Sarah were in the office and David Ingleby arrived while Townshend was pouring himself yet another cup of coffee, having had two at Ginny's. Not for the first time he was reflecting that he drank too much of the stuff.

"No sign of Sharon Doherty, Sarah?" Townshend asked.

"No sir. I decided it was best to leave a uniformed officer there and come back to the office," she said.

"Never mind. It was just a hunch that they'd be back." He turned to Ken Collings. "How about you, Ken? How was Robert Bexton-King?"

"A bit on the quiet side, sir, but I found out what you wanted," Ken said. "He was in a better mood than that sister, though. She was most definitely not a happy bunny."

"Did you pick up my message?" Townshend asked. He'd rung Ken's mobile with instructions to bring any pieces of paper Robert Bexton-King wrote his answers on and to ask a question about Stephen Warner. It had been an after-thought while he was drinking coffee at Ginny's.

"Yes, guv." Ken passed over some pieces of paper covered with Robert Bexton-King's handwriting. "He admitted telling Colman and Yeats about the cars in his brother's garage, but he couldn't give them the keys because he didn't know where they were."

"That explains why they had to break in," Townshend said, almost to himself. "Did he tell them the alarm code as well?"

"Yes, guv."

"Were the cars supposed to be payment for his debt, Ken?"

"Bexton-King said that's what the plan was, guv, and I think the idea was that this London firm would wipe out the whole debt. But he did seem a bit upset at losing all of them. From what he said he had his eye on keeping the Aston Martin."

"Can I ask what's happened?" Ingleby interrupted.

"Oh, yes, sorry David. I should have brought you up to speed first," Townshend quickly told his Detective Sergeant about the morning's events.

"Just how much was his debt again, Ken?" Ingleby asked when Townshend had finished.

"If you remember, my informant was a bit vague about the figure. Around half a million, he said."

"Well, I had the cars down at about four hundred thousand," Townshend said, "so that just about fits. If they're feeling generous."

"It's more likely to be the other way, guv," Ken said seriously. "Bexton-King is likely to find himself still owing this firm a fair bit of money."

"Interest, you mean, Ken?" asked Ingleby. Collings nodded.

"They'll have added a fair bit on," Ken said.

"What are uniform doing about the break-in, sir?" Sarah Miller asked.

"Treating it as just that, Sarah, but the report's coming to me to deal with, as part of this investigation. I'm just going to write it off. We'll put it down as repossession to cover an outstanding debt or just a gift. I haven't decided yet."

"What about the insurance on them, sir?" Sarah asked.

"I can't see Robert Bexton-King claiming, can you, Sarah? He told these two guys from London where the cars were and gave them the alarm code. He wouldn't have a leg to stand on."

"So what about these two men, sir?" asked Ingleby. "Colman and Yeats, isn't it? Are we still treating them as suspects? I don't think having taken these cars that they're going to be hanging around Hereford long."

"No, I agree, David. By now, they're probably on the M4 heading for London. But there is one thing," he added. "If these two are well-known criminals, the Met will know where to find them if we need them to." Ken, an ex-Met man, nodded in agreement. "What seems important at the moment is when they arrived in Hereford, not the fact that they've left. Ginny Marston told me that Stephen Warner met Colman and Yeats about two weeks ago, which would put them here before the murder. What did your informant have to say about that, Ken?"

"He doesn't like talking about those two, guv. They've got quite a reputation, but he thinks they arrived the day after the murder, by train," Ken said.

"Two different stories, then sir," Ingleby said. He was right, Townshend thought. Ginny said before, Ken's informant said after. It was irrational, but he knew which one he was more inclined to believe. Before he could say anything, Ken was speaking again.

"When I came out of the hospital, guv, I nipped over to the railway station and did some checking on their CCTV records. Colman and Yeats can clearly be seen getting off the mid-morning train on the Wednesday after the murder, coming in from Abergavenny."

"Would that be the way they'd come from London?" Townshend asked. "Anyone?" he said into the silence that ensued.

"I'll check," said Ken, moving over to his computer keyboard.

"And would they come by rail and not by car?" Ingleby asked. "I'd think it was unlikely. Could they have done that to give themselves an alibi?"

"If they were planning anything while they were in town, it would hamper any getaway if they had to rely on trains, wouldn't it?" said Townshend.

"Through Abergavenny would be the way they'd come if they left from Paddington, guv," said Ken, "but if they left from Euston, they'd come into the station the other way, from Birmingham."

"That doesn't get us any further forward, does it, sir?" Ingleby said. Townshend shook his head, but something was still bothering him. There was no reason why two criminals from London wouldn't use a train, but it didn't seem right.

"What's the next station down the line, Ken?" he asked.

"Abergavenny, guv." He could see where Townshend was coming from and continued. "It runs through Pontrilas, but doesn't stop. If they had anything to do with killing Richard Bexton-King at Pontrilas, they'd have had to get back to Abergavenny to be coming in on that train, guv."

"How far, Ken?"

"About twelve miles, guv. Not exactly walking distance for city boys."

"No," said Townshend.

"Taxi, sir?" Sarah Miller asked.

"No," said Ingleby. "It would provide a witness putting them at the scene."

"They might have rung one from the pub, though, David," Townshend said.

"There isn't one, sir. The Pontrilas Inn burnt down in the Nineteen Seventies. It's a fair old walk to the nearest ones."

"So they'd have needed a car," Townshend said.

""Yes, sir," Ingleby replied. Townshend thought for a few minutes.

"Right, at the moment, this is getting us nowhere, is it?" he asked.

"We could talk to Stephen Warner or Robert Bexton-King about it, sir," Ingleby said.

"We've got to be careful about Robert Bexton-King, David. We've arrested him, so any interview needs a solicitor present. I may have made a mistake sending Ken to see him today." He didn't really want to think about the repercussions of that move, particularly if Monroe found out about it. Still, his priority was the murder case, not the fire at BKM.

"That leaves Stephen Warner, then, sir," Ingleby said.

"Yes, David, it does, and speaking of him, did you ask Robert Bexton-King that other question I wanted you to, Ken?"

"Yes, guv. Bexton-King was quite adamant that his brother had no knowledge of Stephen Warner being in Hereford, let alone working for BKM. He's not sure how Richard would have reacted, even after all these years."

"Do you remember what Warner told us, David?" Townshend asked of his Detective Sergeant.

"He insisted the welcome he had from Richard Bexton-King, sir, was almost like greeting a long-lost friend. And he said that it was Richard who arranged for a van for him. So that's another point where two stories don't match up," Ingleby added. Townshend nodded. Little discrepancies like this were important and needed to be cleared up.

"What was it Sharon Doherty told us about Warner?" asked Townshend, testing Ingleby's memory once more. "I know she mentioned him in her first interview." Ingleby didn't let him down.

"Something about Warner being one of Robert's pets, or at least I think that's the word she used, sir. She didn't mention Richard in connection with him at all."

"When we do get hold of her for another chat, that'll be one of the questions we ask, amongst others," Townshend said. "Although with what we now know about her, it's going to be difficult to rely on anything she tells us."

CHAPTER THIRTY SEVEN

Broomy Hill in Hereford is a quiet place on a Sunday evening. Townshend had learned a little more about it since his last visit, as part of getting to know the city he'd now made his home. Built in Victorian times, Broomy Hill was regarded at the time as the highly desirable part of the city. The buildings reflected the status of the people who lived there. The streets however were designed for stylish carriages, not modern motor cars. Thankfully at this time on a Sunday, cars were few and far between, weaving in and out of the numerous parked cars, nor were there many people walking the pavements. To make things worse for Townshend and Ingleby, sitting in an unmarked police car outside Sharon Doherty's flat, it had started raining.

The building they were watching, not far from the old waterworks tower, was in darkness apart from the flat downstairs where Sharon Doherty's neighbour, Mrs Armstrong, lived. Townshend was beginning to doubt himself. As he'd put it to Sarah Miller, it was only a hunch based on what Mrs Armstrong had said. Was she right? Were Doherty and Eddison coming back from their trip today?

It wasn't as if that was all that was on his mind about this investigation. There was still so little to choose between all of the suspects and he was torn over whether these two men Colman and Yeats were involved. He kept running scenarios through his mind but he was finding it increasingly difficult to fit Marcella Bexton-King into any of them. People tended to murder for all sorts of reasons, but he couldn't find any way to fit her in.

Then there was Robert Bexton-King. He was a weak man, there was no doubting that. The only way he could have murdered his brother was if he was being helped or even forced, but it seemed from what he'd said about Richard trying to help him that he had no reason for killing his brother and every reason for him staying alive. But that had to be balanced against the fact that Robert was the person who benefitted most from Richard's death.

A movement to one side caught his eye and he glanced around quickly. He was relieved to find it was only a pedestrian walking past on the pavement glancing into the car. Townshend shrugged. The man was probably curious as to why two men were sitting in a car in the dark. As he noticed Townshend looking back at him, the man turned his head away and walked more quickly. The street went quiet again.

What of Sharon Doherty and Stephen Warner? Both were either lying, distorting the truth, or at the very least, withholding information. Whichever it was, they were hindering the investigation by preventing him getting at the real facts. He didn't look very kindly on people when they did that and it naturally ignited his suspicions. Nicholas Eddison he was already forming assumptions about. That the man was aggressive was obvious and the picture that Townshend was building up was of a bully as well. Making assumptions wasn't something he should do as a policeman. Investigations should be approached with an open mind, at least as far as possible, but human nature is what it is, no matter your profession.

And then there was the burden of proof he was working under, that every policeman worked under. His problem was the lack of evidence. Would DNA be enough, combined with information about the car or would more come out of the investigation? If any of these people were the killer, would he get enough of a case together to satisfy the Crown Prosecution Service and get them on side? It was one of the problems the police faced. Someone else always made the decision about whether a case would go to court.

"Sir," said Ingleby, breaking into his thoughts. "I think Eddison and Doherty have just pulled up." Townshend looked down the road, towards where Ingleby was pointing. A car had pulled up outside the building where Sharon Doherty lived. After what seemed like an age, but was probably only a few short minutes, the passenger door opened. Sharon Doherty climbed out, illuminated by the interior light. Reaching back into the car behind her seat, she retrieved an overnight case, which she placed on the pavement. Then she leaned back into the car for a few moments. Straightening up, she closed the door and stood waiting on the pavement until the car had driven off. The driver hadn't even bothered to switch off the ignition.

"Did you get the index, David?" Townshend asked. He'd had plenty of time.

"Yes, sir. I'm just checking it now," Ingleby replied. Townshend didn't see the accompanying slight nod of acknowledgement in the gloom of the car. "Got it," Ingleby added after a few moments. As ever, Townshend was impressed with the technology so easily at hand. It was advancing so quickly. Things were so different from when he started as a copper, but he wasn't going to allow himself to go down that route again. No time for reminiscing, not here. A PNC check used to require a radio call back to the station and then a wait. Now, even the unmarked cars carried the necessary equipment for instant access to police records.

"Go on, David," he said.

"Registered to Nicholas Eddison at the address we visited in Weobley, sir. Insurance and MOT both up-to-date."

"What's the recorded colour and model, David?"

"Black Mazda MX5 Roadster, sir." Ingleby hesitated. "Hardly what you could call a family car, is it, sir?" He could see where his superior officer's train of thought was going. "But it easily fits the description of a flashy black car, doesn't it?"

"Yes, it does, David, but let's not start jumping to conclusions too quickly. There are plenty of flashy dark coloured cars on the roads. We will check it out, though. A visit to interview Nicholas Eddison at work tomorrow will give us the opportunity to have a look at it in the car park, won't it?" Townshend was slightly disappointed that Eddison had driven off. It meant he still didn't know where the man was living. He'd hoped that the man might have been staying here in Broomy Hill with Sharon Doherty since leaving his wife and moving out of his home in Weobley, but never mind. "Right then, David," he continued. "Let's go in and have a little chat with Sharon Doherty, shall we?"

CHAPTER THIRTY EIGHT

There was surprise in Sharon Doherty's voice when she answered the buzzer on the intercom to her flat. She obviously hadn't been expecting anybody. The surprise turned to irritation when Townshend spoke.

"Detective Inspector Townshend and Detective Sergeant Ingleby to see you, Mrs Doherty," he said. "We've some more questions for you." It was obvious to both men from the pause that she was reluctant to let them in.

"At this time on a Sunday evening? I've only just got in," she said, the intercom giving a slight metallic edge to her voice.

"We know, Mrs Doherty, but it is important," Townshend replied.

"Oh, very well. Come in. First floor. Door on the right," she said brusquely. The electronic lock on the front door was released and they were given access to the building. Climbing the stairs, they heard a door above them open and Sharon Doherty, now full of smiles, was waiting for them at the entrance of her flat.

"I've just put the kettle on. Can I offer you a tea or a coffee?" she asked as she ushered them through the doorway. Her attitude seemed to have completely changed.

"No, thank you," Townshend said. "Hopefully we won't keep you long." Was that a look of relief on her face? There was an overnight case in the hallway, presumably the same one he'd seen her carrying in from the car just a short while ago. The lounge beyond was just untidy enough to be described as 'lived-in', a phrase one of his ex-wives had been particularly fond of. There was already music playing gently on the stereo, nothing he recognised, but she turned it off anyway. Turning to face them, she gestured at the sofa.

"Please sit down," she said, seating herself in an armchair, her favourite, Townshend guessed. It was the seat in the room with the most clutter around it and with the best view of the huge TV. "What more can I tell you that you haven't already asked?"

"There are a few things that have come up in the investigation that need clarifying, Mrs Doherty," Townshend said, noticing that Ingleby already had his notebook out, waiting for her answers.

"I'll do what I can to help," she said, looking serious.

"I hope you will, Mrs Doherty," Townshend replied. "Firstly, I'd like to clear up some confusion about your movements on the evening of Richard Bexton-King's death."

"I told you I went to Cardiff to see my step-daughter and her new baby."

"So you did, but that's not true, is it?" Townshend paused to let the significance of his words sink in. She met his gaze without blinking. "The hospital say your step-daughter had no visitors that evening and that they were under instructions not to let you in if you did visit."

"Not let me in?" She sounded shocked.

"And we've talked to Lynn herself…"

"To Lynn?" she interrupted.

"Yes. She confirms that you weren't there," Townshend said. "So where were you, Mrs Doherty?" She didn't answer. "Never mind, we'll come back to that, because I assure you, Mrs Doherty, I will have an answer to that question." His tone was firm. "Now, while you think about an answer to that particular question, there are some more that have come up. For instance, why were you estranged from Lynn Doherty and, presumably, her brother?"

"What's that got to do with anything?" she asked, irritation creeping back into her voice.

"Please just answer the question, Mrs Doherty," Townshend said.

"Typical step-mother stuff," she said. "Nothing more. They were jealous of my relationship with their father."

"Really? They weren't suspicious of your motives in marrying your boss?" She glared at him. "Of course, they didn't know about your past, did they? That might have made them even more wary."

"You know about that?" she said shakily.

"Yes, Mrs Doherty. It's difficult to keep anything a secret in a murder investigation," Townshend said. "I would imagine it's a part of your life you kept quiet about in your job interviews with your late husband and with Richard Bexton-King." She nodded, visibly uncomfortable. "I'll give you the benefit of the doubt that you weren't going to do the same thing to your late husband's company, Mrs Doherty, or with BKM, but the money must have been appealing. Is that why you married him instead? Using your position as an employee to get close to him? Like you tried with Richard Bexton-King?"

"You're being rude and personal, Detective Inspector, and I'd like you to leave. I can't see what this has to do with Richard's murder."

"It has everything to do with the investigation, Mrs Doherty, and I won't be leaving until I have some answers."

"And if I refuse to co-operate?"

"We'll continue at the station in a formal interview under caution with a solicitor present, Mrs Doherty." What was it with the women in this investigation, thought Townshend. Why are they so damned stubborn? He'd had to use the same approach with Marcella Bexton-King.

"Very well. Fire away."

"Having started work at BKM, you began a relationship with Richard very quickly, didn't you? Almost a repeat of the scenario leading to your marriage."

"I couldn't keep him away," she said. "Right from my first day, he was coming on to me."

"That's not quite the way we've heard it," Townshend said, deciding not to pursue it. Surprising changes of subject often led to unexpected results. "What about when Richard ended the relationship? How did you feel?" Again, there was no response apart from another glare. "You led us to believe when we first saw you that you were in a relationship with him, didn't you?" She nodded. "But that wasn't true either, was it? He'd ended the relationship hadn't he? But you wouldn't let it go."

"I loved him," she said, "and I know he loved me."

"But he didn't, did he, Mrs Doherty?" She nodded defiantly. Townshend sighed. "If you loved Richard Bexton-King, Mrs Doherty, why were you seeing another man?"

"Another man?" she said, feigning an innocence Townshend didn't fall for.

"Nicholas Eddison. And please don't demean yourself by denying it," he added quickly. "We know otherwise and I'm well aware you've been away for the weekend with him. How long has this relationship been going on?" She hesitated before answering.

"About two months," she said eventually.

"I see. And at the same time, you were chasing Richard."

"I wasn't chasing him, as you put it. I knew he loved me really and I was trying to make him jealous, to show him what he was missing. I was trying to show him that we were right for each other. It wasn't a matter of chasing him at all."

"And you thought the way to do that was by sleeping with a man he was constantly having arguments with, a man he didn't even know you were seeing?" She didn't say anything. "Did you know about the ill feeling between Nicholas and Richard?"

"No."

"I'm not surprised, because it would have meant that Mr Eddison would have had to explain himself if you did."

"Explain himself?" He'd got her interest.

"About his relationship with Richard's ex-wife, Marcella, Mrs Doherty. It also looks very much as if he was about to be named as the co-respondent in their divorce."

"No, that's not true. He wouldn't, not with her." Townshend didn't respond, wondering if anything else was coming. It was. "Richard was divorcing his wife for me." Townshend nodded.

"Yes, that's what you told my detectives when they came to see you, but it's not the truth, is it?" He gave her time to answer, but didn't get one. "He was divorcing Marcella because he was in a relationship and leaving the country. But you knew that as well, didn't you?" Again she said nothing so he continued. "You knew about Val Pereira and the Greek villa, didn't you? He booked the tickets with the company credit card. Of course you knew." Still no response. "Mrs Doherty, you're making this very difficult for yourself. I'm very aware you've not been telling me the truth and you're not offering me any explanation, are you?" Townshend persisted, despite her silence. "Let's move on to Richard Bexton-King's property portfolio, shall we?" There was a flicker of response this time. "Was he buying you off with it? Was it the final confirmation that as far as he was concerned, you and he had no future?"

"Buying me off? With that? It was worthless." A flash of anger crossed her face.

"I know it was. What I didn't know was if you knew," Townshend said. "It was an insult, wasn't it? You loved him and that's what he offered you, while at the same time making plans to run off with another woman." Was he finally getting through to her, through to the truth?

"I loved him," she persisted. Was she still pretending, Townshend thought, or did she really believe it? "He couldn't treat me like that, could he? I'd tried to persuade him, to make him see and that's what he did."

"Let's talk about Stephen Warner for a few moments, shall we?" Townshend said. "Did Richard meet him? Did he know who he was?"

"No, he didn't meet him. He might have seen him around the yard, but he didn't say anything to me." Interesting, Townshend thought. She didn't show any surprise at being asked if Richard knew who he was.

"I take it from your answer that you knew who he was?"

"Yes. Robert had told me and asked me to keep it quiet."

"So you kept something like that a secret from the man you say you loved," it was more a statement than a question. He received another glare in return, but she didn't answer. "Did you not think it was something he should know? He'd received death threats from his mother."

"Robert said it was years ago," she answered.

"Let's return to an earlier question, shall we, Mrs Doherty? The matter of the evening Richard Bexton-King was killed. Ignoring for now that you weren't where you told us you were, you've told us that you went to Pontrilas because Richard asked you to. Is that true?"

"No, he didn't ask me to go up there."

"Were you on the phone to him in the afternoon? Someone told us they thought he was talking to you."

"Yes. I rang him to tell him I loved him and that I wanted him back," she said.

"Did Richard tell you he was going to be at High Lawns all evening?"

"Yes."

"And did you go up there?"

"Yes. I told you I did. There was no one there, so I came away."

"And you didn't go inside the house?"

"No, I came away," she said emphatically.

"What car do you drive, Mrs Doherty?" She looked puzzled.

"A Vauxhall Corsa," she said.

"And what colour is it?"

"Silver."

"What time were you at High Lawns, Mrs Doherty?" Townshend asked.

"Time? I'm not sure. Mid-evening, I think."

"You don't sound very sure. Were you on your own?"

"Yes."

"And you didn't go inside?"

"No, I've told you I didn't. The place was in darkness," she said.

"Yes, you did say that. But you're not sure what time you were there."

"No."

"Was it early evening? Mid-evening? You must have some idea," Townshend persisted.

"Oh, about seven-thirty, I think," she said finally, obviously irritated by being asked the same question over and over. The same time that Marcella Bexton-King was there arguing with her husband, Townshend thought. He didn't believe she couldn't remember what time she was at High Lawns and didn't believe she was telling him the truth now that she had answered.

"Are you sure you didn't go inside?" he asked again.

"I've told you I didn't. Why would I go inside an empty house?"

"Because you've said that Richard told you he would be there all evening. Wouldn't you go in to check? Just to make sure everything was alright? Or was he in the habit of lying to you?"

"No. I wouldn't go in if it was dark."

"I find it hard to believe it was in darkness, Mrs Doherty. We've talked to another witness who was in the house with Richard at just that time."

"Then they must be lying," she said flatly, but there was just a tinge of uncertainty behind her words.

"One last question, Mrs Doherty," Townshend said, taking note of the look of relief that passed across her face. "Can you explain to me why, if you didn't go inside the house that evening, traces of your DNA have been found at the scene?"

CHAPTER THIRTY NINE

Hindlip Hall, roughly halfway between Worcester and Droitwich, has been the headquarters of the West Mercia Police since 1967, when the force was created by amalgamating the three local county forces. It was an impressive building with a long history, but Townshend found his mind wandering as Ingleby drove them from Hereford, filling him in at the same time with the information. It wasn't that he wasn't interested, it was just that his mind was elsewhere.

Showing their warrant cards, they were waved through the security barriers to make their way to the car parks. Townshend, climbing out of the car, couldn't help but compare Hindlip to the headquarters of the Cambridgeshire police, to which he'd been a frequent visitor. The Cambridgeshire force headquarters in Huntingdon was modern and purpose built, lacking in the character which seemed to be part of every brick of Hindlip. Ingleby followed him into the main reception area.

The foyer was deserted apart from two female receptionists, one young and one seemingly middle-aged. They looked up from their desks as the two detectives entered. It was the younger one who stepped forward to a counter to greet them. Again, both men produced their warrant cards. She looked quite closely and then asked how she could help.

"We're here to see Mr Eddison," Townshend explained.

"Is he expecting you, Detective Inspector?"

"Yes, he is, Joanne," replied Townshend, picking up her name from the badge she was wearing.

"Shall I ring up and tell him you're here?"

"No, no need. Just give us an idea of where his office is and we'll find our own way." She did so as they were signing a visitor book. They went up a grand looking staircase, following her directions and easily found the office, a small plate on the door showing 'Mr N Eddison,' but displaying no job title.

"It looks as if he's got no secretary, David," Townshend said, surprised. "It must have been reception I spoke to when I rang last week. I assumed he had his own secretary." He knocked and a male voice called for them to enter. Townshend entered first.

"Good morning," said Nicholas Eddison, sitting behind a desk in a fairly small office. "What can I do for you?" The smile on his face disappeared when Townshend introduced himself and Ingleby, producing his warrant card for the third time. Ingleby followed suit.

"We've got some questions for you, Mr Eddison," Townshend said.

"For God's sake, I'm at work. You can't come in here questioning me," Eddison said.

"No, Mr Eddison? Well we are here and no one knows why we're here, so we might as well get on with it anyway, hadn't we?" He seated himself in a chair by the desk without waiting for Eddison to offer. Ingleby seated himself in a chair by the door.

"I'm not happy about this," Eddison said. "This is an intrusion."

"Hardly, Mr Eddison. We are police officers in our own headquarters. I'd hardly call that an intrusion."

"Well, Detective Inspector..."

"Mr Eddison, you're wasting your own time. The sooner you answer some simple questions, the sooner we can leave and you can return to your work. Can we just get on with it?" Townshend asked. Very reluctantly, Eddison agreed. "Good," said Townshend. "The first thing I'd like to clear up is your relationship with Richard Bexton-King. A number of people have witnessed the two of you arguing quite heatedly in the weeks leading up to his death. What were these arguments about?"

"It was personal matter between Bexton-King and myself and none of your business," Eddison said.

"That's not very helpful, Mr Eddison. Considering the man you were arguing with was found dead in suspicious circumstances, saying it was personal isn't good enough. I would have thought that as a solicitor you'd be all too aware of that." The aggressive glare Townshend received didn't bother him in the slightest. "Were the arguments to do with Marcella Bexton-King?" He could tell by the expression on Eddison's face that he'd hit the target.

"Yes."

"Can you expand on that a little, Mr Eddison. We're well aware of your relationship with Mrs Bexton-King, but as Richard Bexton-King and his wife were separated, it certainly wasn't a disagreement with a jealous husband. I'll ask you again, try to be a little more helpful and we can get this over and done with. I'll be specific. Was it to do with their divorce?"

"Yes." Townshend sighed audibly.

"Mr Eddison, please. I'm trying to be patient. In what way was it to do with their divorce? Was Richard Bexton-King threatening to cite you as the co-respondent?"

"Yes." Eddison almost spat the word out. There was a pause while he seemed to be thinking over his next words very carefully.

"I suggest you're as frank as possible with us, Mr Eddison. Please remember this is a murder investigation and that you have been seen arguing with the victim," Townshend said firmly. A little of the aggression seemed to fall away from the man sitting behind the desk as he reached a decision of some sort.

"Bexton-King had agreed with Marcella that my name was going to be kept out of their divorce. Being a well-known businessman in Hereford, his divorce would attract a fair amount of local interest and no doubt some publicity." He paused. "I couldn't get involved in that."

"Couldn't get involved, Mr Eddison? I think your relationship with his wife made you very much involved."

"I just couldn't have it," Eddison said. An interesting choice of words, Townshend thought. But were they the words of a man who would take action to prevent it?

"Why not and what could you have done?"

"Two questions in one, Detective Inspector? I hoped to persuade Bexton-King to change his mind. Being involved in something like that wouldn't have been good for my career plans. I've got a very clear plan for my life."

"And this," said Townshend gesturing around the small office, "is part of that plan, is it?" Another glare.

"As a matter of fact, it is. Working in the Police and Crime Commissioner's Office looks good on the CV." Townshend nodded and waited for more. It didn't come.

"Being a suspect in a murder case doesn't though, does it?" Townshend asked, almost absently.

"Suspect? What the hell are you talking about?" Eddison's anger was mixed with disbelief.

"You've admitted having heated arguments with the victim and you've also just said yourself that you couldn't have anything affecting your life plan. Where do you draw the line, Mr Eddison? How far would you go to stop anything affecting this life plan?" Townshend made a deliberate effort to look around the small and unimposing office again. Eddison half rose from his seat, his face growing red with anger. Then he sank back into his chair.

"The arguments were all Marcella's fault," he said. "She'd reached an agreement with Bexton-King about the divorce, a very lucrative agreement as far as she was concerned. Then she got greedy and asked for more. That's when he decided to name me as the co-respondent in their divorce. Whenever I saw him, I tried to get him to change his mind."

"Did he?"

"Eventually, yes. But he only agreed not to mention me after I persuaded Marcella to back down in her demands."

"Very good of him," Townshend said drily.

"It made no difference to him. All he wanted was for Marcella not to contest the divorce and be out of his life, Detective Inspector."

"And how sure are you that things were settled?"

"Why wouldn't they be? Marcella had agreed to what Richard was offering and he'd agreed not to mention me. I had no reason to feel any animosity towards Bexton-King."

"The day before Richard died, Mr Eddison, Marcella had an argument with him in the middle of Hereford over money. She's admitted to us that the argument continued on the evening of his death, at his mother's house."

"My God. Are you saying that Marcella…" Eddison began, then stopped, thinking about the possibilities.

"Where were you that particular night, Mr Eddison?" Townshend asked. The other man looked stunned.

"What? You think I was there with her and might have something to do with it? That's ridiculous!"

"Just answer the question, Mr Eddison. What I might think doesn't really matter."

"To give myself an alibi?"

"If you like," Townshend said. "Marcella might have told you she'd been arguing with Richard again and that would affect your position, wouldn't it? And just to remind you, you've already said you weren't going to have that, haven't you? Now, just tell me where you were that evening and what you were doing. If you were with somebody, that would be very helpful." Townshend was becoming irritated with the man, but was trying hard not to show it. Eddison reached for his desk diary.

"What date was it?" he asked.

"Tuesday the eleventh," Townshend answered as Eddison flipped through the pages.

"Here it is," he said, "and I think you ought to know that the relationship I had with Marcella had finished by then," he added.

"Still, having your name linked with hers in a divorce might have been enough to make you see her again, mightn't it, Mr Eddison. Now, where were you?" Townshend was a little disconcerted when Eddison smiled broadly.

"I was at home in Weobley that night, Detective Inspector and I'm sure my wife will confirm that. In fact, she actually picked me up from Hereford after work that day. I dropped my car off at BKM for service and she drove me home."

"That'll be the Mazda Roadster?"

"Yes."

"And you say you dropped it off at BKM, despite your differences with Richard Bexton-King?"

"I told you," said Eddison impatiently. "That was all sorted. Sharon told me she'd be able to get me a good price on a service. They cost quite a bit on that little beauty. Mind you, the guys at BKM did a really good job. She's running well." He paused. "There was only one problem. They damaged the rear wheel arch somehow. A nasty dent and scratch. I'm not going to get it sorted out with them now, though, am I?"

"Have you got a bill to prove the time the car was there, Mr Eddison?"

"Yes, I have, but not here. I always leave my documents at home."

"Good. I'd like to take a quick look at the Roadster when we leave. I'd like you to come out with us and show us where it is."

"Of course. Now, will there be anything else? I have got work to do, you know." Eddison had noticed that Townshend didn't look like he was going anywhere, despite his last words.

"Yes, Mr Eddison. Your relationship with Sharon Doherty. When did it start?"

"After the relationship with Marcella finished. We'd met once or twice seeing productions at the Courtyard in Hereford…"

"Did your wife not go with you?"

"No. She's not much of a theatre goer. Anyway, we met for drinks and things just went from there."

"Who made the first approach, Mr Eddison?" Townshend asked.

"A strange question, Detective Inspector," said Eddison.

"But one that needs an answer," Townshend said simply.

"Sharon did. She came across and joined me in the bar in the interval of a play we'd both gone to see. Why are you interested?"

"Everything's interesting to a policeman, Mr Eddison," Townshend said, evading the question. "And after starting a relationship with Sharon Doherty, you started a divorce yourself."

"It might seem like that, but things had been going wrong in our marriage for some time," Eddison said.

"Because of your womanising? Or your career plans?" Townshend asked. Eddison nodded, but only after glaring at Townshend again.

"Yes. Both."

"Wouldn't going through a divorce and walking away from a young family be as damaging to your career as being named as the cause of a divorce, Mr Eddison?" Townshend paused, but spoke again before the other man exploded angrily. Then with a change of subject that Ingleby had come to expect from his DI, Townshend asked: "Your pistol. Where do you keep it? You do realise it has to be somewhere secure of course." Townshend had a gut feeling it wasn't and the look on Eddison's face confirmed it.

"In the car," he said. That was worse than Townshend had feared, but at least the man hadn't denied having the weapon. "When did you last use it?"

"At the gun club a few days before the car was serviced."

"Can we take a look at the car now, Mr Eddison? I think we're done here," Townshend said after a short silence.

Downstairs, they were called back to the reception counter, having forgotten to sign out. Eddison waited impatiently while they did so and then took them out to his car. The damage was noticeable, but not as bad as Eddison had made it out to be. But then again, he was the owner of an expensive car. Ingleby crouched down and measured the height of the marks with a tape measure and then looked up at the other two men.

"It's just the right height, sir," he said.

"What do you mean just the right height?" Eddison asked. Townshend ignored the question.

"Mr Eddison, when you finish work, bring the car in to Hereford police station. No ifs or buts, or I'll get a forensics team to go over it here in the car park tomorrow, in full view of all your colleagues. Do you understand? Make sure you've picked up the bill from BKM and bring it with you." Eddison nodded. "And please leave the pistol just where it is, will you? I'll want them to look at that as well."

CHAPTER FORTY

Paperwork. Townshend sighed as he looked at the pile on his desk. It was the bane of every policeman's life, whether a constable or a Chief Constable. There was a form to fill in or a report to write for everything you did during the working day. When he was still a constable they were talking about the advent of the paperless office. It was the 'in phrase.' When was that? It must have been the early eighties, he thought. Thirty years on and not a lot had changed, but at least using a PC was easier than a typewriter. DCI Logan wanted a weekly report on the progress of the investigation. A 'sit-rep' he called it, hinting at military experience somewhere in his background. But the question was, where to start? A lot seemed to have happened in the past few days without any corresponding progress. The phone rang, interrupting him before he'd even typed a single letter.

"DI Townshend, it's Michael Wilson, in Forensics. Sorry to interrupt whatever you might be doing, but it appears we've screwed up a little down here." The man sounded anxious. Mistakes were apparently unforgivable in these days of scientific crime-fighting.

"Screwed up? How do you mean?" Townshend's heart fell to somewhere near his feet, but he tried to keep the feeling from his voice. But what had forensics done? Hopefully it wasn't something to do with Sharon Doherty.

"You sent us a DNA sample from someone named…" there was a pause on the other end of the line. "Oh, yes, here it is, Stephen Warner."

"Yes," said Townshend, "but it was only last Thursday." There was still no clue as to the problem.

"I know, but we actually did the tests as soon as it arrived and no one's got back to you." Wilson sounded apologetic.

"I wasn't expecting them to yet," Townshend said.

"No, but based on what we found, someone should have got back to you straight away." That made Townshend sit up straight.

"What did you find that could be so urgent?" Townshend asked. He'd had enough apologies.

"The DNA sample from Stephen Warner matches the second DNA found during the autopsy, Detective Inspector." Townshend took a deep breath.

"Let me get this straight," he said. He wanted to make sure of what he'd just heard. "You're telling me Stephen Warner's DNA was on the victim's body?" Townshend asked. This was a breakthrough in the investigation.

"On and in," said Wilson. "It was found under the victim's fingernails and in his mouth, according to Karen Welby's report."

"If it was under the victim's fingernails, would Warner have had scratches on him?" Townshend asked. It seemed a reasonable assumption.

"Not necessarily. The victim might well have scratched him in some sort of struggle, but not deep enough to break the skin. Just a surface scratch would still have left skin cells under the fingernails," Wilson explained.

"What about the DNA found inside the victim's mouth?" Townshend asked Wilson, already forming a theory in his mind. "How would that have got there?"

"I've tried to imagine the scene and I can only assume a finger or two was pushed in the victim's mouth to keep it open," said Wilson, "particularly given the cause of death." Which was exactly what Townshend had thought.

"There's no doubt about these results?"

"No, not at all." Wilson, sounding surprised to be asked.

"One last question," said Townshend. "Whereabouts on the victim's body was Sharon Doherty's DNA found?" It was something that might or might not prove important.

"The same, Detective Inspector. Under his nails and in his mouth," said Wilson. "I'll get the details e-mailed to you." Townshend thanked him and put the phone down. Now there's a turn-up, he thought to himself. It seemed that Richard Bexton-King had grabbed out rather than putting up a real fight. A struggle would have left marks on his assailants. He called for David Ingleby.

"I think it's time for another chat with Sharon Doherty, David. Don't you?" he said after telling him about the phone call from forensics. "Let's go downstairs and see how helpful she's going to be."

"I just hope that she's more talkative than she was yesterday," Ingleby said.

The fact that Sharon Doherty was in one of the custody cells was just one of the things that had happened that DCI Logan didn't know about, or at least Townshend hoped he didn't, as he didn't know how he'd take it. She'd been unable or unwilling to answer the question he'd asked her about her DNA being present at High Lawns. He wasn't sure which it was and given the DNA evidence and her general level of unhelpfulness, he'd arrested her on suspicion of being involved in the murder of Richard Bexton-King and of obstructing the police in the execution of their duties.

The first thing she'd done, in line with her legal rights, was ask the desk sergeant for a solicitor. It wasn't a surprise to Townshend that the solicitor she'd asked for was Nicholas Eddison, despite the fact that he wasn't currently practising. Townshend had ruled him out with a curt comment.

"He's involved with the case," he'd said, ignoring her complaints. With Eddison out of the running, she asked for Martin Lacey, the BKM solicitor, but again Townshend had to rule him out. In the end she settled for the duty solicitor who'd spent an hour with her after she'd been brought into the station. Ingleby had been surprised when they'd not questioned her immediately afterwards.

"No, David. We've got time. We'll let her think about whether she wants to be helpful or not and hopefully a night in a cell will focus her mind. Tomorrow will be time enough."

A rather tired-looking Sharon Doherty was waiting in the interview room in which they'd first interviewed her, but this time she was accompanied by the duty solicitor. Ingleby inserted a fresh tape into the tape recorder and switched it on before Townshend spoke. First he ran through the formalities: date, time and who was present.

"Good afternoon, Mrs Doherty. I hope we're looking after you well."

"It's hardly the Ritz, is it?" she said.

"We do our best, Mrs Doherty, we do our best. Now let's get down to business, shall we?" She nodded in response. Townshend felt his hopes rise a little, but not too much. If you expect the worst, anything less is a pleasant surprise.

"For the benefit of the tape, Mrs Doherty nodded her assent," said Ingleby into the recorder. He looked at Sharon Doherty. "Mrs Doherty, it would be helpful if you could say 'yes' or 'no' when replying," he said. When he'd finished, Townshend spoke to her.

"Mrs Doherty, I'm going to ask you the same question you wouldn't answer last night before your arrest. I'm hoping you've had time to reconsider and that you've now decided to give me an answer. Can you explain the presence of your DNA at the scene of Richard Bexton-King's murder when you've stated that you didn't go into the house that night?"

"I was in a relationship with Richard. Of course my DNA would be in the house," she replied. At least it was an answer.

"No, Mrs Doherty you were not in a relationship with Richard Bexton-King. We've already established that," he said. "You told us yourself last night not only that you wanted him back but that you were also seeing another man to make him jealous. You'd not been in a relationship with him for some time, had you?" She didn't answer for a few moments.

"He loved me," she said. There was a stubborn tone to her voice, Townshend thought, his hopes fading that she might be a little more helpful.

"That's not answering the question, Mrs Doherty," Townshend said. "Any relationship you had with Richard Bexton-King outside of a purely working one ended some time ago, didn't it?" She looked at her solicitor, who nodded slightly.

"Yes," she admitted, not looking at Townshend, her voice almost a whisper, but still audible enough for the tape.

"Thank you, Mrs Doherty," said Townshend. "Now, when was the last time you were actually inside High Lawns?"

"Last year," she said, this time raising her eyes to meet Townshend's.

"Why were you there?" he asked.

"I was delivering a package to Mrs Bexton-King, Richard's mother. She invited me to stay for a cup of tea."

"A cup of tea? And that would be enough for your DNA to be found by our crime scenes team, would it?" Townshend asked.

"It must be," she replied, "mustn't it? It can't have come from anywhere else." Townshend held her gaze for a few moments before he spoke. As he'd hoped, it made her uncomfortable.

"Mrs Doherty, by the time our forensics team checked High Lawns, everything had been packed and taken to the sale rooms, every cup, every saucer, and the entire house had been subjected to a deep clean from a professional cleaning company," Townshend explained carefully. "As you probably know, in a clean like that, the cleaners leave nothing untouched. Any traces of anything would have been wiped away. Yet traces of your DNA were found at the scene. I'm going to be much more precise now and I advise you to think carefully before you answer my question." He paused. "With the house wiped clean, there is only one place at the scene of the murder where your DNA could still be found and that is actually on Richard Bexton-King's body. That is where it was found."

"But that's not High Lawns," she interrupted.

"No, I agree, Mrs Doherty. But Richard Bexton-King's body was found in a trunk and there is no way that your DNA could have got into the trunk, is there?" She obviously didn't know what to say. "So, it must have been on the body before it went in the trunk. At High Lawns. Now, given that you hadn't been in a relationship with Richard for some time, how could your DNA come to be on his body?" Sharon Doherty just looked at him blankly. Her expression had been changing to one of concern as Townshend spoke. Then she looked away, turning to her solicitor, who shook his head firmly. That was enough for Townshend to realise he wasn't about to get an answer.

"No comment," she said, extremely quietly, her eyes once more focussed on her hands which were clasped in her lap.

"Can you repeat that a little more loudly for the tape, please, Mrs Doherty?" Townshend said. She did.

"Thank you," Townshend said. "Mrs Doherty, how well do you know Stephen Warner?" She looked up sharply, surprised at the question, as if she'd been expecting him to pursue the question of her

DNA. And was that another look of concern on her face? Townshend wasn't sure.

"Not very well at all. He was a friend of Robert's and was doing some work for BKM, but that's all. I told you this before."

"Yes you did, Mrs Doherty, but you've also told us things which have turned out to be patently untrue. How can I be sure you're telling us the truth this time?" The solicitor looked at him sharply, a frown on his face.

"Detective Inspector, I think…" he began.

"Yes, OK," said Townshend. Obviously the solicitor thought he was being a little harsh. Well, possibly he was. "What do you know of Stephen Warner's background, Mrs Doherty?"

"Nothing apart from what I've already told you," she said. Townshend didn't reply, instead suddenly deciding to terminate the interview.

"Interview suspended at two thirty three," he said, looking at his watch. David Ingleby was as surprised as Sharon Doherty and her solicitor, but still turned off the tape recorder and pocketed the tape. They left Sharon Doherty whispering animatedly to her solicitor.

CHAPTER FORTY ONE

Leaving the interview room, Townshend turned towards the station canteen rather than going back upstairs to the team office. Ingleby followed him, curious. It was just after shift change-over, so there were only a few officers around, grabbing a quick bite to eat or just having a cup of tea or coffee before heading for home. Townshend was relieved to see so many empty tables; it would be a good time for a chat with David. Townshend was keen to bring his sergeant out of himself and see what he thought.

"I missed lunch," he explained to Ingleby. "Get us both a drink while I find a sandwich of some sort, will you, David?" When they were both seated at a table, Townshend, continued, opening the pack of sandwiches as he spoke. "So what do you make of all this, David?"

"What, Sharon Doherty and Stephen Warner, sir?"" Ingleby asked. Townshend nodded silently, his mouth full of prawn mayonnaise sandwich. Ingleby considered his answer. DI Murdoch, his former boss, would never have done this. When they were working for Murdoch, all three of them on the team, himself, Ken and Sarah, were nothing more than information gatherers. It had been Murdoch who made the decisions and called the shots and they'd never been asked for their opinions or encouraged to voice them. Townshend, relaxed, calm and eating his lunch across the table, was nothing like that. It seemed to Ingleby that for Townshend, a team was a team and worked together. Everyone's ideas and suggestions were valuable. It was a very different way of working to which Sarah and Ken had taken very quickly. Ingleby was well aware he was having more trouble adjusting.

"Well, David?" Townshend prompted, one sandwich finished.

"Sorry, sir. I was just thinking it through." He paused, giving himself a little more time by sipping at his drink, knowing that

Townshend's full attention was on him. He wanted to get his thoughts across without making a fool of himself. "The two of them together seems an unlikely pairing. It's not what I would've expected, but the DNA evidence isn't something I can argue with."

"I agree with you, David, but what pulled them together? Any ideas?" That gave Ingleby more confidence.

"I'd say Sharon Doherty knows more about Warner's background than she's letting on, sir, and that she approached him."

"Approached him?"

"Yes, sir. I think she knew about his background and thought Warner could be of use to her."

"How do you think she could have found out about him?"

"The brother, sir? Robert Bexton-King?"

"You think he might have talked to Doherty?"

"Let something slip is more likely and then been asked to explain by Doherty, sir," Ingleby said. Townshend pondered this for a few minutes, eating the second sandwich from the pack.

"She's certainly the sort of person who could get information from someone else, I agree, but what if it was the other way around, David?" he asked.

"Sir?"

"What if Robert Bexton-King had told Stephen Warner about both Sharon Doherty's fixation with his brother and his brother's plans to jet off to a Greek island with Val Pereira?"

"It would definitely give Warner an opening to approach Doherty, wouldn't it, sir?" Ingleby said. "He might have hoped that getting Doherty on his side might give him the opportunity to get at Bexton-King. That was the one thing that would have been a problem for him."

"Are you saying you think his intention in coming back to Hereford was Richard Bexton-King?" Townshend asked. Ingleby nodded. He was thinking faster now, eager talk. Townshend, noticing, smiled.

"Well, sir, I'm not a psychologist, but I think that with his mother's influence, Warner grew up blaming Bexton-King for his sister's death, and we know he adored her." Townshend nodded. "When his mother died, still not having got over her daughter's death, I think Warner added that to the list of Bexton-King's crimes, convincing himself that Bexton-King was somehow responsible for that as well."

"Interesting idea, David, but in what way?"

"We know that the family emigrated halfway round the world to get away from the grief, but for Warner's mother, that didn't work. I think it had affected Warner just as badly, if not more, but because of the mother's problems, no one noticed. We have to remember just how young Warner was. The world is a very black and white place at that age."

"Interesting," Townshend repeated, not wanting to interrupt his sergeant's flow.

"His mother lost her husband when their marriage broke up, presumably over her behaviour, and was left with only her son. Then her sanity finally went and he was left as her carer. The mother's problems could only have aggravated the feelings that Warner already had. In those circumstances it would be natural for him to want to blame somebody and there was already a family bogeyman in the shape of Richard Bexton-King." Ingleby paused as Townshend chuckled at the word 'bogeyman' as if thinking he was saying too much. Townshend urged him to go on.

"That's one way of describing our murder victim," he said, "but go on, David."

"I also think he was playing Robert Bexton-King for information and to get close to Richard, sir," Ingleby added. He seemed to be warming to his subject Townshend thought, something he probably wouldn't have done in front of Sarah or Ken.

"Well, sir, two people have told us that Richard Bexton-King's property portfolio was worthless – his ex-wife and his brother. Warner had got himself really close to Robert, so is it possible they'd talked about it?"

"And you think that Warner passed that knowledge on to Sharon Doherty as well?"

"Yes," said Ingleby, "to push her a bit further."

"Do you think the property portfolio was part of her motive for killing Richard?" Townshend asked and Ingleby had the sudden feeling he was being led, albeit gently.

"Isn't it?" he asked in return, now once more unsure of himself.

"I like your thinking, David, but I'm not sure she knew about the portfolio and I've still not worked out why Bexton-King was transferring it to her. But it's definitely a possibility that he did tell her, if he knew."

"So don't you think the portfolio had anything to do with it at all, sir?" Ingleby asked.

"It's another of those loose ends that keep popping up in this case, David. I don't like them. They confuse things and a loose end gives a good lawyer something to pull on. If they pull hard enough and we've missed something, the whole case could unravel." Townshend paused. "You saw the solicitor, didn't you, David? What did he say about the portfolio?"

"Well, as I said, he said the transfer was watertight and he was sure she didn't know about it," Ingleby said.

"Yes, but was there anything else?" Townshend asked. "Did he say Richard was going to tell her, or were the solicitors going to write a letter?"

"He said Richard was going to handle telling her," Ingleby said, "but if he'd discussed it with his brother Robert, Doherty might already have known before Bexton-King even went to the solicitors."

"Yes, that's right. We also know Bexton-King was in the BKM office the day after seeing the solicitor when he might have told her. Let's go over some of that day again, shall we? First, from the office, Bexton-King had a taxi pick him up from BKM to take him to High Lawns and stopped off at his doctor's. He was at High Lawns to meet an antique dealer about some of the items in the house." Ingleby nodded. "And we picked up all that from Sharon Doherty's statement at her first interview, didn't we?" Ingleby nodded again. "Now, it was the foreman who told us that he thought Bexton-King was on the phone to Sharon Doherty when they left, wasn't it?"

"Yes, sir, Tim Stevens."

"But he didn't say why he thought that, did he, or if he heard anything to make him believe it was Sharon Doherty?"

"No, sir," Ingleby said.

"And it was Sharon Doherty herself who told us he'd rung her to ask her to go up to see him after she'd been to Cardiff Hospital, wasn't it?" Ingleby nodded, happy to let Townshend speak. "Why would he do that, David? It fits in with what she told us when she wanted us to believe she was still in a relationship with him, but she wasn't. It wouldn't make any sense for him to invite her there."

"Unless he was going to tell her about the portfolio, sir."

"No, there's something else, David. Something about the phone calls. As far as the property portfolio goes, the more I think about it, the more I think that it was aimed at being a back-handed pay-off for her after he'd left the country. And that makes me think she wasn't supposed to know about it until he was safely tucked up in Greece with Val Pereira." Both men were quiet for a few moments.

"So it wasn't a motive for Sharon Doherty, sir," Ingleby said before the silence became strained.

"I think the key to motive for Sharon Doherty is in her relationship with Richard Bexton-King," said Townshend. "Or lack of it."

"She wanted him back, but he didn't want her is the bottom line, isn't it?" asked Ingleby.

"Exactly. And what did she do about getting him back?"

"She started a relationship with another man," replied Ingleby.

"Yes, David, with another man who Richard Bexton-King was already having problems with," Townshend said. "Not a good move on her part, even if she wasn't aware of it."

"What are you thinking, sir?" Ingleby asked, curious.

"How would she feel if she found out he was leaving for Greece with another woman? Particularly as she didn't seem to be thinking straight anyway."

"You think it would tip her over the edge enough to make her want to kill him?"

"To stop another woman having him, David? It's possible. Murders have been committed for less." Townshend paused, as if something new had just come to him. "Airline tickets," he said almost to himself. "We need to trace how they were bought, David."

"Yes, sir," said Ingleby, making a mental note to get Sarah on to it as soon as they returned to the office.

"An approach from Stephen Warner would fit nicely with her plans. He'd be the obvious accomplice with his background and for his part, he must have had doubts about whether or not he could pull it off on his own." Townshend paused once more. "That was the problem with

Stephen Warner right from the beginning; he seemed too obvious. In fact, he was so obvious that he was almost ruled out after we'd talked to him, wasn't he?"

"Yes, sir," said Ingleby, "but where does Nicholas Eddison fit into all this?"

"Yes, Nicholas Eddison. I'm not sure he does, David," said Townshend. Ingleby was surprised.

"No?"

"Eddison is an aggressive bully, David. He thinks he knows what he wants out of life and says he won't let anyone or anything stand in his way, but it's all bluff. He's certainly no killer."

"What about the car? And the pistol?" Ingleby asked. "We've asked him to bring it in for forensics, haven't we? And asked him to prove his alibi. Do we need to if he's not a suspect?"

"Yes. Think about the possible scenarios again, David." Ingleby did while Townshend studied his empty coffee cup.

"You think that Sharon Doherty and Stephen Warner used Eddison's car that night and that forensics will find evidence, don't you, sir?" Ingleby said after a pause.

"Yes," said Townshend. "What I'm hoping is that we can at least prove that it was Eddison's car that was there that night. Forensics have traces of two types of paint from the gate and will be looking for a match."

"What about other evidence?" Ingleby asked.

"It would be good to place Warner in the car, if we get that lucky, but as Sharon Doherty was away for the weekend with Eddison, there'll probably be evidence of her all over the car, which could cloud things unfortunately," Townshend said. "We need to prove that Warner and Doherty took the car out of BKM's workshops. It might be an idea to have a chat with the workshop manager from BKM this afternoon before Eddison gets here. Are you all right with that?"

"Yes, sir. Do we know who the manager is or where he lives?"

"Hopefully it'll be on the disk that we retrieved from Burghill. You know, the one that Sharon Doherty looked at. Sarah can look at it for us, then you can see what you can get out of him, OK?" Ingleby nodded and rose from his seat as Townshend stood up. "Good. Come on, let's get back to the office."

CHAPTER FORTY TWO

"I've found the workshop manager's name, Sarge. It's Colin Harrison," Sarah said after a few minutes of searching through the contents of the BKM disk.

"Thanks, Sarah. Write down the address, will you?" Ingleby asked over his shoulder while leafing through some papers on his desk. He hadn't bothered to sit down. No polite 'please,' Townshend noticed. Did Ingleby have a problem with his female colleague or not? Sometimes it looked like he did, but at other times not. And was he going to have to chat with him about it? He watched as Sarah held out a piece of paper to Ingleby without replying. "Oh, right. Out on the Ledbury Road, then," Ingleby said, turning to her.

"On the estate leading up to the colleges," she said helpfully. The look on his face said he wasn't quite sure where the street was.

"OK, thanks," Ingleby said, then turned to face Townshend. "Do we need DNA or fingerprints, sir?"

"No, David, not from him. Just see what you can get out of him about Eddison's car." As Ingleby left the office, Townshend carried on talking to Ken and Sarah. "Don't worry, I've got something for you two to get on with as well," he said, laughing. "Firstly, Sarah, see if you can find out how the airline tickets Val Pereira gave you were paid for. The airline itself is probably the best place to start." He paused.

"And me, guv?" asked Ken.

"Phone records, I'm afraid, Ken," said Townshend and the big man groaned theatrically. "Always the best for last," added Townshend, grinning. It was usually a long hard slog going through lists of phone calls.

"What am I looking for specifically?" Ken asked, grinning back. "Takeaway orders? Chatlines?" Sarah snorted at this last suggestion.

"Sometime during the afternoon before his death, Richard Bexton-King made a call from High Lawns. One of his employees, the foreman actually, thinks it was to Sharon Doherty. I need you to check on it and find out who it was to. Have a look at anything else interesting as well, OK? There might be other calls."

"Is that the landline at Pontrilas or Bexton-King's mobile, guv?"

"I hadn't thought about it, Ken," Townshend admitted. "Make it both." The landline would probably have still been on, but people these days used their mobiles no matter what, he thought.

"Yes, guv." Townshend left them to it and went into his own office. There was still that sit-rep for DCI Logan to write while the others were working, but it didn't stop him wondering how Ingleby would get on. David Ingleby was actually quite happy to be out on his own, despite the rain which had started yet again just as he settled himself into his car. Pulling up outside the address Sarah had given him, he took a few minutes to look over the property from his car before venturing out into the rain and dashing for the front door. It was a semi-detached house, probably built in the nineteen fifties, nothing too grand, but well looked after. The small front garden, even given the wet weather, looked neat and tidy. Harrison or his wife? Ingleby wondered. The middle aged paint-spattered man in overalls who answered the front door did so with a friendly welcoming smile on his face, which to his credit, at least in Ingleby's eyes, didn't fade at all when Ingleby introduced himself and produced his warrant card.

"Come in out of the rain, Detective Sergeant, and I'll get the kettle on," Harrison said. "A cup of tea is just what I need what with all this decorating. It's good to have an excuse for a break."

"Decorating?" Ingleby could smell the fresh paint, somewhere upstairs, at a guess.

""Unfortunately, yes," said Harrison with a resigned shrug of the shoulders. "With BKM burnt to the ground, I'm on what you could call gardening leave, but as my wife pointed out, the weather's too bad for gardening, so decorating it is." The two men were still standing in the hallway and as he spoke Harrison gestured towards the open kitchen door. "I presume it's to do with BKM and Richard's death that you're here, but I don't know how I can be of any help to you." He gestured for Ingleby to sit at the kitchen table and started washing his hands.

"It's only a few questions, Mr Harrison and you never know, any little piece of information might help our enquiries." God, thought Ingleby to himself, I'm already starting to sound like Townshend. Harrison fiddled with the kettle and got two mugs ready, dropping tea bags into them. Ingleby took out his notebook.

"Fire away then," he said. "Biscuits?" Ingleby shook his head. Harrison took a packet out of the cupboard anyway and placed them on the table between them.

"Something's come up in the investigation and we need some information about a car," he said. "It was brought into the workshops at BKM for a service," he added. Harrison frowned slightly.

"Which car in particular, Detective Sergeant and when? We did see a fair few, you know. The workshop wasn't only for BKM vehicles." He poured boiling water into the mugs, stirring as he did so.

"No? I thought the workshops were just for..." Ingleby didn't finish, letting his words tail off as Harrison interrupted him.

"We'd have been sitting on our bloody backsides most of the time if they were," Colin Harrison said. "So come on, what about this car? Milk?" he added.

"Yes, please, but not sugar," Ingleby said, following it up with a "Thank you," when Colin Harrison handed him a steaming mug of tea. "I'm hoping you'll remember this particular car as it was a bit out of the ordinary. A black Mazda Roadster, brought in on the same Tuesday a couple of BKM vans were out in Pontrilas."

"The same day Richard died?" Ingleby nodded. "Oh, yes I do remember that car, for a couple of reasons, but especially the driver. A bloody minded arrogant so and so, he was. More suited to a bloody BMW than a Mazda, if you ask me." He looked at the smile on Ingleby's face and took a sip of tea. "You don't drive a BMW by any chance, do you?" Harrison asked, smiling himself.

"No," Ingleby replied, "just the chance would be a fine thing," he added, smiling to himself at the man's conversation being liberally peppered with 'bloodys'.

"You'll have to forgive me. It's just a silly personal prejudice." Harrison took a biscuit, pushing the packet towards Ingleby who shook his head. Harrison dunked his in his tea.

"The driver's name was Nicholas Eddison," Ingleby said.

"Is that what it was? I didn't like the man, so I didn't ask or even take much notice to tell you the truth." He laughed. "That's a funny phrase to be using to a copper, isn't? Anyway, Sharon did all the paperwork. I did notice that this bloke…"

"Eddison," prompted Ingleby.

"Yes, well this Eddison seemed a bit overfriendly with Sharon, if you ask me, but he wasn't going to get anywhere there. She was all for the boss."

"For Richard?" Harrison laughed at Ingleby's question.

"Well, she wouldn't have had much luck with Robert, would she, Detective Sergeant, but you probably knew that already. She was certainly holding this fella, Eddison at arm's length." In public at least, Ingleby thought.

"So who actually booked the car in?"

"As I said, Sharon will have done the paperwork. She'd asked earlier that afternoon if we could do it last minute as a favour. We were quiet first thing the following morning, so I suggested this man Eddison brings it back early. Sharon didn't like that for some reason and got quite stroppy. She was adamant he leave it overnight so we could start on it straight away to not waste any time. It was no skin off my nose, so I agreed, even though it wasn't what we normally did. Eddison insisted it was kept in the workshop overnight though and Sharon agreed. It was a nice car, so I suppose he had a point."

"What time was all this?" Ingleby asked.

"Late afternoon," Harrison said, then thought for a few moments. "No, nearer to going home time for the lads. I suppose Eddison would have been on his way home from work."

"So it was kept locked in the workshop all night," Ingleby said, trying to confirm what had happened. "Who had the keys? You?"

"No, it wasn't in the workshop. We didn't have the room, no matter what Sharon had said, but we didn't tell the driver that. It was put in the secure yard where we keep the fleet vehicles."

"And where were the keys to the car kept, Mr Harrison?"

"In the main office, locked away."

"What about the yard keys? You did say it was secure, didn't you?"

"Again, they'd have been in the office. Sharon would lock them away every night," Harrison said, taking another biscuit.

"You said there were a couple of reasons you remembered this particular car, Mr Harrison. What was the other one?"

"There was something else a bit strange, Detective Sergeant. I parked the car in the yard myself after this Eddison fella had left and handed the keys over to Sharon. In the morning, I wouldn't let any of the lads drive it even though they wanted to, so I went out to the yard for it myself. It was in a different part of the bloody yard to where I'd left it."

"So someone moved it?" Harrison nodded. "Do you know who?" Ingleby asked.

"Only three people had access to the keys. Richard, who according to Sharon was staying in Pontrilas…"

"She told you that?" Ingleby interrupted.

"Yes. Then there was Robert and he was off to Lichfield on some sort of business, and Sharon herself."

"So are you saying it was Sharon Doherty who moved it?"

"No one else could have done it, so, yes I would think so. Maybe she just fancied a drive in it. There was definitely extra mileage on it, that's for sure." Harrison said. "I recorded the mileage when I booked it in and it was different in the morning when I filled in the service history."

"How much?"

"About thirty miles."

"That was some joy ride," Ingleby said, thinking to himself that it would cover the distance to Pontrilas and back. "Are you sure?"

"Yes. We'd recorded the mileage when it was booked in."

"And that was the other reason?" Ingleby asked. Harrison nodded.

"Yes it was. There was a hell of a row about the Mazda when the driver came to collect it as well," he said.

"Over the mileage?" Ingleby asked.

"No, it wasn't the mileage. There was a dent and a deep scratch by the rear wheel. Apparently it wasn't there when he dropped the car off with us. She must have done it getting it in and out of the yard." Harrison laughed and finished the last of his tea. "Silly bitch!" he added.

"Sharon Doherty?"

"Yes. She should never have taken it out, should she?" Harrison said. "The driver…"

"Eddison."

"Yes. Eddison said he wanted the damage fixed free of charge or he'd take it further. So naturally Sharon agreed to us doing it if he brought the car back, but then the place got burned down." Colin Harrison looked at Ingleby. "And now there's no telling what's happening, is there? I don't even know if I've got a job."

CHAPTER FORTY THREE

"Ken, the security company that monitors the houses in Bulmer Close, the one we got the CCTV footage of the BKM fire from," Townshend said. "Get in touch with them and find out if they've still got footage of the Tuesday evening a few days before the fire, will you?"

"Yes, guv, I'll get on to it straight away," Ken replied, reaching for his phone. Townshend nodded at Ingleby.

"It could be a good call of yours, David," he said. On his way back from seeing Colin Harrison, Ingleby had remembered the damaged CCTV camera in Bulmer Close which had given them the lead over the fire. When he mentioned it back in the office, Townshend had immediately picked up on it, hence the instructions to Ken. Their hope was that it might just show who had moved Nicholas Eddison's car.

"So Harrison said this was a last minute booking, David?"

"Yes, sir," Ingleby said. "But how did Sharon Doherty persuade Eddison to go along with it?"

"I think that's a question for Mr Eddison himself, don't you?" Townshend said. Ken Collings appeared in the doorway.

"The security people have still got the footage, guv. It's been archived on an external hard drive, and it should be here in half an hour or so. They're sending it over by courier," he added.

"Thanks, Ken. Any joy with the phone records?"

"A start. There was only one phone call made from the landline at High Lawns that day. To BKM."

"So Tim Stevens could be right," Ingleby said. "Richard Bexton-King could have been on the phone to Sharon Doherty."

"Yes," said Townshend. "It was definitely an out-going call, Ken?"

"Yes, guv."

"Chase it a bit more, Ken. I want to know what time it was made and how long the call was," said Townshend. "Find out what calls were made from BKM that day, after Bexton-King rang in. And don't forget his mobile."

"OK, guv. I'll see what I can dig up."

"Thanks and get Sarah onto that CCTV footage as soon as it arrives." Sarah was deep in conversation on her phone.

"What's she looking for guv?" asked Ken.

"Anything strange after the place was shut up," Townshend said. Ken turned to go back to his desk. "Has she come up with anything on the tickets, do you know?" Townshend asked.

"They were paid for by credit card apparently, guv. She's got the card details and she's chasing up the payment just to be sure." That was good news. A credit card payment should be easy enough to check out.

"Thanks, Ken." The big man walked back over to his desk in the main office, grumbling to himself about phone records. "The question still remains about Sharon Doherty and Stephen Warner," Townshend continued, turning back to Ingleby. "I've been giving some more thought as to who approached who. If Doherty found out about Warner, then how, David? Robert didn't know, Richard didn't know, so how?" Ingleby couldn't think of an answer. "It seems more logical that he approached her."

"Would it be of any use to ask her?" he suggested.

"The only people who can tell us are going to be her or Stephen Warner, David. I don't think anyone else is going to have an answer," Townshend said. "But then again, are we actually going to get an answer from Doherty? She's not being very co-operative, is she?"

"Are we going to pull Warner in, sir?"

"Oh, yes, David, but he'll wait a bit. Let's get forensics to go over Eddison's Mazda first. That'll give us time to see what more we can dig up." He took a look at his watch. "Come on, let's go and see what forensics might have found already, shall we?"

"Is Eddison here, then, sir?" Ingleby asked.

"Yes. He arrived just before you came back. He was a bit earlier than I expected. I haven't had the chance to mention it to you." As they left Townshend's office and crossed the outer office, it was Ken's turn to be on the phone, Sarah replacing the receiver on hers as they neared her desk. Townshend stopped and told her they were going down to the station garage and then to have a chat with Nicholas Eddison.

"Just in case anyone wants us," he added.

"Can you give me just a minute before you go, sir?" she asked. "It's about these airline tickets."

"Why, have you found something, Sarah?"

"They were paid for by credit card," she said.

"Yes, Ken told us a few minutes ago. But whose card was it?"

"It was the BKM business card, sir."

"Now that is interesting," Townshend said, but to Ingleby he didn't seem surprised.

"Why would he do that, sir? Why not his own card?" Sarah asked. It was exactly what Ingleby was thinking.

"Surely he would have known that Sharon Doherty would see the account," he said.

"And I think that was the point," Townshend said to both of them. "She wasn't listening to him telling her that their relationship was over, was she? I think that this was his way of making a point, that he was going away with somebody else."

"If it was, it backfired on him," said Ingleby. Sarah agreed, as did Townshend.

"Yes, it looks that way, David," Townshend said. "Thanks for your good work, Sarah. Can you give Ken a hand with the CCTV footage when it arrives? Or if you feel generous, take over the phone records and do him a favour. He hates them."

"Yes, sir," Sarah replied, smiling.

Two forensics officers, in full scenes of crime clothing were busily working on Nicholas Eddison's car when Townshend and Ingleby entered the garage.

"How's it going?" Townshend asked them. One of them straightened up from ferreting around in the boot space.

"It's early days, but already interesting. Obviously the driver's prints are all over everything, but we've found a second set of prints on the passenger side..."

"Almost certainly Sharon Doherty's," Townshend said to Ingleby. "Sorry," he said to the forensics officer, "I didn't mean to interrupt. And I didn't catch your name."

"Wilson, Detective Inspector. We spoke on the phone earlier."

"Oh, yes, about the DNA. I thought the voice sounded familiar."

"Yes and I assume we're looking for more of the same?" Wilson asked.

"Not just DNA. I'll settle for anything you can find," said Townshend. "You'll find a locked box in the boot," he added. "Hopefully the driver gave you the key. Be careful with it. There's a pistol in there and it might be loaded."

"I've already seen the box and the pistol and it wasn't locked, Detective Inspector."

"It wasn't locked?" Townshend was incredulous. "If Eddison's stupid enough to leave it in the car, there's every possibility he could leave it loaded as well. The weapon might prove interesting, though, so give it a good going over."

"Do you want ballistics to take a look?" Wilson asked.

"No. It's not a murder weapon. As far as I can see it was just used as a threat. It's prints and DNA I'm after." He paused, looking thoughtfully at the car. "How long do you think you'll be? Do we need to send driver home or make him wait?"

"It'll take as long as it'll take, I'm afraid, Detective Inspector. Send him home and tell him to come back in the morning. We should have finished with it by then," said Wilson, obviously anxious to get back to the car. "And you can tell him we'll take good care of his precious car!" Obviously there had already been words between Wilson and Eddison. Grinning, Ingleby led the way through to the interview rooms where Nicholas Eddison was waiting. He didn't look happy.

"I hope those clowns are going to be careful with my car," he said before Townshend or Ingleby had a chance to speak.

"They've assured me they will, Mr Eddison. You won't even know they've checked it," Townshend said. "But they do want to keep it overnight."

"Overnight? You never said anything about that!"

"Needs must, Mr Eddison. They are extremely thorough men. I can either arrange a lift for you…"

"What? In a police car?" Eddison burst in before Townshend could finish. "That would look good, wouldn't it? No, thank you, Detective Inspector, I'll make my own arrangements when you've finished with me. Which I hope won't be long, by the way." Townshend sighed audibly as he and Ingleby took seats on the other side of the table to Eddison. It seemed that everyone he spoke to in this investigation was tetchy of downright difficult. His reaction didn't do anything to improve the other man's temper. Eddison glared at him.

"I did mention I might have a few more questions for you, Mr Eddison, but as you're well aware, you're not under caution and you are free to leave whenever you choose.

"No, there's no need for that, Detective Inspector," Eddison said quickly. "but let's get on with it, shall we?"

"Fine," said Townshend, fighting back a smile. "Now, about the servicing of your car. How far in advance was it booked?"

"It wasn't. I had a phone call from Sharon and took it in the same afternoon."

"Why BKM, Mr Eddison?"

"I told you this morning. Services on the Mazda are expensive and Sharon had told me she could get a good price. I knew BKM had workshops with a good reputation and I'd mentioned the car needed a service to her. It was a no-brainer, even if it was at short notice, though."

"That'll be on the Tuesday afternoon?" Townshend asking, confirming the day.

"Yes, I was on the verge of leaving the office when she rang."

"So it was late in the afternoon?"

"Yes. When I got to BKM, this guy in the workshop, the manager or someone, said they'd start on it first thing in the morning."

"You didn't want to leave it overnight?"

"No, it wasn't that. Taking it in at that time of day, I'd expected it to be there overnight. Sharon had warned me it would be and I'd already arranged for my wife to pick me up. What I told this workshop manager was that if I didn't get an assurance the car would be securely locked in the workshop overnight, I wasn't leaving it. He said they didn't leave cars in the workshop unless they'd already started work on them. He said something about putting it in the yard. Sharon put him in his place and sorted it out with him, though."

"And you left it there?" Townshend asked.

"Yes. She told me they'd look after it and keep it inside and I believed her. I still don't know what happened to it," Eddison said.

Townshend wasn't about to enlighten him as to what had gone on. Instead, he changed the subject.

"I'm surprised Mrs Doherty didn't suggest you stayed at her flat that night, Mr Eddsion. After all, you were in a relationship with her, weren't you?"

"I suggested it when she rang, but she said she was busy all evening," Eddison said. "That's why I rang my wife."

"Did she say what she was doing?" Townshend asked.

"No, she didn't. Just that she was busy." He still sounded upset about it, even now, Townshend thought. He was quiet for a few moments before speaking again.

"Mr Eddison, let's talk about your pistol. You told us you kept it in the car. Did Sharon Doherty ever touch it or handle it in any way?"

"No." The answer was quite emphatic, but Townshend wasn't convinced. A man like Eddison would quite likely be the sort to boast to a woman about having a weapon in the car. He would at least have shown it to her, if not actually let her hold it. Most people didn't get to handle guns.

"Did she know it was there, Mr Eddison?" There was a long pause, as if his solicitor's training had suddenly kicked in and he was thinking of the possible consequences of his reply. Townshend prompted him. "I would like an answer, Mr Eddison. Did she know it was there?"

"I…I might have mentioned it," Eddison said quietly after another brief hesitation.

"Thank you, Mr Eddison. Just one last thing. Did you bring the paperwork I asked you for?"

"Yes, I did, even though I had to go all the way to Weobley for it," said Eddison. He took it out of his jacket pocket and passed it over the table. Townshend unfolded it but gave it only a cursory glance before passing it back. "Is that it? I drove all the way to bloody Weobley for it and you just wanted a quick look?"

"Did you check the mileage on your car when you collected it from BKM, Mr Eddison?" Townshend asked.

"No."

"Thank you, Mr Eddison," Townshend said, not expanding on his question and rising from his seat. "Our forensics people will be in touch in the morning when they've finished with your car to tell you when you can collect it." Before Eddison could complain or say anything, he added, "Detective Sergeant Ingleby will show you out. You did say you were happy to arrange your own transport home, didn't you?"

CHAPTER FORTY FOUR

Tuesday morning. Two weeks since Richard Bexton-King had been killed and a week and a half since his body had been discovered at the auction rooms. Was it all coming together? It looked that way, but Townshend remained unsure. He wouldn't let himself believe it until someone was charged with the murder. There was always something else to discover, some other little piece of information waiting to take its unwelcome place as a major spanner in the works. But even with all that, he had to admit that this case was looking good.

He'd arrived in the office before the other three, anxious for the forensics results from Eddison's car. While waiting for them to contact him with what they'd found. He busied himself with the coffee machine, a part of his mind waiting, a part thinking that a kettle, a mug and a jar of instant coffee was much less bother. When the phone on his desk rang he quickly crossed the main room to his office to answer it.

"Townshend," he said into the receiver.

"Jimmy Wilson, forensics, Detective Inspector. Good morning."

"Good morning, Mr Wilson, or at least I hope it's going to be," Townshend said. "What have you got for me?"

"Enough to brighten your morning, I think," Wilson said. That sounded positive, Townshend thought. "We found the inside of the car to be fairly clean. As you said to your colleague last night, the second set of prints we found were those of Mrs Doherty and the main set were of course from the car owner, Mr Eddison. The good news is that we found some extra prints on the glove compartment and on the passenger seat adjustment lever which didn't belong to either of them."

"And?"

"They match the prints that you had sent to you from the Auckland police for Stephen Warner."

"And that definitely places Warner in the car, yes?" Townshend asked. He wanted no doubt in his mind.

"In that model of car, you have to be sitting in the passenger seat to use the lever, Detective Inspector, but that, along with a fingernail, definitely places him in the car at some point or another," Wilson said.

"Did you just say 'fingernail,' Mr Wilson?" He wasn't sure if he'd heard properly.

"Yes, Detective Inspector, a fingernail, on the carpet in the passenger foot well. It matches Warner's DNA."

"How did it get there?" Townshend asked.

"Who knows?" said Wilson. "It was there, so from a forensics point of view, it hardly matters. But some people do pick at their fingernails, instead of using clippers as most of us do. It's a nervous thing. Watch out for him doing it if and when you interview him."

"What about the pistol?" Townshend asked.

"Strange, that pistol and its box," Wilson said. "Someone's tried to wipe prints from the weapon itself, but we found some anyway. Eddison, Doherty and Warner's were all on it."

"All three of them?" Townshend asked. That was a surprise. Two out of the three he might have expected, but all three? Still, it was something else to work with.

"Yes, but like I said, someone had tried to wipe them. Same with the box, but both Eddison and Warner's prints were still on it."

"It's all been good so far, Mr Wilson, but there's one thing you haven't mentioned."

"What might that be, Detective Inspector?"

"The paint on the gateway at Pontrilas and on the car. Do they match?" Townshend asked.

"Yes, they do, Detective Inspector. And the height of the damage was just right as well against the measurements from the gate. Is that all?"

"Yes, it is, Mr Wilson. More than enough, believe me," said Townshend. "Thank you for your good work. I appreciate it."

"All part of the job, Detective Inspector. I'll get the report written up and on your desk by lunchtime," said the forensics officer and the line went dead. Townshend dropped himself into his chair and then remembered the coffee machine. He was just pouring himself a cup when Sarah and Ken walked in, closely followed by Ingleby. As soon as they had their coats off, Townshend explained what he'd just been told.

"I think we're there with this one. Forensics have given us some solid evidence from the car."

"So we've got Doherty and Warner, sir?" said Ingleby.

"It looks like it, David. There are some loose ends to tie up, obviously the phone records and the CCTV footage, but I think it's time to bring Mr Warner in for some serious questions." Ingleby turned to put his coat back on, but Townshend stopped him. "No, have a coffee first and then take Ken with you when you go." He turned to Ken and Sarah next. "Sarah, can you carry on with the footage and phone records while Ken goes with David?"

"We finished those off last night, guv," Ken said.

"Last night?" He'd known Ken and Sarah were still talking to Ingleby when he'd left, but he was still surprised.

"Yes, after you'd gone. The three of us talked about it and the Sarge agreed."

"So did you find anything?"

"As far as the phone calls go, sir," Sarah said, "immediately after Richard Bexton-King's call to the BKM from Pontrilas, there was a call from BKM to a local taxi firm. When I checked it with them, they'd logged it as cancelling a return pick up to Hereford from Pontrilas."

"So that confirms that Sharon Doherty knew Richard Bexton-King was staying at Pontrilas," Townshend said.

"Which was also confirmed by Colin Harrison," Ingleby added. Townshend nodded.

"What else, Sarah?" he asked.

"There was another phone call from BKM to a Worcester area number, which just happens to be a line into the Police Headquarters," she said. "I'm assuming Nicholas Eddison?"

"I would think so, Sarah," said Townshend. "He did tell us that he received a call from Sharon Doherty that same afternoon telling him they could fit the car in for him at BKM."

"Why would Sharon Doherty go to all this effort about the car, sir?" Sarah asked.

"I can only imagine she didn't want to use her own car in case someone saw her in it and recognised her," Ingleby said.

"Or what if she hoped the opposite, that someone would see the Mazda and remember it. There aren't that many like it in the area," said Townshend. Ken picked up on his meaning straight away.

"And assume it was Nicholas Eddison driving?" Townshend nodded.

"But that's crazy, sir," said Ingleby. "She'd given him an alibi herself. She couldn't be trying to implicate him."

"It does seem crazy, David, but sometimes you can over-plan, David, and miss the obvious," Townshend said, "and that's what I think she's done here." He paused. "Right then, before we bring Warner in, tell me about the CCTV footage."

"Was I right?" Ingleby asked Ken and Sarah. "Does it help?"

"Spot on, Sarge," said Ken. "At about seven forty five, there's a clear view of both Doherty and Warner at the gate of the secure yard. She unlocks it, drives the Mazda out and he locks the gate behind her and gets into the car. Then they drive off. They come back together at some time around one o'clock in the morning and repeat the procedure and leave together."

"Fantastic," said Ingleby. "Just what we needed."

"Good work, both of you," Townshend said to Ken and Sarah, then continued to Ingleby "I think it's time you and Ken went to fetch Stephen Warner."

CHAPTER FORTY FIVE

Although neither of them wanted Townshend to think they were eager to be out of the office, both Ken and Ingleby were happy to be on their way to Yazor Road to pick up Stephen Warner. Ingleby was enjoying a sense of responsibility that DI Murdoch had never given him. Murdoch never gave anyone else the chance or the kudos of being the arresting officer on a case, while Townshend had already allowed him to do that for both Robert Bexton-King and Sharon Doherty. As for Ken, Ingleby knew that when he'd been working for the Met in London, a former DI of his had described him in a report as 'a doer who liked to get stuck in and get his hands dirty.' Ken would be the first to agree with that assessment. He'd only been half joking when he was grumbling about having to check phone records.

Pulling up outside the house in Yazor Road where Stephen Warner was lodging, both detectives noticed a taxi waiting in the rain, windows steamed up and engine running.

"Looks like someone's planning a trip," Ken said.

"We'll see about that," said Ingleby. He parked their car directly in front of the taxi to stop it driving off before he could get to the driver. Both policemen were quickly out of the car and into the rain and as he approached the car, Ingleby saw curtains moving in an upstairs window.

"Ken, I think Warner's just seen us. Get around to the back of the house just in case he's decided he doesn't want to talk to us. I'll have a chat with this taxi driver and then go to the front door." For a big man, Ken Collings could move quickly when he wanted to and had soon disappeared around the corner of the house and into the back garden, heading for the back door. Ingleby tapped on the taxi driver's window, which was wound down slowly.

"Who are you picking up?" he asked the driver.

"What's it to you?" was the aggressive response, but the man's attitude changed remarkably quickly when Ingleby produced his warrant card. "A guy named Warner for a fare to the station," he said, slightly more amiably.

"He won't be needing you," Ingleby said.

"No?"

"No. I'd be on your way." The driver didn't need telling twice and after reversing back to give himself room to get out, had gone before Ingleby was halfway along the garden path to the front door. The welcome he received when it was opened was much less welcoming than the one he'd received from Colin Harrison the previous day.

"What are you doing back here? Didn't I tell you the other day that I don't like having policemen on my doorstep." Ingleby couldn't remember the woman's name, but she was right, she'd been just as unwelcoming on his previous visit. "And I'm not answering any more questions," she added firmly.

"I'd like to see your lodger, Mr Warner please," Ingleby said.

"He's just leaving," she said.

"So I gathered from the taxi driver a second ago," Ingleby said. "Did he tell you where he was going?"

"Back to New Zealand." Ingleby nodded.

"Where is he now?" he asked. She pointed upstairs, but was interrupted by Ken before she could speak.

"I've got him here, Sarge," he said. She didn't seem at all happy to have the big detective appear in her hallway, coming from the direction of the back door with Stephen Warner. "He was thinking of using the tradesman's entrance." Ingleby smiled. He could just imagine Warner's reaction at finding Ken waiting for him at the back door. The landlady moved to one side to let Ken and an unhappy looking Warner through, treating Ken to a glare as he passed.

"I'm sorry to hear you were leaving, Mr Warner," Ingleby said. "Your taxi's gone by the way, but we'll be happy to give you a lift, won't we, Ken?" Collings nodded, a big grin on his face. "New Zealand, was it?"

"I thought it was time for me to be heading home and pick up my life again," Warner said. "I've been away from home for a while now."

"You can tell us all about it at the station, Mr Warner," Ingleby said. Seeing Warner about to say something further, he continued. "No, don't argue, Mr Warner. Not when we've come out in the rain to arrest you."

"Arrest him?" asked Warner's landlady. Ingleby ignored her, his attention all on Stephen Warner.

"Stephen Warner, I am arresting you on suspicion of being complicit in the murder of Richard Bexton-King. You do not have to say anything, but it may harm your defence if you fail to mention when questioned something which you may later rely on in court. Anything you do say may be given in evidence. Do you understand?" Warner nodded, visibly crestfallen, his shoulders sagging. His landlady however was furious.

"You're arresting him for murder?" she shouted. "He's been living in my house! A murderer! Get out! Get out all of you!"

"Ken, get him into the car, will you? I'll deal with this," he added quietly. The big man guided Warner down the garden path and into the back of the car. Ingleby meanwhile stopped on the doorstep and turned to talk to the almost hysterical woman, hoping to calm her down a little.

"Whatever it is you're about to say, don't bother!" she yelled at him and slammed the door in his face. He shrugged and walked to the car without looking back. Don't take it personally when this sort of thing happens, the instructors said. It's the uniform they're shouting at, not you.

It was all very well to hear that in a classroom. Out in the field, it was harder to accept.

"Right Mr Warner, let's get you to the station," he said as he settled himself behind the steering wheel."

"Shame it's not the station you were intending to go to," Ken said wickedly from the back seat, where he was sitting next to Warner.

Neither Stephen Warner or the two detectives said anything during the short trip to the police station in Gaol Street and on arrival the two policemen took him directly to the custody suite.

"We'll arrange for the duty solicitor to see you as soon as possible, Mr Warner," Ingleby said and then handed him over to be booked in by the custody sergeant. After he'd signed the custody record confirming the property that had been taken from him and that he was feeling well and was led to a cell, the two detectives went upstairs to their office.

"Everything go OK, David?" Townshend asked as they entered.

"Yes, sir. When we arrived he had a taxi waiting to take him to the station," Ingleby said.

"Did he now? That's something to talk to him about, isn't it?" Townshend said as the two detectives took their coats off.

"And the custody sergeant's arranging for the duty solicitor to see him," Ingleby added.

"Fair enough. We won't be able to talk to him without one present anyway."

"Townshend and Sarah had obviously been busy while Ken and Ingleby had been off arresting Stephen Warner. Blown-up still photographs taken from the latest CCTV footage of the yard at BKM were adorning the evidence boards, on which new details and lines had been drawn up. Townshend saw them looking.

"Belt and braces," he said. "It's a matter of checking everything hangs together and ties up before I present the case to Logan for his approval. We're all going to go over it together. Four minds are better than one."

"Is there any doubt about it hanging together, guv," Ken asked.

"I don't think so, Ken," said Townshend smiling, "but if there is, I'd rather find out about it now than when DCI Logan reads it. And that's the point of this exercise."

CHAPTER FORTY SIX

"Interview resumed at eleven fifteen am. Those present are Detective Inspector Derek Townshend, Detective Sergeant David Ingleby, Mrs Sharon Doherty and Mr John Carey, solicitor." Ingleby spoke clearly and carefully, then paused and looked at Townshend sitting next to him.

"Mrs Doherty, I trust that in your discussions with Mr Carey he has advised you to be more forthcoming in your answers to our questions and I hope you will follow his advice." He looked at the woman sitting opposite him in the interview room. There was no response from her as she calmly met his gaze.

"Detective Inspector Townshend," began the solicitor, "I have been instructed by my client to tell you that she has no intention of answering any questions you might put to her. She considers herself to be here under false arrest and asserts that you can have no evidence that she was in any way involved in the murder of the man she loved." Townshend looked at the man in disbelief and then at Sharon Doherty who continued to show no emotion whatsoever. For a brief moment he considered turning the tape recorder off and telling them both what he thought of them, but resisted the temptation and swallowed his irritation. At least the solicitor had the grace to look uncomfortable. Never mind. He could play silly games as well if that was what Doherty wanted.

"That is unfortunately going to make this a very one-sided interview," he said addressing the solicitor, who nodded slightly. Then Townshend switched his attention. "But firstly let me assure you Mrs Doherty, whatever you believe, you are not being held under false arrest. You were not only arrested under suspicion of being involved in the murder, but also for obstructing the police in the course of their duties, as we pointed out to you. You are still continuing on that course. You have not been charged with the actual murder of Richard Bexton-King.

And I'm sure Mr Carey will have pointed this out to you, while at the same time as he was hopefully trying to talk you out of such a futile protest." Another slight nod from the solicitor. "I would also like to assure you that the amount of evidence we have is enough to hold you for at least forty eight hours and is almost certainly enough for a judge to grant us an extension on that period. Given that, I would ask you to consider being slightly more helpful." He could see he had her interest, but apart from a few whispered words with her solicitor, she still didn't respond. Carey shook his head.

"Mrs Doherty has again indicated that she will not respond to questions," Ingleby said for the tape.

"Very well," said Townshend, resigned to what was about to happen. "Let me ask you again, Mrs Doherty where were you on the Tuesday evening you told us you were going to Cardiff hospital, an explanation that turned out to be untrue?" She just looked at him. "For the benefit of the tape, Mrs Doherty has declined to answer the question," he continued.

"Let me ask you another question about your activities on that evening, Mrs Doherty," Townshend persisted. "Did you return to the premises of BKM Ltd after the business had closed for the evening?" Again no response, not even a flicker of emotion. Townshend turned to the solicitor. "Mr Carey, would you please point out to your client that should she wish not to answer a question, a response of 'No comment' will be sufficient?" There was a short whispered conversation between the solicitor and his client.

"Mrs Doherty has pointed out, against my advice I might add, that as part of her protest at being held here, she refuses to say anything for the benefit of the tape," the solicitor said.

"You are doing yourself no favours, Mrs Doherty," Townshend said. "But instead of asking you questions, let me outline a scenario to you, which you are of course at liberty to discuss with your solicitor after this interview. Please feel free to interrupt me at any time should you decide you want to say anything."

"On starting work at BKM," he began, "you saw an opportunity to form a relationship with your new boss, Richard Bexton-King, whose marriage you found out was breaking down. This is of course, a scenario you have been in before, with your late husband." Townshend had the satisfaction of her briefly glaring at him. "Mr Bexton-King did indeed become involved with you for a short period, but that relationship went sour, didn't it Mrs Doherty? Despite your best efforts, Mr Bexton-King wanted nothing more to do with you outside of the workplace, confining your relationship to that of employer and employee. I do hope I've got everything right so far?" She didn't respond, but he hadn't expected her to. "If not, please feel free to correct me."

"By your own admission, to Detective Sergeant Ingleby and myself, you started a relationship with another man to make Mr Bexton-King jealous, a rather schoolgirl-ish idea in my opinion. But that didn't work either did it? You also weren't aware that the man you started a relationship with, Nicholas Eddison, had only just finished a relationship with Mr Bexton-King's ex-wife. In fact, he may well have still been sleeping with her when he started seeing you. You didn't know there was ill-feeling between the two men, did you? Or did you, Mrs Doherty?" He paused, but only to make another comment for the tape. "Mrs Doherty neither confirmed nor denied what has been put to her."

"As part of your duties at BKM you were in charge of the company accounts, although it appears from comments made by Mr Bexton-King's brother Robert, that you also actually dealt with most of the day to day management of the business. A responsible position, Mrs Doherty, but you still weren't made aware by the brothers that the business was heading for financial difficulties, were you?" His attempts to provoke some sort of reaction didn't appear to be working, but he hoped they were gradually wearing her down or at least giving her something to think about. Nobody likes to believe they are deliberately being kept in the dark. "But that's by the by, really. While working with the company finances, you recently became aware of a personal transaction made on the company credit card by Richard Bexton-King, didn't you, Mrs Doherty? Two airline tickets to Greece, one in his name and one in the name of the new woman in his life, Val Pereira. What did you think, Mrs Doherty? Was it why her and not me? Why a cleaner? Did it finally get the point across to you that he wasn't interested in you, that there was someone else he cared more about and wanted to share his life with? Because that's what was happening. Richard Bexton-King was leaving the country to live in Greece. The company was going down the pan and couldn't be sold. He and his brother had actually agreed to set fire to the business as part of an insurance scam to help Robert out with debts. There was no thought for you in any of this was there? No thought of the woman who loved him so deeply she slept with another man." He paused again, aware of subtle changes in her body language, but there was still no response.

"What did you think, Mrs Doherty?" he persisted. "If I can't have him no one else will? Was that it? Or were you so angry with him that you just wanted him dead?" Despite her self-control, Sharon Doherty was beginning to fidget and look pale.

"Detective Inspector, I feel that you're surmising what my client may or may not have been thinking," the solicitor said.

"Mr Carey, with all due respect, we're in an interview room and not in court and I'm simply outlining what I believe was going on. You'll also notice that at no time have I said that any of this is actually what Mrs Doherty may or may not have been thinking. I've asked her if it's what she was thinking. She's at perfect liberty to deny it and tell me what she was thinking at any time." The solicitor nodded in reluctant acceptance.

"Let me continue and move on to the day on which Richard Bexton-King was killed at Pontrilas, shall we, Mrs Doherty? He was in the office at BKM in the afternoon, but had to go to Pontrilas to see an antique dealer about some items of his late mother's. You arranged for the taxi, didn't you? A return trip to Hereford, with the taxi picking him up from Pontrilas in the evening. He also stopped at his doctor's to collect his prescription of oxycontin on the way to Pontrilas, didn't he? A full month's worth of painkillers with him at the house. And then late in the afternoon, at around four thirty," he paused to check the time on his notes, "he rang you from his mother's house, didn't he? To cancel the taxi. For some reason, he'd decided to stay there for the night, possibly to oversee the last of the clearance the following morning and to lock the premises. We've checked with the taxi firm and they've confirmed that you rang them to cancel the return trip. You then rang Nicholas Eddison at Hindlip, didn't you, Mrs Doherty? To arrange for his car to be left in the workshop overnight for a service the following morning. If you were doing him a favour, why couldn't it just come in the following morning, Mrs Doherty? What was so important about having it there overnight?" Townshend paused again. Was it his imagination, or was she showing just a little more interest in what he had to say?

"Mr Eddison wanted the car left in the workshop overnight, but that didn't happen, did it? It was left in the secure yard instead. A yard for which only you had access to the keys. The other people who could otherwise get hold of the keys from the office were the Bexton-King brothers weren't they? And Richard was in Pontrilas with no transport while Robert was on a business trip to Lichfield. But let's move on. We have clear CCTV footage of you opening the yard after business hours and driving Mr Eddison's Mazda Roadster out through the gate. It wasn't returned until five hours later in the early hours of the morning when again we have CCTV footage of you, Mrs Doherty. The question is why use a car that was likely to be remembered if it was seen? Were you hoping suspicion would fall on Mr Eddison? Where did you and the other person caught by the camera go in that car, Mrs Doherty and who was that other person?" There was nothing to be gained by telling her they knew who it was at the moment, Townshend thought. That could wait. "There is no response from Mrs Doherty," Townshend said, tiring of repeating himself, but having to go by the book.

"The following morning, there was extra mileage on the Mazda from when it was booked in, Mrs Doherty, about thirty miles, which would easily allow the car to be taken to Pontrilas and back." The solicitor looked at him again questioningly, but Townshend continued before the man could speak. "Of course, that would be supposition on our part if we didn't have a witness statement placing the car not only in Pontrilas, but actually at the house in question during that period of that five hours. There is physical evidence on the car as well, placing it at the scene. A dent and scratch contain flecks of paint from a gate hinge at High Lawns which our witness says the car collided with on its way out of the drive. Paint taken from that gate hinge matches the paintwork on the car."

"And then of course, we come to your DNA, Mrs Doherty, which I have questioned you about. If I recall correctly you said you'd only been to the house once, sometime last year, when you had a cup of tea with Richard Bexton-King's mother. That was the reason you gave for your DNA being there, wasn't it?" She didn't answer, but he hadn't expected her to. "The only problem was I hadn't told where your DNA was found, so your answer didn't hold up." He paused again, instead deciding he was going to leave her some questions to think about.

"How did it feel, Mrs Doherty, watching the man you say you loved being tied up on a chair and being force-fed a drug that would kill him? Was there fear in his eyes? Did he struggle? Did he ask you why? Did he beg? And why were you in such a hurry to leave that you crashed the car against a gate hinge? Did someone disturb you? Did you see someone in the lane outside the house? Is that why the body was dumped in a travelling trunk? And of course, you couldn't get back the next day, because the items had already been moved out first thing in the morning, hadn't they?" Townshend motioned to Ingleby to be ready to turn the tape recorder off. "Interview suspended at eleven fifty am." As Ingleby flicked the switch, an agitated and shaken Sharon Doherty was having another whispered conversation with her solicitor.

CHAPTER FORTY SEVEN

"I hope we've given you plenty of time to talk things over with your solicitor, Mr Warner?" Townshend asked. When Stephen Warner simply nodded, the DI sighed, hoping this interview wasn't going to be a re-run of the interview earlier in the day with Sharon Doherty. "And you do understand why we're holding you here, don't you, Mr Warner?"

"Yes, Suspicion of being complicit in the murder of Richard Bexton-King," he said, quoting Ingleby's words exactly and grinning amiably at the Detective Sergeant. It was Townshend's turn to nod.

"Let's start at the beginning, shall we, Mr Warner?" Warner's body language seemed relaxed as he sat across the table, next to his solicitor, who Townshend was thankful was not Mr Carey. Most people in this sort of situation, an interview under police caution, were on edge, guilty or innocent, Townshend thought. It wasn't quite a devil may care attitude that Warner had, but it was certainly close. "Why did you come back to Hereford, Mr Warner?"

"Why do people return to the place they grew up, Detective Inspector? I wanted to see the place I was born and where I spent the young years of my life."

"How old were you when your family left for New Zealand?"

"I was nearly eleven."

"Hardly old enough for too many memories," Townshend said, and those probably fading, he thought but didn't say. "I would imagine it's changed a great deal."

"No, it hasn't changed that much really," Warner replied. "Mum and my father talked about our life in Hereford all of the time and there were lots of photographs. I wanted to come back and see it for myself."

"Have you always wanted to come back to Hereford?"

"Yes, ever since we left. I just thought I'd see a bit of the rest of the world as well, on the way here," Warner said. "Where is this going, Detective Inspector?" he asked. Townshend ignored the question.

"Did your parents miss their life in Hereford?"

"Yes, both of them. Mum more so, I suppose, because of Kim. It's where she's buried," he explained. "It was my father who insisted that we go, but even he missed it."

"Why New Zealand, Mr Warner?" Townshend asked.

"Sorry?"

"Why did your parents choose New Zealand to move to?"

"I don't know. They never talked to me about it. I suppose they thought I was too young to be involved. There were arguments, though, lots of them and they continued in New Zealand."

"Between your mother and father?"

"Yes. As I said, it was my father's idea to leave Hereford. He thought it would do Mum good to make a clean break. It didn't though and she never really forgave him." There was a difference in Warner's relationship to his parents, Townshend noticed. It was 'Mum' on the one hand and a more formal 'my father' on the other.

"They did leave under a cloud. Is that why they went so far? Before your mother did something stupid?"

"What do mean stupid?" There was a flash of anger in his voice, a flash of defensiveness for his mother?

"Well she blamed Richard Bexton-King for your sister's death…"

Of course she blamed him!" Warner interrupted. "It was his fault!"

"Not according to the inquest, Mr Warner," Townshend said calmly. "The verdict was accidental death."

"He killed her. He was driving, so it was his fault. He lived and she died, her and the baby." His voice had risen to a near shout and he angrily shrugged off the hand the solicitor had placed on his arm.

"Baby, Mr Warner? What baby?" Townshend asked. This was the first he'd heard of a baby. Townshend glanced quickly at Ingleby, who understood the unspoken question immediately. He shook his head, equally puzzled.

"Kim was expecting a baby," Warner said, calming slightly. "Mum always said that Bexton-King not only killed her daughter but her grandchild as well." Although he appeared to be calming, Warner's relaxed attitude had gone, leaving him animated and fidgeting in his seat. He was also fiddling with his fingernails. Thank you for that, Mr Wilson, Townshend thought.

"Did your mother tell you how far into her pregnancy your sister was?" Townshend asked.

"About three or four months."

"Did you notice at the time?"

"No. I don't remember it," Warner admitted.

"Did your father ever mention the baby?" Townshend asked.

"No."

"Why was that?"

"It was never mentioned until he left us. Mum said talking about it upset him too much."

"Mr Warner, the question of your sister being pregnant was not mentioned at the inquest. It surely would have been if she was expecting. Could your mother have been mistaken?"

"Mistaken? About her own daughter? Of course not!" Warner seemed agitated again. "She would never have been wrong about anything to do with Kim. Kim meant everything to her." His voice was rising again. Townshend decided to push this further.

"Your mother became mentally unstable, didn't she, Mr Warner?"

"No, she was a loving caring person."

"The medical records say different, Mr Warner," Townshend said. "Your father left her because he couldn't cope with her mental state, didn't he?" There was no answer. "She wouldn't accept the fact of your sister's death, would she? She sent death threats to Richard Bexton-King, Mr Warner. Did you know that? Is that why your father took you and your mother to New Zealand? Because he was afraid that she'd try to kill the person she thought killed her daughter?" Townshend rattled the questions at Warner.

"You know nothing about my mother!" Warner exploded. "She had her daughter and grandchild taken away from her…"

"There was no baby, Mr Warner," Townshend said. "It was a figment of your mother's imagination." This was too much for Stephen Warner.

"What the hell do you know? My Mum would never lie. That bastard Bexton-King destroyed all our lives. It was his fault we had to leave Hereford. And it was his fault my Mum's marriage split up."

"Leaving you to look after your mother on your own," Townshend interrupted.

"She was everything I had. Bexton-King destroyed her life and mine. I was happy in Hereford. I didn't want to go away. I hated him for what he did."

"Your mother told you it was his fault?"

"Yes. She told me I had to leave my friends because of him."

""Have you seen any of them since you've been back in Hereford?" Townshend asked. Warner nodded, his anger disappearing, in a sudden mood change, leaving him upset instead.

"Detective Inspector, can we take a break?" asked the solicitor, worried about Stephen Warner. "I think my client could do with a few minutes to compose himself. Townshend wasn't sure he wanted Warner to be composed.

"Yes, certainly," he answered, "after Mr Warner's answered one last question. Can you tell me the names of any of the friends you've seen? We might need to talk to them."

"I've only seen one, my best friend Nick," said Warner.

"Detective Inspector, I must insist on a break," the solicitor said, much more firmly. Townshend nodded.

"Nick who, Mr Warner?" he asked.

"Nick Eddison. Though he prefers to be called Nicholas now," he added. Townshend and Ingleby glanced quickly at each other. "We met for coffee and a chat," Warner continued, regaining his composure a little. He obviously felt on safer ground than when answering questions about his family.

"I would imagine it was good to catch up," Townshend said. "Where did you go for coffee? Somewhere in town or out?"

"In town, Costa in High Town. Why do you want to know?" Warner looked puzzled at the direction the questions were taking, while his solicitor looked ready to speak up again.

"I just wondered if he'd driven you anywhere," Townshend said. Warner shook his head.

"I don't even know if he's got a car," he replied. Townshend smiled and terminated the interview before the solicitor could say anything more.

CHAPTER FORTY EIGHT

"Has Nicholas Eddison been in to collect his Mazda yet?" David Ingleby was on the phone to the police garage, a not very confident DI Townshend standing by his desk. It was a long shot, but if Eddison hadn't been in yet, Townshend wanted a word with him about Stephen Warner. Ingleby, still listening on the phone, turned towards him, shaking his head, then replaced the receiver. "He picked it up first thing this morning, sir," he said.

"Never mind, David. He'll wait," said Townshend. "It'll just give us more time to see what we can find out from Stephen Warner," he added.

"It was a bit of a surprise finding out that Warner and Eddison knew each other, sir."

"Yes, David. But does it help and make things easier or or does it make things more difficult?" He wasn't expecting an answer.

"Do you think they'll be long, sir?" Ingleby asked.

"Who? Warner and his solicitor? No, I don't think so, David. They haven't got a lot to talk about and I think the solicitor just wants a chance to calm Warner down a bit." He chuckled. "He realised I was trying to push Warner and wanted to stop it."

"Can we get it back to that point, sir? He might just say something without thinking about it."

"That's what I'm hoping, David," said Townshend, "but I'm not sure it'll work now. Warner might be better prepared. We'll try a different tack when we go back in and do the same as we did to Sharon Doherty. But for now, let's get some coffee on the go." The coffee machine was bubbling away nicely when the phone rang. Ken Collings answered it.

"CID. Collings speaking," he said. "OK, thanks. Someone will be right down," he continued after listening for a few moments. Townshend looked at him enquiringly as he put the phone receiver down. "Custody sergeant, guv. Warner and his solicitor are ready to carry on."

"Thanks, Ken," said Townshend. He turned to Ingleby. "Let's get to it, David. Shame about the coffee, though." It took them only a few minutes to go downstairs to the interview room, where Stephen Warner, now apparently returned to his earlier relaxed attitude, was sitting waiting with his solicitor. A uniformed constable, standing just inside the door, left the room as the two detectives seated themselves.

"Rather than pick up where we left off, Mr Warner, I'd like to put a scenario to you," Townshend said after Ingleby had turned on the tape recorder and dealt with the formalities.

"Certainly, Detective Inspector," Warner said politely. If he was surprised, he hid it very well, Townshend thought.

"I'll be honest with you, Mr Warner, I don't think you came back to Hereford to visit the place you were born or to see your old school friends, Mr Warner. I think Richard Bexton-King was the sole purpose of your visit." There was no reaction from Stephen Warner, who did however seem to be listening to him with interest. "After all, you must have wanted to get close to him to involve yourself with his brother and get a job with BKM."

"I needed money. I told you that I was working my way around the world," Warner said.

"So you did, Mr Warner. But why BKM and why a relationship with Robert Bexton-King? Surely you could have got a job somewhere else?"

"I didn't know who Robert was. I only knew him as Robert at first."

"You must have found out. When was it? After you'd slept with him?" Warner nodded. "And yet you carried on seeing him, using him to get close to his brother. You must have been wondering how you'd get to meet Richard, so using Robert to get a job at BKM was just the opportunity you needed, wasn't it? A real piece of good luck." Townshend paused, giving Warner the chance to say something. He didn't, so Townshend carried on.

"Let's turn to Richard Bexton-King himself. We've established that you didn't like him and blamed him for a lot of things in your life…" Warner looked like he was going to interrupt, but Townshend held up his hand to stop him. "No, Mr Warner, let me continue. You'll get a chance to have your say. In fact, I think rather than not liking him, you actually hated him, didn't you? And yet when we first spoke, you told us that Richard welcomed you like an old friend. Why did you lie to us, Mr Warner?" No answer.

"No? You haven't got an answer for that one? Shall I answer it for you? You lied to us because you didn't want us to know how you really felt about him. And why was that? Because you thought it might make us suspicious of you, didn't you?" Again, no answer.

"You're a pharmacist, aren't you, Mr Warner?" Townshend asked. This time he waited for an answer.

"Yes, but you know that, Detective Inspector," Warner said, "we've already discussed it."

"It's for the benefit of the tape, Mr Warner," Townshend explained. "What do you know of oxycontin?" Warner looked puzzled. Was it Townshend's imagination, or did the question make Warner uncomfortable?

"Oxycontin? It's a painkiller. A strong one. Usually prescribed in capsule form."

"Why in capsule form, Mr Warner?" Townshend persisted.

"Because it's a slow release painkiller, Detective Inspector. The capsule slows down the drug entering the bloodstream."

"And what would happen if it was administered directly to someone in powder form in large doses?"

"It would make someone very ill. If the dose was large enough, it would kill them, very slowly." Realising what he was saying, Warner stopped and looked directly at Townshend and then glanced at his solicitor, a growing look of horror on his face. "Are you saying..." he began and then stopped again, turning back to his solicitor. They talked quietly for a short while, their voices too low for the tape to pick up or for Townshend and Ingleby to hear. The two detectives waited, glancing at each other.

"Detective Inspector," Warner said, "I think I need to know how Richard Bexton-King died."

"Are you telling me you don't know?" Townshend said. He didn't believe it.

"I wouldn't ask otherwise."

"Oxycontin poisoning," Townshend said, deciding to go along with it, watching closely for Warner's reaction. "Bexton-King was taking it because of injuries he sustained in the accident which killed your sister."

"Oh, Christ," was all Warner said. There was another hurried discussion with his solicitor. They seemed to reach a decision between them. "Detective Inspector, a couple of weeks ago, I was asked the very same questions about oxycontin, but I swear I didn't know Richard Bexton-King was taking it."

"And who was it who asked you, Mr Warner?"

"Nick Eddison," Warner answered after a slight hesitation.

"Did he tell you why he wanted to know?"

"No."

"And you didn't think to ask why?"

"No." That was hard to believe.

"About Mr Eddison," said Townshend, noticing as he spoke that Warner had gone pale. "Do you need a glass of water, Mr Warner?"

"No. Let's continue."

"Have you seen him much while you've been in Hereford?"

"A few times, yes."

"And when was it he asked you about the oxycontin?"

"The second or third time we met, I think."

"And you really didn't think to ask why or even wonder why he might want to know?" Townshend asked. Warner shook his head

"I've already said no."

"Did you know he was having an affair with Sharon Doherty?"

"No." There was an element of surprise in his voice and on his face, but Townshend wasn't convinced. He was also unsure about the whole Eddison and oxycontin issue. It seemed too glib, too convenient. Was Ingleby right? Were Doherty and Warner trying to set up Nicholas Eddison?

"You were helping clear out the house at Pontrilas, weren't you?"

"Yes, on both days, the Tuesday and the Wednesday, until we'd finished."

"I'm glad your memory's so good. Now, where were you on the Tuesday evening and what were you doing?"

"The evening?"

"Yes, after you got back to Hereford from Pontrilas."

"I had something to eat in town, then met Sharon Doherty."

"Where did you meet her?"

"At BKM. She rang me and asked me if I could give her some help with a car."

"What sort of help?"

"With the gates on the yard. Apparently they're very stiff and she can't manage them."

"And she wanted to get a car out? Hers?"

"I don't know. I suppose so."

"And why did she not get it out before the gates were locked?"

"I don't know."

"Did she say why she needed it so urgently?"

"She said she was seeing someone that night. I suppose from what you've just told me, it might have been Nick." Townshend sat and just looked at Warner without saying anything. Tension began to build in the room the longer the silence went on.

"So why did you go back to BKM in the early hours of the morning?" he asked eventually. There was a fleeting flicker of reaction on Warner's face, but Townshend caught it.

"She asked me to," Warner said simply.

"Because she asked you to? I don't understand, Mr Warner. I can't help but ask myself why you? And why you agreed." This provoked another hurried and whispered conversation between Stephen Warner and his solicitor. Townshend waited patiently.

"Sharon knew who I was and was threatening to tell Richard and Robert, so I just did as she asked," Warner eventually said.

"Would it really have made that much difference?" Townshend asked.

"I liked the job and the people I was working with, Detective Inspector. And I didn't want Robert to know."

"Because?"

"We were becoming quite fond of each other," Warner said reluctantly.

"And what about Richard?"

"I had nothing to do with him."

"But you told us he greeted you like an old friend, didn't you Mr Warner? And now you're saying you had nothing to do with him," Townshend said. Warner didn't reply.

"How did Sharon Doherty find out about you, Mr Warner?"

"Nick told her," said Warner. Townshend nodded. From what he'd learned in the last few minutes, it didn't surprise him.

"Let's get back to that Tuesday evening. Did Sharon Doherty take you anywhere in the car?" he asked.

"No," Warner said firmly. "I only helped her with the gates."

"Would it jog your memory if I told you we have CCTV footage of you getting into the car after locking the yard gates? It's funny. Your memory doesn't seem quite so good all of a sudden. Where did you go?"

"Back to my lodgings," Warner said after another slight hesitation. "Sharon dropped me off there."

"And later on?"

"She picked me up to help her with the gates again."

"So you spent all evening in your lodgings?"

"Yes."

"Can your landlady verify that?"

"Mrs Bellamy? No. It's her bingo night on Tuesdays and she's out all evening. I heard her come back, but she was in bed when I went out again."

"OK, Mr Warner. I think we'll leave it there for now while we make a few more enquiries. Interview terminated at fifteen thirty hours."

CHAPTER FORTY NINE

"What do we do now, sir?" Ingleby asked after the solicitor had left and Stephen Warner had been taken back to his cell by a uniformed constable. He and Townshend were still sitting in the interview room.

"We need to talk to Sharon Doherty again, David, but while I'm doing that with Ken I'd like you and Sarah to go out to Weobley and have a chat with Nicholas Eddison's wife. Find out what was going on that Tuesday evening and whether Eddison's alibi stands up."

"Is there anything we need to know in particular, sir?"

"No. Just corroborate what we've been told and see what comes out of talking to her," Townshend said. Ingleby returned to their office to collect Sarah Miller, while Townshend went to the custody suite for a word with the duty sergeant.

John Carey, Sharon Doherty's solicitor, had gone back to his office in town after the earlier interview, but had left instructions at the custody desk to be rung if Townshend wanted to interview her again. He'd promised to return to the station as quickly as possible. The custody sergeant made the call.

"His secretary said he'll be here in about half an hour, sir," he reported to Townshend as he put the phone down.

"Time for the coffee I missed earlier, then," said Townshend with a smile. "Give me a buzz when he arrives, will you? I'll give him a few minutes with her before I come down."

It took David Ingleby and Sarah Miller over half an hour to get from the city centre to the Eddison's house in Weobley, with Ingleby complaining about the traffic every minute, from city drivers to slow tractors with oversized trailers. When they arrived, there were two vehicles parked on the gravel driveway, a green people carrier and Eddison's black Roadster. Ingleby hadn't expected to see Eddison here.

He parked near the gate on the verge where he and Townshend had parked on their previous visit.

"We need to talk to Mrs Eddison on her own," he said to Sarah. "If Eddison's around, I'll get him into another room for a chat and you can question his wife, OK?"

"She might open up more to a woman," Sarah agreed. The two detectives hadn't spoken much during the journey from Hereford and Sarah had been wondering why Townshend had sent them out together. Sergeant Ingleby always seemed uncomfortable when working with her and she didn't know why. She'd tried hard and knew she was a good detective, but there always seemed to be some sort of barrier between them. She was surprised when he suddenly smiled at her, agreeing with what she'd said.

"Hopefully, Eddison will make himself scarce. I think he's seen enough of policemen for now," he said. "But I think you're right. She'll probably be more comfortable talking to you, Sarah, so I'll let you lead the questioning anyway. If that's alright with you, of course." She nodded, delighted with this development. She was still smiling as they crossed the gravel drive, squeezing between the two cars.

When Mrs Eddison opened the front door to them, she looked visibly shocked when they announced themselves. Sarah spoke before the other woman could say anything.

"Mrs Eddison, I'm Detective Constable Sarah Miller, Hereford CID," Sarah said showing the woman her warrant card. "We've got some more questions to ask you, if you can spare us a few minutes."

"Me? Not my husband? He is in, you know," Mrs Eddison said, a puzzled look on her face.

"We saw his car," Ingleby said, as Mrs Eddison ushered them in, "but it is you we want to see, Mrs Eddison." Ingleby then went quiet. Nicholas Eddison being at home was a problem as far as he was concerned. He didn't know what to do about it. It was plain from the two interviews with Stephen Warner that Eddison would have to be interviewed again, but neither he nor DI Townshend had even considered the possibility of him being at Weobley. Should he talk to him or not? He was still thinking about it while partly listening to Sarah talk to Mrs Eddison.

"Two weeks ago, Mrs Eddison, you picked your husband up from a garage in Hereford, when he'd left his car for a service," Sarah began.

"Trish," said Eddison's wife.

"Sorry?" said Sarah.

"My name's Trish. I prefer it to Mrs Eddison."

"OK, Trish. Do you remember that evening?"

"Yes, I remember. I was furious. He'd rung me from the office, asking me to meet him at BKM on the Worcester Road. He didn't give me much notice, just said 'be there.'"

"Where did you go after you picked him up?"

"Go? Nowhere. We came straight back here."

"Both of you?" asked Sarah. "You didn't drop your husband off anywhere on the way?"

"No, we both came back. Nick said he had some things to do here and told me I had to take him back to Hereford in the morning."

"So he stayed the night."

"Yes. In the guest bedroom," Trish added quickly, colouring up and obviously embarrassed.

"I was told about the situation between you and your husband, Trish," Sarah said sympathetically.

"It's for the best for both of us," the other woman said, but without much conviction. Sarah nodded, then returned to her questions.

"Was he here all evening, Trish, or did he go out?"

"He went out. Someone came to pick him up."

"Do you know who?"

"No, he didn't tell me. We don't talk much."

"What time did he go out, Trish?" Sarah asked.

"Eight-ish, I think. Somewhere around there, anyway."

"Any idea where he went? Did he say?"

"No. All he said was that he was meeting someone about work."
Ingleby, listening for nuances, heard disbelief in her voice.

"But you didn't believe that, did you?" he asked.

"No," she said quietly.

"Did he say who he was meeting?"

"No and I wasn't really interested, I'm afraid."

"What time did he come back to the house?" asked Sarah.

"I'm not sure, but it must have been midnight or just after. I was already in bed, so I didn't take that much notice." The noise of a car pulling rapidly out of the driveway distracted all three of them. Moving quickly to the back door, Ingleby saw Eddison's Roadster disappearing out into the lane. Turning back to the two women, his first thought was that at least he didn't have to worry about talking to Nicholas Eddison. It was also plain that the man didn't seem to want to take the chance of talking to the two detectives.

CHAPTER FIFTY

As Sharon Doherty and her solicitor were ushered into the interview room, Townshend sat quietly, watching them as they settled into their seats. Was she going to be more helpful in this interview or was it going to be a re-run of the last one? He was also unsure of how he was going to handle this himself. Flying by the seat of your pants was not the best approach for interviewing a suspect. She returned his gaze without giving anything away. Ken, sitting next to his DI, turned on the tape recorder and dealt with the formalities of who was present. Townshend turned his attention to the solicitor.

"Thank you for coming back in, Mr Carey," he began. "I hope after this morning's interview you've advised Mrs Doherty to be a little more co-operative and open with her answers." The solicitor shook his head almost imperceptibly; certainly Sharon Doherty didn't notice.

"My client insists that the police caution advises a suspect that they don't have to say anything, Detective Inspector. It might not be called a right of remaining silent any more, but it appears that for the present at least, she has chosen not to say anything."

"Is that correct, Mrs Doherty?" Townshend asked. Her only response was to nod her head. He decided that the slight smile he thought he'd seen was only a figment of his imagination and suppressed a sigh. Ken's audible sigh of irritated disapproval more than made up for his own self-control. "Never mind, Mrs Doherty, we'll continue anyway. Feel free to join in at any time if you have anything to say." No reaction. But there definitely was a smile. He wasn't imagining it.

"We've been talking to Stephen Warner and some things have come up that we need to confirm with you," Townshend began. "According to what we've discovered, on the Tuesday evening of Richard Bexton-King's death, you rang Mr Warner and asked him to meet you at

BKM to help you with the yard gates, because you can't manage them. Is that correct?" No answer. "No matter, as I told you earlier, we have CCTV footage of both you and Mr Warner at BKM, unlocking the yard gates. I just wanted to confirm why you were both there. He said you wanted to get a car out of the yard as you were going to meet someone that evening. The footage shows Mr Warner getting into the car with you. He says you dropped him off at his lodgings and then went on to wherever it was you were going." Still no answer. "Please remember, Mrs Doherty, you have lied to us concerning your whereabouts that evening and when we pointed that out to you, you refused to tell us what you'd been doing. It does appear that even without your help, we're building up a picture of your movements."

"Now, Mrs Doherty," he continued, "why was Stephen Warner the person you chose to help you? He was just someone doing a little bit of part-time work for BKM, wasn't he?"

"Detective Inspector, isn't there more than a little presumption in all this?" the solicitor asked.

"Without any confirmation or otherwise from Mrs Doherty, I am only describing a possible scenario, Mr Carey. Please bear with me," Townshend replied. Carey nodded, despite looking unsatisfied with the answer.

"One of Robert's pets is the way you described Mr Warner, isn't it, Mrs Doherty?" Townshend continued. He wasn't expecting an answer and didn't get one, only that infuriating smile. "So why him? I couldn't work that out, Mrs Doherty. As far as I knew, there was only one person in Hereford who knew of Warner's past, and that was Robert Bexton-King, but then I found out from Mr Warner himself that there was someone else, a person you know very well. An old school friend of his. Nicholas Eddison." Was that a flicker of reaction? Did she pale a little? It was probably just wishful thinking on his part. If she was playing games, she was doing it very well. He had to give her credit for that.

"He told you who Warner was, didn't he, Mrs Doherty? I think that you then coerced Warner into helping you, but that raised another question. How far did his help for you go? Of course, both you and Nicholas Eddison were aware of Warner's knowledge of drugs. Did you ask Eddison to pump him for information? The questions that Mr Warner says Nicholas Eddison asked him were very specific, Mrs Doherty, but where did they come from? Nicholas Eddison couldn't have known Richard Bexton-King was taking oxycontin. But you did, didn't you? So it seems sensible to assume that it was you who asked Eddison to question Warner, doesn't it?" Townshend had given up expecting answers from Sharon Doherty. His sole intention was to give her plenty to think about while she was sitting on her own in her cell with time on her hands.

"Who was with you when you went to Pontrilas, Mrs Doherty? Stephen Warner or Nicholas Eddison? The CCTV shows you driving the car away from BKM with Stephen Warner. Later that evening, we have a witness statement placing the same car in Pontrilas. Then we have further footage of you returning it to BKM, again with Stephen Warner. As we have DNA evidence placing you in Pontrilas that evening, it seems reasonable to assume you were still in the car. But who was with you? The Mazda Roadster is a two-seater sports car and two people were seen in it in Pontrilas. Now both Stephen Warner and Nicholas Eddison say they were at their respective homes that evening. We're verifying Mr Eddison's alibi as we speak, while we'll be checking Mr Warner's very soon. There's one thing for sure. It couldn't have been both of them, could it?"

Sharon Doherty continued to look at him with that slight smile on her face. Townshend suddenly found it disconcerting. She wasn't oblivious to what was going on, he was sure of that much and it was a deliberate policy on her part not to say anything. It was the smile that was throwing him. It gave the appearance she knew something he didn't and that unsettled him. Doubt was a part of the job. You couldn't be a good detective without ever doubting yourself. Blind certainty was always going to lead you into trouble. Questioning other people wasn't the be all and end all of detection; you had to question your own conclusions as well. Was that what she was up to? Making him doubt himself? He dismissed the thought; if anyone was going to be playing mind games, it would be him not her. The courts had agreed to her being held for ninety six hours because of the seriousness of the crime involved, and she'd not been in custody for half of that yet. He decided to terminate the interview.

"We'll speak again, Mrs Doherty, after we've had a word with Nicholas Eddison. Ken, switch off the tape recorder and have Mrs Doherty returned to her cell, will you?"

CHAPTER FIFTY ONE

Wednesday morning. Another day into the investigation and Townshend couldn't shake the worry that they were building up a case against Sharon Doherty without getting any information or even much response out of her. She was the key, he was sure of that and as guilty as hell. It was who was with her that was the question. She couldn't manage to tie Richard Bexton-King to a chair on her own, so inevitably, there had to have been someone there with her. He had DNA evidence for Stephen Warner being at Pontrilas, but what was Nicholas Eddison's involvement? Townshend sighed in frustration. He had Sharon Doherty for about another thirty six hours before he had to formally charge her. Thankfully, he had longer than that with Stephen Warner, but there was still pressure. On top of everything, DCI Logan was soon going to be asking questions about what was going on because Townshend hadn't updated him with a sit-rep. It was almost a relief when David Ingleby arrived in the office.

"David, grab us both a coffee and we'll have a chat," he called out.

"Do you want to start with the chat Sarah and I had with Trish Eddison, sir?" Ingleby asked, putting the coffees on Townshend's desk and settling himself onto a chair. Townshend shook his head.

"We'll get to that, David, but I want to talk about Nicholas Eddison first. Do we know what's happened about the charges Marcella Bexton-King brought against him?"

"No idea, sir, but it'll only take a quick call." Townshend gestured at the phone. As an assault of that nature didn't normally fall within the remit of CID, it had somewhat slipped Townshend's mind. As he was now re-considering Eddison's involvement in light of what Stephen

Warner had said, the assault charge against him might prove a useful lever towards making Eddison more helpful. David put the phone down.

"Apparently they've been too busy to look into it yet, sir, but they have only just received the medical report from the hospital. They were going to chase it up today, but they're going to sit on it until we come back to them. Did you have something in mind?" he asked.

"We need to talk to him again and we haven't got enough evidence to bring him in for questioning on anything relating to Richard Bexton-King, but I think we can get away with linking this attack on Marcella Bexton-King with our investigation," Townshend said. Ingleby looked puzzled. "If she's pressing charges, we can arrest him," Townshend continued, "and that gives us time to talk to him and maybe apply a little pressure. What was the actual charge?"

"The charge sheet says common assault, sir," Ingleby replied. "Six months maximum, if he's convicted."

"Or a community order, David," Townshend said. "Still we'll pull him in for it. You did take his address on Monday, didn't you?"

"Yes, sir. A flat in Bromyard."

"Leave it until he's finished work and pick him up from there, will you, David? Take Ken with you again. We'll do Eddison the favour of not doing it at his office. DCI Logan would give us a rocket if we waltzed into the police headquarters to arrest him." Just the thought of it brought a smile to Townshend's face. Despite the smile, Ingleby could sense an undercurrent of tension in the DI's voice.

"I take it that yesterday's interview with Sharon Doherty didn't go well, sir," he said hesitantly.

"No. She didn't say a bloody word again. I'm wondering if she's doing it deliberately to annoy me or if it's some vain attempt to go for a psychiatric assessment," Townshend said. Ingleby grinned.

"If anyone needs that, it's Warner, sir," he said.

"It wouldn't surprise me, David. Now how did it go with Eddison's wife? Did she say anything interesting?"

"It was good, sir. I let Sarah lead the questioning and the two women seemed to get on quite well." It was a surprise for Townshend for Ingleby to have that much confidence in Sarah Miller, but he refrained from saying anything, just mentally filed it away. "Eddison was there when we arrived, by the way," Ingleby added.

"Was he in the room while you were questioning her?" Townshend asked anxiously. That wouldn't be good.

"No. He was in the house, but he left while we were talking to her. We didn't even see him." He explained about Eddison driving off while they were talking to his wife.

"He knew you were there?"

"I should think so, sir. He left in quite a hurry, so I had the impression he didn't want to run the risk of us talking to him."

"We'll get to that later today when you bring him in, David. Let's get to what his wife had to say."

"Firstly, he wasn't there all evening, sir, despite what he told us. He was picked up by somebody, something to do with work, she said."

"She didn't know who?"

"No. She didn't ask and he didn't tell her."

"What about time, David? That could be important."

"She said around eight o'clock, sir."

"And what time did Sharon Doherty get Eddison's car from BKM?" Townshend asked.

"I'm not sure, sir. I think it was around that sort of time, but I'll just check it with Ken." He started to rise from his chair, but Townshend stopped him.

"Just give him a shout, David," he said. Ingleby did so.

"A quarter to eight," Ken called back after a quick check.

"Right, let's work this into the scenario we think we've got. If Stephen Warner is telling the truth and Doherty did drop him off at his lodgings, would that give her time to get to Weobley?" Townshend asked. Despite having the incontrovertible proof of Warner's DNA in Pontrilas, Townshend wanted to have the arguments in place to contradict anything Warner might say.

"Probably, at that time of night, and Eddison's wife wasn't very precise. She did say eight-ish, so I'd say yes." He paused. "There is one other thing for us to factor in, sir."

"If there's only one, we're doing remarkably well. What is it?"

"The extra mileage on the car, sir," Ingleby said. "It's not enough."

"Not enough?"

"No. It would be if she drove directly from BKM to Pontrilas and back, but it's nowhere near enough if she went through Weobley to pick up Eddison."

"Are you sure, David?"

"Yes, sir. I was thinking about it last night. Colin Harrison told me the difference was about thirty miles. To go to Weobley and then on to Pontrilas and to do the return trip you'd have to add at least forty miles on to that, if not more," Ingleby answered.

"So whatever Warner says, we can rule out Doherty picking up Nicholas Eddison?" Townshend asked.

"It looks like it, sir."

"Good," said Townshend.

"But it does mean Eddison lied to us about being at home all evening, sir," Ingleby said. Townshend nodded. "Why would he want to do that if he went out legitimately?"

"It can only be something he wants to keep quiet about, legitimate or not," Townshend said, thinking to himself but what? Another question for Nicholas Eddison when they talked to him. "OK, David, enough about Nicholas Eddison. We need to talk about Stephen Warner."

"What about him, sir?"

"I want you to go and talk to his landlady." Ingleby groaned. "Check out his alibi with her."

"How, sir? He said no one knew he was in because his landlady was at bingo."

"I know, David, but she might just remember something."

"You know she slammed the door in my face when we arrested Warner, don't you, sir," Ingleby said.

"Well, let's just hope she doesn't do it again, David," said Townshend, smiling again as Ingleby rose from his chair. "And send Ken in, will you?" Ken Collings always seemed to fill the office with his presence.

"Yes, guv?" he said.

"Sharon Doherty's car. You said she didn't have one when you checked, yet she told us she had a Vauxhall Corsa. If she has got a car and we can find out where it is, we can get forensics to give it the once over, but she was probably lying."

"I've already been in touch with DVLA about that, guv. They've got no car registered to her, either as Sharon Doherty or Sharon Lilley. But she has got a valid driver's licence. Maybe she was using a company car."

"That will have gone up in flames. I think she used Eddison's car in an attempt to throw suspicion his way. Maybe we should pin driving without insurance and taking a vehicle without the owner's consent on her as well," Townshend said, then paused as a thought occurred to him.

"When you were interviewing the neighbour in Pontrilas, he couldn't give you a description of the two people in the car could he?"

"No, guv. He said it was too dark and the car went past him too quickly. But he was adamant that there were two people in it."

"OK, Ken, thanks."

CHAPTER FIFTY TWO

David Ingleby wasn't looking forward to knocking on the front door of Stephen Warner's lodgings. Mrs Bellamy, the landlady, had made her feelings clear when they'd taken Warner in and it didn't help that Townshend seemed to find it quite funny. If the DI hadn't wanted Ken in his office as Ingleby left, the sergeant had thought about asking the big detective to go with him.

"Man up, Ingleby and get on with it," he muttered to himself and knocked firmly on the door. "What's the worst that can happen?" he added as he heard footsteps approaching the door. A friendly looking Mrs Bellamy opened the door, but her face darkened when she noticed who was standing on her doorstep. At least she didn't immediately shut the door on him, Ingleby thought positively.

"Haven't you finished here? I wasn't expecting to see you back." She didn't give him a chance to answer. "It's not enough that I've been sheltering a killer and might have been murdered in my bed, now I've got policemen turning up on my doorstep all the time…"

"Mrs Bellamy…" Ingleby began.

"Why are you here now? To tell me I've got drug dealers hiding under the stairs? Or terrorists in the box room? I've got nothing to say to you." She made to slam the door in his face again, but he took the door to door salesman's approach and put his foot in the way, trying to ignore the pain.

"Mrs Bellamy, please. I've got just a couple of questions for you. I don't even have to come in."

"You weren't coming in, young man, whatever you might have thought. I don't know where you got that idea from. Now move your foot," she said.

"When you've answered some questions," Ingleby persisted. She hesitated and then eased the door off his foot.

"Make it quick, I've got a sponge cooking." She might have given in, but the dark frown didn't leave her face. "Come on, ask the questions, so I can get on," she said, when he didn't say anything straight away.

"You go to bingo on Tuesday nights, don't you, Mrs Bellamy?" Ingleby asked, relaxing and moving his foot back.

"Usually, yes. I don't drink and I don't smoke, but I do like my bingo."

"So you're always out on a Tuesday night?"

"Yes," she said but then her frown deepened. "No. I've not been for a couple of weeks. It's all to do with that bitch in Number Twenty Two. She's started going and I won't have anything to do with her. She's a nasty piece of work, she is." Before she could continue with that particular tirade, Ingleby interrupted.

"How many have you missed?"

"With last night, three, I think. Let me see. I didn't go last night, or the week before and that's right, the previous week was the first one I missed because she started going."

"So you didn't go a fortnight last Tuesday, Mrs Bellamy?"

"That's what I just said. Weren't you listening?"

"Yes, I was, Mrs Bellamy. I'm just confirming what you said. It's important. Were you at home a fortnight last Tuesday?" He quoted the date as well. She sighed in frustration.

"Yes. All night."

"Was Stephen Warner at home that evening?"

"How am I supposed to remember that? No, let me think a minute. Ah, I do remember it now because I gave him a piece of my mind over breakfast the following day," she said.

"And why was that, Mrs Bellamy?"

"He was out and came home in the early hours of the morning making a hell of a bloody row and waking me up. So I told him what I thought the next day." Ingleby could imagine she did. "I do like a bit of respect from my lodgers."

"Thank you, Mrs Bellamy," said Ingleby. "You've been very helpful."

"Is that all you wanted to know?" she demanded. Ingleby nodded, but before he could say anything more she slammed the door.

Ingleby took it well when Townshend, Sarah and Ken all laughed back in the office.

"She was a bit of a fiery one, Sarge," Ken said. "I wouldn't want her for my landlady."

"But at least she's told us what we need to know, David," Townshend said. "Let's see what Mr Warner has to say about his alibi turning out to be a lie." They had to wait while the duty solicitor was summoned to the station, but this gave Townshend time for not only yet another coffee but also time to consider how to approach both Warner and Sharon Doherty.

Stephen Warner entered the interview room with the same relaxed attitude as he'd started the previous two interviews, but Townshend hoped to change that as quickly as possible. Formalities over and the tape running, he just looked at Warner for a few minutes, without saying anything, hoping the silence and his gaze would unsettle the other man.

"You lied to us again, didn't you, Mr Warner," he said finally. "We checked your alibi, weak though it was, with Mrs Bellamy, your landlady. It would appear that she hasn't been to bingo on a Tuesday evening for some time and the evening on which Richard Bexton-King died is the first one she missed. You told us you were at your lodgings alone all evening. Your landlady said that on that particular evening, far from being at home, you were out and didn't come home until the early hours of the morning. Apparently there was quite a row about it the following day. Have you anything to say?" No reaction. "Mr Warner refused to answer the question," Townshend said for the tape and then looked Warner in the eye.

"Did you tell Richard Bexton-King who you were when you had him tied to the chair, Mr Warner?" he asked. Even Ingleby looked surprised at the question.

"What?" asked Warner.

"Was it satisfying telling him you were Kim's brother? Did he try to explain what had happened?"

"I don't know what you're talking about, Detective Inspector."

"Yes, you do," Townshend said flatly. "You enjoyed that moment, didn't you, Mr Warner? Did you tell him you were doing it for your mother? That you were taking the revenge she hadn't been able to?"

"No. I wasn't there," said Warner.

"Did you explain to him exactly what the oxycontin would do to him? Did he look scared? How did you feel holding the gun on him while Sharon Doherty tied him up? Is that when you told him? Your mother would have been proud of you, wouldn't she? Finally, she was getting what she wanted."

"Don't bring my mother into this again."

"No? But it's all about her, isn't it? Bexton-King ruined her life. That's what you've grown up being told, Mr Warner and if he ruined her life, he ruined yours as well didn't he? You even said yesterday that everything was his fault, didn't you?" The relaxed attitude was starting to slip. "It was his fault your father left. His fault you were left to waste your own life looking after your mother. And his fault that your mother went mad, wasn't it?" Warner thumped the table angrily.

"She wasn't mad!"

"She needed someone to look after her and that person was you, wasn't it? She'd lost your father and her daughter. No wonder she wanted Bexton-King dead and that was what she made you believe needed to be done. But you couldn't do it while she was alive, could you? Who'd look after her? Your father wasn't around, was he? He'd run off and left you to it."

"You're talking absolute shit!" Warner shouted, rising to his feet and jabbing his finger in Townshend's direction, glaring angrily at him. His solicitor's hand on his shoulder gently pulled him back into his chair. "I don't want to hear this," Warner added, almost snarling.

"No, I don't imagine you do," said Townshend, "but you're going to. It was the perfect opportunity for you when you found out how Sharon Doherty felt about Richard Bexton-King, wasn't it? Was it her idea to go to Pontrilas, or yours, Mr Warner? The oxycontin was a good idea and must have been hers. It was slow, though, wasn't it? Plenty of time to watch him suffer…"

"Suffer? He didn't know the meaning of the word!"

"Did he suffer, Mr Warner? Was he scared? Did you wish your mother could have seen him?"

"How do I know? I wasn't there! I wasn't in that kitchen!" He was shouting again.

"Kitchen, Mr Warner? What kitchen?" Townshend asked.

"The kitchen at Pontrilas where he was killed. Where you said he was tied up." Warner looked slightly relieved at having explained himself.

"I didn't mention a kitchen, Mr Warner," Townshend said quietly. Warner sagged back into his seat. "Why the trunk, Mr Warner?" Townshend added.

"Trunk?" Warner's thoughts seemed to be elsewhere.

"Yes, the trunk. Why did you put the body in the trunk? Did somebody disturb you or did you think they were about to?" No answer.

"For the benefit of the tape, Mr Warner declined to answer the question," Townshend added. He waited before speaking again, considering his next question.

"Tell me about Nicholas Eddison's pistol, Mr Warner."

"What about it?" asked Warner. A little of his confidence seemed to be coming back with the change of subject.

"Why are your fingerprints on it and on the box it's stored in?"

"Because he showed it to me and I've used it."

"Used it? Where?"

"At his gun club. He took me there," Warner said. Townshend turned to Ingleby. "Interview suspended at twelve fifteen pm." Ingleby, surprised, switched off the tape recorder. "Get him back to his cell, David," Townshend said. "I've had enough of this," he added under his breath so only Ingleby could hear. Ingleby beckoned in a uniformed constable from outside, and Warner and his solicitor were led out of the interview room.

"Damn!" It was Townshend's turn to slam his fist down on the table, his suppressed anger bursting out in one furious blow.

"Something wrong, sir?" Ingleby asked after a short pause. "You did catch him out about the kitchen. He couldn't talk his way out of that one."

"We're getting there in small steps, but it was a bloody awful interview, David. I didn't handle it at all well and it didn't go the way I wanted it to. It was a bloody waste of time!"

"We all have our off days, sir," said Ingleby, regretting the words the moment he said them. Townshend didn't seem worried.

"Yes we do, David, but you can't afford to have them in the middle of a murder investigation. Come on, I need a coffee and some lunch."

CHAPTER FIFTY THREE

Even after he'd had two cups of coffee and something to eat, the whole team could tell that Townshend's mood hadn't improved much. He'd thought about ringing Ginny Marston to see if she was free for lunch, but had decided not to inflict his mood on her as well as the team. He was aware there was a definite atmosphere in the office when he called them all together and was trying to play it down, but still paced up and down in front of the white boards, while the others pulled their chairs around their desks to be closer. He was almost talking to himself.

"You start with a list of possible suspects and eliminate them one by one, which we've done. Robert Bexton-King and Marcella Bexton-King have been eliminated. I'm not sure about Nicholas Eddison. He's involved in this somehow, but how? Anyway, when you've done those eliminations, the people you're left with are most probably the people who've committed the crime. Yes?"

"Yes, guv," said Ken, responding first to what was probably a rhetorical question.

"In this case, that's Sharon Doherty and Stephen Warner, possibly, no probably, with the help of Nicholas Eddison. We're talking to him later, so that might become clearer. Two main suspects for a crime we've already established needed two people. Both of them have lied to us during the course of the investigation and neither can give us a good alternative alibi for where they were on the night of the murder." He didn't wait for anyone to say anything, but carried on speaking. "We've got CCTV footage of them taking a car without permission on that same night and returning it in the early hours of the morning, the times of which fit in with the time the murder took place." Ken interrupted.

"Don't you think Nicholas Eddison knew Sharon Doherty was taking his car, guv?"

"No, I don't, Ken. He's very precious about it and I think she lied." He took a breath and continued. "We've got a witness who told Ken that he saw that same car leaving the house at Pontrilas at some speed and saw it collide with a gatepost. Forensics have confirmed that the paint on the gatepost and the paint on the damaged car match." He looked at each of them in turn. "Am I right so far?"

"Yes, sir." It was Ingleby's turn to answer.

"As well as the CCTV footage of them in the car, we've got forensics evidence, fingerprints and DNA, of them having been in the car. Sharon Doherty has a valid reason for that in that she went away for the weekend with Eddison. Warner says Sharon Doherty gave him a lift to his lodgings, which we now know was a lie, but has at least admitted he was in the car. Most damningly, Nicholas Eddison stupidly kept a pistol in the boot of that car, for which he will be having his gun licence revoked, by the way. Forensics have proved that both Warner and Doherty have handled the weapon and that some effort has been made to remove their prints. Nicholas Eddison insisted that Sharon Doherty hadn't handled the weapon, but did admit he'd told her about it, boasting more like. It would explain how she knew it was there. Warner has said his prints are on it because he fired the pistol at Edison's gun club. That needs checking. Can you do that when we finish talking, Ken?"

"Yes, guv," the big man replied.

"Anything else before I carry on?" Townshend asked. Sarah, Ken and Ingleby all shook their heads, so he continued, hoping this was proving as useful for them as it was for him.

"As far as Sharon Doherty goes, Forensics have matched her DNA to DNA found in the victim's mouth. As they were no longer in a relationship, despite Doherty's statements to the contrary, I can't imagine any reason for that other than one. And that is that she put her fingers in his mouth to prise it open while something else was put in there to wedge it open. Fair assumption?" he added. There was a chorus of agreement.

"Now, Stephen Warner. He's a qualified pharmacist who knows all about oxycontin. We know that Nicholas Eddison asked Warner questions about it. Warner has said that much, and it seems a fair bet that Sharon Doherty put Eddison up to it. She would have known the victim was taking it on a regular basis. And that's something we're going to talk to Eddison about." He paused, gathering his thoughts. "They both have motives, Warner's stronger than Doherty's admittedly. David and I have already talked about the possibility of a psychiatric report for Stephen Warner. With his background and the level of hatred he was brought up in, I think it's a certainty. With Sharon Doherty, she believed she was in love with Richard Bexton-King. We've been told that she threw herself at him and that he was quite willing to go along with it for a time. When he changed his mind, she kept trying for him, to the point of desperation. People have depths of feeling that can be quite unbelievable and she admitted she started seeing Nicholas Eddison just to make Bexton-King jealous. So how can we tell what effect finding out about his plans to move to Greece with Val Pereira might have had?"

"Is it worth pushing that with her in another interview, sir?" asked Sarah Miller. "Perhaps show her the photo of Bexton-King and Val Pereira outside the villa."

"That's not a bad idea, Sarah. Dig it out, will you? I think we're in the position where we need to get a confession out of one or the other of them, because there's one thing for sure: I don't think we've got enough hard evidence to make a real case against either of them at the moment," Townshend said. There was a long silence in the office.

"So what is it we need, sir," asked Ingleby.

"In an ideal world, a murder weapon, David. But in this instance, our murder weapon is a spoon, or two rather, because Karen Welby said the signs were that they propped the victim's mouth open with one. The other question is, what happened to the empty capsule cases of the oxycontin. They must be somewhere."

"Could they have been thrown out of the car, guv, or dumped somewhere?" Ken asked.

"They could well have been, Ken, but short of searching every roadside verge between Pontrilas and Hereford, I think that could be a lost cause," Townshend said.

"Sir, talking of long shots, I've got an idea," Sarah Miller said. "It's probably silly, but..."

"Never mind, silly, Sarah, let's hear it."

"Have the bins from Pontrilas been checked?" she asked.

"The wheelie bins? Forensics went through them," Ingleby said.

"No, Sarge, the house bins, especially the kitchen bin," Sarah persisted.

"You think they might have dropped the rubbish in the kitchen bin?" asked Ken. "Wouldn't that be asking for trouble?"

"Yes and no," she said. "We're pretty much agreed that the victim's body was dumped in the trunk in a rush, aren't we?" The three men nodded. "And we think that's because they thought they were being disturbed when they heard the neighbour's dog barking?" More nods. "Well what if they disposed of the spoons and drugs just as quickly and dropped them in the kitchen bin."

"But they must have known they'd be found by the cleaners. Sharon Doherty had arranged for the cleaning, Sarah," said Townshend.

"The cleaners wouldn't have looked at what was in the bin, sir. They'd just have emptied the contents. Maybe Sharon Doherty was banking on that or on Warner going back in the morning to get hold of the contents then. The thing is, what if the bin wasn't in the kitchen and Warner couldn't find it? The BKM men were completely clearing the house weren't they? Could they have taken the bin and put it on one of the vans, contents and all, without checking?"

"Warner would have spotted that, wouldn't he?" Ken said.

"There were three other men there and two vans," said Townshend thoughtfully. "He might well not have noticed where it was or been able to get hold of it without anyone noticing."

"So it would have gone with everything else to the auction rooms and once it was there, it would be out of his reach," said Ingleby. "And we've got everything that went in secure storage."

"Yes we have, David," said Townshend, "and forensics haven't checked it yet, or I don't think they have. Sarah, it's your idea. Get down there with someone from forensics and check it out. And don't let them tell you they're busy or no-one's available."

CHAPTER FIFTY FOUR

With Sarah off with Forensics and David and Ken having left for Bromyard to collect Nicholas Eddison on his return from work, Townshend took advantage of the peace and quiet in the office to have a relaxed cup of coffee before starting work on his sit-rep for DCI Logan. It could only be the bare bones. Things could change drastically in the next few hours, particularly if Sarah came up trumps with her hunch.

He'd decided to interview Nicholas Eddison before re-interviewing Doherty and Warner. There was information he hoped Eddison would give him that would hopefully further wear down the two main suspects and if he handled it properly, Eddison might just incriminate one or other of them. Time would tell. He hadn't got very far with his report when Sarah came back into the office. One look at her face told him she had good news.

"We've got it, sir," she said, unable to keep the excitement out of her voice. "It was all in the kitchen bin. Forensics are examining it as we speak."

"It was a good shout, Sarah. Well done," Townshend said. "Now what exactly did you find?"

"Spoons, empty capsules, empty medication boxes and the repeat prescription form that Richard Bexton-King would have been given when he picked his medicine up," she replied.

"Do Forensics think they'll get anything from it?" he asked.

"It was a Mr Wilson, sir. He seemed very confident."

"Did he say how long?"

"As quickly as he could was all he'd say, sir." That sounded like Wilson, Townshend thought.

"Then we'll have to go with that, Sarah," he said. "Anyway, well done again. It was a good call." Looking pleased, she returned to her desk. Townshend turned back to his report, with new information to add. He was still aware that after any one of three interviews, things would change again. He was soon lost in his work to the extent that he didn't hear David and Ken come back until Ingleby knocked on the door frame.

"Nicholas Eddison's downstairs, sir," he said. "I think it's safe to say he's not a very happy man."

"Hardly surprising, David," Townshend said. "You're back early," he added.

"He was at the flat when we arrived, sir, so we picked him up and came straight back."

"Good," said Townshend. "Has a solicitor been arranged? I think we need to talk to him as soon as possible."

"He doesn't want one, sir. Says he can handle it himself."

"It's unusual, David, but I suppose we can go with it. Let's go and see him." They stopped by Sarah's desk for a few moments. "If Wilson comes back with anything, Sarah, I want to know even if we're still in the interview room, OK?"

"Yes, sir," she said. Townshend and Ingleby went downstairs.

"What the hell is this all about, Detective Inspector?" Nicholas Eddison demanded as they walked into the interview room.

"In just a moment, Mr Eddison," Townshend replied as he and David sat down opposite Eddison. "David, can you do the formalities?" Ingleby placed a new tape into the deck and turned it on.

"Interview commences at five forty five. Nicholas Eddison, Detective Inspector Derek Townshend and Detective Sergeant David Ingleby present." Nicholas Eddison was growing visibly more irritated.

"Before we start, Mr Eddison, I have been informed that you have waived your right to a solicitor. Is that right?" Townshend asked.

"Yes. I'll represent myself. Now what is this about?" It would probably help that he was angry, Townshend thought as Eddison carried on talking. "I asked your sergeant here to explain himself but all he said was that we'd talk about it at the station."

"Surely you understand why you've been arrested, Mr Eddison? Detective Sergeant Ingleby will have made it clear."

"Some tosh about common assault. Absolutely bloody ridiculous. A man of my position?"

"It's not tosh, as you put it, Mr Eddsion. Mrs Bexton-King has been into the station and wishes to bring charges of assault against you for an attack which she alleges took place in her apartment last Friday." Eddison didn't say anything. "Nothing to say, Mr Eddison? I interviewed her myself, along with Detective Sergeant Ingleby and I have the medical report here. Shall I read you some of it?" Townshend asked opening a file. He waited a few moments for an answer, but he wasn't really expecting one. "A broken cheekbone, extensive bruising to the face and two loose teeth." He closed the file and looked Eddison in the face.

"And you say this was last weekend?" Eddison asked.

"Yes."

"And you're aware that I was away with Mrs Doherty last weekend?"

"Yes."

"So how could I have been there?"

"You were absent from work all day and from the timeline we've established from Mrs Bexton-King and a neighbour of Mrs Doherty's you had ample time to visit Mrs Bexton-King before going away," Townshend replied.

"And yet you didn't mention this on either of the occasions you spoke to me on Monday," said Eddison.

"It was in the hands of uniform at the time," Townshend said, happy to go along with Eddison wanting answers instead of the other way around. Allowing him to ask the questions might make him feel in control of the situation.

"I would have thought that in a case of common assault it would be uniformed officers who dealt with it," Eddison said, "not CID."

"Not if it happens to fall within the scope of a murder investigation, Mr Eddison. Now, you explained to us how you felt about Richard Bexton-King when we saw you at Hindlip and that you felt no animosity towards him, despite the heated arguments that we've learned about."

"No I didn't. I just wanted him to see reason."

"But there was no mention of animosity towards Mrs Bexton-King, was there?" Eddison began to shake his head.

"Animosity? To Marcella?"

"Please, Mr Eddison, don't bother to deny it," Townshend said. "We have her statement. You're a bully and you let your anger get the better of you. The question is: why were you angry with her in particular?" Eddison took some time before answering.

"I blamed her for getting me involved in a murder investigation, Detective Inspector. I didn't think it would look good for me in my position."

"Even less so than a divorce," Townshend said drily, remembering their conversation in Eddison's office.

"Yes. Anyway, we argued and she denied it."

"Quite rightly. She seemed determined to keep your name out of it. Your name came from other sources." Eddison at least had the decency to look a little shame-faced, Townshend thought.

"I was angry," he said. "I over-reacted and I shouldn't have…I mean, I didn't mean to…" He stopped. "What happens now? Will I get bail?" he asked.

"As you know, it's a police decision, but I see no reason to object. We'll sort it out with the custody sergeant later and he'll tell you when you'll be due to appear in court. In the meantime, I have some other questions for you."

"About Marcella?" Eddison looked resigned to answering whatever Townshend might ask.

"No. Further questions relating to Richard Bexton-King's death." Eddison looked surprised. Townshend continued. "On the evening you left your car at BKM, you told us your wife picked you up and took you back to Weobley. You said you were there all evening."

"Yes. That's right, I was."

"But you weren't, were you, Mr Eddison. Someone picked you up from the house at about eight o'clock and you went out for the evening." A frown crossed Eddison's face, but he didn't say anything. "Where did you go and who did you go with?" Eddison seemed reluctant to answer. "I must insist on you telling me, Mr Eddison," Townshend said.

"I went to The Salutation in the village," he said.

"Who with, Mr Eddison," Townshend persisted. "We'll need to verify this."

"Gerald Brotherton of the local Conservative association for the constituency. We were discussing the possibility of my standing as a candidate at the next election. There's no hope of that now," he added bitterly.

"He'll be happy to confirm that for you, will he?"

"I don't know if happy is the right word, but yes, he'll confirm it."

"How well do you know Stephen Warner, Mr Eddsiosn?" Townshend asked. The question must have surprised Eddison judging by the look on his face, Townshend thought.

"He's an old school friend from primary school. I've seen a bit of him while he's been back in Hereford."

"And you mentioned him to Sharon Doherty?"

"Yes, I knew she'd know him as they both worked at BKM."

"Did she ask you much about him?" Townshend asked. There was a distinct hesitation.

"We talked about him, yes. She was interested, in the same way as you'd be interested in anyone you worked with," Eddison said.

"Did you talk about where he'd been living and why his family left Hereford?"

"Yes. She thought it was a huge coincidence that their families had been linked in such a tragedy all those years ago."

"And you told her he was a pharmacist?"

"Yes."

"Was it Mrs Doherty who asked you to talk to him about oxycontin, Mr Eddison?"

"Yes."

"Did you not wonder about the detail of the questions she wanted answers to?" asked Townshend.

"She told me she was writing a story and needed the information for her book," Eddison answered.

"So you didn't think it was strange that she wanted to know?

"No."

"Did you ever see any of her writing?"

"No. She was very secretive about it and didn't want anyone to see it until it was finished."

"Mmm. Let me ask you about your pistol," Townshend said, changing the subject.

"What about it? I thought we'd been through all that." There was a light tap on the interview room door.

"Come in," said Townshend. A young WPC entered the room and gave Townshend a piece of paper.

"For the record, WPC Williams has entered the room and passed Detective Inspector Townshend a piece of paper," Ingleby said for the benefit of the recording.

"Detective Constable Miller asked me to give you this, sir," the WPC said.

"Thank you," Townshend said absently, reading the note. With a smile, he passed it to Ingleby as the WPC closed the door behind her on her way out. Townshend turned his attention back to Nicholas Eddison. "Have either Sharon Doherty or Stephen Warner handled the weapon you keep in the boot of your car, Mr Eddison?"

"No. Neither of them. Stephen Warner didn't even know about it."

"Then can you explain to me how both of their fingerprints have been found not only on the weapon but also on the box you keep it in?" By the stunned look on Eddison's face, it was plain he couldn't. "Let me ask you one more question which may give you pause for thought. As a solicitor, if I told you that Richard Bexton-King was killed by oxycontin poisoning on the evening that you left your car at BKM and that we have CCTV footage of Sharon Doherty and Stephen Warner driving away from BKM in that same car, what would you think?" There was a much longer hesitation before Nicholas Eddison spoke.

"Oh, Christ," was all he said.

CHAPTER FIFTY FIVE

I didn't really need to do that, Townshend thought as he made his way back upstairs to the office, but it did feel quite good. He'd taken an instant dislike to Nicholas Eddison the first time he'd met the man and scoring points off him, however trivial they might be, was quite satisfying. Eddison had been used, he was sure of that, an unwitting dupe in what had been going on. It pointed everything further at Doherty and Warner. David Ingleby caught him up as he reached the office door.

"He'll be in court on Friday, sir," Ingleby said.

"Good," said Townshend. "I can't see him getting a custodial sentence, but a community order and hopefully anger management classes might do him some good. As soon as we get his gun licence revoked that'll be Eddison sorted."

"What'll happen about his job, sir?" Ingleby asked.

"I've no idea, David. That decision will be down to the Police authority, but I think it might mark an end to his political ambitions."

As they walked through the door, Sarah was waiting for them with the results from Forensics.

"Mr Wilson rang with the Forensics results, sir," she said. Townshend had actually been surprised to receive the note. Forensics had surpassed themselves with the speed in which they'd analysed the evidence. "Both Sharon Doherty's and Stephen Warner's fingerprints were all over the stuff we found inside and Richard Bexton-King's DNA was on both of the spoons." Townshend smiled. He couldn't help it and Ken improved his mood.

"The secretary at Eddison's gun club almost laughed when I asked him if Eddison had ever taken any guests or visitors along, guv," he said. "Apparently Mr Eddison has never introduced any visitors to the club, nor did the secretary think he was ever likely to."

"Thanks, Ken. That confirms what Eddison has told us and proves Warner is lying again. Good work." With all of the other evidence, the Forensics results were enough for Detective Chief Inspector Logan to give Townshend the go-ahead to formally charge both Warner and Doherty with Richard Bexton-King's murder and for the case to be passed to the Crown Prosecution Service. Their decision was final, but in murder cases, it was rare for them not to proceed with a prosecution. In the mean-time however, both Doherty and Warner had to have a final interview and be formally charged.

"It was a good call, Sarah," Ingleby said.

"Yes," said Townshend, "and it's going to give us what we need to charge them both. Well done." He turned to Ingleby. "Can you arrange for both of their solicitors to be called in, David? I think we'll try to get this wrapped up this evening. As long as Logan agrees," he added as an afterthought. DCI Logan agreed straight away when presented with the evidence and the solicitors were soon at the station. Then it was just a matter of which one to interview first. Townshend decided on Sharon Doherty.

"I appreciate, Mrs Doherty, that you possibly thought that if you didn't say anything in your interviews, we'd reach the limit of the time we could hold you without formally charging you with a crime. And as I'm sure you're well aware, that limit runs out sometime this evening." Sharon Doherty said nothing, maintaining the silence she'd pursued since her first interview. For Townshend, it was still proving an irritating performance, but one that was shortly to come to an end.

"Would you like to tell me about that evening at Pontrilas? Was Richard surprised to see you? Or was he annoyed? What did he say, Mrs Doherty, when Stephen Warner walked in with you? And which of you was holding the gun?"

"Detective Inspector, I really do think that is supposition," said John Carey, the solicitor.

"Which part, Mr Carey?" asked Townshend. "There was a gun and it has Mrs Doherty's fingerprints on it, as well as Mr Warner's, so I think a question about which of them was holding it is reasonable, don't you?"

"Why would either of them be holding it, Detective Inspector?" Carey asked.

"I think if neither of them were holding the gun, Mr Carey, then Richard Bexton-King wouldn't have allowed himself to be tied to a chair," Townshend said. "Isn't that right, Mrs Doherty?" The solicitor looked at his client as if expecting her to say something. She didn't.

"Just out of interest, Mrs Doherty, have you an explanation for your fingerprints being on Mr Eddison's gun? He says you never held it." There was no answer. "No? I'm not surprised. What happened in that room, Mrs Doherty? What was it like after you'd put your fingers in Richard's mouth to force it open? Stephen Warner wedged it open with a short spoon, didn't he? That can't have been very pleasant. Did Richard look scared? The man you say you loved. Was he trying to appeal to you while Warner spooned oxycontin into his mouth? Warner hated him, Mrs Doherty. You knew that. But you? You told us you loved him, that you wanted him back." He could tell that what he was saying was getting through, but with the results they'd obtained from Sarah's hunch and the Forensics tests, he didn't need a confession now.

"Mrs Doherty, have you anything to say?" he asked. No response but a smile. "Sharon Doherty, I am arresting you for the murder of Richard Bexton-King on the evening of the eighteenth of February 2014. You do not have to say anything, but it may harm your defence if you do not mention when questioned something on which you rely on in court. Anything you do say may be given in evidence." Finally, there was a reaction from her, Townshend thought as she turned to have a short whispered conversation with the solicitor. She was pale when she turned to look back at him, but still said nothing. "You still have the chance to make a statement if you wish, Mrs Doherty and I have to point out to you that given the seriousness of the charge, you'll be kept in police custody until your initial court hearing. Interview terminated at nineteen twenty hours."

With his last interview with Stephen Warner not having been very productive, something which he was sure Warner was aware of, Townshend wasn't surprised to see him looking relaxed again.

"Mr Warner, fresh evidence has come to light, linking you even more closely to the murder of Richard Bexton-King," Townshend began.

"I wasn't there. I told you that yesterday," Warner said.

"So you did, Mr Warner, but I didn't believe you then and I still don't. With the evidence we now have, I'm not inclined to believe you at all. Now, you told us that you'd fired Nicholas Eddison's pistol at his gun club. That was another blatant lie, Mr Warner. Mr Eddison has told us that not only had he never let you touch his gun and he'd never even mentioned it to you. His gun club have confirmed that he hasn't introduced any visitors during the whole course of his membership." Townshend sighed. "You were there in that kitchen, Mr Warner, forcing oxycontin into Richard Bexton-King's mouth. We've found the spoons and the empty oxycontin capsules, all with your fingerprints on, so please don't do me the discourtesy of lying to me any further." Townshend was surprised at Warner's reaction and a quick glance at Ingleby told Townshend that he felt the same. The man just seemed to slump in his seat, muttering.

"Stupid bloody bitch! I told her not to put that stuff in the bin! But no, she said it would be all right, that the cleaners would just take it without looking." To Townshend's satisfaction, it was loud enough to register on the tape, but only just.

"Did you want to elaborate on that, Mr Warner?" he asked, but got no answer. "Never mind, you'll have a chance to make a full statement later and I'm sure your solicitor will advise you that it's in your best interests to do so. Stephen Warner, I am arresting you for the murder of Richard Bexton-King on the evening of the eighteenth of February 2014. You do not have to say anything, but it may harm your defence if you do not mention when questioned something on which you rely on in court. Anything you do say may be given in evidence." Townshend paused, looking squarely at the man on the other side of the interview table. "One last thing, Mr Warner. Because of the seriousness of the charge being made against you, we'll be keeping you in custody until your court appearance."

CHAPTER FIFTY SIX

The atmosphere in the office on the following Thursday morning was very much that of a job well done, but as Townshend pointed out to them, without wishing to deflate their enjoyment in any way, there was still a lot of work to do in writing reports and tape transcripts. He took the opportunity to remind them that solving a murder is a mixture of footwork, fact-checking, deduction and sheer good luck, but there's always the paperwork. Then he told them he'd buy them all a drink when they finished work that day.

Sitting at his desk, Townshend considered the frustration of the past two weeks. The team were delighted with their efforts, as well they should be, he thought, but there had been mistakes made, questions not asked and things not handled well. If it hadn't been for Sarah Miller's flash of inspiration, who knows where things might have gone? He tried to console himself that it was their first murder enquiry as a team and anyone would expect teething problems.

There was a clear picture of what had happened on that Tuesday night in Pontrilas in Townshend's mind, with one or two minor loose ends that would have to be tied up. Richard Bexton-King had been on his own in the house after a row with his ex-wife, an argument over money as most of their marital rows had been, from what they'd gathered during the investigation. It must have been a surprise for him when Sharon Doherty turned up uninvited at his door. Did he invite her in, or did she and Warner force their way in past him. The most likely scenario, Townshend thought, is that Warner had Eddison's pistol and that once Bexton-King had opened the door to Doherty, they'd forced their way in before he'd got over his surprise.

Under threat of being shot, Bexton-King had allowed himself to be tied up, tight bonds leaving marks on his wrists and ankles. If he'd known what was coming, Townshend thought Bexton-King might have preferred the bullet. What went through his mind when Sharon Doherty put her fingers in his mouth and Warner wedged it open with a teaspoon? It was one of Townshend's failings that he found it much easier to put himself in the mind of the victim than the murderer. Try to put yourself in the mind of the villain, one of his early bosses had advised. Try to think like they do. He'd never managed it.

Did Warner tell Bexton-King who he was in some grand theatrical denouement as he was breaking up the capsules and feeding it to him? Almost certainly. Brought up by his mother to hate the man, it was unlikely that Warner would have missed an opportunity to do so. He would have had plenty of time to gloat. Killing him in such a way would have taken time, as proved by the time the car was away from BKM. It certainly wasn't a heat of the moment passion killing and it was more than likely that Warner had taken the lead. Townshend still wasn't sure that Sharon Doherty would have killed Bexton-King. It seemed more probable that she had the idea but would never have carried it through, and then got caught up in something that she couldn't get out of. With her refusing to say anything, he couldn't be sure.

And of course there was the apparent rush to get away from the place. Did they think they were being disturbed by the neighbour when they heard his dog barking? Possibly, he thought, but then again, they were in a two-seater car. They wouldn't have been able to take the body away. So was it deliberate to put the body in the trunk? No, they must have been in a rush. Why else would the car have been driven recklessly enough to collide with a gate post? The witness had said they were driving too fast, hadn't he?

He tried to put the questions out of his mind. The case would soon be in the hands of the Crown Prosecution Service. He needed something else to think about. On impulse he reached for the phone and dialled a local Hereford number.

"Hello, Ginny, it's Derek. Do you fancy dinner tonight?"

Other books by Gary Cann:

'Smallbrook': The year is 1916. Nathan Holt, a soldier wounded on the battlefields of France, returns to the village of his youth whilst recovering. Jenny Tiley is a young woman struggling to keep her farm, having been widowed. Their paths cross as they struggle to adjust to the effect the Great War has had on them. But are they able to find happiness?

'Greenhill': The green hills of the Welsh border offer peace and solace but for Malcolm Gregson they are also a place to hide from the present and remember the past. His wife's funeral gives him time to reflect on his own rather ordinary life, but that takes a new and confusing turn when he meets an old school friend, the glamorous and attractive Sonia Fox. He finds himself embroiled in events he doesn't understand and a shadowy world of lies and deceit opens wounds he didn't know existed. Who can he trust? Who can he believe?

Made in the USA
Charleston, SC
12 April 2016